SIGHT FRO

To Richard & Suzanne

With very best wishes

Charles 11/24

PS. Please keep the secret!

Sight from Sound

by

Abeni Chopra

('Abeni': 'we asked for her and behold we got her'.)

YOUCAXTON
PUBLICATIONS

ISBN 978-1-915972-21-7
Published by YouCaxton Publications 2023

YouCaxton Publications
www.youcaxton.co.uk

To Hannah,
a most remarkable woman for whom
my enduring love knows no bounds.

Chapter 1

'THE EYE DOCTORS are here! The eye doctors are here!' shouted Absko excitedly as he ran up the drive towards Bottlesford Hall. As he drew closer to the four storeyed Georgian mansion his shouts became louder, more urgent until he was at the front door banging and shouting, making as much noise as he could.

'Jumapili, you must come! You must come! *Lazima uje*,' he yelled, switching between English and Swahili. 'The eye doctors are in Thindigua. *Madaktari wa macho wako Thindigua*. They'll cure your blindness. *Wataponya upofu wako*. They'll make you better. Jumapili, they will make you better!'

Jumapili abruptly stopped playing the piano in the west front drawing room and listened hard. She had never heard such urgency in her brother's voice before.

'I've seen them. I've seen their caravans!' shouted Absko through the front door breathlessly. 'They're parked at the Baptist Church. It's proper, I promise you. It's proper western medicine!'

With her heart beating faster, Jumapili rose from the piano stool, reached for her white cane, and started to click her tongue against the roof of her mouth to help orientate herself in the room and locate the door to the hall.

'Jumapili, Jumapili you must come. You must come now! They are in Thindigua for just one more day, then they go.'

Jumapili reached the cavernous entrance hall at the same time as Colin Downsted. He was the imperious headmaster of Bottlesford Hall, an independent girls' boarding school on the outskirts of Nairobi. It had taken Jumapili in when she was eleven years old, and since then she had never found a reason to leave. In fact, it was the opposite, she loved the place and wanted to stay.

Andrew Buckam Colin Downsted was known to everyone as either 'Headmaster' or 'Mr Downsted', although to his friends as 'Colin'. Since none of his pupils knew what the initials 'A' and 'B' stood for, he had earned the nickname (naturally behind his back) of 'Anyone But Colin'.

His wife, Joyce, arrived and demanded to know what the din was about. She commanded that it stop immediately and, a few seconds later, Hawla, the housekeeper, came rushing, pushing past everyone to get to the front door first. It was her job to open it to guests, and no one was going to take such an important task away from her if she could help it. It was, therefore, a large deputation which, upon the door being open, greeted Absko and his news.

'What are you saying?' demanded Downsted.

Absko took a moment to gather his breath before thrusting a leaflet into Downsted's hands. There was a mobile clinic in town doing cataract eye surgery, he explained, and it would cure Jumapili's blindness. She needed to come urgently as they would soon be gone.

Jumapili heard Downsted turn the leaflet from one side to another.

'Only one more day?' he asked in that disbelieving tone adopted by experienced teachers.

'Yes. Then they go to the next town, and then they go home. So she needs to...'

'Where's their home?' interrupted Downsted.

'England. I think they've come from England, maybe Holland, so she must come now, she must, she must!'

'We don't have to do anything right away,' declared Downsted with his usual air of authority. 'Mrs. Downsted and I will investigate. We'll consider it, and then we'll decide.' There was a heavy emphasis on the word 'we'.

'There is no time for that,' shouted Absko. He pushed past Downsted and his wife and grabbed Jumapili's sleeve, attempting to pull her out of the house. But he was not quick enough for Hawla, who stamped hard on his foot before kicking him sharply on the shin.

'What does Jumapili say? It's her decision. You can't decide for her,' said Absko, as he jumped about nursing his wounds from Hawla's heavy shoe. 'Jumapili, what do you say? What do you want?'

But Jumapili did not know what she wanted. She remembered the slums, the poverty, the hunger, and she knew she didn't want to disobey Mr. Downsted and possibly return to all that, but to be able to see like everyone else… well, what a magical thing that would be!

'I don't know, Absko,' she said lamely. 'I'm not sure.'

'But you'll be able to see. You'll have a whole life if you can see. Please, Jumapili, you're a Mwangi. We Mwangis, we make brave decisions.'

The mention of their family name prompted Jumapili to step forward to go with him, only to find herself being pulled back sharply by Hawla.

'Mr. Downsted hasn't said you can go!' And with that one tug the decision was made.

'Look Absko, you know you can't come here in term time. In the holidays you're most welcome. You know that,' said Joyce trying to calm the situation.

'You want her blind! You want to keep her blind so she can play her music, sing her songs, everyone knows that's why you want her here. She's your plaything, your musical box,' bawled Absko scathingly.

'Look, would you like something to eat, to drink?' asked Downsted calmly. 'You've come a long way. If you go to the back door, I'm sure Hawla could find you something.'

'No, I don't want to eat, no thank you,' he answered brusquely. 'I just want my sister to come with me. She's mine; she's not yours.'

'Well, that's not possible,' said Downsted. 'As I've said, I will check it out in the morning, and we'll decide what's best. Now, if you don't want anything to eat, then I think it's time you left. You're disturbing the whole school. Jumapili must get back to her studies.'

'Hawla, shut the door,' ordered Joyce.

Jumapili felt the wind of the door pass her face then she heard it slam shut.

'Please Jumapili, please come,' begged Absko through the thick timbers, his voice weakening in defeat.

'Hawla, if he's not gone in five minutes, release the dogs,' instructed Joyce in an unusually fierce manner. If Downsted had not been insulted by Absko's accusations, she had most certainly been.

'Absko go!' yelled Jumapili frantically. 'They're going to let the dogs out!'

'Jumapili,' Absko shouted over his shoulder, 'I'll wait for you by the gate until moonshine. I'll be there until moonshine.'

He was true to his word. Jumapili heard him call for her long after the full moon had risen high in the sky and the 9 pm school supper-bell had been rung.

Chapter 2

JUMAPILI MWANGI WAS born blind in a shack in the Kibera slums of Nairobi. She was the second child of Odikinyi and Nyawira Mwangi.

Their first child, Absko, was five years old when his sister was born. Neither of them knew their birth dates. Birthdays meant nothing to them because they were never celebrated. Like hundreds of thousands of children born each year in the slums around the world, their births were never recorded, and therefore, they did not officially exist.

In a world where there is not much, Odikinyi and Nyawira took enormous pride in their windowless one-room shack of twelve square feet, with its mud, wood and corrugated tin walls, tin roof and dirt floor. It was their home and having such a home gave them status in a society where so many were homeless. Most importantly, in a slum where the majority of shacks were rented, they were owners. However, all this belied the bravery that Odikinyi had to exercise time and time again as the Kibera mafia sought to evict his family or press him for protection money which he refused to pay.

Their pride in themselves and their home was shown in the way that their shack was kept neat and tidy, with a place for everything. It was as spotlessly clean as they could keep it. Although, at any moment, a rainstorm might overwhelm the defences Odikinyi had built, and raw sewage would pour through their home.

Although much was missing from Odikinyi and Nyawira's home in the form of tangible assets, it lacked nothing in love and ambition. Almost every waking moment was spent thinking about how they would earn the money needed to pay for Absko's school fees, because they knew education was the way to a *proper* house.

Odikinyi was proud of his son, but he worshipped his daughter. Despite Jumapili's blindness, he knew from the moment he touched her that she possessed something very special. It was why he refused to take her out to the wilderness where, according to tribal custom, he should have abandoned her to die.

At the age of four, Jumapili was badly scalded when she accidentally pulled a pan of boiling water onto her body. Odikinyi was distraught beyond despair. He left their shack immediately with his daughter's screams yelling in his ears promising he would return with medicines.

He was never seen again.

There were many rumours as to what had happened to him. Some said he was caught trying to raid the pharmacy and ended up in jail; others said that when he went to the moneylenders to borrow more money to buy painkillers, the beating they gave him for not repaying past debts went too far, and he was killed. Nyawira was certain of one thing: Odikinyi had not absconded nor abandoned them. She knew he loved his children too much.

From the moment Jumapili was burned, she became a child without joy, a child who lived in fear that she would be struck again with an indescribable, never-ending pain which, in an adult, would have had them praying to die.

The pain went on for many weeks because the treatment of Jumapili's burns was as crude as it was ancient. Egg white was used to seal her skin and then Nyawira would painstakingly dress her wounds, both morning and evening, with fine cotton cloth laden with a gel made from a concoction of pig fat, honey and wine, yielding all the love that a mother in anguish and a broken soul could lavish on her daughter. She knew the White men had better treatments, but that took money – and she had no money. As she cradled her daughter in her arms for hour upon hour, her resentment grew at the injustices she could see all around. So much of Kenya's wealth was in the hands of the White settlers while her tribe, the Kikuyu, had been forced from their lands and had so little.

Jumapili's burning meant she would not move a fraction outside of any space which she didn't already know and had mentally defined. It was only her mother and brother whose leadership she would trust. No one, no visitor, no friend nor neighbour could persuade her to explore new surroundings. Any attempt would bring forth her screams, the likes of which were only made by the tortured and were enough to terrorise anyone into inaction.

Odikinyi's disappearance marked the end of Absko's childhood because it then became his job to earn money for the family. He was about nine years old. Any ambition Absko had for going to school to learn to read, write and do sums disappeared with the same certainty as his father had done. Two hours each Sunday morning at Sunday School would be the limit of his education.

Two years after Odikinyi's disappearance, Nyawira caught tuberculosis, because it was rampant throughout the slums. Over the next year, slowly but surely, Nyawira started to drown in what was to become a long and painful death. The medicines which might have saved her were as remote in her world as finding gold, frankincense and myrrh in the next.

A few days before Nyawira died, with agonising shortness of breath and the pain of despair etched on her face, she told Absko and Jumapili that she had to go to hospital and would never be coming back. As tears fell silently from her eyes, she told them that they only had each other and their friendship was the most important thing they would ever possess. She said they should not ask anyone, not even the neighbours, for any help, as the neighbours would only use any favours given to trick them out of their home. She warned of the Mafia gangs and the risk of Jumapili being stolen. She told them of the bravery of their father in protecting their inheritance and made them repeat several times the name of 'the dog man' whose animals would see any squatter leave their shack if it was ever illegally occupied.

Nyawira then made Absko promise that he would look after Jumapili.

'Do you promise faithfully?' she asked persistently, and despite his repeated assurance, she told him that she would know if he ever broke this promise, and if he did, she would make a point of haunting him for the rest of his life.

Absko was confused as he did not understand that his mother was dying, but Jumapili understood completely. Even though Nyawira used all the power she could muster to keep her voice strong, Jumapili could detect the tiniest of trembles and thus the distress in her mother's voice.

After her talk, Nyawira ceremoniously gave Absko the little money she had and ordered him and Jumapili to go to the shop to buy vinegar and bleach, adding instructions that they were to wash and wipe down everything immediately they got back.

As soon as Absko and Jumapili left their shack, Nyawira placed the gifts she had made in preparation for this moment on their small, bare table. For Absko, she had made a traditional kente kufi hat which she had covered with orange, green and black beads, together with a matching leather belt. Conscious that Jumapili needed shape and texture, not colour, she made a set of traditional beaded toy animals comprising a zebra, hippopotamus, and giraffe, which she placed on her favourite headscarf. Finally, she put a plate of samosas made from maize rice and beans on the table. They were the last items of food she had cooked for them at the community cooker because she could no longer collect, let alone afford, charcoal or firewood for her oven.

Coughing blood into her scarf and with her chest heaving with sobs, Nyawira left home. Making sure she didn't use any of the major paths in case her children saw her, she stumbled towards the hospital, stopping every few steps to rest, lean against whatever was available before coughing herself to beyond a point of exhaustion.

As soon as Absko returned home and saw the gifts on the table, he realised what his mother had been telling him. He collapsed on to Nyawira's bed and sobbed, grasping her pillow and sheets close to him. They were still soaked in her blood and sputum. Jumapili reached out to comfort him, her own tears flowing. Absko grasped at his sister. In turn, she held him very tight, as if to stop him shattering into a million tiny pieces like a china doll.

Apart from when they went out to collect water, they stayed at home for the next three days, hoping beyond hope that their mother would return. They washed and cleaned their shack as she had ordered, but for most of the time, they did nothing but hibernate in a depression as deep as any two souls have known. They were just seven and twelve years old and received not a single visitor.

Chapter 3

LONDON HAS THE black taxi; New York has its yellow cabs; Nairobi has its *matatu*. These are privately owned, highly decorated buses and minibuses which are far more than the transport lifeblood of the city; they represent the spirit of Nairobi, the glue which holds the community together.

Despite being obscenely overcrowded, uncomfortable and, for the most part, in a dreadful condition, matatus are the living embodiment of President Jomo Kenyatta, the first President of Kenya's, political policy of *'Harambee'* ('Self-Help and Unity'). And despite the pirate matatu drivers suffering from an overload of bribery, corruption, fines and police harassment, they flourish because the people of Nairobi need and want them.

Matatu drivers take passengers where the state-run Kenyan Bus Company never goes. They make diversions off their regular routes as their customers' needs or traffic changes dictate. They will wait if a regular customer is running late and, if raining, it is common for a matatu driver to drop a passenger at their front door.

Matatus thrive because their drivers provide their customers with the service they need and, because of that, they enjoy huge customer loyalty. For example, if a matatu doesn't start because it has a flat battery, its customers will get out and push to get it started. If a bus is stopped by the police, as they often are, then the passengers quickly disappear or if they stay it is to argue that they are all friends and travelling for free.

The matatu charge used to be typically about 30 cents, sixty per cent of the regular bus fare.[1] For those without money, the drivers take

---

[1] The name Matatu comes from the Kikuyu word for 'three' in recognition of the three big ten-cent coins once charged for a ride into the city.

goods in barter, give credit, and are happy to accept small livestock, even chickens, on their buses as guests.

But above all, the matatu were and remain a symbol of the rejection of Kenya's colonial past - of being kept in one's place by colonial officials. In any battle between '*their*' flexible rebellious matatu and the rigidity and officialdom of the Kenyan Bus Service, then matatu win every time because they are of the people and not of the state.

After his father died, Absko got himself a job working on a matatu as a *manamba*.[2] It was Absko's job to crank the engine while the driver drenched the carburetor with a petrol-soaked rag to get it started. He had to keep the radiator topped up with water, to pump up the tyres, which had invariably gone down overnight, and remove the stone chocks that kept the wheels in place for hill-starts, as there was no certainty that the parking brake would work. Once underway, it was Absko's job to push people onto the bus, force his way amongst the passengers to collect fares, and above all, to keep a beady eye open for the police.

After three days of abject depression at his mother's passing, and with his hunger growing, because her samosas had long been eaten, he knew he had to get back to work. The competition for *manamba* jobs was fierce and he knew that if he had another day off, there would be no job for him to return to. He therefore got up an hour earlier than normal, while it was still very dark and the slum around him still slept. He fumbled around getting himself dressed before he lit the oil lamp. His mother had impressed on her son the need to ration their use of kerosene. It meant he had a guilty feeling every moment it was on.

'Wake up, Jumapili! Wake up!' He rocked his sister. 'I need to go to work. You must come too. You'll ride with me, on my matatu today; you'll be safe there.'

Jumapili got dressed and Absko found her white-washed tapping stick and led her outside. There she waited and listened as he wrapped the heavy chain around the door to their shack to keep it shut, just as

[2] Means junior bus conductor'.

their mother had done. They had no padlock. They could not afford one.

At the public lavatories, Absko helped Jumapili use the toilet and wash her hands and face as he had done a thousand times before. He then did the job his mother had always done and wrapped Jumapili's hair in a headscarf. Since their mother had left their home, Jumapili had been compliant with Absko's wishes, but in the matter of her headscarf, she had very strong views as to how it was to be tied, which she expressed firmly.

From Absko and Jumapili's shack to the bus depot was normally a walk of around forty minutes, but Absko knew that with Jumapili it would take twice as long – this was why they were up so early. Holding her arm just above the elbow, he marched her at such a speed that the tapping of her white cane was not of much use.

'Tsk, Tsk, Tsk.' Jumapili clicked her tongue against the roof of her mouth, mimicking the sound and rhythm of her cane but, for the most part, it was silent because it rarely touched the ground.

'Tsk, Tsk, Tsk,' continued Jumapili who, for the first time, heard something. It was the sound of her Tsk, Tsk, Tskes, returning to her. The retort was quieter, duller, delayed, but for the first time, Jumapili became conscious of hearing her echo.

Chapter 4

THE EARLY SHIFT matatu drivers and their *manamba* were standing around drinking coffee and discussing the football scores of the night before when Absko and Jumapili arrived at the matatu park. It was a wasteland where ten or eleven buses, all of different makes, shapes, colours and sizes, were tightly packed together, having been parked up overnight.

Absko waved his greeting towards his colleagues before he squeezed Jumapili through the narrow gaps between the buses to his own matatu. There, he carefully helped her climb the steps and led her to the back seat of the bus, out of the way of everyone else. He handed her the toys their mother had made for her, but Jumapili was not interested because she had never travelled on a matatu before. She concentrated intensely, reaching out slowly, cautiously exploring the space which surrounded her. Her hands moved only a millimetre at a time before she would withdraw them, fearful that, at any time, she would touch something dangerous or difficult.

'Stay there, Jumapili,' he told her. 'I'll be back.'

'Well, *kumanina*[3]' said Absko's driver. 'Where the fuck have you been?'

'I'm sorry. My mother had to go to hospital.'

This was the only explanation he ever gave. From then on, whenever he thought or spoke about his mother, he didn't want to think of her lying unrecognised in a municipal grave, but as though she was still in hospital being looked after.

'An' look at you in your new 'at! 'Ave you been working somewhere else? Is that 'ow you got it? Why 'ave you not been 'ere?' asked his driver.

---

[3] Bloody Hell.

'My mother made it for me before she went to hospital.'

'I should've hired someone else, someone more reliable, but all the passengers wanted to know where you were,' lamented his driver.

'But I've never had a day off, not one!'

'Good job too. Now go 'n get the bus started. We need to get out.'

Absko's driver didn't notice Jumapili on his matatu when they came to leave the parking lot, because it had already started to fill up with customers. It was only when they stopped for lunch and Absko took time out to care for a blind girl, taking her to the lavatory and making sure she had something to eat and drink, that the driver took notice.

'Who's the blind girl?' asked the driver as the matatu was being locked up for the night.

'My sister,' said Absko. Sometimes the truth is best.

For the next few days, Absko and Jumapili's routine was the same. They would arrive at the parking lot early in the morning and walk back in the dark. They lived from hand to mouth. Absko's pay each day gave them enough money to eat but with very little left over.

Absko's driver, for the most part, ignored Jumapili's presence.

'It's a shame she's blind,' he said casually in front of her as they rested between journeys. 'She has a pretty face. One day it will be beautiful. With a face like that, she would have made a fine wife, but who's going to take a cursed blind girl?'

Late that night, in the pitch black of their shack, when they were lying on their beds, Jumapili lay awake.

'Am I cursed, Absko?' she asked.

'Why do you say that?'

'It's what the driver said. He said no one was going to take a cursed blind girl.'

' He's silly to say that. Remember what Baba said; he said you were different, that's all.'

'I don't want to be different; I want to be the same.'

'One day, I'll make you the same.'

'Do you promise?'

'Yes, I promise,' said Absko, 'but do you remember Baba's saying about the birds?'

'How they're all birds, but they sing different songs?' answered Jumapili.

'Yes.'

'I don't want to sing a different song. I want to sing the same one as everyone else, the same one as you.'

There was a long silence.

'Absko, do birds see?' asked Jumapili.

'I think so.'

'Are there any blind birds?'

'Bats are blind.'[4]

'Bats can't see – like me?' Jumapili found this oddly reassuring.

'Yes.'

'So how do they get around? Don't they bump into things?'

'They use their ears. At least that's what Baba said. They make high-pitched squeaks and listen for the echo to tell them where they are.'

[4] It is a myth that bats are blind; they are not. They have small eyes that are capable of seeing, not with the sharp colourful vision enjoyed by humans but with a sensitivity to the minimum of light that helps them see in almost pitch-black conditions. They also have the ability to 'see' with their highly sensitive ears which they use to detect variations in the reflected sound waves - the echo - of the high-pitched squeaks they emit. They process this auditory information in their brains into visual maps which they use for finding and feeding on fruits, insects, and other small animals.

Chapter 5

IT WAS A heart-stopping shock to Absko when his driver declared that he had to stop bringing Jumapili to work.

'The passengers don't like her here,' he said.

'That's not true! They like her. Once they know her, they like her,' protested Absko.

'It upsets them first thing in the morning. They don't want to be depressed at the start of the day.'

'It shouldn't make them depressed; it should make them pleased at their own good fortune.'

But the driver was adamant. 'She's taking up a space which could be used by paying customers,' he said. 'We take less money ... unless you want to pay for her seat?'

Absko shook his head mournfully.

'Listen Absko,' said the driver. 'You need to take Jumapili to the nuns. It's best for you and her. It's their job to look after girls like her.'

It wasn't the first time Absko had heard that. Several of the passengers on his matatu had told him. He hated it. It was as though they wanted her locked up and out of the way because she was different. There were thousands of able-bodied Kenyan children living on the streets of Nairobi who were dependent upon orphanages for food and night-time shelter. They were despised by many and seen as pests by most. He knew that Jumapili had no chance in that environment.

Above all, the thought of putting her in the care of the Catholic Church was abhorrent to him because his mother had been violently opposed to the idea. She thought the Catholic Church was the devil incarnate, a view formed when she learned that priests and nuns were not allowed to marry.

'It's not natural,' she would argue, 'and if it's not natural, it's not God's way. Anyway, they all do it but pretend not to.'

Absko had no idea what 'doing it' was, but it was enough that his mother thought they were liers and hypocrites, whatever 'it' might be. Thus, it was easy for him to decide that no self-respecting person should ever get involved with them.

Nyawira's opinion was confirmed when she learned that 'good' Catholics practised penance to get forgiveness for their sins, and they think everyone else should practise penance too. But it was when she discovered that ultra-orthodox Catholics practise self-flagellation, that the whole notion of Catholicism was put beyond bounds.

'It's kinky,' she said, although Absko had no idea what she meant.

Worst of all, she believed that the priests and nuns would think that Jumapili's blindness was God's punishment for a sin she had committed, and this made the whole idea of putting Jumapili in a Catholic orphanage a no-no. She was certain they would make Jumapili's life doubly bad.

That night, in the mud and steel womb of their shack, Absko was wide awake. His driver had made it very clear that tomorrow would be the last day that Jumapili could travel on his matatu.

'Do you remember Baba's saying?' Absko asked into the darkness.

'I don't know,' whispered Jumapili. How could she? She was only four when their father disappeared. 'But I'd like to hear them if you know them.'

'He was a wise man. He had wise sayings. He used to say there's always a solution to every problem. It just requires thinking to find the answer. He would say it was a lack of thinking that got you into a mess, and it's only thinking which will get you out.'

'A bit like Mama's saying: "when in a hole stop digging".

'I suppose so. He would always say you had to listen to God because God would give you the answer. I've been listening for God, Jumapili, I promise you. I have been listening hard, but God doesn't talk to me; I hear nothing.'

'Perhaps you're facing the wrong way. When I hear something, I turn my head to hear better. Why don't you turn over and face the other way?'

He did as Jumapili suggested.

'Baba would say: "there's no rhyme, there's no reason, but we all have a purpose". Why doesn't God tell me my purpose?' said Absko towards the wall.

'You have a purpose, Absko – to look after me. I couldn't manage if you weren't here. I don't know what I'd do – but me, what's my purpose?'

'You're young. Your purpose will come.'

'Did Baba have other sayings?'

'He had great belief in coincidences,' said Absko, after a long pause. 'He would see something for the first time and then claimed he would see the same thing time and time again until he'd seen it so many times he stopped noticing. He had a saying for it: "once is an incident, twice is a coincidence, three times a sequence, four times a pattern, and the fifth time it's a law.'

'What law would that be?' asked Jumapili.

But Absko didn't answer. He had fallen into an exhausted sleep.

Chapter 6

IT WAS WITH a heavy heart that Absko led Jumapili to the matatu station the next day. As a result, they did not walk at their usual speed. It meant that Jumapili had more time to swing her cane and tap the ground, concentrating hard to decipher the meaning of each change in vibration or sound. Absko was so deep in thought, worrying about how he was going to look after Jumapili, that he was guiding her on autopilot, no longer hearing the clicking sound of her tongue.

Absko's matatu's route was an irregular figure-of-eight towards the north of Nairobi, running through the Central Business District towards Mathare in the east and the Karura Forest in the west, their main run being up and down Kiambu Road with diversions off towards the Windsor Country Club. It was at their stopping point near Tayiania and what might loosely be called a parade of shops, that Absko found a solution to his problem.

Near Tayiania, there was a bakery run by a modest Omani family whose history dated back to the time when Kenya was a colony of Oman. They were renowned for their chapati, mahambri, samosas, and bajias, which they adorned with an unusual arrangement of Indian spices. Twice a day, sometimes three times, Absko's matatu would stop and he would be ordered inside to stock up with fresh warm food which he was instructed to sell, because one thing was certain about Absko's driver and that was his ability to turn a profit from every opportunity.

On one side of the baker's was a small artisan coffee roaster run by another Omani family whose coffee was sought out by coffee aficionados throughout Nairobi. The roast-master knew intimately the local coffee plantations and the nature of their coffee beans. As a result, he changed the proportions of his blend of arabica and robusta beans according to where the beans had come from, thus creating what he thought was the perfect roast every time. However, it was his insistence that his coffee beans were drum-roasted with the heat from wood, which made him unique; as he proudly boasted: 'no filthy oil fumes are ever going to come close to one of my roasts.'

On the other side of the bakery was what might best be described as a newsagent's or general trading store, run by a Portuguese family. It sold everything that a local village shop might sell, but it was its collection of European alcoholic drinks and Kenyan wines which made it a destination for the European expat community, and what set it aside from most stores of its nature in Nairobi was its neatness. The fruit and vegetables placed outside were not straight from the field but presented washed, cleaned, and orderly.

There was one strong reason why these Omani and Portuguese families behaved modestly, impeccably, and without fuss: their ancestors had all been involved in the slave trade with the Omani Arabs first using Africans captured along the coastline in their plantations. Later, the trade was taken over by the Portuguese who tried to continue with their transatlantic slavery trade for some years after it had been abolished by the British, whose navy was by then under strict orders to stop the trade for every other country as well as Britain. These Omani and Portuguese families had decided long ago that they did not want their past discussed, and for that reason they made sure that they were discreet and did not stand out.

As Absko was walking into the bakery, he noticed the alleyway which ran between the back of the baker's shop and the coffee roaster's. On either side of the alleyway, stacked up against the length of wall, were wooden logs ready for the oven and roaster. They were being kept dry under a makeshift plastic roof. He had seen it a hundred times before, but it was the higgledy-piggledy collection of wooden fruit boxes which caught his eye. They had been discarded by the general store and left there so they could be chopped into kindling wood ready to start the fire for the bakery ovens and coffee roaster at the beginning of the day.

'Could my sister sit outside your shop for a little while?' Absko asked the baker, after he had placed his extensive order for bread and delicacies. 'She's feeling a bit poorly on the matatu.'

'She's not going to be sick, is she?'

'No, no, nothing like that; she just needs a rest from travelling.'

Adopting the philosophy of his father that it was always much easier to get forgiven than get permission, Absko assumed that the baker's non-committal reply had given him consent. Leaving his shopping in the bakery, he darted back to the matatu and led his sister off the bus towards the alleyway.

'You must sit here, Jumapili,' he told her while sorting out an orange box before helping her turn around to sit on it.

'My stick, my stick!' she wailed.

Absko darted back to the matatu.

'My toys!' she shrieked louder.

But Absko was already ahead of the game because he returned with both stick and toys.

'You must stay here,' he commanded, speaking quickly. 'Here's the wall.' He took her right hand and placed it on the wooden boards of the shop to the side of her. 'In front of you is the road. If you go into the road you'll get hurt, so you must stay here. Do you understand? – you could get hurt. I'll be back. I promise you. I'll be back.'

'No, Absko, please don't, don't, don't...' Jumapili reached out, waving her hand frantically in the air as she tried to touch her brother, but he had already stepped back.

The matatu driver sounded his horn and Absko raced back into the bakery and grabbed his shopping.

'Thank you, thank you, thank you,' he said.

'Don't move, don't go away ...' Absko reminded Jumapili as he stepped past her.

The driver honked his horn again, impatiently.

'I'll be back, I'll be back, I promise!' he shouted and, with arms full, he boarded the matatu.

Jumapili felt helpless, frightened witless, and abandoned. She wrapped her arms around her body and broke down in heart-wrenching, sobbing tears.

No one took any notice. She was, to passers-by, just another street child of Nairobi.

Chapter 7

'WHO'S GOD?' ASKED Jumapili when she was lying in her bed at the end of her first day of being abandoned in the alleyway beside the bakery.

Absko had been as good as his word. He had managed to persuade his bus driver to return to Tayiania three times during the day. For Jumapili, the time between Absko leaving and him returning had seemed endless. Her anxiety was made worse because each time she heard a matatu her hopes rose that Absko had returned, so when he did not reappear her disappointment was so deep and her fear so great that she felt as though she had been stabbed in the heart.

Each time Absko returned she felt fractionally less insecure, but when you are aged just seven and you are blind, your function is to sit still and you are petrified to move, then time is a meaningless continuum, with no beginning, no middle, and no end.

'I don't know who he is,' replied Absko. 'Why do you ask?'

'A customer asked the baker what the chokora[5] was doing outside his shop,' answered Jumapili. 'I think he was referring to me. The baker said, "God knows". Another man asked the same question, and that time the baker said, "Heaven knows". You said Baba talked of God, so who is he and who is Heaven, and why do they know I'm there?'

'I don't know. I don't think Baba knew,' replied Absko. 'I heard the priest once tell Mama that Jesus was the Son of God and that she would find God through him. But Jesus died hundreds of years ago,

---

[5] Chokora is the name given to the street children of Kenya. The word comes from the Kiswahili language and refers to scavengers who poke at dustbins or garbage heaps in search of food and other valuables.

so I don't know how he was going to help Mama find God. It makes no sense.'

'The man from the coffee place wasn't that nice,' said Jumapili. 'He told the baker that he wasn't to give me any food. He said if he did, the place would soon be swarming with chokora, and they'd lose all their business. I don't think he wanted me there.'

'Did he say anything else? Did he complain?' asked Absko.

'No, but the European lady from the shop on the other side of the bakery came and spoke to me to make sure I was all right. I told her about you. I said you worked on the matatu, and I was waiting for you. She seemed nice.'

'I think it's a good place for you to be while I'm at work, at least for a little while,' said Absko. 'The alleyway's got a roof to keep their firewood dry, so if it rains, you can shelter. Also, when my matatu comes by, I can stop and make sure you're OK. I'm sorry but I must earn money for us, and I don't know what else to do.'

'As long as you come back for me, Absko, I'll be OK. If you bring me home, bring me back here, I'll be alright.'

Chapter 8

THE NEXT DAY, Absko went prepared. He had a cushion for Jumapili to sit on and her mother's toys in a plastic bag. On the walk to the matatu station, he filled a bottle with water and purchased some samosas, fruits and nuts for her to eat. This was to become their daily routine.

'She's getting off at Tayianna,' said Absko, brusquely in response to the driver's frowned look of disapproval.

In the alleyway, between the bakers and the coffee roaster's, Absko found the orange box from yesterday. He set it by the side of the corner of the alleyway with the street, and out of the way. He placed the cushion on top of the orange box, and guided Jumapili backwards before encouraging her to sit down.

'Here's the wall,' he said as he guided Jumapili's right hand to the warm wooden boards of the baker's shop. 'Take this.' He placed the plastic bag and her cane in her other hand. 'There's food, water, and your toys in there. There's enough for today. I'll be back. Stay here.'

Jumapili heard her brother disappear into the baker's shop to place his order. When he reappeared, he stopped, put down his shopping and instinctively placed both his hands slowly and very gently on the top of her head. It was the touch of reassurance Jumapili so desperately needed.

'I'll be back, I promise,' he said.

'Absko, no!' Jumapili experienced an overwhelming sense of being abandoned, joined with loneliness, hopelessness, and fear. She rose to follow him, taking a pace towards the road and, as she did so, her cane dropped to the ground.

'STOP!' yelled Absko, 'the road, the road .....' but it was too late for him to go back as his matatu was already moving away.

Jumapili stood rock still. She did not know whether to go forwards or backwards. Every touch, every twitch, every muscle movement was conditioned by her subconscious and the burns she had suffered as an infant. In her nervousness, she started to make the same clicking sound she made when she walked with Absko and then, with every one of her senses heightened, she heard her echo. She lifted the plastic bag Absko had given her closer to her chest and clicked some more. She immediately noticed how its echo sounded different. It was quicker, denser, with its own timbre. She turned her head, continuing to click as she did so. This time she heard the echo from the baker's building. It returned more slowly with a hollower sound, and then, as she faced opposite the alleyway and clicked, she noticed her echo was not there at all. It had gone. Still without moving her feet, Jumapili turned back and, as she continued to click, the echo of the bakery returned to her ears.

Tentatively, and with her hand outstretched, she turned and shuffled her way back towards the bakery corner, noticing how the returning sound of her clicks sped up and changed as she got closer. In her nervousness, she was hardly breathing.

Almost tripping over her white cane, she found the corner of the building. She did as she always did whenever she touched anything unexpectedly, she withdrew her hand sharply before moving it forward again, but very cautiously with her fingers outstretched. Nothing, absolutely nothing was going to put her in the same pain as her burning.

It took time for Jumapili to organise herself so she could sit down on her cushion on the orange box, as her brother had left her. She was worried as her cane was out there somewhere, but she didn't know where and without it she felt vulnerable – but mostly she feared what her brother might say at its loss.

'Is this yours?' asked a young male voice.

Jumapili didn't answer because she had no idea as to what he was referring.

The cane was placed firmly in her hand.

'Thank you,' she said, noticing the change in his echo as he walked away.

Time is a strange commodity. It speeds up as you get busier, or older, or you deeply lose yourself in some activity. It slows down when you are bored or waiting for something to happen. The perception of time is personal to every individual and circumstance. When you are a seven-year-old blind girl who has been told to sit in one place and is scared to move, time is almost indeterminable. It was therefore unsurprising how quickly Jumapili drank her bottle of water and ate the food she'd been given.

Her bladder began to fill until it was quite painful. She squeezed tight, praying that Absko would return to help her, but he didn't come. Her forehead started to perspire and, as the pain grew, her mind could think of nothing else. She sat rigidly still and started to cry. She wept for a long time without anyone noticing, because no one notices the tears of the chokora of Nairobi.

'Are you OK?' asked the same young male voice associated with the return of her cane earlier. He had walked past Jumapili, turned around and walked back to her when he had seen her tears.

'*Nahitaji kukojoa*,' she said in Swahili, before repeating in English, 'I need to pee.'

'You want the toilet?'

'Yes, *kwenda chooni*. I need to go to the toilet. *Nimekata tamaa,* I'm desperate.' She was doing as her mother and brother did: repeating their Swahili in English when talking to strangers.

'OK, stay there. I'll find you a toilet.' The owner of the voice disappeared first into the baker's shop and then into the coffee roasters. 'There's a toilet at the back of the alleyway you can use,' he said on his return. 'I'll lead you.' He took Jumapili by the hand.

The toilet block at the back of the shops was a shared outside facility, because lavatories were not usually built indoors when the row of shops was originally built. They were spotlessly clean.

The young man helped guide Jumapili around the cubicle. He took her hand to find and lower the lid seat, then to the chain, the toilet paper and finally to the wash basin. All the time she was in agony willing him to close the door and leave.

'I'll wait outside,' he said.

When she came out of the cubicle, he had her white cane in his hand. He had returned down the alleyway to fetch it. With the boy's gentle guidance and her stick, Jumapili was able to tap her way back to her orange box.

'Are you OK now?' asked the young man.

'Yes, thank you. I'm expecting my brother to come back for me. He won't be long. I'm sure I'll be OK.'

Jumapili listened to the young man's walk as it faded away and started clicking her tongue against the roof of her mouth. As the late morning sun started to shine on her face, she started to use the echoes of her clicks to create a mental picture of the world around her. Every sound had its own imprint, as different as every human voice, and she was beginning to learn those sounds and their meaning.

Chapter 9

OVER THE NEXT few weeks Jumapili and Absko developed a routine, and this allowed Jumapili's anxiety levels to fall. Small changes were made. For example, Absko stopped buying Jumapili's food on their morning walk to the matatu station after the baker protested that she was eating samosas outside his bakery which had not been bought from him.

'That's plain bad manners,' he told Absko crossly.

Slowly, Jumapili became part of the furniture of that small village and regulars to the shops started to wish her well as they passed. Her day was timed by everyone else's routine.

The most interesting part of each day turned out to be a gathering of friends at around 11:00 o'clock on the pavement outside the café on the other side of the road directly opposite her. Three or four tables were pushed together so that between six and eight European men could gather for morning coffee. Using the papers purchased from the general store as their agenda, they would discuss the issues of the day.

Jumapili did not know it then, but she was getting a life's lesson in politics, because these men represented the dying embers of the British Empire and colonialism. On most occasions, they would discuss what these changes meant for them personally. Their meetings had started during the Mau Mau rebellion as a strange act of public defiance against the Kenya Land and Freedom Army ('KFLA') who were in a war against Kenya's white European settlers, with the overall aim of removing British authority and the white settlers from '*their*' land.

The men who gathered for morning coffee had two things in common. They were the product of the English public school system. If, as the Duke of Wellington claimed, the Battle of Waterloo was won on the playing fields of Eton, it would be equally fair to say that the British Empire was run by men with overwhelming self-confidence, a strong sense of entitlement, and a rigorous application of the idiosyncratic customs of the public schools which had educated them.

The second thing they had in common was that they had each served in the British military in either World War I or, and mainly, in World War II. Those who grew up in Kenya naturally joined the King's African Rifles, and because they were white and from a public school, were immediately made commissioned officers, because the racial segregation policies of the time meant that Blacks were not able to rise above the rank of Warrant Officer.

One of their number, Colin Downsted, had been stationed with the British Eastern Naval Fleet at Kilindini, near Mombasa. His work involved deciphering Japanese naval codes at the Kenyan outpost of Bletchley Park, the British codebreaking centre. Afterwards, he was seconded to military intelligence and Kenya's Governor's office. In accordance with his signing of the Official Secrets Act, he never breathed a word of what he did.

Whether they were second-generation settlers, whose fathers and mothers had taken bare land and planted the now famous coffee and tea plantations of Kenya, or whether they had remained in the country after the war had ended, each man took credit for twenty years of post-war hard work, either improving what they had or creating something anew. Each was in no doubt they had been responsible for creating well-paid jobs and wealth where there had been none before. It was a fact that to be forced from '*their*' land or '*their*' businesses was as anathematic to them as was the undeniable fact that six-million Black Africans in Kenya outnumbered white Europeans by one hundred to one.

To a man, this café group supported the 1957 direct elections of Africans to the Kenya Legislative Council (Legco) but their support was conditional upon Britain remaining in overall charge. They feared what would happen to them under Black rule.

Thus, it was with regret for a past never to be re-seen, and deep anxiety for their future that, on 12th December 1963, the eight men from the café, together with their wives, gathered at their Country

Club to watch television. There they saw the Union Jack flying over the State House lowered and the Kenyan flag raised, as Kenya became an independent country under a new constitution and Jomo Kenyatta became its first president.[6]

Each of the eight men had studied the new Kenyan constitution, drawn up for the Kenya people by the British government, and they had debated endlessly its contents among themselves. They all knew by heart Clause 19 of Chapter II, which made it clear that none of their property could be confiscated. However, they were also aware of the inadequacies of the subsequent provisions on compulsory purchase which would allow *'their'* land to be taken without the payment of adequate compensation. Each was too much of a realist to know that it would not be long before the constitution was changed, and each was certain that their own children had no future in Kenya.

Their hope was that any subsequent changes would be made slowly, so they could keep working safely until their retirement, at which time they would go home – back to Britain. It was because of this that an exodus of white capital to Britain began to accelerate. People, like these eight men, needed money in England for when Kenya would no longer welcome them.

There was another reason they were depressed: Kenyan independence came just a few days after John F. Kennedy, President of the United States, was assassinated. The appalling treatment of Blacks in America had created a deep anger throughout the whole of Black Africa. In Kenya, the resentment had grown into a slow-burning rage – as though the 60,000 Whites in Kenya were responsible for the unfair treatment of the 11% of the 189 million population of the USA who were Black.

It had been the fervent hope of these eight men that Kennedy's civil rights work would help correct the wrongs, not only in the USA, but also in South Africa where apartheid was raging. Their wish was that, through his good offices, Kennedy would bring about change which would help relieve the antagonistic pressure building against

---

[6] Kenya gained its independence on 12th December 1963. In the same year Kenya joined the British Commonwealth.

them. But Kennedy's death saw the end of their hope with the same certainty as Lee Oswald's bullet had ended Kennedy's life.

With the weight of politics in their mind, it was not surprising that none of them noticed Jumapili sitting opposite them. Homeless children on the streets of Nairobi were an everyday occurrence. But these men provided fascinating entertainment for Jumapili as she listened to their conversation. Without sight, she had no idea that these people had different skin colour or hair types or even different coloured eyes. She had no idea what White rule meant, but she knew that each of them thought it had been beneficial to Kenya even if she couldn't work out why. And she had no idea why, when the eight white men arrived for their morning coffee, all the Black customers, with their different sounding voices, went inside, only coming out when they were gone.

A casual observer might remark that the Black men's move was out of age-old colonial deference but, as Jumapili was to learn from listening to their conversations, they did not want to be seen mixing with White Europeans. That was why, as soon as the eight White men had gone, men of the Kikuyu tribe would come outside again to reoccupy the places they had given up in silent protest. Racial prejudice works in a host of strange ways.

Chapter 10

'WHAT ARE YOU doing?' Absko shouted at the strangers inside his shack. It was the first anniversary of his mother's disappearance but without the ability to use a diary he didn't know that. Life, while harsh, had fallen into a routine for him and his sister. It had become just about manageable.

Absko had thought something wrong when he saw the chain which he used to seal his cabin lying loose on the floor, but now, inside his shack, his adrenalin was pumping, his heart was thumping, and fear had raised the hairs on the back of his neck.

'What are you doing here?' he repeated.

Five youths were spread about his home.

'Fuck Off!' said one of them. 'Who are you? What do you want?'

'This is mine. This is my home! You've got to get out. You've got to leave!'

'It's ours now.' Another youth rose from Jumapili's bed to tower above Absko.

'It's not; it's mine ... it's *ours*,' he said, glancing towards Jumapili.

'It's not. Not now we've paid the rent.'

'What rent? We don't pay rent. My parents have never paid rent,' declared Absko proudly.

'Explains why it's ours,' said the tall youth who moved threateningly close. 'You ain't paid the rent so you've been evicted. It's obvious, ain't it!'

Absko knew he stood no chance of evicting the squatters by himself. He negotiated the collection of a few of his and Jumapili's possessions which he thrust rapidly into plastic bags before retreating to the door.

'Have they stolen our home?' asked Jumapili in a whisper.

Absko was in too much of a shock to answer.

'What do we do, Absko? What do we do?' Jumapili asked. 'Where are we going to sleep?'

'I don't know – I don't know.'

Absko walked away with his head down, leaving Jumapili standing where she was.

'Absko where are you going? Don't leave me. Don't leave me!' shouted Jumapili frantically.

He stopped walking, returned slowly to his sister's side and gently took hold of her arm.

'Come on, let's go,' he said softly. There was defeat in his voice.

'Where?'

'I don't know. The matatu station perhaps. Maybe we'll sleep in our matatu tonight. I can't think where else, can you?'

He walked in silence, deep in thought, not hearing Jumapili's constant clicking.

'Do you remember the name of the dog man?' he asked after they had been walking for twenty minutes.

'What, the name Mama gave us? Yes, Chacha Zuberi.'

'Do you remember where she said he lived?'

'Yes, Mathare.'

He held her arm and kept walking, deep in thought, without the commentary he would usually give to keep Jumapili safe. Meanwhile, she tapped with her cane and clicked with her tongue. She was continuing to learn how to gauge the world around her.

Chapter 11

ABSKO HELPED JUMAPILI settle down for the night on the back seat of the bus. She was very frightened. Through discipline and adherence to a strict routine, she had been able to manage for herself when she was in their shack – she knew exactly where she had placed everything, so it was always quick to her touch – now, with her few possessions thrown into a couple of plastic bags, she felt completely lost.

'You're not going to give me to the nuns, are you?' she asked. 'You're not going to take me somewhere and leave me, are you?'

Absko didn't answer; he too was frightened.

'Absko answer me!' commanded Jumapili.

'No, only by the bakers during the day as we've agreed,' he answered crossly.

'It's just you did once.'

'I didn't.'

'You did. Mama got really angry with you.'

'I was always there. I just pretended to be away, that's all.'

Absko could remember the occasion as though it were yesterday. He'd been having enormous sport with Jumapili, teasing her as every brother teases their sister. He was doing it by moving her things, so they were never where she thought she had left them. It was when his sport moved to hiding from his sister when he was supposed to be looking after her that Nyawira, his mother, had flown into an uncontrolled rage. She had picked up a heavy canvas shopping bag and forced it down over Absko's head. She then threw him to the ground and kicked him into a corner of their shack before she piled clothes, then sheets, then blankets and finally their straw mattresses on top of him. Absko couldn't breathe. The canvas hood was suffocating him. He panicked. The more he fought the more the weight of everything around him made his escape impossible, which made him panic even more and fight even harder. He was semiconscious when the bag was eventually removed from his head because his mother could sense that the fight had gone from him. Still enraged, she threw cold water on him before she sat him down on his bare bed, tears flooding from his eyes.

'Was that horrible?' she had asked.

Absko had nodded.

'Well, that's what it's like for Jumapili, but all the time. You couldn't see; she can't see. You couldn't move; she doesn't know where to move. You were frightened; she's frightened all the time. But there's one big difference – that moment ended for you; it never ends for her.'

His mother then took a cloth and wiped his face.

'I don't think you realise how lucky we are to have Jumapili. Do you know why we have her?'

He shook his head.

'To teach us kindness, to teach us to see the world through the eyes of others, to teach us to love. We're so lucky to have her.'

Absko never forgot those final words – We're so lucky to have her.

Chapter 12

THE MATATU DRIVERS are as individual as they are a collective. You wrong one matatu driver and you wrong them all. And the men of Absko's matatu bus park rowed behind his need to get his shack back.

'Do you know the gang that put them in there?' he was asked, because quiet diplomacy, rather than physical force, might provide the solution as gang[7] culture was only just beginning to take hold in the Kibera slums.

The Kibera Battalion and the Nubians were then the two largest and toughest gangs in Kibera, and whereas new gangs might arise, the Kibera Battalion was usually very effective in smashing their activities before they got started. And the only thing more frightening than the gangs of Kibera was the dog man of the Mathare slums. If you had the protection of the dog man then you were inviolate because he had three dogs, and it was well known that these had torn many a man to his death.

Many attempts had been made to kill the dog man and his dogs, but they protected each other as though their lives depended upon it, which they did. Many times, his dogs had been reported to the authorities as being dangerous with demands that they be put down. However, at his home where they roamed freely, his dogs were treated and behaved as though they were the gentlest of family pets. It was the cine films of his children and grandchildren playing roughly with his dogs and their docile response which defeated the many requests made to the magistrates to have them put down. The fact was that

---

[7] By 2010 there were 33 recognized gangs in Kenya. By 2017 that number has risen to 364 and rising with politician in Nairobi and Mombasa paying gangs for their political ends

Chacha Zuberi was a first-class dog trainer and his dogs loved him for it.

The dog man of Mathare lived on the edge of the Mathare slums. Whereas his shack was built from the same timber and corrugated iron as all the others, perhaps a little bigger, he had land which went all the way around his hut. Most importantly, he had free electricity courtesy of a transformer which he had connected to the powerline which overflew his property. Many times the electricity company had sent men out to disconnect him but they never did. Such was the reputation of the dog man that no one was brave enough to go onto his land to cut him off.

Mid-morning the next day, when the passenger load would usually be light, Absko's driver took Jumapili and him to see the dog man.

'Wait here,' commanded Absko to Jumapili, who was more than happy to do as she was told.

'Is anyone here?' shouted Absko from the gate. 'Is Chacha Zuberi here? I'm looking for Mister Zuberi.'

'Who wants him?' shouted a voice from inside the shack.

'Me ... my mother said we had to come and see him if we had a problem.'

'Who's your mother?'

'Nyawira ... Nyawira Mwangi.'

'Never heard of 'er.'

There was a long pause before Chacha Zuberi lazily made an appearance. He was nothing like Absko or the bus driver had imagined. He was tiny in both height and build, but it was his dress which shocked them. It was immaculate. His white shirt was starched and ironed, his navy trousers pressed with a sharp crease, and his black shoes were polished to a shine. The dog man of Mathare was making a statement.

Zuberi beckoned Absko and the driver in. They looked at the three dogs laying lazily in the yard.

'They won't bother you,' he said with a smile of perfectly white teeth.

The dogs lifted their heads lazily and their tails beat once or twice on the ground, just hard enough to kick up some dust in acknowledgement of Zuberi's guests.

'You want me to evict squatters from your home, is that right?' asked Zuberi when Absko had finished his tale of woe.

'Yeh, please.'

'Where are your mum and dad?'

Absko explained.

'How do I know the place is yours?'

'You can check. Everyone will tell you.'

'Any women, children, babies in the shack?'

'Not that I know of – just five boys – much older than me.'

'Are you Kikuyu?'[8]

'Yes, can't you tell?'

'Are they Kikuyu?'

'I don't think so.'

'Are they Nubians?'

'No.'

'We Kikuyu, we must stick together, mustn't we?'

Absko nodded hard.

'Has anyone told you what it will cost?'

Absko shook his head.

'I need twenty-five shillings up front and then one hundred and twenty-five shillings when they're gone. And for that, I guarantee they'll stay away for a year.'

'I don't have that kind of money,' protested Absko.

'Nah, most people don't. My other deal is twenty-five shillings up front and then 10 shillings a week for one year.'

'Thats over five hundred shillings. It's over three times more,' protested the driver.

'Yeah – it's called interest. Needs to be high 'cause I get bad debts, you know. Fuckers disappear, but the dogs nearly always get 'em in the end. Know what I mean.'

[8] The Kikuyu are a Bantu ethnic tribe native to Central Kenya

Absko rubbed his hand into his face in despair. These were impossible sums of money; he only earned sixty shillings a week.[9]

'On the one-year payment deal, I'll guarantee no one will be back for two years' added Zuberi, thinking it was time to offer a sweetener.

There was silence while Absko and the driver looked at the ground. Zuberi unwrapped a stick of chewing gum and started to chew.

'Look. I'll provide the twenty-five shillings to get you started, and if you work seven days instead of the six days you do now then that would give you the other ten shillings which you need,' said the driver.

'Yeah, yeah, thank you.' Absko paused, wincing as he did so. 'And what if it goes wrong and I can't pay?'

'The dogs will give you a bloody good nip,' interjected Zuberi, his face turning into a smile as he spoke.

'Look boy, learn,' said his driver firmly. 'The reality is that some choices ain't choices at all. The alternative is you and Jumapili are homeless, and that's not a choice, is it?'

Absko's driver made the decision for him by producing the twenty-five shillings upfront payment.

'When can you do it?' asked the driver, allowing the money to hover in the air.

'Pick me up at eight o'clock tonight. You can show me where to go and I'll have 'em out by tomorrow afternoon, latest.'

'It'll be dark then,' protested the driver.

'Yeh. I don't want people to see me before, otherwise they'll know, they'll prepare. It'll all get messy.'

At exactly 8 o'clock Absko and his driver watched, and Jumapili listened, from the safety of the matatu, as Zuberi chained up his dogs to three points strategically placed in his yard, designed to protect both his shack but, most importantly, his illegal electricity supply.

Absko and Zuberi were dropped off at the nearest point to Absko's shack, and then using moonlight, some torchlight, the flickering shadows of oil lamps and fires, they made their way to Absko's shack.

---

[9] In 1965 the average wage in Kenya was 450 East Africa Shillings a month-roughly 18EAs a day for working a six say week.

There is never silence in the slums because they never sleep. Even in the deadest of night there is the sound of shouting, screaming, music and laughter. It never ends.

'This is it,' said Absko as he reached his home.

'You sure?' asked Zuberi.

'Of course I'm sure.'

'Keep cool. I'm just checking. Go back to the matatu. I'm going to wander around here for a bit. I don't want you seen, so piss off back to the bus.'

'You're coming back to the matatu?' asked Absko.

'Yeh, I ain't fucking walking 'ome,' said the dog man.

The next day at 12 noon, and holding them tightly on their lead, Zuberi and his three dogs made their way to Absko and Jumapili's shack. Expecting Absko to return, and determined to retain their new possession, the youths had left one of their number behind and equipped him with a heavy three-foot wooden pole and a machete so he could repel any borders.

The sharp scraping pull of the shack door by Zuberi took the youth completely by surprise, but it was the three snarling dogs which caused him to retreat both empty handed and with shaking fear against the shack wall.

'Get those fuckers off! Get those fuckers off me! Get 'em out of here!' he yelled.

The louder the youth screamed, the more the dogs got frightened. One word, one signal from the dog man and the youth would have been torn to shreds.

'Shut up! Shut up!' shouted Zuberi. 'You'll frighten them, then you'll get bitten. The Mastiff will go for your balls. The Alsatian and Doberman will go for your face and throat. You won't stand a chance, so shut the fuck up! Anyway, what are you doing here? It's not yours.'

'It is! It is, sir. We've rented it. We've paid fifty shillings as a deposit and another fifty shillings for the first week's rent. Its ten shillings a week each.'

'Who did you pay?'

'I don't know 'is name. He's always based outside the liquor store. The one near the Catholic church.'

'Well, he's rented you something he ain't got no right to rent, so you've gotta fuck off out of 'ere.'

'But we've paid to be here!'

'Well, you paid wrong. You'll 'ave to go and get your money back.'

'He won't give it to us.'

'Look, take this,' said Zuberi, handing the youth a white card with a pencil drawing of three snarling dogs on it. Show it to the geezer that cheated you and tell 'im he'll have me to deal with if you don't get your money back.'

The youth stared at the card. 'What you'll come and help us?' he asked.

'Nah, of course not, but 'e don't know that does 'e. Now get your things and bugger off before me dogs get 'ungry'

The youth moved gingerly about the shack stuffing his things into a couple of bags which he placed outside the door as the dogs, sitting alert, sat and watched his every move.

'What do I do with my mate's stuff?' asked the youth.

'I dunno, but it ain't stayin here,' said Zuberi. 'Take 'em to the liquor store. I'm sure they'll all be going there when they find out what 'es done. And don't take anything that don't belong to you.'

Zuberi watched as the youth filled more bags, this time with his compatriot's possessions. 'These dogs, they know what's right 'n wrong. They can smell it.'

As the youth, relieved to be out of the dog's glare and loaded with bags, made his way to the liquor store, Zuberi went outside and nailed on the front and side of Absko and Jumapili's shack more cardboard drawings of his drooling dogs. It told the people of Kibera that this property was protected by the dog man. It was a sign which would ensure there would be no reoccupation.

Each of the youths arrived at the shack in turn to be faced down by Zuberi and his dogs, some more aggressively than others, until eventually the liquor man arrived. Five angry youths demanding their money back required at least some investigation.

'I'm glad you've come,' said Zuberi to the liquor man as his dogs, now off their leads, wandered freely. 'I wanted to see your face. I'm good with faces. I remember faces. Anything 'appens to my clients, well you'll be their dinner that night.' He looked at his dogs. 'Know what I mean!'

The liquor man said nothing. Win some, lose some, he thought. There would be other shacks to steal. He'd take the money and allow the owners and interlopers to fight it out. It was the way of Kibera. The toughest won. The liquor man knew he wasn't the toughest, but he knew he was one of the smartest because, if anyone demanded their money back, he always gave it to them less a charge for rent for the nights they were in occupation and, if he could get away with it, a handling fee. It was money for nothing.

When Absko and Jumapili arrived back at their shack loaded with the bags taken at the time of their retreat it was noticeably calm. Zuberi was sitting quietly in the dark, his dogs laying peacefully around him.

'No padlock,' said Zuberi accusingly as Absko lit the oil lamp. No fucking padlock.' Those were his first words.

'Our parents couldn't afford one,' explained Jumapili who rarely found her voice and certainly not at a time like this.

'Your eyes roll when you talk, do you know that?' said Zuberi taken aback by Jumapili's interjection.

'She's blind,' said Absko.

'Yeh yeh, I know. I can tell by the way her eyes roll, but it's odd when someone's talkin' 'n they don't look at you,' said Zuberi. 'Look, I've been out and bought a heavy-duty padlock for you.' He threw it across the room toward Absko, who failed to catch it, causing it to clank on the ground.

'Thank you!' said Absko surprised.

'Make sure you use it, and remember – ten shillings every week,' said Zuberi. 'Don't forget. Don't be late. If you ever go from 'ere I'll find you. I always have my money, remember that.' Then he asked: 'Do you have a cloth?'

Jumapili reached into a drawer, took out a clean rag and offered it.

'Thank you.' Zuberi poured water on to it from a jug. Then placing his shoes, one at a time on the chair, he wiped them spotlessly clean. He was leaving as immaculately as he arrived.

Snapping his dogs to attention, Zuberi clipped on their leads.

'Make sure you lock the door the next time you leave,' he said as he pushed his way through the corrugated iron door, the dogs at his heel.

It was late by the time Absko and Jumapili had everything sorted. For the first time in their lives, they chained themselves inside their huts before they went to bed. They were fearful that the youths might return angry and in force.

'You know you've broken your promise to Mama, don't you?' said Jumapili from the still of her bed. 'You promised her you would always go to Sunday School to learn to read and write and do arithmetic. You can't work and go to school, can you?'

'I know,' said Absko, 'but we can't have both. We can't have a home and me go to school. It's one or the other.'

'But Mama wanted you to read and write. Above all else it was what she wanted for you. She said it would be your way out of here.'

I know Jumapili, I know.'

Absko turned his face into his pillow and cried himself to sleep.

Chapter 13

'I HAVE A present for you,' said Absko as he and Jumapili walked back to their shack from the matatu station after a very ordinary day. 'It was left on the matatu about three days ago, but no one has claimed it, so Bosi has said I can give it to you.'

'Your driver has said I can have a present?' said Jumapili surprised. 'I didn't think he liked me.'

'I'll give it to you when we get home.' Absko was excited because this would be his sister's first present since their mother had died. Despite him working seven days a week, their budget could only ever manage the bare essentials. On the plus side, 'Blind Jumi', as Jumapili had become known, had become quite a feature of Tayiania to the point where people would often place some coins on her lap or tip them into her bag. These gifts were never enough to pay the dog man the full ten shillings he had to be paid each week, but every few cents Jumapili collected were gratefully received.

When they were home, their jobs done, and the shack was quiet, Absko reached into his bag and presented Jumapili with a full-sized mouth organ.

'What's this?' she asked as she fumbled with the strange object in her hands.

'It's a mouth organ. It's used to make music.' He helped turn it around in her hands. 'You must put it to your lips and blow.'

Jumapili put it close to her mouth and blew.

'No, no. You need to put it to your lips, so it touches, almost in your mouth, and then you blow and suck.'

Jumapili did as she was told only to emit an unpleasant rasping sound.

'Let me,' said Absko snatching the mouth organ and putting it straight to his lips before he emitted an equally unpleasant sound.

His unmusical noise changed significantly in pitch as he blowed and sucked. Giving up, he wiped the mouth organ on his sleeve before placing it back in Jumapili's hands.

She tried again. This time more successfully even if there was no recognisable tune.

'Maybe it's because you've lost some of your back teeth. Perhaps that makes a difference,' suggested Absko. 'Try softer blowing and sucking.'

Jumapili moved to lie on her bed, and, following her brother's instruction, started to teach herself to play the harmonica.

Before the baker's shop and coffee roaster's opened for customers and turned off their radio sets, Jumapili would sit on her orange box and listen to the music played to her in stereo from these two shops. On the day after she had been given the harmonica she surreptitiously started to play. Very quietly and modestly she tried to find the notes which matched the sound of the songs being played. Day after day she practiced until she was confident to keep playing the most popular songs of the day after the shops had turned their radios off.

Slowly, the songs of Aretha Franklin, Stevie Wonder, Marvin Gaye, Tammi Terrel, The Supremes, Dion Warwick, and The Four Tops became her staple repertoire. As she grew more self-assured in her playing, so she played louder, and started to draw more attention to herself. Undoubtedly, she had a rare gift amongst mouth-organ players because she was able to use her lips and tongue to get the pure sound of one note. It meant that people would stop what they were doing and take time out to listen to her.

With this came Jumapili's first self-taught life lesson and one she never forgot: no skilled person needs ever to be a beggar. Instead of throwing coins in her direction, shoppers began to pay to hear her play.

'Can you sing Jumi?' asked Rishi McGeown, the boy who had helped Jumapili find a toilet two years before. They had become quite friendly since then with him buying her the occasional cup of tea, donut, or bar of chocolate.

'I don't know.'

'If you can sing then you can use the harmonica in the introduction and in the chorus between the verses.'

'I don't know.'

'You should try. Do you have a favourite song?'

'*Over the rainbow*. It's the one I get asked to play most often.'

'What – from the Wizard of Oz? Have you seen it?'

Jumapili pulled a disapproving face.

'Sorry, dumb question, but you know what I mean. Come on, have a go,' Rishi continued enthusiastically.

'I don't want to.'

'Look, I'll start, and you join in.'

'*Somewhere over the rainbow, Way up high*,' sung Rishi, taking Jumapili's hand to strike out the beat.

'*There's a land that I heard of*,' they sung together.

'*Once in a lullaby*,' sung Jumapili on her own, and her voice quietly crackled as she continued through the next couple of versus.

'You need to do it standing up,' commanded Rishi, after she had stopped singing. 'It will be better standing up.' He reached for her hands. 'Come on, we'll do it again. I'll beat us in like before. On three - one ... two ... three.'

At the very moment Jumapili started singing, the traffic cleared allowing the purest of voices to travel to the café tables opposite where the eight European men were debating the news of the day. They knew she was there but few, if any, had taken much notice of Jumapili before, simply tipping her a few coins as they walked past. They'd heard her play the harmonica, but that was just background muzak. Now, to a man, they stopped what they were doing, turned to look at her and listen. She had captivated them. It wasn't just her voice which was perfect, but her breathing, phrasing and emotion. These attributes made Jumapili's singing quite exquisite, to the point that, when she ended, the men at the coffee tables stood up to give her a standing ovation.

Graeme McGeown, Rishi's father and the youngest of the Europeans sitting opposite scraped back his chair. Stumbling and swaying he crossed the street to where Jumapili was sitting.

'Here's two shillings. Sing that again,' he ordered rudely, before throwing money into her lap. From the slur of his voice and the overpowering smell of alcohol, it was obvious he was drunk.

'Do you want to, Jumi?' asked Rishi concerned. 'You don't have to if you don't want to.'

Jumapili nodded; she sensed something was wrong.

'Pa, if you return to your seat then I'm sure she'll be happy to start. You'll hear it best from over there,' said Rishi.

For the first time Jumapili sang for her supper, and with it, she suddenly felt good, very good indeed.

Chapter 14

'I'VE GOT TO go back to school,' announced Rishi McGeown as he stood before Jumapili who was sitting on the same upturned orange box in front of the alleyway in Tayiania. 'The term starts on Tuesday.'

'It sounds as though you don't want to go,' said Jumapili, picking up on the sadness in his voice.

'Not really,' he answered. 'It's not much fun.'

'Would you do me a favour before you go?' she asked nervously.

'Sure, but I've got something for you ...'

'It's something I'd normally ask my brother, but he's never got the time,' she interjected before Rishi had finished his sentence.

'I thought you might like these,' said Rishi and he reached down to take Jumapili's hand, placing two objects in her grasp.

'What is it? What are they?' she asked moving her hands slowly up and down in fractions of an inch until she was sure that the objects he had given her would not hurt, and then she took hold of them fully.

'The thin one, the metal one, that's a penny whistle. The wooden one, that's a recorder. They're mine. I first learned to play music on them. I thought you might like them ... to learn with.'

Jumapili smiled as she toyed with both instruments in her hand.

'Look, I'll show you,' he said, taking back the penny whistle and placing it to his lips. He started to play the first few bars of *When The Boat Comes In*.

'I know this,' said Jumapili before joining in: *'Dance to your Daddy, my little laddie, Dance to your Daddy my little man. Dance to your Daddy, sing to your mommy. Dance to your Daddy my little man.'*

'How do you know that?' asked Rishi, surprised.

'Oh, it's played on the radio quite often.'

'You try,' he said thrusting the penny whistle into her hands. 'The plastic end goes into your mouth. No not like that. Like ... rest it on your lower lip, close your mouth and then blow. That's it! Now feel the holes. Your fingers must cover the holes to make the notes. Each finger must cover a different hole.' He forcefully spread her fingers out. 'Blow some more.'

Jumapili smiled the widest smile she had ever smiled.

'Listen to this one,' said Rishi, now putting the recorder to his lips. 'You play it the same way as the whistle, but it has a mellower sound.'

This time he played the first few bars of *The Skye Boat Song*.

'I know that one too,' exclaimed Jumapili. 'I heard it discussed on the radio. Also, your father speaks of it often when he's having his morning coffee. The story's fascinating.'

'You know the story?'

'Yes, the song's about the escape of Bonnie Prince Charlie to the Isle of Skye after losing the Battle of Culloden.'

'You know of the Battle of Culloden?' Rishi was astonished.

'Yes, I get a lot of learning sitting here.'

'It's quite funny because the Skye song has become the informal national anthem of my school. It's the first thing the music teacher teaches when you arrive.'

'Why?' asked Jumapili.

Because it's where Prince Charles, y'know, the future King of England, went to school. He's just left.'

'Well, he's not the rightful king, is he?' said Jumapili stridently.

'Yeh, that's why they play it,' explained Rishi, 'but how do you know that?'

'It's a descendant of the Stuarts who should be King of England, not a family from Germany. The man on the radio said we shouldn't have a false queen as our queen. They gave it as one of the reasons why Kenya needed to be a republic.'

'I didn't know that.' Rishi's forehead creased in a frown.

'But it's a good job the Stuarts were thrown out,' continued Jumapili. 'They wanted to bring back the Catholics and that would have been a disaster.'

'Why?' asked Rishi who had been baptized a Catholic.

'Fancy selling indulgences to rich people so they can buy the forgiveness of their sins and go to heaven in the next life. It's not just stupid; its crooked, but it's what the Catholics did!'

'You wanted a favour?' asked Rishi, deliberately changing the subject.

'I was wondering if you would walk with me. I would like to walk to the other side of here and over the road. After the first time I'll be OK, but I ...'

'Of course I will.'

Jumapili arranged and stored her things around her orange box, before she reached for her cane which was leant up against the wall. She turned towards Rishi, who'd been waiting patiently.

'Hold my arm here,' she instructed, tapping her biceps. 'You'll find it works best from here as it is easier to twist me the way you want me to go. I find it better than me holding your arm. I get better guidance this way.'

Rishi felt embarrassed, almost coy, at the familiarity involved in taking her arm. They turned left, first walking past the coffee roaster's before proceeding at a fairly normal pace down the street. Jumapili tapped her stick ahead of her and clicked her tongue as she walked.

'Be careful of the lamp post. There's a waste bin just ahead. There's a sign post,' warned Rishi.

They crossed the road and walked back on the other side.

'Would you like a tea or coffee?' asked Rishi as they were approaching the coffee shop opposite where Jumapili would sit out her day; the coffee shop where the White men took their coffee each morning.

'Do you think I'm allowed? They probably have a very strict no chokora rule.'

'But you're not a chokora.'

'I am to most people.'

'Well, you're not when you're with me!' said Rishi. He led her to a seat.

'Would you like a bacon sandwich?' he asked. 'Honestly, they make the best bacon sandwiches in the world here.'

Jumapili smiled and nodded.

'What would you like to drink, coffee?'

She nodded again.

For the first time in her life Jumapili was about to have a conversation with someone other than her brother.

Chapter 15

'DO YOU KNOW the men who sit here in the morning?' asked Jumapili as, cautiously she found the cup and saucer that had been placed in front of her. She grimaced at the bitterness of coffee which she was tasting for the very first time.

'Do you want sugar in that?' asked Rishi.

'Yes, please.'

He moved the sugar bowl towards her but said nothing more. He was studying the way her hands were moving around the cup and then the movement of the cup to her mouth.

Jumapili heard the bowl move and knew it was the sugar Rishi had offered. She slowly reached out to touch it.

'Would you like help with that?'

She nodded and what followed was an intensity of emotion which took them both by surprise. It was not the first time Rishi, a fifteen-year-old boy, had touched hands with Jumapili, an eleven-year-old girl, but as he helped her first hold, then load, and finally tip a spoon full of sugar, they became shyly embarrassed at the intimacy they found in the softness of each other's fingers.

'We should practice that,' said Rishi abruptly, before disappearing inside to return a minute later with an empty cup.

There was jocularity in their discussion as spoon-full after spoon-full of sugar went everywhere until, taking a break, Jumapili had another sip of her coffee and grimaced again.

'Oh God. I'm sorry. I forgot to tell you to stir it,' said Rishi. He placed the handle end of her teaspoon in her hand again. 'You put that in your cup and whisk it around. Seriously, have you never done this before.

'Never, every drink I've ever had has come already made in a cup or a bottle.'

'My father and grandfather come here most days,' said Rishi, returning to Jumapili's very first question.

'I know which one's your father,' said Jumapili. 'He's usually the quiet one – until he gets excited about something.'

'Yes, that's my father.'

'But which one is your grandfather?'

'He tends to sit at the end, I think.'

'Do you know, they have the most earnest discussions. Time and time again I want them to explain something, but I don't ask. I daren't. I am sure they wouldn't like to think that someone is listening to them.'

'You can hear what they're saying from over there?' asked Rishi, amazed, pointing in the direction of Jumapili's orange box.

'Yeh, unless there's a vehicle in the way. Are your family the tea buyers?' she asked.

'Yes.'

'Does one of them own a Rolls Royce?'

'My grandfather.'

'He's very proud of his car, and everyone else is very envious!'

'Yeh, he likes his cars, but I don't know why they're envious. Karl Stenner could buy a hundred of 'em. He's the richest man there by far.'

'Which one is he?' she asked.

'He's the publisher, prints magazines.'

'Oh, the crook,' said Jumapili.

'Schhh, you can't say that, Jumi. Its rude!'

'Well, everyone else around the table says it about him ... but only when he's not there.'

'Why's he a crook?' asked Rishi. 'What do they say?'

'You don't know?'

'No.'

'He gets copies of magazines, trade newspapers from the UK and from America which he copies word for word, line for line, picture for picture which he prints up at his printers and then sells them throughout Africa as though they were original.'

'What's wrong with that?' asked Rishi innocently. 'We all copy everything. Every time I write an essay at school, I copy whole pages of text.'

'It's counterfeiting,' she answered.

'Is it?'

'Yeh, its stealing someone else's intellectual property.'

'What's that?' asked Rishi.

'One of the men's a headmaster, isn't he?'

'Yes, Colin Downsted.'

'He's the cleverest by far, isn't he?'

'I don't know,' admitted Rishi.

'He's not an easy man to argue with,' explained Jumapili. 'He's very precise. He takes what someone has said and then through careful questioning makes them seem naïve, almost stupid. He doesn't speak often but I love listening to him as I always learn lots of new words. You should hear him sum up a debate or argument they've had; he can dissect the arguments against something and then go on to list double the arguments in favour.'

'And he thinks Karl Stenner's a crook?'

'Yes, but he doesn't think he'll ever get caught.'

'Why not?'

'Although stealing intellectual property is a crime, he doesn't think the police in Nairobi will prosecute him. He says they will see it as a White man stealing from another White man. The only thing he thinks might happen is that one of the magazines Stenner copies might sue him for damages, but then Mr. Downsted doubts it because the costs would be more than the gain.'

'And you've learnt all this just listening to their conversation?'

'I can give you a definition of intellectual property if you want it.' said Jumapili enthusiastically.

'Go on then.'

'Mr Downsted said, and I quote.' She took a deep breath: *'intellectual property is work which comes from creations of the human mind.'* She beamed a wide confident smile.

'He said that, and you remembered it? Wow.'

'He most definitely said it.'

'Do you remember everything anyone ever says?' Rishi was both worried and amazed at the same time.

'Not always, but Mr. Downsted said it twice, so I know I've got it right.'

Chapter 16

'ABSKO, WHY DON'T I go to school?' asked Jumapili when they were both tucked up in their beds for the night, her recorder and tin whistle safely in her grasp.

''cause you're blind,' answered Absko abruptly.

'Rishi says there are special schools for the blind.'

'In England maybe, but not here.'

'Rishi says that they're here in Nairobi too.'

'But it takes money to go to school, and we don't have money.'

'He says these schools are charities, and I won't have to pay.'

'Oh.'

'I think we should find out, don't you?' she asked, after a long pause.

Absko grunted.

'It would be so much better if I could read and write.'

'You can't read 'cause you can't see!' said Absko raising his voice in frustration. 'You're being silly. Stop it!'

'Rishi says that there's a special writing for blind people called braille.[10] It enables them to read and write, just like everyone else.

---

[10] Braille is written on paper held in a slate. This slate contains a range of grids along and down the page. Typically, an A4 slate will have 27 rows with 30 grids in each row. In each grid, there are two parallel vertical lines of three holes (six holes in total). These holes are arranged like the dots placed on the side of a six on a dice cube. A stylus is pressed through a hole to create a tactile dot in the paper which can then be felt by tips of one's fingers. From these six dots, sixty-four alternative combinations can be created. For example, the letter 'a' is represented by a single dot in the top left of the grid, the letter 'b' by two dots in the top and in the middle rows on the left of the grid, and the letter 'c' by two dots in the top row. Braille is written from right to left so that when the paper is turned over to feel the indentations, reading is made from left to right.

Do you know there are lawyers that are blind, and they do all their learning using braille.'

'Don't be silly. Just think about it for a moment. How can there possibly be blind lawyers. You'll be telling me there are blind doctors next.'

'There was one once, in Chicago, but not now. Rishi looked it up.'

Absko said nothing. The fact was that working every day, together with all the chores, while being the main carer for his sister was knocking the stuffing out of him. In times gone by, he would have enthusiastically risen to the challenge to get Jumapili into a school for the blind, but this extra task was perhaps the one which was going to break the camel's back. Slowly but surely Absko was being driven into a deep depression. He knew he had to go on; he just did not know where he was going to get the strength.

Chapter 17

'RISHI HAS ASKED me to sing at a family funeral,' said Jumapili as she and Absko walked home after a long shift.

'Who's Rishi?' asked Absko. He had forgotten.

'You know, Richard McGeown, the boy who encouraged me to start singing. I've told you about him. He's the one who gave me the tin whistle and the recorder. His father's a tea buyer ... always drunk by lunch time.'

'I thought he was away in England.'

'Scotland. He's at school in Scotland, but he's come back early because his grandfather's died.'

'And they want you to sing at his grandfather's funeral?'

'He's said they'll pay me twenty shillings.'

'Twenty shillings! For singing?' The surprise in Absko's voice was palpable.

They walked on in silence.

'But he says I must have a new dress. He says I can't go to church in this dress.'

They walked on. A new dress was completely beyond their means.

'Does he mean a new dress, or can we get one from the bazaar?'

The bazaar was where almost everyone in Kibera bought their clothes, mostly second hand.

'I dunno.'

'I suppose he wants you to wear black?'

'You know I don't know what that is,' said Jumapili crossly. 'Black, white, I've no idea what you're talking about.'

'People wear white dresses to weddings, black dresses to funerals. They're different colours, that's all.'

'Then obviously it will have to be black.' There was frustration in her voice.

'Suppose I could steal one. Everyone around here steals.'

'No! Absko no,' said Jumapili rounding on him firmly. 'If you get caught they'll send you to prison, and then I'll have no one.'

'Perhaps I should have kept working seven days a week like I used to when we had to pay the dog man. There are so many things we need to buy but can't afford.'

'No Absko, that was killing you. You weren't nice to know because you were so tired all the time.'

They said little more as they walked back to their shack. It was when they were lying in their beds that the subject of the funeral returned.

'Have you noticed how we have no friends?' said Jumapili.

'What do you mean, no friends?'

'We don't have any friends. Everyone else has friends but us.'

'Why do we need friends?'

'If we had friends, I might be able to borrow a dress,' answered Jumapili.

'Mama and Baba had no friends,' said Absko defensively.

There was a long pause.

'Chummy boy will have to pay you upfront,' declared Absko. 'If he wants you to have a new dress, he should pay for it.'

'Absko ... do you think I might have some eye shields, something to hide my eyes,' she asked shyly.

'Why? Does the sunlight hurt you?' There was sympathy in his voice. There always was when they spoke about her eyesight.

'You know I don't know what sunlight is. It's just that people comment on how my eyes move. You've heard them. Remember the Dog Man. They say they revolve, going in all directions. They say it's strange. They say it makes people think of my eyes, not me when they're talking to me.'

'You mean sunglasses, like Stevie Wonder or Ray Charles wear?'

'I don't know.'

'They're famous singers. They're blind too. You'll know their songs.'

Jumapili shrugged.

'It will be your money. You've earned it. So, you can spend it on what you want,' said Absko.

'It's not like that. You always talk about the money you've earned being our money so the money I earn must be our money too. You spend your money on me; I must spend my money on you. That's only fair, isn't it?'

'You'll need a haircut if you're going to sing in public. It's too long – I'll cut it,' volunteered Absko, 'and after that we'll go to Bibie Wasuse. She won't charge as much because it'll be shorter, but she'll finish it off and make it nice for you.'

Chapter 18

RISHI'S FATHER, GRAEME McGeown entered the Royal Military College, Sandhurst in 1937 straight from school. As the son of a Scottish colonialist from a second-rate English public school, it was inevitable his first commission would be in the British Indian army. His first and last posting was to III Corps in Dimapur, India.

III Corps' role was in mountain and jungle warfare. It was therefore inevitable McGeown would be posted to fight against the Japanese in Malaysia in World War II. Suffering defeat after defeat, and retreat after retreat, the British Army was constantly outmanoeuvred by the Japanese army. McGeown's company was eventually order to Singapore to defend the Island. They were not in good order.

After a short battle, the British Army surrendered Singapore on 5th February 1942 and Captain Graeme McGeown became one of the 140,000 Allied troops who became Japanese prisoners of war, of whom 30,000 were to die in captivity. As McGeown found, everyone who became a Japanese prisoner of war had their lives irrevocably changed by the experience.

McGeown was taken to Fukuoka 17 Prisoner of War camp on mainland Japan and was put to work as a slave at the Mitsui Miike Coal Mine. Conditions were unbelievably harsh and cruel because, to the Japanese, a surrendered soldier's life was worthless. You were there to be worked until your death.

The men who found freedom on 15 August 1945 when Japan surrendered, had only survived their captivity through enormous willpower. Like many others, as soon as McGeown was released and taken into the care of the US Army, he fell desperately ill. The US Army's care for the Japanese POWs was impeccable because much had been learned from the rehabilitation of German concentration-camp victims. The fact was that the fight part of the brain which had kept

McGeown, and many others, alive during their captivity switched itself off, and with the bodily resources all gone, death suddenly became a hair's breadth away.

The US Army repatriated McGeown back to his regiment in Dimapur where he was hospitalised for a year. With independence and the partition of India and Pakistan on the close horizon, McGeown resigned his commission and returned to his family in Nairobi. He took with him a newly acquired, much younger Indian wife called Lakshmi, who had helped nurse him better.

McGeown joined his father's tea-buying business which acted as agent for many tea importers and blenders around the globe. The war had badly affected his father's trade, but with peace came prosperity and this brought additional business and good fortune which father and son enjoyed. In 1953, McGeown's only son was born. His father called him Richard, but his mother nicknamed him Rishi in recognition of his Indian heritage.

Except then, no one knew anything about Post-Traumatic Stress Disorder, a mental health condition caused by a traumatic experience, which Graeme McGeown was suffering from in spades. Vivid flashbacks and nightmares made it seem as though his past trauma was happening in the present, bringing him out in sweats, feeling nausea, trembling uncontrollably and stomach-aching pain. In his agony, he found that whisky was the only thing which could help him sleep, first having just a dram, and then two. It was not long before he was drinking a bottle a night. There were long bouts when McGeown would be teetotal but then the flashbacks and nightmares would recur, and he would be back on the bottle again.

The problem was that alcohol had dulled McGeown's senses and this meant that they started to lose customers and friends. Those friends they did retain were fellow regulars at the Tayiania café. When McGeown was sober he was eloquent and engaging, sharing a perspective on issues not swayed by group thought; when he was drunk, he was silent and maudlin.

After McGeown's father fell ill and was unable to make their morning coffee rendezvous, McGeown would continue to come but always drunk. The fact was that he would have been uninvited long ago if it hadn't been for the respect the others had for his father, and the sympathy they had for him for his war years.

Wearing a shorter version of the black dress worn by Audrey Hepburn in *Breakfast at Tiffany's*, and with her fingers and toenails painted courtesy of her hairdresser, Jumapili looked stunning when she came forward to sing at Graeme McGeown's father's and Rishi's grandfather's funeral.

Rishi had spent time coaching Jumapili how to sing Psalm 123, *The Lord is My Shepherd*, so she was comfortable with him when he led her to a place in front of the congregation. However, it was her singing of *the Skye Boat Song*, and her note-perfect playing of the harmonica in the places normally reserved for the bagpipes which made the service memorable. It reminded everyone of the family's Scottish roots. Her singing of the words '*burned are their homes, exile and death, scatter the loyal men*' chilled everyone's hearts, because there was not a European there who, at that moment, did not yearn for their homeland.

Rishi invited Jumapili to the wake where almost every member of the congregation congratulated and thanked her. Even the undertakers asked for her contact details because they were sure other people would want her to sing at their funerals.

The day after the funeral, Jumapili was back at her usual station between the bakers and coffee roaster's in her normal clothes. Yesterday, all eyes were on her. Today she was virtually invisible to those that walked by.

As Jumapili had observed, Graeme'McGeown's father's pride and joy had been his silver-and-maroon painted Rolls Royce Phantom V. Although it had been purchased second-hand and was now ten years old, it was his statement of success. The day after the funeral, McGeown chose to drive it for the very first time to the café in Tayiania.

Other than being unfamiliar with the car or being blind drunk, there could be no explanation for McGeown having lost control of the Rolls Royce. He turned first to hit the corner of the coffee roaster's at the alleyway where Jumapili sat, before accelerating and driving into the opposite corner of the bakery.

Jumapili didn't stand a chance. She was hit with the full two-and-a-half tons of car, breaking both her legs and smashing an ankle before she was pinned against the timber wall of the bakery. Her body was thrown forward, forcing her head to smash into the bonnet of the car, knocking her unconscious.

McGeown clambered out of the car without a scratch, almost oblivious to what he had done.

Chapter 19

COLIN DOWNSTED WAS on his feet the moment the Rolls Royce hit the coffee roaster's. He was on the other side of the road only seconds after Jumapili was hit. He was standing by the door of the car when McGeown climbed out.

'Reverse man, reverse!' yelled Downsted, but McGeown was too drunk to react. Pulling him to one side, Downsted climbed into the car and with the engine still running, he slammed it into reverse freeing Jumapili's body. The other Europeans from the café were now on the spot too, and it was they who held up Jumapili's limp body as, being free, it began to collapse to the ground.

'We need an ambulance, phone for an ambulance. Go into the bakers and get them to call for an ambulance,' shouted Downsted. 'Get the police here too, but an ambulance first.'

'It'll cost. Who's going to pay?' asked a voice.

'McGeown,' responded Downsted, with all the authority of a headmaster, 'and for God's sake, someone, get 'im out of here. Get 'im home otherwise the police will pick 'im up and then everything'll get out of control.'

'She's alive,' pronounced another voice. 'She has a good pulse and her breathing's strong, but we don't know if she has any internal bleeding, so she's got to get to the hospital fast.'

'The ambulance will be here in thirty to forty minutes,' declared the baker returning from phoning the emergency services.

'Jesus, that's too long, far too long!' exclaimed Downsted. 'We'll have to get her there ourselves. We'll need an estate car, not a sedan so she can stay lying down.'

'We'll use my van,' said the coffee roaster. 'It's a bit dirty but it'll be big enough.'

'What are we going to use as a stretcher?' someone else asked.

Slowly, but surely under the leadership of Colin Downsted, problems were solved so that, before the ambulance had even started making its way, Jumapili's legs had been put into temporary splints and she was on her way to the emergency room of the Kenyatta National Hospital, Nairobi.

Chapter 20

ABSKO SAT NEXT to Jumapili's bed for the next three days and nights, holding her hand and talking to her while she lay motionless in a coma. The femur of her left leg had been snapped in two because it took the full impact of the Rolls Royce's bumper. A metal plate had been screwed along the two halves of the bone to keep them aligned, and a pin inserted so that her leg could be kept in traction.

Jumapili's tibia and fibula on her right leg were also both broken, as was her ankle. These were repaired with plates and screws. It would be a miracle if she would be able to walk again without a limp.

'You know she's blind,' Absko would say to every doctor and nurse who came into her private room to examine her. There would be words of commiseration, but no one suggested what he was secretly hoping – that she might be able to see after this bang on her head. His logic was simple: when the engine on the matatu didn't start they would bang the carburettors and battery points with a hammer, so the connections were remade. Could this have happened in her brain, he wondered.

Downsted and Rishi visited Jumapili every day to check up on her. There was no debate between the two of them. The McGeown family were going to pay for all Jumapili's hospital costs. Absko had to go back to work, so it was Rishi who was sitting with Jumapili when she slowly regained consciousness. It was a slow process as she drifted in and out of sleep. Encouraged by the nurses, Rishi gently held and stroked her hand.

'Water, I need a drink,' whispered Jumapili turning her head to look towards Rishi. If she had been able to see she would have seen his smile of relief, of joy - and of love. Because although Rishi was just fifteen years old, there was something which this brown-skinned boy with his thick black wavy hair found utterly beguiling about the eleven-year-old blind black girl with her tight curly hair.

'I'll check with the nurse,' said Rishi disappearing out of the room, before returning with a nurse and a small drinking teapot.

'Where am I?' asked Jumapili in the faintest of voices.

'You're in hospital. You've had a bad accident,' said the nurse. 'You've got to stay still, very still. You mustn't move.'

'I hurt, I really hurt. My head hurts, my legs hurt, everywhere hurts.'

'I'll get a doctor and he'll organise some pain relief for you,' said the nurse, leaving the room quickly.

'I'm so sorry, Jumi,' said Rishi as soon as the nurse had gone. 'It was my father. He lost control of grandfather's car and drove it into you.'

'Why?'

'He was drunk.'

'Drunk? It was the morning... I heard it come. I couldn't understand why it wouldn't stop. It was all so fast.'

'He's always drunk,' said Rishi in a resigned tone, as he continued to stroke the back of her hand with his thumb, before watching her fall back to sleep.

It was some while later that Rishi stood away from her bed and watched admiringly as a nurse fed Jumapili with sips of water from a small teapot and then as a young doctor performed a series of tests about her body before injecting her with morphine.

'Well, she's not paralysed,' the doctor announced. 'We were fearful ... there's always the risk...'

Jumapili heard him but without appreciating that the doctor was talking about her. She continued to drift in and out of sleep, only waking properly when Absko came into the room.

'Can you see, Jumi?' he asked. It was late in the evening and his first question on seeing her awake.

She turned her head slowly from side to side.

'No, why?' she asked.

'Father's been arrested and charged,' said Rishi not giving Absko time to answer.

'Drunk driving?' asked Absko.

'No - dangerous driving, leaving the scene of an accident and having no insurance.'

'Downsted says your father was falling-down drunk, so why hasn't he been charged with drink driving?'

'He left the scene, so the police didn't get the evidence.'

'Everyone saw him, ask anyone there. They'll all say he was blind drunk! I went there. I've asked 'em.'

'I'd say he came home blind drunk too, but it's not enough,' explained Rishi. 'There are masses of medical conditions which make people look as though they're drunk when they're not, and he could invent one of those. The police have said they'll tell the courts he left the accident 'cause he was drunk, but they say that's the best they can do.'

'He'll bribe 'em. It's what all you lot always do. It'll never get to court.'

'This time it will. My mother's determined. She's locked him out of the house. He's sleeping in the shed with his train set. She wants him in jail.'

'Jesus, ... and you, do you want that?'

Rishi didn't answer. Above all, he wanted his father to stop drinking, to be sober.

'Did you say he ain't got no insurance?' stormed Absko. 'Fuck, how's this lot going to be paid for?' He waved his arms around the room. 'The headmaster said you were paying. He said you had insurance.'

'It's father's company insurance that's paying, not the car one. Somehow, he's wangled it saying Jumi was one of his workers ... because he paid her to sing at Grandpa's funeral.'

'That ain't right. Jumi and me – you call her Jumi too, don't you? – we might be from Kibera and have no education, but we know what's right and wrong, and that's just wrong.'

'I agree, it's dishonest,' replied Rishi, 'but it's the only way this is going to be paid for, 'cause we don't have the money.'

'course you do. You bleedin' lot, you're the rich ones. You've all the money. It's our land and you've been making loads of money from it, and from us.'

'That may have been before Kenyatta, before independence but things have changed,' argued Rishi.

'Well, one thing is fuckin certain,' said Absko who rarely swore. 'Your fuckin house is a million times better than ours, and that ain't fair!'

'I agree. It's not fair. It's what the courts are for, to make it a bit fairer.'

The two boys sat in silence watching Jumapili sleep.

'She did the singing 'cause she wanted some sunglasses,' said Absko after a long pause. 'She was going to buy them with the money she had from singing at your grandfather's funeral. She's been told her eyes roll and it embarrassed her. She wanted sunglasses to hide her eyes.'

'No! that's absurd,' protested Rishi. 'Have you seen how beautiful they are. Just look at the colour, the brightness. They're beautiful. Have you noticed how most people's eyes have bits of yellow, green and blue? Jumi's have none of that. They're pure mahogany and look at the whiteness.'

'Do you think that's why she's blind?' asked Absko, forever seeking the reason Jumapili couldn't see.

'No, its in the genes. It's hereditary. It's your mum and dad who gave her those eyes.'

'They're gone,' said Absko abruptly.

'Yeh, I know, I'm sorry.'

'It's because her eyes don't stay still like everyone else's, that's what worries her,' said Absko. 'She says people comment on it, never to her, but she hears, and it upsets her. Someone once told her that the eyes are the windows to the soul, and they couldn't look into her soul 'cause her eyes moved all the time.'

Rishi said nothing but he took careful note because the next day he arrived by Jumapili's bed with a set of Ray-Ban, Wayfarer sunglasses.

'You had her dress, so I thought you should have her sunglasses too,' said Rishi as he handed over the spectacle case.'

'Who's dress?' asked Jumapili.

'The dress you wore. It was like Audrey Hepburn's in the movie. I said about it. Well, she had sunglasses too; I've got the same for you.'

Jumapili opened the case carefully and took out the glasses.

'Show me,' she commanded.

'Rishi took back the glasses, unfolded them and placed them on her nose.

'Just the rock star,' he commented as he stood back to admire her. 'They suit you, Jumi. They really suit you.'

Jumapili's confidence soared.

Chapter 21

LAWYER'S OFFICES ARE intimidating places for the unfamiliar. For an illiterate sixteen-year-old in second-hand clothes, the offices of Kimutai & Makokha Advocates were frightening, but even more terrifying was the woman Absko was meeting.

Aminifu Kiprono had worked as a legal assistant in KMA for over ten years. Her experience made her as good a lawyer as any of the partners in the firm. She had worked her way through the University of East Africa becoming one of the first women to gain a first-class law degree. She had planned on becoming an advocate. However, with a busy husband, three children and a target of 2,200 billable hours a year, she had not yet had the time to complete the six months advocacy course. It meant that she was going to fail in her ambition to be the first woman lawyer in Kenya.

When Absko was promoted from a *manamba* to a *utingo*[11] he had to become a member of the Matatu Crew Welfare Association, their trade union, and membership gave him access to one hour of legal advice. KMA were the lawyers retained by the MCWA, which was how he came to be sitting in front of Mrs. Kiprono.

Absko had four questions: could Jumapili sue McGowan for her injuries? How much would she get paid for those injuries? How much would it cost? And how long would it take before she was paid?

He succinctly set out Jumapili's circumstances and the details of the accident, stressing time and time again that it was entirely McGeown's fault. Despite preparing hard to tell Jumapili's story, he was not prepared for the questions which came back to him. He knew how to spell his and Jumapili's names, but the trouble started when he was asked about his and his sister's dates of birth. He did not know

[11] Bus conductor

them. It was when he explained that their parents were both dead and neither he nor Jumapili had birth certificates, that the problems really started because, as far as Mrs. Kiprono was concerned, the lack of birth certificates could only mean that he and his sister could not have been born in Kenya. The matter was confirmed in her mind when Absko told her that neither of them had the antenatal passbooks which Mrs. Kiprono was certain that their mother must have been given if they were born in Kenya.

Absko's next problem was the lack of an address. As far as the Nairobi council was concerned there were no legal properties in Kibera; everyone was an illegal squatter. As far as the courts were concerned, Absko and Jumapili had no fixed abode. Mrs. Kiprono laboured the point that the Nairobi courts were not sympathetic to petitions from homeless people, and certainly not those from the Kibera slums.

However, the most depressing news was on the size of Jumapili's damages. Mrs. Kiprono patiently explained that Jumapili would be paid compensation based on the loss of her earnings, but as she had never been to school and her earnings comprised only the few shillings she earned from busking, the amount paid in compensation for loss of earnings would be miniscule.

'If your sister's claim was based just on her loss of earnings, it would not be worth bringing the case,' advised Mrs. Kiprono. 'The costs would exceed the likely award for damages. You'd be out of pocket.'

However, there would also be an award for pain and suffering, and based on the extent of Jumapili's injuries, and the likely long-term harm, Mrs. Kiprono advised that the amount of money paid out would be as life changing as the original car accident had been.

'Every child has a right to a name and nationality from birth,' said Mrs Kiprono. 'If your sister wants to sue Mr. McGeown then both of you will need to have Kenyan ID cards. She's too young to sue on her own, Absko, so you will have to sue on her behalf, as her guardian. Take your mother and father's ID, and their death certificates, to the Assistant Chief at your nearest District Office. Get registered, get your ID cards and come back to me. There is nothing I can do until then!'

Absko walked dejectedly back to his matatu station. The tasks he had been set were impossible for him to achieve. However, Mrs. Kiprono was not going to be defeated so easily. She was quickly on the phone to Nairobi's children's welfare services.

'There's a blind girl in Kenyan National Hospital, called Jumapili Mwangi,' said Mrs. Kiprono, pausing to look at her notes. 'She's had a bad car accident. She's an orphan who's being looked after by her brother, but he's illiterate and too young. She needs to be made a ward of the court.'

Mrs. Kiprono's thinking was simple and mercenary. If Jumapili was a ward of court, her identity would be established. She would then have a client, and a client means billable hours and fees.

Chapter 22

'DID YOU WATCH it, sorry ... did you *listen* to it?' asked Rishi.

'What?' asked Jumapili.

'The moon landing, of course.'[12]

'Yes, the nurses had the television on in the patients' dayroom, but I listened to it on the radio in my bed.'

'Didn't you think it exciting?'

'When they were landing, I held my breath and held my breath until they were down. I was bursting.'

'And the walk?'

'I didn't get that as much. It didn't seem as exciting. I'll just be glad when those men are home. They've all got children, and I don't know how they can think of leaving them.'

'It's how discoveries are made,' explained Rishi.

'The thing is, they have no idea, they can't imagine, what it's like to grow up without a father. Well, Absko and I know. They should have sent men without a family.'

Rishi knew it was not an argument he was going to win so asked: 'What do you know about the moon?'

'Everything you do, except I can't see it. The KBS[13] have given me a cassette player and lent me a cassette they've made to explain the moon, the moon landings, and space exploration, and when I can read braille, I'll know so much more.'

'When are you going to learn braille?' asked Rishi.

'As soon as my compensation gets paid, and I can pay for it.'

---

[12] Neil Armstrong and Buzz Aldrin landed on the moon at 20:17 GMT (23.17 EAT) on 20th July 1969. Neil Armstrong was the first man to walk on the moon at 02.56 GMT (05.56 EAT) on 21st July 1969.

[13] The Kenya Society for the Blind.

'Mummy's very angry about you suing Daddy. She thinks there will be much less for her after their divorce.'

'You said my hospital costs were being paid by your father's work insurance' said Jumapili. 'Well, it's not true, is it?'

'Isn't it' said Rishi, palpably shocked.

'Your father had insurance on his own car which covered him when he drove another car like the Rolls Royce which he hit me with. But it's only for the damage done to other people, like me and the shops. It's his car insurance which is going to have to pay.'

'I don't know, but Mummy has said that the insurance company has told him they're suing him for their loss because he was drunk and that voided his insurance. They want to recover from him anything they pay to you.'

'Is that why you're being nice to me. So, I don't claim so much?' There was a bite in her voice.

'No, of course not! I felt kinda responsible in a way. Don't know why. I wanted to make sure you're ok, that's all.'

'It's just, it's got nothing to do with me,' explained Jumapili. 'A lawyer and a lady from the council, and someone from the hospital, have taken it all over. Not even Absko is allowed to have a say. They just shut him up. It's 'cause he can't read. It's why I must learn to read.'

There was a long, strained silence between them.

'I'm sorry, Rishi,' said Jumapili. 'I shouldn't have said that. I'm really sorry.'

'Do you know how to use a telephone?' she asked after a little while. 'It's just, I don't know how to use one. I hear I can speak to someone on the other side of the world.'

'You've never used a phone?' asked Rishi surprised.

'No, there are a thousand things I never knew about until I came in here, and the phone is one of them.'

'Who do you want to phone?'

'I don't know, anyone. I just need to learn how to use it.'

Actually, Jumapili did know; she wanted to talk to the lawyer and council officer who were now ruling her life without her consent, but now was not the time to mention it.

‘Yeh, yeh. There’s a pay phone in the main lobby of the hospital. We’ll go there,’ he said. ‘But I would like to ask a favour too.’

‘What?’

‘When you look, what do you see, Jumi?’ he asked. ‘Lots of blind people see shades. They know dark from light. It means they know night from day. You go around things so you must see something.’

‘I see nothing, just blank. I can put my hand right in front of my face, like this, but it’s not there. I know it’s there because I know where my hand is, and I can feel the draught it makes when it moves, and I hear. I hear really well. The doctor’s say I have a sixth sense.’

‘And night and day. Do you know when it’s nighttime?’

‘No, I don’t know what that is at all, except its when people go to sleep. The best I have is to know that when I start to feel the warmth of the sun day time has started.

Chapter 23

'I HAVE TO go back to school tomorrow,' said Rishi as he sat by the side of Jumapili's bed. She had been out of traction for a few weeks and had been moved from the Kenyatta National Hospital, where she had first been taken, to the specialist orthopaedic unit at the former British Military Hospital in Kabete.

'Your public school that's not for the public?' commented Jumapili.

'Yeh, that one, Gordonstoun.'

'How long will you be away?'

'It's a long term, twelve weeks. I come home just in time for Christmas. Although I'm not sure what home will be like then.'

'I'll miss you being here,' said Jumapili. 'The only visitors I have are Absko, a new fussy woman from the government, you and Mr. Downsted. He's very nice. He's teaching me to play chess.'

'You any good?'

'He says I'm getting better. He's also started to teach me to play the violin. They told me I couldn't play my mouth organ in here, so he pushes me out into the garden for a lesson whenever he's here.'

'He's pretty darn cross with my father,' said Rishi.

'I'm sure it was an accident.'

'It's not an accident to get drunk. Certainly, my mother thinks it's inexcusable, and I do too! I told you she's filed for a divorce, but the rules appear to be very complicated and are making her really mad. To make matters worse, my father's been told that he should expect a jail sentence when he comes to trial next year.'

'Why?'

'He could have killed you.'

'But he didn't.'

'They need to make an example of him. He's a White-privilege man in a Black country. They want to show that the Whites aren't privileged anymore.'

'Are you saying that they wouldn't send a Black man to jail for the same thing?'

'Most Blacks don't have cars to drive,' retorted Rishi, side-stepping her question.

'I really don't get this White/Black issue.'

'It's because you can't see.'

'I know. I think it's better I only hear voices. I make my judgement based on voices. I don't understand what you gain by making a judgement based upon skin colour.'

'You're right Jumi. We live in an absurd world, but it is not all about skin colour. A lot of it's about wealth. There's such disparity in wealth between Blacks and Whites.'

'Why's that?'

The Whites are accused of stealing Kenya's land, but we didn't. All we've done is take land which was not being used, not owned by anyone, and turned it into plantations.'

'How come the Whites did that and not the Blacks?'

'They could have done, but they would not have known that there was a market for tea and coffee back in England.'

There was a long pause.

'I've learnt so much since I've been in here,' said Jumapili. 'Do you know until I came here I didn't know another blind person, but now I've met someone else who's blind and I've realised I can do almost anything. There is so much to help blind people like me. The tape machine they lent me to explain the moon landing means I can listen to stories and have lessons like everyone else. The cassette is teaching me how to do arithmetic. I can now add and subtract. I didn't know how to do that before. I even know how to do money.'

'You didn't know how to count your money?'

'Oh yes, I've always been able to count how much I've been paid in a day, but I didn't know how to add today's money to yesterdays and the day before unless I counted it all. Now I can add it up. Honestly, the amount I've learnt since I've been here is amazing. To think, I wouldn't have learnt any of this if your father hadn't crashed into me.'

'You make me feel better by saying that,' said Rishi sheepishly.

'You know I won't be here when you get back. They tell me I'll be here for another two weeks and then they'll discharge me.'

'Where will you go?'

'I don't know. Home, I suppose, but this fussy woman from the City Council is telling me she will decide. Absko doesn't like it one bit.'

'Will you still be in a wheelchair?'

'I have physiotherapy twice a day to get me walking again, but it hurts and exhausts me. All I want to do afterwards is sleep. But the plan is I walk out of here. I may need crutches or a walking stick, but they've yet to work out how I can use my cane and crutches at the same time. It's quite funny as they keep trying to invent new ways.'

'How will I know where you've gone to?' asked Rishi, concerned.

'There was a long pause as Jumapili thought.

'You can send me a cassette, like a letter? Then I'll record on it telling you where I am and will send it back.'

They both laughed as they mimicked their imaginary recordings in different accents.

'Look, I must go,' said Rishi when their laughter had died down. 'I'll write and come and see you when I'm back.'

'Yes, please. I'd like that.'

Rishi leant forward and, squeezing the side of Jumapili's arms, he kissed her gently on the side of her cheek. The warmth of his breath on her ear and around her neck gave her a tingling feeling because she had never been kissed like that before.

'Bye Jumi,' said Rishi leaving. 'Good luck. See ya.'

Chapter 24

JUMAPILI HEARD DOWNSTED announce himself at her ward's nurses' station, so she set off in her wheelchair to greet him from the day table where she'd been working.

'How did you do that?' asked Downsted, amazed.

'What?'

'Manoeuvred your way around the bedstead, the one that's sticking out.'

'I knew it was there.'

'How?'

'I heard it.' There was innocence in Jumapili's reply.

'How?'

'It tells me it's there.'

'But it doesn't speak. It doesn't say anything,' said Downsted puzzled.

'Of course it does!'

Downsted shook his head not understanding what Jumapili was telling him.

'Shall we go outside?' he asked. 'You can practice the violin, then we'll play a game of chess.'

Jumapili said nothing, instead she whirled herself around in her wheelchair, tore down the ward to her bed where she whisked herself around both sides before steaming back, this time avoiding a different bed which had been pulled out to clean behind it.

'Do you know where you're going? Do you want me to push you?' asked Downsted, a frown now deep on his forehead, but Jumapili was already racing ahead of him, so she didn't answer.

Downsted stood in amazement and watched as Jumapili brought her wheelchair to a rapid stop just in front of a set of double metal doors with paned glass before she opened them to let herself out. She clicked as she independently moved herself around and through the garden until she came to the table they always sat at for their lessons and games.

The Jumapili who sat in front of the headmaster was a changed person for, in her wheelchair chariot, she held none of the fear which had inhibited her when she walked.

'We'll do scales in D Major and A Major, in two and three octaves,' said Downsted as he handed Jumapili the violin and bow she had brought out with her, 'and then we'll go on to learn the scales in E Major.'

'You haven't been practising,' scolded Downsted when Jumapili came to the end of her first set of scales. 'Do them again,' he ordered, and was to order time and again until she produced a sound which, if not pleasing, was, in Downsted's opinion, satisfactory.

'Please can we stop and play chess?' asked Jumapili.

Downsted rapidly set up his travelling chessboard and grasped one of the pieces in his hand. 'Left, right?' he asked.

She pointed whereon Downsted declared that he had won, would play white and would start.

'Does white always start?'

'It's convention,' answered Downsted without really thinking.

'Isn't it racist if black always goes second?'

'I don't know, does it matter? I'm moving the pawn in front of my king forward two places. That's my opening move.'

'I'll do the same.'

'We always say black and white, not white and black. Is that also racist?' asked Downsted before he declared that he had moved his queen to H5.

'My king to E7, please' said Jumapili. 'I'd like to get him out before he's trapped.'

'That's just stupid, checkmate,' said Downsted crossly. 'What did you think I'd do?'

Jumapili realised her mistake. 'You're lucky. You can see the pieces. I must remember them.'

'That's just an excuse. You're better than that. Much better. We'll start again. We won't count that one,' said Downsted using his sympathetic but headmasterly tone.

'A woman from the council came to see me this morning,' said Jumapili. 'She told me I'm to be made a ward of court. Apparently, the priests at the Kibera Catholic Church have kept a record of every person they've ever visited in Kibera and from that they've discovered I was born in 1957, or that's what they think.'

'What, so you're twelve years old?'

'That's what the lady says. She also said that Absko's seventeen and too young to look after me. They're going to take me away from him, to where I don't know. God knows why when he's looked after me every day since my mother died.' There was deep distress in her voice as though she were holding back tears.

'I know,' said Downsted.

'You know. How? exclaimed Jumapili surprised.

'Well, I knew it was a possibility,' said Downsted. 'Before Rishi went back to school, he phoned. He said you told him there was a risk of this happening. He asked whether my wife and I would look after you. Whether you could come to our school, my wife's school really. How would you feel about that?'

Chapter 25

'LOOK AT THIS,' said Jumapili excitedly to her brother as he approached her bed. The sound of his walk told her he was coming towards her.

'What is it?' asked Absko, as Jumapili handed him her full supper plate. She always saved her last meal of the day for him so he would be able to have a free dinner. Money was always so short and there was no guarantee that Absko would have enough money to feed himself.

'It's an abacus; it's used to do sums.'

'It looks like a child's toy. Can you use it?'

'Yes, but only for simple sums, like add and takeaway. I'm told it will do multiplication and division, which is fairly obvious because it's only adding and taking away many times, but they say there's a simpler way to do it with this.'

Absko placed the dinner plate on his lap and took the abacus in his hand before flicking the beads backwards and forwards.

'Where did you get it?'

'The KBS[14] gave it to me.'

'The blind people?' said Absko with his mouth full. 'I went to the church today. 'The woman from the council is right. I'm seventeen and you're twelve. We don't know the day or month, but we know the year we were born, so it's enough to get us identity cards.'

'That's good.'

'Yeh, but it means it's four years before I can get a licence to drive a matatu. I don't think I can wait that long. I need to earn more money now. And there's another problem.'

'What's that?'

I need to have High School Certificate and I can't get that, can I.'

---

[14] The Kenya Society for the Blind

'Do all the matatu drivers at your parking station have High School Certificates?'

'No, but they've all been doing it a long time, so they got their licences before the rules changed.'

'So our plan's not going to work then, is it,' announced Jumapili, sighing.

She sensed Absko's shake of his head. Their plan had been to use Jumapili's compensation from the accident to buy a matatu which Absko would drive, and she would be the conductor. That way, they planned that they could be together all day and make a good living for themselves.

'We must be able to do better for ourselves than this,' said Absko dejectedly.

'Did I tell you Mr Downsted has offered me ten shillings if I can work out how long it would take to walk to the moon using this.' She waved the abacus in the air. 'He's told me to work on the basis of it taking twenty minutes to walk one mile and then walking for ten hours every day,' said Jumapili.

'Do you know the answer?' asked Absko recovering some of the enthusiasm which carried him through his daily life.

'Not yet, but I'll work it out.'

'Do you know how far the moon is away?' asked Absko.

'He didn't tell me, but I've found the answer and that's created another problem – it's not in the same place,'

'What do you mean, it's not in the same place? Of course, it's in the same place. I can see it's in the same place. OK, it moves just a bit each night as it grows into a full moon, but not much.'

'Well, I can't see it, and I've been told sometimes its 221,000 miles away and another time its 252,000 miles away. It goes around, not in a circle but an eclipse.'

'So it was a trick question. If you gave one answer, he'd say it was the other.'

'I don't think so, but I'm going to do the sum twice just to make sure.'

'Has he said anymore about you going to live with them?'

'No, I must meet his wife first, and then we have the council meeting. I really don't like her.'

'Who?' said Absko surprised, 'Mrs. Downsted?'.

'No! The woman from the council. She talks and never listens. She bullies her way through everything – threatening all the time.'

'You shouldn't let her,' said Absko.

'You try,' retorted Jumapili.

The two sat quietly contemplating how suddenly a stranger had come in from outside and taken control of their lives.

Chapter 26

'HOW DO YOU navigate your way around, Jumi?' asked Joyce Downsted using the nickname Absko had given her. 'You can't see and yet you manage to move around things without too much difficulty.'

'Yeh, it's very strange, the doctors here seem to have become fascinated by the way I find my way around,' confirmed Jumapili. 'They've spent hours testing me as they don't believe I can't see. They've given my technique the name of "echo-location".'

'Is this why you make a clicking sound whenever you move?'

'Yes, the doctors tell me that from the echoes of my clicks I construct a mental picture of what's in front of me and the world around me, but I don't know. I can't describe it that way. They think, but are not sure, that I'm using the visual part of my brain to create something which in its manner is similar to vision.'

'How accurate is this echolocation ability?'

'It's pretty good at position, distance, location, and I have a fair grasp of contours and densities, so for example going up stairs or appreciating how steep a hill is, that's easy. It's the voids I have difficulty with. Where something falls away suddenly, like going downstairs, that's a real problem.'

'And do you do it consciously or subconsciously?' asked Joyce, quite fascinated.

'Mostly subconsciously. It's when something has changed, or when I'm somewhere new, that I become very conscious of what I'm doing. Then I listen intensely to the information which is carried back to me in the echo.'

'This world which you create within your own mind, are you able to differentiate between things?'

'Oh yes, of course. Wood, metals, tin, paper, all different types of paper, they have their own sound. Do you know that an apple and an orange have a different sound?'

'Are you the only blind person with this ability?' asked Joyce.

'I don't know. The doctors at the hospital are going to make enquiries with other blind institutes around the world to see if anyone else does what I do, but most importantly they want to know whether it can be taught.'

'Do you think it can be taught?' asked Joyce.

'I don't know, but we should find out, shouldn't we?'

And it was with those final few words that Miss Jumapili Mwangi passed Joyce Downsted's interview, because Joyce looked for three traits in a person before she allowed them into her lifeboat. They were the same traits held by those who are successful and live a long life: they need to have a sense of purpose, an ambition; they need to be optimistic, positive in nature; and they need to be resilient with the ability to rebound after a setback. Jumapili Mwangi had these three characteristics in spades.

'My husband tells me you're a good musician,' said Joyce.

'He tells me I must be much better!'

'Ah yes, that's Colin for you, always the perfectionist.'

'He says you have one of the best singing voices he's ever heard.'

'That's nice,' acknowledged Jumapili with a smile.

'He says it needs training, but it's probably fine enough for the most demanding of operas. Would you be happy to have singing lessons and, of course, learn Braille?'

'Yes, I must. I got paid to sing at a funeral before this,' said Jumapili as she waived her hands around her wheelchair and the room.

'Yes, I know. I was there. You sang exquisitely.'

'Thank you.'

'Look,' said Joyce, her voice adopting a business-like manner. 'Would you like to come to us when you get out of here? I understand you can't go back to Kibera, and the council want to put you in a home somewhere. We've a small girls' boarding school. The girls are all White, but I don't see why that should be a problem, do you? Colin think's it's a good idea and I do too.'

Jumapili nodded and shook her head, while tears gathered in her eyes. The relief that someone wanted her was truly overwhelming, such that she was unable to speak.

The expression of happiness on Jumapili's face was the only answer Joyce needed.

Chapter 27

JUMAPILI AND THE nurse who accompanied her were the last people to walk into the room. Jumapili sensed it was overcrowded, not with people but with desk furniture.

Absko, Mrs. Kiprono, Mr. Downsted and his wife Joyce, and Miss Gasira Onyango from Nairobi Child Services Department were already there. Also, in attendance was the senior administrator of the hospital who had a very large bundle of papers in front of him.

Jumapili who was walking without support, just with her white cane, struggled to find a seat.

'I think everyone's here, although I am surprised we're joined by Mr Mwangi. I didn't know he'd been invited,' said Miss Onyango in a disapproving tone. 'Miss Mwangi is now a ward of court and I've been appointed one of her legal guardians,' she announced.

It was news to everyone in the room.

'We're here to agree the next stage of her care, and the suggestion is that she's placed with Mr. and Mrs. Downsted who will look after her,' continued Miss Onyango.

'Excuse me,' said Downsted, 'but shouldn't we introduce ourselves so that Miss Mwangi knows who's here and in what capacity.'

'Yes, sorry,' said the lady from the council. 'My name is Miss Gasira Onyango. I run children's welfare services for Nairobi Council.'

'I'm Mrs. Aminifu Kiprono of Kimutai & Makokha Advocates. I represent both Miss Mwangi and Nairobi Council.'

'I'm sorry, but you cannot represent both Miss Mwangi and the council, can you?' interjected Downsted. His hackles had been raised by the condescending way in which Miss Onyango had dismissed Absko's presents. 'Surely, Miss Mwangi should have had her own legal representation?' He turned towards Jumapili. 'Have you appointed a lawyer to represent you?' he asked.

'I don't think so,' replied Jumapili.

'Your brother came to see me about representing you in your personal injury claim against Mr. McGeown,' explained Mrs. Kiprono. 'We couldn't file a claim because Miss Mwangi is both a minor and an orphan, so an application was made to the court to appoint Miss Onyango and me as her guardians.'

'And who spoke for Miss Mwangi at the hearing?' asked Downsted.

'I did,' said Mrs. Kiprono.

'Who spoke for the Council?'

'I did,' said Mrs. Kiprono again.

'Was Miss Mwangi at the hearing?'

'No, she was in hospital, too poorly.'

'Was Jumapili's brother, Mr Mwangi, invited?'

'No. In fact, there was no hearing. The judge simply signed the order we had already prepared for the court.'

Downsted resisted shouting out loud, 'Gotcha!' Instead, he looked at his wife who discreetly nodded. The exchange with Mrs. Kiprono confirmed the rumours which now abounded: just six years after Kenya became independent and the courts were already corrupt.[15] It was now well known that, upon the payment of a few hundred shillings, a court order could be magicked out of the system. If Downsted was right, Mrs. Kiprono would have already offered Miss Onyango a buckshee payment to come out of any compensation that Jumapili might receive.'

'Do you have an appointment letter for Miss Mwangi?' asked Downsted.

'Yes.'

'Signed by Miss Mwangi?'

---

[15] But this is to assume that the Kenyan courts were not corrupt before independence, which would be wrong. Before independence, the East African and Kenyan Courts practiced what might best be described as 'good cause' or 'noble cause' corruption. For example, the British Government locked up Kenyatta and the men of the Mau Mau on the basis of knowingly tainted evidence wrongly produced so as to achieve the British Government's aims of keeping these men out of circulation. Following independence the corruption was more transparent. Money purchased power in the courts.

'No. It's signed by Miss Onyango on behalf of the council.'

Then surely Nairobi Council are your clients,' observed Downsted. 'Has Mr. Mwangi on behalf of his sister, agreed to your terms?'

'No. He's only seventeen. In any case he can't read.'

'You could have read them to him. The fact is that he has looked after his sister over the last five years remarkably well, and that's without your, or the council, or anyone else's help. I would have thought that, in these circumstances, he would have deserved some courtesy and consideration. Apart from Jumapili, he has the best case to speak on her behalf, to know what she would want if she could not speak for herself, and yet he has been ignored.'

Five years of Absko's struggle, five years of hardship, five years of being ground down had, at last, been recognised. For the first time in Absko's life, his efforts had been acknowledged. He squeezed his eyes tightly so as not to cry from the emotion he was suddenly feeling, but no one was looking at the illiterate boy from the slums, so they didn't see – except Joyce Downsted. She knew how important her husband's words had been to him.

'I think we're getting off the point,' interrupted the senior administrator. 'There are only two things which must be decided today: Who's going to look after Miss Mwangi when she's discharged from hospital tomorrow? And who's going to pay our not insignificant hospital bill? Miss Mwangi has been with us over seven, eight months. She's had a lot of care and attention in that time, and we've not had a penny. Well, tomorrow she leaves because, quite frankly, enough is enough. We've been told ...' The administrator paused to consult his file. 'We've been told that Mr. Graeme McGeown or his insurance company will pay.'

'That's right,' confirmed Downsted.

'Well, it seems to me time has gone on and little progress has been made in sorting out even the fundamentals.'

'These matters are complex,' protested Mrs. Kiprono and Miss Onyango almost in unison.

'Mr. Downsted, you were one of the people who brought Miss Mwangi here,' continued the administrator. 'You said that Mr McGeown would pay. It's on the admission form which you signed.

When you signed the form you gave us your undertaking, your surety, your guarantee, that our bill for looking after Miss Mwangi would be paid by you if not paid by Mr. McGeown.'

Joyce looked at her husband shocked. She had no idea that they were liable for Jumapili's hospital costs. Whereas, when he looked back at her, he was hoping that she was enjoying, as he did, the way the administrator was using three words, which all meant the same thing, to bolster his authority in the meeting.

'If those are the issues then the matter is simple,' declared Downsted. 'To the first issue, unless anyone objects, Miss Mwangi will come and live with my wife and I at our girls' school. It's licensed by the Nairobi City County and, as Miss Onyango will know, it has an excellent reputation. I presume the council has no objection to that?'

'Jumapili, is that what you want?' asked Joyce gently, first in English and then in Swahili.

'Yes, to go with you please,' said Jumapili, first in English and then repeating herself in Swahili. She had the distinct impression from the sound of their voices that something was wrong, that she was being fought over, but she didn't understand why. It made her feel nervous. 'Is that alright Absko?' she asked anxiously.

'If you want. I'm sure I'll be able to see you. Won't I?'

Ominously neither Downsted nor Joyce said anything.

'As to the second point,' said Downsted. 'Mr McGeown or his insurance company will pay your reasonable costs. I guarantee it. But I stress *reasonable* costs.'

'I'm making a note you said that in front of all these people,' said the administrator quite pleased with himself. 'I'll write to you to confirm your words. I don't think there is anything more we can do now.'

'Mr. Downsted and I will arrange for Miss Mwangi to have her own legal representation as I'm sure she's allowed,' chipped in Joyce. 'They will review all the papers and will advise Jumapili and Absko if everything is satisfactory.'

'Mr. Downsted, Mrs. Downsted,' said Mrs. Kiprono. 'Will you be charging Miss Mwangi for staying with you? Will she be another pupil paying your exorbit ...' She stopped herself... 'enormously large fees?'

If Kimutai & Makokha Advocates were not going to be able to milk Jumapili for fees, as Mrs. Kiprono had originally hoped, she was darned if anyone else was going to do well instead of her.

'Good question – but no!' replied Joyce strongly. 'We want nothing for Jumapili coming to live with us. We only ask she behaves properly and continues with her music studies, that's enough. If the time comes when we think it appropriate to charge a fee, we would, of course, make the proper arrangements with the court at that time.'

Downsted was thrilled at what he saw as the *coup de grace* delivered by his wife. It confirmed what he had thought many times before: they made a good team. He folded up the single piece of paper in front of him with his scribbled notes and tucked it, together with his fountain pen, in his inside jacket pocket. He too had concluded that the meeting had ended.

'We haven't met,' said Downsted as he went with his hand outstretched to greet Absko in the corridor as people began to disperse. 'This is my wife, Joyce.'

As Absko shook both their hands he was conscious that he had never touched the hands of a White man or woman before.

'You've done a fantastic job,' said Joyce. 'You should feel really proud of yourself. Keeping your family together in such circumstances has been a remarkable achievement.'

'Thank you,' acknowledged Absko, swallowing hard.

'What happens now?' asked Jumapili, almost ready to burst into tears. 'It all seemed horribly strained to me.'

'I think the lawyer and the lady from the council are in cahoots to share a large part of your compensation,' said Downsted. 'I've been in touch with both McGeown and his insurance company. They tell me they've made a settlement offer which includes making a payment on account of the hospital fees. Mrs. Kiprono has rejected the offer as she doesn't think the money is enough. They're still in negotiation.'

'So, McGeown's insurance company is going to pay Jumapili's hospital bill then?' asked Joyce, sounding relieved.

'Yes, no doubt,' confirmed her husband.

'So, we'll collect you tomorrow?' asked Downsted, looking straight at Jumapili.

Joyce saw her lips quiver and, moving to comfort her, she took Jumapili into her arms. It was the first time since Jumapili's mother had died that anyone had held her like that. It was too much. Five years of pain fell out as tears onto Joyce's dress as Jumapili clung on to her for dear life and sobbed.

Absko turned away and faced close to the wall. He didn't want anyone to see he was crying too.

Chapter 28

IN 1922 THE directors of Irvine, Friedman and Gilman Capital Bank had a problem: they were awash with depositors' cash, largely from America, which they didn't know how to deploy.

World War I had ended, peace had come to Europe, and they needed to find sound investments for their customers if they were to sustain the same high level of profits made over the previous three years. The perceived opportunities in British East and South Africa could no longer be ignored. For that reason, they decided to open branches in Nairobi, Kenya, in Salisbury, Southern Rhodesia, which had just received 'Responsible Government' status, and in Cape Town, South Africa.

The bank's business plan was sound. They planned to limit their asset lending, instead their lending would go into financing the trade between these African countries and the United Kingdom. Their profits would come from currency exchange and from commissions charged for transmitting money between their branch offices and London.

The first two years trading in their Nairobi branch were incredibly profitable, so the board committed the bank to build a house suitable for a future managing director of their East African operations. The local branch manager found thirty acres of plateau land, a UK architect was chosen, and the board approved the building of a four-storey Georgian house redolent of earlier times.

The daylit basement housed the kitchen and all the working areas of the house. The ground floor was configured around a large hallway and staircase, which was reached by climbing a few stone steps. Large double doors led off the hall to six large reception rooms each with a majestic fireplace. The first floor had the same configuration. The attic floor, at the top of the house, was made up of small bedrooms and washrooms as quarters for the servants. There was one giveaway that the house had been designed by an Englishman with little knowledge of Kenya – his specifications included a cast-iron central heating system with coal boiler.

When the construction photographs showed the building as an unattractive stump protruding from the ground, the board ordered two large conservatories to be built on the east and west sides of the house in iron and glass along the lines of the Temperate House at Kew Gardens. At every stage the project became more extravagant with land flattened for, not one, but two polo pitches and, of course, with the pitches came the stables for the polo ponies.

By 1929, the building was finished, and the board was receiving reports of the magnificence of the building, with its wooden panelling throughout, from Mr. Bottlesford, the Nairobi Branch Director.

It was Bottlesford's hope that he might be authorised to live there, but it was not to be. In 1931, Irvine, Friedman and Gilman Capital Bank and its directors filed for bankruptcy. It was unable to survive the economic depression which followed the financial crash of 1929 when depositors withdrew their money in panic.

Bottlesford Hall, as the house became known, passed to Sir Patrick Haynes in part-payment for his fees as the lawyer in the liquidation of the bank. He never visited it. Instead, it sat, uncared for, for the next decade until it passed to The Hon. Miss Joyce Haynes on the death of her father.

Joyce was teaching at the King Edward VI Grammar School in Nuneaton when her father died. He had retired to Royal Leamington Spa after a bout of ill health and, with Nuneaton just forty minutes away by train, it meant that, for a few years prior to his death, Joyce was able to combine her teaching career with regular visits to see him.

Eschewing an air-raid shelter, Joyce stood on the hills just outside of Nuneaton on the night of the 14th and 15th November 1940 with two fellow teachers to whom she was letting rooms in the house she had purchased there. They watched as over five-hundred German Bombers flew overhead to drop over five-hundred tons of explosives on Coventry and Coventry Cathedral. The fire was so huge that no one who saw it would ever forget that night, nor the 550 people who perished. Not least Joyce, as her fiancé worked and lived in Coventry as an engineer, designing aero engines. She was petrified for his safety.

However, it was the early hours of 17th May 1941 which were to have the greatest impact on her life. The bombs which fell on Nuneaton that night killed 130 residents. They included her fiancé who, at her behest, had taken digs there to be safely away from Coventry, and closer to her.

Her father's death, which came a year after her fiancé's might have come as a shock, but he had been very poorly; it was the war years, and death was all around. Further, as was common in those years, the school was so short of staff that all teachers did double shifts, teaching the boys in the morning and the girls in the afternoon. It meant Joyce was too exhausted to grieve for either her father or fiancé properly. Prime Minister Winston Churchill had an expression which summed up the times. 'KBO'[16] he would say publicly, and so, like everyone else, that is exactly what Joyce Haynes did until the Summer of 1947.

---

[16] KBO = Keep Buggering On

Chapter 29

USING HER SEVEN-WEEK summer holiday and with leave of absence for the 1947 Michaelmas Term, Miss Joyce Haynes took the boat train from London to Paris. There she caught the train to Rome where she boarded a boat, which, after calling in at Valetta in Malta, and Alexandria in Egypt, took her through the Suez Canal, across the equator and into Mombasa.

Before 1939 it would have been thought mad for a young woman to have made a journey like that on her own, but the war years had, in many ways, made things safer, because there was military discipline everywhere. However, it was the encouragement of a gentleman from Thomas Cook which persuaded her. Asked by Joyce to advise on the journey, he was adamant that it could be made safely by a single woman if she did as he advised. Therefore, buoyed with nervous excitement, she booked what she saw as her once-in-a-life-time trip.

Following her travel agent's advice, Joyce stayed one night in a hotel he recommended in Rome. This was so the hotel chauffeur could greet her at the train station and deliver her the next day to the port and her boat. It was, he told her, the riskiest part of her journey.

However, it was the journey from Mombasa to Nairobi which worried Joyce the most. Upon disembarking the boat, she had to take the 'Lunatic' Express Sleeper Train, a renowned small gauge railway, for the fifteen-hour journey between the two cities. The gentleman from Thomas Cook was most reassuring on this part of the journey. He was certain that Joyce would make plenty of friends on the boat, many of whom would be travelling to Nairobi too, and would help look after her, and so it proved.

In Nairobi, Joyce booked into the Stanley Hotel, the oldest in the city, and known the world over as the place to meet and rest before going on Safari. It was from there that Joyce was going to find

Elephant Hall, as Bottlesford Hall had been renamed by her father in recognition of its White-Elephant status. White Elephant or not, it was part of her inheritance and Joyce was going to reclaim it.

It was with a mixture of excitement and mild trepidation that Joyce travelled in the front seat of the taxi arranged by the Stanley Hotel. About thirty minutes from the centre of Nairobi they turned right, onto a well-made dirt track. After about five-hundred metres they came to a break in the hedgerow. There, a large, very tall, set of double gates, more suited to a stately home, presented themselves. They were wide open. Looking through them, Joyce's eyes fell on Bottlesford Hall, a building identical almost in every way to the photographs she had brought with her from her father's files. At the moment she saw Bottlesford Hall, she fell in love with it. The attraction was as instantaneous as it was powerful. It was a home too good to be true.

'This is it,' declared Joyce to the driver, as she leant forward enthusiastically. 'Turn left here.'

Their path was blocked by a rickety homemade fence, clearly designed to be moved, but it was only when they had broken through that the reason became obvious. Spread throughout the gardens and the never-played-upon polo pitches were a flock of Red Massai sheep grazing contentedly. The visibly thick ring of jatropha, which went all the way around the grounds was doing its job of acting as a natural barrier, keeping the sheep in and the wild animals, looking for their supper, out. The taxi wheels crunched their way up the drive to the portentous parking area in front of the house steps where it stopped.

'Don't go, will you,' instructed Joyce as she climbed out, before standing and looking around her.

The peeling white paintwork of the French shutters and the cracked cream rendering did nothing to dampen her ardour as she climbed the steps, anxious to open the magisterial front doors. She already had in her hands the keys to the house which hung on fraying string from a heavy block of wood. Attached to the block was a worn label with the name 'Elephant House' written on it in her father's handwriting. She took a few seconds to think of him and how she came to be here but, just as she was turning the key to open the door, she heard a shout.

'*Unafanya nini. Unafanya nini!*' yelled a man, running across the polo field.

'What's he saying?' Joyce asked the taxi driver.

'He wants to know what you're doing.'

'*Huwezi kuingia hiko*,' shouted the man, waiving a stick in the air.

'He's saying you can't go in,' said the taxi driver.

'Tell him its mine. Tell him I own it.'

'*Ni yake, anaimiliki,*' said the taxi driver before repeating what he had said in English. 'It's her's, she owns it.'

There then proceeded a heated argument in Swahili between Geteye Odhiambo, the man with the stick, and the taxi driver, none of which Joyce understood. Eventually the taxi driver turned to Joyce.

'He's agreed you can go in if your key opens the door. He's accepted if you have the key, you must be the owner. But he's also made it clear that these are his sheep and not yours. He wants them to stay here.'

'Of course,' conceded Joyce. 'Please tell him I don't want his sheep.'

'He thinks you will try and claim them for rent,' said the taxi driver.

'Why would I do that?'

'Because they're feeding on your land.'

'Please tell him I'm not interested in his sheep,' said Joyce as she inserted the largest of the keys in the lock and turned it.

'I've told him that,' said the taxi driver, before he joined Joyce in putting his weight behind the heavy doors to force them to swing open.

It was the first time they had been opened in sixteen years. They moved with grace, allowing beams of light to flood into the hall and on to the wide staircase. It was reminiscent of days long gone, a testament to the skills of the carpenters and the pedantry of the supervising architect to have everything perfect.

'You don't have a torch, do you?' asked Joyce.

The taxi driver shook his head. So it was with great care that Joyce's posse of three walked around the ground floor, bashing down spiders' webs, opening doors and windows before forcing the shutters wide to let in fresh air and light. Apart from the obvious signs that a few rodents had made Bottlesford Hall their home, there was little damage downstairs.

Joyce climbed the stairs to the first floor and the galleried landing, but in the semi darkness she refused to venture any further without a torch, which she cursed herself for not bringing, only to curse herself once more when she found the stairs to the kitchen. These would have to be explored later, for one thing was certain. Miss Joyce Haynes would be returning tomorrow.

The two conservatories on either side of the main building provided the first and most obvious problem because the vegetation growth was as thick as any jungle, to the point that the two rooms were impossible to enter. Over the years, the plants had grown so tall that they had forced panes of glass off the roof which had then allowed the rain to get in, creating a never-ending cycle of growth.

After walking around the hall a few times, Joyce went outside, and her posse joined her. They toured the grounds, admiring the house. It was, she admitted, huge, far too big for a home. What was she going to do with it, she wondered. It would have to be sold. It was the only answer.

Returning inside to close the shutters, windows, and doors, Joyce felt pangs of regret at her decision, but she knew it was the only one she could take. She also knew she would regret it for a long time.

The next day, Joyce returned to Bottlesford Hall with torch, cleaning cloths, dustpan, broom and mop, plus an electrician and plumber. The electrician had the lights working with the flick of a switch. He was amazed at how, after so long, every bulb came on without a hitch. The magnificence of the chandeliers in the hall were further proof that no expense had been spared in the building works.

The plumber's job was not so easy, but with Joyce stoking the boiler with coal and with the electrician having fixed the pump on the central heating system, there was, by late afternoon, hot water throughout the house from kitchen to attic.

With the plumber and electrician set to their tasks, Joyce swept and washed the floors and wiped down all the surfaces. With every touch, she reaffirmed her love for the building and questioned her decision to sell it.

'It's amazing this place has come through unscathed,' said the electrician, before he left. 'If any Kikuyu had known this was here and owned by a colonialist, they'd have stripped it bare.'

'Yeh, I agree. You need to put a guard on it otherwise you'll end up with only a ruin to sell,' said the plumber who was leaving too.

Just as Joyce was leaving, the shepherd from the previous day returned carrying two boxes of papers, primarily unopened envelopes, delivered over the years to the letter box built in the gates at the entrance to the drive.

'These are yours,' said the taxi driver, translating for the shepherd. 'He says there are some important papers in there.'

'Ask him if he will act as security guard for here,' said Joyce to the taxi driver. 'Tell him I'll pay him.'

After negotiations in Swahili, which Joyce didn't understand, a bargain was struck – fifteen shillings a week for the shepherd, five shillings a week for his boy, and their sheep could graze for free.

How right the shepherd was – included in the envelopes were several letters from the local authority with possession orders. They were seizing the property to recoup years of unpaid local taxes. Joyce had arrived just in the nick of time if she was not to lose the hall completely.

The contents of the envelopes were frightening enough to force Joyce into a whirlwind of activity involving the council, lawyers, estate agents and banks as she fought to stabilise the affairs of a property which she was now certain had been aptly named by her father as White-Elephant House

'The best you can do is to get the Governor's Office involved,' advised the hotel manager, after Joyce had complained that no one in Nairobi City Council seemed authorised to take her money. 'If the Governor's involved, the matter will automatically get raised to someone senior enough who will be able to make a decision. Also, you won't have to pay any baksheesh.[17] That's probably why they're messing you around. They're expecting to enjoy a little windfall.'

'What's baksheesh?' asked Joyce naïvely.

---

[17] Bribe

Chapter 30

'I'M SORRY TO have kept you, .er, Miss Haynes,' said Colin Downsted looking down at his papers as he addressed Joyce, who had been sitting patiently in the foyer of the Governor's Mansion for what she thought had been an inordinately long time.

'The KLFA[18] are being frightfully busy ...,' he continued without finishing his sentence. 'How can I help you?'

Just as she was about to speak, Downsted interjected. 'We met on the train from Mombasa, didn't we?'

'No,' replied Joyce curtly.

'I could swear we were on the same Lunatic Express,' continued Downsted confused.

'We were, but we didn't meet. I would've remembered.'

'Yes, you're right,' acknowledged Downsted, 'awfully sorry.'

'You were in naval uniform.' observed Joyce.

'Yes, I've been seconded here. Third Attaché they call me, but as yet I still have to find the brief case which goes with the job,' he jested.

If the job title 'Third Attaché' was not demeaning enough, Downsted's small and sparsely furnished office would have confirmed his lowly status, but that was to mislead. Downsted's new task was to head up military intelligence in the Governor's Office. His job was to help secure the peaceful end of British rule in Kenya. Independence was coming to East Africa. Not only did the poor state of the British economy make it an imperative, but the Americans were insisting upon it. But the operative word was 'peaceful', and the Kenyan Land and Freedom Army were already making it far from peaceful.

---

[18] Kenyan Land and Freedom Army later to become known as the Mau Mau

Downsted escorted Joyce to his office where, as duty officer for the day, he listened to her plight before he opened the adjoining door to an adjacent office and put his head around the corner.

'Miss Haynes, this is Miss Mutinda,' he said, introducing a tall, elegant woman. They acknowledged each other with a nod.

Downsted summarised Joyce's predicament, adding. 'It's a building we're interested in. Would you be so kind as to speak to the council chief and put a stop to anything going on with Bottlesford Hall.'

'I may have been here only seventy-two hours,' continued Downsted, 'but I've already worked out that Miss Mutinda is the linchpin to making anything happen in this office, in fact, probably the whole of Nairobi. If you take her phone number and work with her, I'm sure everything will get sorted.'

The two women smiled politely and said nothing.

'I wonder if I might see Bottlesford Hall. It sounds quite delightful,' said Downsted, his gaze firmly set on Joyce's eyes. 'We might be able to use it.'

'Yes, certainly, when?'

'This afternoon, say three-thirty? Staying at the Stanley?'.

'Yes,' answered Joyce, not at all certain she had made a wise decision in telling him where she was staying.

'I'll pick you up, three-thirty at the Stanley,' he confirmed.

Their meeting was over.

Chapter 31

IT WAS A pool car from the Governor's Office that took Joyce and Downsted out to Bottlesford Hall. They sat side by side in the back, but it was the raise of his finger which indicated to Joyce that he didn't want to talk.

'Sorry about that,' said Downsted as soon as they were out of the car and walking towards the steps of the house. 'Walls have ears, if you know what I mean.'

Joyce smiled sweetly.

'It's magnificent, isn't it?' said Downsted as he stood on the driveway.

'Yes,' replied Joyce, 'and it will be darn expensive to run.'

Once inside, Downsted paced rapidly from room to room on the ground floor.

'Perfect, perfect,' he muttered to himself before climbing the stairs. He toured the bedrooms on the next floor before announcing from the galleried landing that it had the same footprint as downstairs, and how unusual it was that a 1920's house had been built with so many ensuite bathrooms. 'Very avant-garde,' he commented. He skipped through the house from kitchen to the attic only to declare: 'bloody hell,' when presented with the jungles in the two conservatories.

'Let's walk,' said Downsted to Joyce when they were both back in the hall. He pointed to the front door.

'What do you do, Miss Haynes?' he asked when they were outside and some way from the house.

'I'm a teacher.'

'Where?'

'Nuneaton Grammar School. I teach a bit of everything – classics, history, geography.'

'University?' he asked.

'Bedford College.'

'In Regent's Park?'

Joyce nodded.

'I know it. I've been there several times. I'm a King's man.'

'London?'

'Where else? Yes, physics and chemistry. I imagine if it hadn't been for the war I'd have stayed there as an academic.'

'How long were you at sea?'

'Four damn weeks in the North Sea, then three months in Brighton for officer training. Long enough to make me realise I hate boats. I like my feet on dry land. The longest sea trip I've ever made was to come here, to Mombasa. It's been my only posting, thank God.'

Downsted missed out telling her of his secondment to SOAS[19] to learn Japanese before going to Chicksands, a listening station for Bletchley Park, and then on to Mombasa and another listening station where he listened to poor recordings of Japanese pilots talking to each other, writing down phonetically what they were saying before translating them into English.

What did you do in Mombasa?' Joyce asked.

'Moved paper,' he replied.

'What do you do now?' she continued.

'Move more bits of paper, just in a different place, that's all.'

Joyce stopped walking, took Downsted by the arm and looked into his eyes as though he was one of her pupils and about to be told off. She deliberately raised a disapproving eyebrow. It was as plain a message as she could give that she knew he wasn't telling the whole story, and she was not going to ask any more.

When they were in the middle of the field and with his face turned away from the Governor's pool car, he asked: 'How would you feel about lending us this place, to the British Government, for a little while? Say a year or two?'

'Why?' asked Joyce astounded.

'It's just, we have some very sensitive training courses and negotiations coming up. In secret. Best no one knows. We can't hold

---

[19] School of Oriental and African Studies, part of the University of London

them in the Governor's Office, and all other places aren't suitable because they're so darn public. This would be ideal.'

Chapter 32

THERE ARE COCK-UP theorists and conspiracy theorists. The fact is that you needed to be a mastermind in prediction and planning to have foreseen the way things were to develop.

The first stage, and the easy bit, was the renting of Bottlesford Hall by the Governor's Office for two years. The next stage, which was harder, was the recruitment of Joyce as Housekeeper of Bottlesford Hall. Feeling there was little reason to return to Nuneaton, Joyce accepted on the condition that someone from the Governor's Office lived in the house with her. She was not going to live on her own in a strange house, in a strange country, and certainly not one where she was told she needed guards. The obvious and most willing candidate was Downsted.

With the lease signed, some things just happened, like the fitting out of the house with the Governor's Office spending a small fortune providing everything the hall needed to host conferences of between twenty to thirty people. Tables, chairs, sideboards, plates, cutlery, and bedroom furniture, mostly second hand but all good quality, arrived quickly. In the kitchen everything was extra-large and purchased brand new. The Governor's chef was not going to cook anything unless his kitchen was in tip-top condition. By Easter 1948, Bottlesford Hall was fit to host a king.

Other things got locked up in endless rounds of political pettiness and intrigue as the rules of the Colonial Office overrode common sense, nearly causing the plans for Bottlesford Hall to fail.

Joyce wanted her salary paid to her in pounds sterling and in London, and at the same rate as she would earn as a teacher in England. The embassy insisted it could only pay her at the rate paid to local domestic staff, and in East African Shillings. The solution was for Joyce to be employed as a teacher by the Colonial Office to teach the diplomat's children. The fact that all these children were at boarding schools in England, already paid for by the Colonial Office was conveniently ignored.

As time progressed there came a cautious shift in Joyce and Downsted's relationship. At first it was very formal but gradually, as they worked together, they developed a friendship. Slowly, as they realised they preferred to be with each other than anyone else, there developed a platonic romance. Joyce became Downsted's constant companion at the Governor's numerous social events.

It was Sir Philip Mitchell, Governor of Kenya, who told Downsted he should marry Joyce.

'It would be darn good for the career. The diplomatic service likes wives. It means they get two for the price of one. Also, stops security wondering if you might be queer, you know, a bit of a risk.'

Downsted already knew he wasn't going to be a career diplomat. The short time he spent in Nairobi's Colonial Office had convinced him that the job was not to his liking. He had already made up his mind that, as soon as this secondment was over, he was going back to London, to do what, he didn't know.

One evening, long after the sun had fallen from the sky, Downsted and Joyce sat close to each other. They were staring vacantly at the hazy pattern of stars making up the magnificence of the Milky Way which streamed through the glass ceiling of the eastern conservatory. They had listened to the evening news from the BBC's colonial service and the room was now in silence.

'When are you returning to Nuneaton?' asked Downsted. 'You said you had to go back to tidy up some things.'

'I want to be back in time for Christmas. I don't think I could bear to miss another Nine Lessons and Carols nor Midnight Mass. I know I'll be on my own, but I always get a lot of joy from the carols.'

'I have some leave,' said Downsted, 'and there are briefings and other things the Governor wants me to do for the Colonial Office in London.'

Joyce said nothing.

'Shall we go back together?' he asked. 'I'll be flying back. Will you be able to change your ticket?'

'I don't know.'

'I've been thinking about this for some time,' he said: 'when we're in London, back in Britain, would you like to get married?'

'Are you asking me to marry you?' asked Joyce almost jokingly.

'Yes, I think so.'

'It's not the most romantic proposal a girl's ever had.'

'Maybe, but I bet it's one of the most romantic settings. Just look at those stars.'

They both stared skywards.

'I've been thinking,' he continued. 'I've realised, I couldn't bear it if you married anybody else.'

'So, you're asking me not out of love, but jealousy. Is that right?'

'Oh no, it's not meant like that. It's more that I couldn't bear for you not to be with me.'

'So, you're asking me not out of love, but to make me a possession. Is that it?'

She was smiling but Downsted was beginning to feel uncomfortable.

'No, not like that,' he protested. 'We can do the ring thing when we're back in London –Burlington Arcade or Hatton Garden.'

Joyce did not answer him.

He got up, selected Moonlight Serenade by Glen Miller from the pile of gramophone records and set it to play.

'I've just thought,' he said as he offered her his hand. 'How can you possibly marry a man you've never danced with?'

In the still of the conservatory and under the stars, the two danced together, their feet barely moving as they rocked in time to the music.

Joyce thought of her fiancé and wished things had been different; she knew she had been in love with him from head to toe, his touch, his laugh, his smile, everything. But Colin Downsted, she wasn't sure. There was too much in his past, and present, which he was keeping secret.

It was the incessant scratching of the record at the end of the song which brought her back to reality.

'Yes, please,' she said looking at him directly in his eyes. 'Thank you. It would be nice. But I'm sorry, I have one condition.'

Downsted looked mortified.

'You must shave off that ridiculous moustache. I couldn't possibly marry a man who is not clean-shaven,' she said before kissing him briefly on the lips.

Chapter 33

JOYCE, AND A clean-shaven Downsted, were hugely excited, if not a little trepidatious, as they boarded the BOAC Avro York aircraft at Nairobi Airport to fly to London, because to fly like this was to enter the glamorous world of the superstar.

There were stopovers at Entebbe, Khartoum, a night stop in Cairo before they made their way to London via a meal stop in Rome. With so many take-offs and landings, they both felt quite seasoned fliers when they touched down for the last time at Heathrow Airport.

They travelled by taxi into London where they said a stiff and formal goodbye. Joyce took the train to Nuneaton while Downsted stayed in London to attend to the schedule that the Kenyan's Colonial Office had set him. Both knew that they would not see the other again until the day before their wedding. It would be fair to say that, as they parted, both were a little worried that the other might not turn up.

In Nuneaton, Joyce visited Oaston Road Cemetery where she placed a bouquet of flowers on the memorial stone laid to commemorate those who died in the May 1941 bombing. It was the only place she could go to honour her first fiancé because he was one of those whose body was never identified. As she stood by the stone, she swore undying love to his memory and trembled, not from the cold, but from the memory of the fears she felt that night hiding in the Andersen shelter in her garden, feeling the earth tremble and watching the soil of their dugout rattle to the ground with every bomb that fell. That evening, she wrote to her first fiancé's parents telling them she was getting married, and that their son was her first love whom she would carry in her heart until the end of time.

Joyce went to see her old school and catch up with her teacher chums. They were happy for her as she shared her story. Although they reported that things were hard, she was buoyed by the optimism everyone felt for their future.

Joyce's lodgers had already vacated her Nuneaton home, so she quickly stripped it of her possessions, sending them to the family home in Leamington Spa, with the rest going to the local rag-and-bone man. Then, she instructed a local estate agent to put the house on the market. She felt comfortable knowing that, after the mortgage had been repaid, she would have a reasonable sum of capital to keep her secure for a little while until she got a proper job again.

Downsted and she had never discussed what she would do after they were married, but she could not believe that he wouldn't be happy in her not working, because she knew every day had to be filled with a purpose.

At her father's house, Joyce selected the best items of furniture: his baby grand-piano, his silver, paintings, his collection of china, the whole of her father's library and a few mementos which she packaged up and arranged to have shipped to Bottlesford Hall. There were more meetings with more estate agents and the result was that her former family home was let to Warwick University, keen to expand by recruiting the best professors from around the world.

At Holy Communion the next day, she saw, in the daylight, the crater damage done by a bomb which had fallen in the church ground eight years before. Once again, she remembered her first fiancé and wondered about marrying Downsted. There was a true physical passion in her relationship with him, whereas Downsted had been restrained to the point of wonder.

On 2nd January 1949 Joyce closed the door of her Leamington Spa home for the last time and caught the train to London. In the whole time she had been in the town she had spoken to no one other than those whose services she had needed. It made her realise how lonely she had always been there. So very different to the life she had made for herself in Nuneaton.

Joyce and Downsted's wedding was a small intimate affair held in the beautiful Chapel of King's College, London. Downsted's brothers fought for the roles they were going to play, decided by a toss of the coin. The elder was delighted to have won the privilege of giving the bride away, whereas his younger brother took the role of the best man and the daunting task of making the best man's speech.

The winter sun streamed through the chapel's beautiful stained-glass windows, reflecting beams of light onto its stunning ceiling and on to the couple as they stood resplendent in front of the altar. Joyce was in a white long shapely wedding dress, chosen to show off her slim figure. She looked quite stunning. Downsted, in his Commander's uniform, certainly thought so, as his face lit up as he watched her walk towards him on his brother's arm.

At the altar, and by his side, Downsted lifted Joyce's veil and looked into her face. He was instantly captivated, causing his heart to thump out of control, his stomach to churn and his breathing to speed up. She smiled because she was happy too, but she had no appreciation of the euphoric turmoil racing through Downsted's whole being.

The wedding breakfast was held in the East India Club where Downsted had hurriedly become a member. Although his membership was sponsored by fellow naval officers, it was a tradition of the club that he needed a letter from his public school's headmaster before he could be admitted. This simple task created an administrative hiccup which took longer to resolve than it took to plan the whole wedding.

As Joyce came into her wedding breakfast by the backstairs, because the East India Club would not allow women through the front door, she wished he hadn't joined, and they'd gone to the Waldorf Hotel on the Aldwych instead. It was where she and a few of her family and friends were staying, because it was a mere stone's throw from King's College Chapel.

However, there was one thing about the East India Club; they knew how to throw a party, and Downsted, his close family, her distant family and their friends knew how to join in, making it an occasion to remember.

Their wedding night was spent in the Waldorf Hotel and Joyce's concerns about Downsted's manhood and his desire for her were quickly abated.

Early the next morning, they delivered Joyce's wedding dress to the hotel concierge asking him to return it to the hire company, because she did not have enough rationing coupons to have one made. Then, weighed down with luggage, they crossed Waterloo Bridge, stopped for a few moments to watch the sunrise above the Thames, then both, with heavy hearts, said goodbye to London.

At Waterloo Station, they caught the boat train to Paris because they were making the same journey Joyce had made when she travelled to Nairobi the first time, just eighteen months before. And when they climbed on board the Lunatic Sleeper Express to take them from Mombasa to Nairobi, they were as contented and happy in their relationship as any two people could be. They were, in their own way made for each other and undoubtedly in love.

Chapter 34

'I SAW CHURCHILL when I was in London,' said Downsted. They were sitting in the eastern conservatory on the evening of their first full day back in Bottlesford Hall.

'You never said,' replied Joyce.

'Walls have ears.'

'You said that when we first came up here. Do you remember?'

He nodded.

'What did he say?' she asked.

'Churchill, he's old, very old.'

'They say he's had a stroke.'

'I heard that too, but he seems determined to go on. It was mid-afternoon when I saw him in his room in the House of Commons. He was already drinking a whisky and soda.'

'Was he drunk?'

'No, far from it. Our meeting was supposed to be just thirty minutes, but it went on for an hour and a half. It was a peculiar conversation because it was strangely nuanced. It was obvious that he was angry with the Indians for increasing their population by fifty million over the last ten years, and he wanted to know what had happened to the population in British East Africa.'

'Were you able to tell him?' asked Joyce.

'No, but I promised to find out. Interestingly, he has a real soft spot for the Kikuyu. He told me he was out here in about 1907 and remembers them as a happy, naked, and charming people. But, like the Colonial Office, he is worried that they are now being infiltrated by the Russians to rebel against us.'

'Is that what's happening?' asked Joyce.

'That's the view in London. They believe the Russians want us to keep an army down here so as to weaken our forces in Europe, but I'm not sure. I've seen no evidence of it and if one person should know it's me.'

'Makes sense though if they're right.'

'Churchill's appalled at the way the magistrates here are unfairly ordering the thrashing of Blacks for what he said was no discernible reason. He was adamant it had to stop.'

'Well let's hope he can order it, because it's about time someone did,' commented Joyce firmly.

'Strangely, Churchill referred to the Kikuyu as savages while at the same time saying they're people of considerable fibre, ability, and steel. Those were his exact words. He got quite emotional about the way they're being treated. He's sure they need to be looked after better, which he doesn't think's happening. Not to be repeated, but he said he thought many of the settlers in Africa were no better than the savages themselves.'

'Savages, that's a horrible term. Why does he use it? In any case, what's this got to do with you?' asked Joyce.

'I agree, it's strange him using such a word given it contrasts with his view that we should not think the Indians or anyone in Africa as being in any way inferior. His plea, and I quote, is that we must be great pals together.'

'Amen to that. But what's this got to do with you?' repeated Joyce.

'Not to be repeated...'

Joyce frowned.

'My job is to find the next generation of leaders in the Kikuyu, Meru, Embu, Kamba and Maasai tribes,' said Downstead, 'so they can be educated and taught how to run the country. The government's very clear. They want to be out long before the end of the next decade.'

'So, the British want to be gone, sometime soon.'

'That's about it. Churchill's petrified there's going to be civil war down here and Britain's good name is going to get dragged through the mud. He was adamant that a modern nation mustn't use its power to kill natives, and yet he thinks the behaviour of the Kenyan Colonial Office is about to make that happen, and it scares him.'

'Do you think that's what's going to happen?' asked Joyce.

'If we behave as ourselves, no. If we kowtow to the demands of the extremist White settlers, like South Africa is doing with the Boers, then it's a certainty.

'And the odds?'

'Sixty-forty.'

'Which way?'

'We'll give in to the White settlers and get civil war,' said Downstead. 'Maybe the odds are even worse, seventy-thirty.'

'So, we need to plan to leave. How long have we got?'

'Seven, ten years .... plus, or minus a bit– but why do you say that?'

'I've attended enough parties at the Colonial Office to know everything is about land. The Kikuyu are convinced that the Whites have taken all their best land. They're going to fight to get it back, aren't they? And even if they don't fight, when independence comes, as you now say it will, then they'll change the law to confiscate the land from the Whites. It makes me glad I've kept the house in Leamington Spa.'

'You should have been in Whitehall with me,' said Downsted. 'It's probably high in their top-ten worry list for the whole of Africa. They keep talking about the problem, but don't have a solution. At least, not a long-term one.'

'Are the Russians really here?' asked Joyce, deliberately returning to the subject.

'So they tell me, but I'm not sure. As I say, I haven't seen them at work. They don't seem to be funding anything I know of. What is happening, and I'm sure of this, is that a Marxist-Leninist ideology is being peddled, which the Blacks are lapping up because they've got nothing and it's a political philosophy which gives them a share of something.'

'Why have they asked you to get involved?'

'Because I speak Swahili,' replied Downsted, relieved that the subject had been changed because his mission was not as simple as he had described. Underneath his cover story were his instructions from British intelligence. These were to get close to the Kikuyu, Meru and Embu tribes throughout the whole of Kenya, and in particular those people who were leading the Kenya Land and Freedom Army. It was a huge task.

'You never said,' protested Joyce, sitting back in her seat realising, once again, how little she knew of her husband. 'When did you learn?'

'In Mombasa. I didn't have to. I did it to avoid the boredom, and now they want me to use it.'

'There's a lot we don't know about each other, isn't there?'

'Yes... it makes it fun,' acknowledged Downsted.

There was another long pause.

'Which bedroom are we making our own?' asked Joyce. 'Am I coming into you or are you coming into me?'

Downsted chuckled at the innuendo and then at her naivety, not realising what she had said.

'I don't think I need answer that, do I?' For the first time, but not the last, he winked playfully.

Chapter 35

IT WAS FIVE days short of their ninth wedding anniversary.

'Well, that's a life-lesson for the learning,' said Downsted as he sat down in the room Joyce had chosen to make her study. There was a strain in his voice. 'You never know who's employing you until you really know who's paying your salary.'

'Why do you say that?' asked Joyce, looking up from the book she was marking.

'I've been sacked, dismissed, made redundant.'

'Why? How?'

'All the time I've been working in Kenya I've been employed by the navy but seconded to the Colonial Office who've been paying the navy to have me. Well, there's been a reorganisation in London; everyone employed by the Colonial Office has been transferred to be employed by a new body called the 'Overseas Civil Service'. When they looked at my file to transfer me across they found I was still with the navy and not with them. Money being tight, they told the navy the navy had to pay me from now on. Of course, the navy didn't want a commander who hadn't been to sea, hated going to sea and lived three-hundred miles from the sea.'

'I am so sorry,' said Joyce. 'That's horrible for you.'

'In some ways I'm relieved. They've made the decision we've been discussing I should make over the last couple of years. It's been an awful, disgusting job, and a complete waste of time, a total failure.'

'Not just disgusting but with those idiots in charge, impossible too,' sympathised Joyce for, like Downsted, she had become convinced that every time the Kenyan Colonial Office had a choice to make they always chose the wrong one. 'But it's not nice when someone decides for you, when it's taken out of your hands.'

'Hearts and minds, hearts and minds, that's what Churchill wanted' said Downsted dejectedly, 'and what did we get - the Mau Mau rebellion, massacres, war crimes everywhere, and on both sides, and flaming British gulags, bloody concentration camps! Who'd have thought it of us!' [20] There was boiling anger in Downsted's voice.

'You can't send soldiers to do the job of policemen,' he continued. 'We should have bloody learnt that in Ireland, but of course we didn't. Damn stupid to allow the KAR to go haywire. [21] So stupid, so darn stupid.' He hung his head at the shame of it all.

'What do you think you'll do?' asked Joyce shocked at Downsted's swearing, because usually he was very restrained.

'It was Baring [22] who told me,' said Downsted ignoring her question. 'Darned decent of him. Nasty job, and he didn't have to do it. He's fairly certain that now Dedan Kimathi's been captured, the rebellion's over, so there's no more need for me.' [23]

'The papers say Kimathi's going to be hung next week, for whatever good that does,' said Joyce with sighs of sadness. 'Apparently, his plea for clemency has been denied.'

'Do you know how many Mau Mau we've killed?' asked Downsted. 'Baring told me.'

Joyce shook her head.

'The Governor's office estimates it's over eleven-thousand people, that includes nearly 1,900 we've executed. And do you know how many we've trained to take over running this country, their country?'

Joyce shook her head.

Downsted raised his hands and opened and closed his fingers twice.

'Twenty people, only twenty people?' said Joyce disbelievingly.

---

[20] Churchill was Prime Minister for a second time from October 1951 retiring in April 1955 following a serious stroke on 23 June 1953

[21] King's African Rifles

[22] Evelyn Baring, 1st Baron Howick of Glendale. Governor of Kenya from 1952 to 1959

[23] Dedan Kimathi, leader of the Mau Mau rebellion, was captured on 21st October 1956. He was executed by hanging on 18th February 1957 in Kamiti Maximum Security Jail. Before Kimathi was killed, he told his wife: My blood will water the trees of independence.

He nodded. 'Do you know what? they're not even the people who the majority of Kenyans want running them. That's not a great outcome for nine years' work, is it? Do you know what makes it worse? Do you know the one guy who's going to rise to the top of the ant hill?'

Joyce knew it was a rhetorical question so said nothing.

'Jomo fucking Kenyatta,' said Downsted answering his own question.

'Please Colin, stop it, don't swear.'

'He tiptoes around, leaving bad debts wherever he goes, hating everything decent we stand for. For God's sake, the man's in favour of female genital mutilation. Churchill called them savages; perhaps he was bloody right.'

'Does Bobby Erskine[24] know? You always got on better with him than Baring.'

'Yeh, I liked Bobby, at least he would make decisions,' said Downsted. 'Did you know he had a letter from Churchill authorising him to declare martial law at any time?'

Joyce shook her head.

'He'd never said until today, when I told him I was leaving. He was bloody furious. He wanted to get the decision revoked, but I told him it was time for me to move on. He kindly said he'd give me a darn good chit if I ever needed a reference.'

'That's nice of him – but what are you going to do?'

'I don't know. I've been given three months' notice and I'm getting three months' redundancy pay plus my overseas living allowance, so we're going to be alright for money for a little while.'

Joyce smiled encouragingly.

'I get to keep the Land Rover and all the camping equipment as part of my leaving package. It wasn't on offer, but it's something I sort of demanded and Baring agreed. Oh, and by the way, I'm getting a runners-up prize. They're giving me a C.'

---

[24] General Sir George Watkin Erskine GCB, KBE, DSO (23 August 1899 – 29 August 1965), known as Bobby, was a British army officer who after World War II commanded counterinsurgency operations against the Kenyan Land and Freedom Army during the Mau Mau rebellion.

'What's that when it's at home?'

'They're making me a Companion of the Order of St Michael and St John.'

'Are you being knighted? Do I call you sir?' she asked laughingly.

'No, I'd need to be made a knight commander for that. This is about the lowest medal they can give anyone.'

'What's it for?'

'Baring said it was for my distinguished service overseas, but in reality, it's a reference for civvy street.'

'Well, that's nice, isn't it?'

'I thought if I did a good job I'd be looked after, but...' Downsted's voice petered out with regret.

'Some of those jailed. Some of those hung... that wouldn't have happened if it hadn't been for your work, would it?' asked Joyce. Her voice was soft and gentle because she didn't want to criticize. She could see the tremendous strain he was under whenever he left or returned from one of his many journeys.

'You knew?'

'Yes, I knew.'

'How?'

'You were away for days. Your reports. Your witness statements. Even your job title.'

'You read them?'

She nodded.

'But you never said'

'I didn't want to ask, to make you explain. I thought if it was important to me, to us, you'd say something. You were under so much pressure, and in any case, if I'd said anything you'd have started hiding things, wouldn't you?'

Downsted didn't reply. He was deep in thought. Many men, too many men, had been imprisoned and hung as a result of the intelligence he had gathered in the field. At that moment, he felt both exhausted and terribly ashamed.

'I'm probably going to take some of the next few months to write,' he said. 'I'm going to tell the story of the foul-up down here. I'm going to put the blame where it well and truly lies – with the politicians in

London. It was the vagueness of their policy and the way it changed every eighteen months that created the leadership vacuum down here, mainly militarily, from which brutality and chaos were allowed to reign. Too many, far too many, suffered as a result. Do you know why the British came to Kenya, Uganda, East Africa, first of all?'

'I was told it was to bring Christianity, to stop the slave trade from the interior of Africa to the coast. It's why they built the railway line from Mombasa to Kisumu to ensure British dominance of the Great Lakes Region.'[25]

'Yes, a nice laudable aim,' said Downsted sarcastically. 'It's right, but only in part. It was never thought enough to justify investing so much money on a railway line, so the Colonial Office came up with the potty notion that if any other country controlled the region, they could dam up the headwaters of the Nile and desiccate Egypt – and we forget how important Egypt was at that time. Britain had invested heavily in the Suez Canal, which was vital to its India interests, and the stability of Egypt was vital to the Suez Canal. Everyone in government knew that to lose Suez would mean the loss of India. It was why Egypt became a British protectorate. The Egyptians ruled themselves, under our influence, and the rest of the world knew they had to leave the country alone. The idea of building a bloody expensive narrow-gauge railway line to protect the source of the Nile was thought so stupid by so many people in London that it was given the nickname – 'the Lunatic Express'. Downsted slowly shook his head from side to side before adding, 'and in such way are the crass decisions of government made.' He then let out a heavy sigh of despair.

'I thought it got its name because of the large number of men eaten by lions when they were building it. It was said you had to be mad to work on it,' interrupted Joyce.

'Set a hare running and millions of pounds of public money suddenly appears and then everyone's snout is in the trough.' There was quiet resignation in Downsted's voice as if he realised that it had ever been thus, and nothing was ever going to change.

---

[25] A city in Kenya on the shore Lake Victoria

'Of course, this was all done under the banner of civilising the Blacks here, ending savagery,' said Downsted ignoring Joyce's comment. 'What a fucking joke! We turned out to be the biggest savages of all.'

'Please Colin, don't swear,' reprimanded Joyce again.

'Sorry but it's the only word which will do. Our rule down here can only be described as awful, fucking awful!'

Chapter 36

THE TRANSFORMATION OF Bottlesford Hall from an unused but well-maintained conference centre to a fully-fledged boarding school was a gradual affair.

By the time the British Government had decided it had no use for Downsted's services, Joyce had already established a thriving tutorial business coaching both boys and girls to pass the Common Entrance exam.[26]

As soon as Downsted was unemployed, he was quickly roped in to tutor maths, physics and chemistry to Joyce's ever expanding customer base. The writing of his book started well, and he found it quite cathartic, but about two thirds of the way through he lost his energy as his vision of its audience got narrower and narrower. It would, he concluded, be a scribe for prosperity, and a bitter one at that.

There was no discussion between Joyce and Downsted on strategy or tactics when, following parental demand, they acceded to requests from parents living too far away for their children to commute, that they take girls in as boarders. Every discussion was on the practicalities of creating dormitories, classrooms and a dining room. One thing was certain in Joyce's mind. She didn't want boys as boarders. Her experience of teaching them at the Grammar School in Nuneaton had convinced her that she was incompatible with the adolescent male.

The next stage happened seamlessly as Bottlesford Hall slowly transformed itself into a crammer for girls seeking to pass Common Entrance.

---

[26] Common Entrance examinations are taken by pupils at the age of 13 as part of the selective admissions process to independent school pupils in the UK (also known as public schools, albeit that that are not open to the public, only to those who can afford to pay the fees.)

'We're not in the business of education,' Joyce would say to anxious parents. 'If your daughter is coming here, then it's too late for education. We're in the business of teaching our victims to pass an exam, and we do it through repetition, repetition, repetition.'

It was Downsted who set the school's very strict timetable, basing it on Joyce's mantra for repetition and his own experiences at boarding school. Everyone was up at seven o'clock. By 7:30 am they had to be in their classroom where there would be a list of thirty facts pertinent to the exams which had to be learnt by heart: the countries and cities of Europe; the Kings and Queens of England and their dates; French and Latin vocabulary, all of which would be tested in a fifteen-minute test starting on the dot of 8 o'clock. The results were meticulously recorded.

Breakfast followed, until 9 o'clock when school would start in earnest with a series of four, forty-five-minute lessons. Lunch was served on the dot of 1 o'clock. Immediately after lunch everyone retired to their beds until 2:30 pm for quiet reading time. The afternoon was committed to a range of games, some organised, some completely wild held in the woods outside of the school grounds. There would be tea at 4.30 pm and, at five o'clock sharp, school lessons would recommence for another two hours. At 7.00 pm there would be supper, and after that essay-writing practice when a subject matter would be set. The outline facts would be given to write the perfect answer. It was the job of the pupil to mould one fact alongside another, all in the space of forty-five minutes. In this way, Bottlesford Hall girls learned to write essays on completely diverse subjects ranging from the evidence available to suggest that Richard III was responsible for killing the two Princes in the Tower, to what were the main exports of India and who did it trade with. Every exercise was designed to pump more knowledge into the pupils' brains with the sole purpose of passing exams.

Bedtime was 9 o'clock with lights out a 9.30 pm. Those who had more than two mistakes in the morning test would, just before lights out, meet Joyce in their pyjamas on the galleried landing for one stroke of, what she called, the beam, on their backside for every mistake above the two they were allowed to make. Three mistakes and she would smack them once quite hard, always lessening the power of her blows for each mistake they had made after that. Her objective was to make the stinging effect the same. Then after all the girls had returned to their beds Joyce would shout out: 'And now you know why we don't sjambok the Blacks.'[27]

It was an unusual but effective way for Joyce to weed out those who were never going to get the required marks to meet their parents' ambition, because the persistent miscreants nearly always matched those who had done poorly in the intelligence tests she had started doing.

'It's time,' she would say to parents whose daughters she had met too often on the landing, 'to reconsider your daughter's educational career.'

By the time half term came, there was rarely a meeting of beam with bottom. The principles of maximum effort which Joyce required had, by then, been well established.

The results Joyce achieved at Bottlesford Hall were so good that it was the parents who encouraged Joyce and Downsted to allow their children to stay, first taking 'O' Levels which required a heavy investment in physics and chemistry laboratories, and when that proved successful, they extended the school even further to teach A-levels.

By the time Jumapili came to join Joyce and Downsted at Bottlesford Hall, the school typically had between forty and forty-five girl borders with ages ranging from eleven to eighteen. They all lived and worked together in surprising harmony, perhaps because Joyce would take no truck with any pupil. She was not beyond phoning a parent to demand they took their daughter home because no one's fees were above the good reputation of her school.

---

[27] A thick, heavy leather whip made of hippopotamus or rhinoceros skin used relentlessly by the white security forces against blacks during the apartheid era.

Chapter 37

JOYCE WAS FULL of nervous excitement as she walked the hospital corridor to collect 'Little Jumi' as she and Downsted had started referring to Jumapili.

In all her years of marriage she had never been able to conceive the child that both she and Downsted yearned for. There was nothing medically wrong and it was not for lack of trying, but it was not to be. Adopting Little Jumi would give them the family they missed, and they found the thought exciting.

Both Joyce and Downsted knew they liked Jumapili because they had already spent many hours with her. The fact was that she had emotional wisdom and intellect beyond her years which, despite her blindness, made her an easy companion.

It was during holiday times when Bottlesford Hall was empty that Joyce was most conscious of their lack of family because it created a loneliness which she found hard to ignore. If Joyce and Downsted had taken a moment to think about it, they would have realised that they needed Jumapili to make their lives fulfilled and complete, as much as she needed them.

Jumapili was equally nervous as she sat on the hospital bed, waiting. She had been ready since early light. She had established a routine for herself in hospital. She felt safe and secure. Everything had a rhythm, a pattern about it. Most of all, Jumapili's body had benefited from regular meals causing a girl of skin and bones to fill out slightly, making her face less angular and thus softer. But it was warm baths, a luxury Jumapili discovered for the first time in the hospital, which she could not imagine being without. Would Mr. and Mrs. Downsted allow her to have baths, she wondered time and time again.

Jumapili heard Joyce arrive long before she said anything. The fact is that every human walks with their own gait. It makes the sound of their footprints slightly different. It was this, coupled with the echo from her clicks, that allowed Jumapili to know that Joyce was walking towards her. In response, she pushed her backbone to be ramrod straight.

'Hello. Are you ready? Are you excited?' asked Joyce when she was by Jumapili's side.

Jumapili nodded as she grasped the edge of the bed tighter with her legs now swinging frantically underneath her.

'Is everything okay?' asked Joyce.

'Can't I stay here? I'm happy here. They're nice to me here.'

'My little darling,' said Joyce sympathetically as she sat down beside Jumapili and extended her arm around her.

'I want to go back to my brother. Back to the time before ...' pleaded Jumapili. 'I know we can manage. We've always managed.'

'There's no going back,' said Joyce softly. 'Everything moves on. Think about it, today can never be the same as yesterday. When you put your feet into a stream for a second time, it might be at the same place, but it is not the same stream as the water's moved on.'

There was silence before Joyce continued: 'There's an author, C.S. Lewis, you'll read his books one day.'

'Read?'

'Yes, most definitely,' said Joyce, her headmistress voice returning. 'The first thing you'll learn to do at Bottlesford Hall is to read and write. It will be braille, of course, but we'll learn it together.'

There was another pause before Joyce continued: 'C.S. Lewis famously said: "*You can't change the beginning, but you can start where you are, and change the ending*". So,' said Joyce as she slapped her hand on the mattress before pushing herself up, 'the hardest part of any journey is the first step, and we'll make it together.'

'I'm sorry,' said Joyce, her voice softening. 'I ordered a couple of sets of new school uniforms for you from Harrods, but they haven't come yet, but I think these will fit. They're perfectly fine. They've been washed, and the vests, knickers and socks, they're new. So are the court shoes and gym shoes. I've got three sizes for you to try on and we'll take back the ones that don't fit.'

'But I've already got dressed,' protested Jumapili.

'I know, but I think it's important you wear the same school uniform as everyone else,' said Joyce. 'It'll help you fit in.'

Very gently and with tremendous patience Joyce helped Jumapili dress, allowing her time to feel the cloth and find the buttons, belts and zips.

'This is like the sensory cloth my mother made for me when I was young,' said Jumapili as she worked out how each of her new clothes were worn.

'Sensory cloth?' repeated Joyce.

'Yes, a cloth with all different things sown on it. I used to touch, play with it. It's made with different types of material: cotton, silks, cords, leather, and wool. It has zips, buttons, button-holes, buckles, hooks on it, even cord, rope, cork, and string to learn to tie knots. Everything is different.'

'And your mother made this for you?'

'Yes, I have it here. In this bag,' said Jumapili as she reached across, knowing instantly the bag she was looking for. She felt deep inside it.

'I have this too,' said Jumapili excitedly. 'Look, it's my grandfather's mbugi.[28] I have one and Absko has one too, from the other grandfather.

Joyce took the pathetic roughly caste tin box in her hand and marvelled at Jumapili's joy from such a worthless object. Had she been so deprived that a pitiful item had such value to her? Joyce wondered.

Jumapili dug into her bag again and took out her sensory cloth. 'It's the only thing I have left of Mama's,' she said in a matter-of-fact way, as she handed it to Joyce.

Joyce didn't respond because she was fighting back her tears. She could see in every stitch Jumapili's mother's painstaking work.

'This is remarkable,' said Joyce eventually, struggling to talk as her cheeks were tight with emotion. 'Your mother was very talented.'

---

[28] As part of their colonial rule of Kenya, the British demanded that all African men who left their allotted reserve had to carry a pass or kipande with them. This recorded their name, fingerprints, ethnic group, their employment history and their current employer's signature. It was the most detested symbol of colonial power throughout all of Africa because failure to carry it resulted in a hefty fine, imprisonment or both. The Kikuyu used to put their pass in a small metal container, the size of a cigarette case, called a mbugi or goat's bell, which they would wear around their necks.

The significance to Jumapili of this small, tired, worn, almost miserable cloth, contrasted sharply to its total insignificance to anyone else. Once again, Jumapili had reaffirmed to Joyce the fact that life was desperately unfair. Joyce had so much, and Little Jumi had so little. As that recognition struck home, as it often did for Joyce in Kenya, she had an overwhelming sense of guilt and shame which caused her to ache physically inside.

'She made me some sensory toys as well, animals, just before she died,' said Jumapili, 'but I lost them on the day of the accident. I don't know where they went.'

'A zebra, hippopotamus, and giraffe made out of pipe cleaners and beads?' asked Joyce.

Jumapili nodded.

'Rishi's got them. He's keeping them safe.'

'Rishi's got them? Really, Rishi's got them, has he?' Jumapili repeated. 'He never said!' The excitement in her voice was obvious to hear.

'These go on your feet,' said Joyce as she handed Jumapili a sock. In all her twelve years Jumapili had never worn socks before. Her footwear, like her brother's, had always been sandals.

Jumapili struggled with the socks and then with her new court shoes. She had never worn anything as uncomfortable on her feet before.

'Do you wear these?' asked Jumapili.

'Yes, all the girl's do.'

'Why, what have you done wrong?'

'Done wrong?'

'Yes, they hurt. You must have done something wrong to be made to wear these!'

'I admit they hurt at first, but when you break them in you'll find they soften, and you won't notice them anymore,' said Joyce, remembering the blisters which came with every pair of new shoes.

Once Jumapili was dressed, they gathered her things and said goodbye to the nurses, showering them with her profuse thanks, and then her fellow patients. As they walked the hospital corridor towards Joyce's car, Jumapili heard a new echo. It was the heels of her shoes clacking against the floor. The returning sound was another source of sight.

Chapter 38

JUMAPILI HAD NEVER travelled in a car before. Her mode of transport had either been her feet or a matatu, so it was with a mixture of excitement and trepidation that she was helped into the front seat of Downsted's Land Rover for the journey to Bottlesford Hall. Everything was new to her touch: the leather, the plastic, the metal, the glass. For the first few seconds of taking her seat Jumapili clicked furiously, only falling silent when the engine started, because the noise drowned out any echo.

'There's a handle on the left, just above your head,' said Joyce as the bumps in the road started to throw the car and Jumapili around.

Joyce was a fast and determined driver. The sad fact was that carjacking and kidnapping by Janjaweed,[29] particularly of a woman in a car on her own, happened far too often to be ignored.

But these were the only words Joyce spoke on their journey because she was reflecting on the talk she had given to the whole school at breakfast that morning and was wondering whether she had been wise.

'Ladies,' said Joyce after she had brought the dining room to order. 'We have a new pupil joining us today. Her name is Jumapili Mwangi. She's blind.'

On the news that their new girl was blind, the room fell into a deathly hush.

'As you'll discover for yourselves,' continued Joyce. 'Jumapili has some remarkable gifts but there are some things we need to talk about before she joins us. As you may guess from her surname Mwangi, Jumapili is Black. She's Bantu, from the Kikuyu tribe, and

---

[29] Translates into English as 'devils on horseback.

her ancestors enjoyed this country long before ours. She will be the first Black pupil we'll have had in this school.'

Joyce paused as her husband walked into the room.

'Being totally blind, Jumapili cannot see colour,' said Joyce. 'She does not know black nor white, and neither will we. We all know, or at least I hope we do, Martin Luther King's dream: that his children will not be judged by the colour of their skin but by the content of their character. Well, that's one of our unsaid school rules. Unquestionably, this school is colour blind and racially agnostic. You, me, we, are each going to be judged on our character and our contribution. That's it.'

Joyce paused again.

'You girls are very fortunate. Your good fortune, like mine, comes from our birth. You've done nothing to deserve being here except to be born to parents with love and means, and although I've studied, strived and worked hard to get here, I too was fortunate to have parents who made sure I had the best start in this life. Some of you will argue – I can hear it now – that you passed exams and are here on your merit, but that's only partially true. You're also here because of your parents' good fortune. Your opportunities in this life started on the shoulders of your parents. These are many rungs higher than those who have no parents, or whose parents are so poor that they can't afford to educate their children. The arrival of Jumapili will remind us daily how blest we are.'

Joyce looked towards Downsted for his approval. He smiled, quickly raised and lowered his eyebrows, and nodded. She discreetly nodded back.

'There's a tendency to think that those who are physically disabled are also mentally less able,' Joyce continued. That's not true. 'I can assure you Jumapili is not stupid. She can do things you couldn't even contemplate tackling. You don't have to look after her, she's more than capable of doing that, but you can help. There's an etiquette for dealing with blind people which you must know. I'm going to go through some of the key points, but they're based upon courtesy and common sense. For your part you must follow the Golden Rule, which we've discussed many, many times. Claudia what's the golden rule?' shouted Joyce to one of her pupils.

Claudia shot bolt upright. 'I dunno Miss.'

'Catherine, what's the golden rule?' asked Joyce again, as she started to pace between the dining room tables.

'You treat another person as you would wish to be treated,' answered Catherine succinctly.

'That's right, Catherine, thank you. You treat another person as you would wish to be treated,' repeated Joyce. 'It's no different when dealing with the blind. You treat them as you would want to be treated if you too were blind.'

Joyce started to run through some of the basics. 'Always treat a blind person normally; speak first and introduce yourself. Jumapili will soon learn your voice,' she told them, 'but until then you must assume she doesn't know who you are.

Always ask before offering any help, and don't be offended if Jumapili refuses. Look at her during a conversation and adopt the same position. If she sits, you sit; if she stands, you stand. And don't be afraid of using normal language, words like 'look', 'see', 'read', as the blind have the same vocabulary as us. Once into a conversation with Jumapili never leave without saying you're doing so. It might be funny, but it's not fair to leave a blind person alone talking into the air! Remember, be precise if giving instructions – giving directions by pointing and saying, 'it's over there' is not much help and very thoughtless. When guiding Jumapili make sure you give adequate room around obstacles and hazards and plenty of time for response, and when tackling stairs say whether you're going up or down, and for Pete's sake, warn her before she gets to the top or bottom of any step. Also, please remember to point out things like changes in ground surfaces, kerbstones, and lamp posts. It's all so obvious if you just think – think ahead!

'Claudia, what do you have to do?' asked Joyce, giving the girl the opportunity to redeem herself.'

'Think ahead.'

'Good, excellent. Think ahead. We think ahead.'

The assembly then practiced taking each other's arms at the triceps, one guiding the other around chairs and through narrow doors, and when they had got used to guiding their friends, Joyce divided them up, so they began to guide those they did not know so well. The exercise produced lots of giggles, laughter, and excitement.

'Ladies,' shouted Joyce several times before her school came to order. 'Two final things. Jumapili sees with her ears and her hands. When she gets to know you well, she might ask to feel your face. Don't be surprised; feel flattered. Finally, I need some volunteers to show Jumapili around the first few days. Hands up all those who are willing.'

Every hand went up in the air, but not Downsted's. He was silently clapping his wife's efforts in approval.

Chapter 39

JUMAPILI AND JOYCE arrived at Bottlesford Hall just as the girls had finished their morning lessons and were going into lunch. Naturally, a large number congregated around the front steps to watch Joyce help Jumapili out of the car and see their new 'celebrity' pupil.

'I'll show you to your bedroom first,' said Joyce as soon as they were in the hall. 'I'm always far more relaxed when I know where I'm going to sleep, and I guess you'll be the same.

Lucy,' she called out to one of the girls standing by, 'would you please ask Hawla to save two lunches for us. We'll be in later.'

Joyce helped Jumapili climb the stairs to the top floor of the house, pointing out banisters, walls, doors, and obstacles as they went. She helped her run her hands along the walls so she could get a sense of where she was. At the same time Joyce was making a mental note of things that had to be moved because there was no need for unnecessary obstacles in what would be Jumapili's most obvious path.

'This is a huge room,' commented Jumapili as they climbed higher, and the echo of her clicks from around the hall took longer to return.

'You're sharing with two others,' said Joyce as they came to Jumapili's bedroom. 'You could have a room on your own, and probably will in holiday time, but I think it's important you share to start with, so you get to know the ropes. You'll need help until you know where everything is and get familiar with the routine.'

Joyce led Jumapili through the narrow door of her new bedroom before gently guiding her turn. 'This is your bed,' she said, as Jumapili's white cane touched against the metal bedframe.

Jumapili bent down to touch the bed, already made with sheets and blankets, before turning around, sitting down, and bouncing on it as everyone always does when introduced to a new bed.

'As I've said, there are two other girls sleeping in here, Alison and Catherine, so there are three of you. You'll like them. They're a bit older than you, not much,' said Joyce, before pointing out Jumapili's bedside locker and wardrobe.

The pair then made their way to the bathrooms where the working of basins, showers, and toilets were carefully explained before they went downstairs again, with Joyce describing every move as Jumapili tapped and clicked in accompaniment.

'I'm sure you'll soon get used to it all,' said Joyce confidently as they entered the dining room, while she remembered how difficult she found it to locate light switches when they had to be found in the dark.

Lunch was just finishing, and the girls were all dispersing slowly to lie on their beds as the school routine dictated, so it took some time for Joyce and Jumapili to navigate to the clean table laid for them.

Joyce took Jumapili's hand and placed it on the back of the chair, from which Jumapili was able to sit down.

'I've laid the napkin out as you asked,' said Hawla, as she brought in two steaming hot lunch plates. 'Be careful,' she ordered as she placed them down. 'They're very hot.'

'Thank you Hawla. Jumapili, meet Hawla,' said Joyce. 'She's our housekeeper. She keeps everything here shipshape and Bristol fashion'.

'Hello,' said Jumapili.

'Jumapili,' continued Joyce, 'we've laid everything out based on the oblong of your napkin. If you find the long edge at the bottom, nearest you, and you work your way around, you'll find your fork on the left and your knife on the right.'

'Miss,' interrupted Jumapili, 'I've never used a knife or a fork before. In hospital they gave me a spoon to use, but I rarely used it.'

'Ok,' said Joyce calmly. 'That's something we'll have to teach you, because I know blind people can and do use them. But, for now, you'll find your spoon directly on the other side of the plate, at the top of the napkin, in the twelve o'clock position.'

'Twelve o'clock?' questioned Jumapili.

'You don't know the positions on the clock?' asked Joyce sounding surprised.

'No, of course not,' said Jumapili sounding quite hurt. 'I can't see a clock, can I.'

'No, you can't. So, we'll have to teach you the clock positions. Not so you can tell the time, but so we can better describe where things are,' responded Joyce positively, before adding, 'you'll find a glass of water at the top right of your napkin.'

Joyce watched as Jumapili felt around the napkin edge until she came to the glass of water. She took it steadily in both hands before proceeding to drink it empty. Then, very methodically, she returned it to precisely the same place.

'Please Miss, what's on my plate?' asked Jumapili.

'There's steak and kidney pie, with mashed potatoes, peas, carrots and cabbage,' answered Joyce.

'What's that?' responded Jumapili sounding quite shocked.

There then proceeded a long conversation in which Joyce described each item on her plate, while Jumapili explained that she had always eaten with her fingers or drunk from a cup. Everything cooked had been prewrapped or, like rice, squeezed together to be mopped up with bread, even when she had been in hospital. By patient negotiation, they agreed that Jumapili would eat with a spoon today as the food was hot and the other implements would come later.

There was a grimace on Jumapili's face as the texture of her first spoonful of steak and kidney entered her mouth. '*Mzungu*,' she swore. [30]

'Jumapili!' rebuked Joyce. 'Please.'

'You put pain on my feet. You put rubbish in my mouth,' protested Jumapili in Swahili. 'Your things are supposed to be better than ours, but they're not, they're not!'

Joyce fell back in her seat, shocked at the vigour of Jumapili's outcry. She had always been so timid, so compliant before. Then it dawned on her. There wasn't just the issue of dealing with Jumapili's blindness and her lack of education because she was confident of dealing with those. But now, for the first time, Joyce was seeing a chasm in their cultures, and it began to worry her.

---

[30] Means European and is an often used swear word in Swahili.

Chapter 40

'I SUGGEST WE return to your bedroom,' said Joyce after she had cleared away their lunch things. 'We all rest for between half and three-quarters-of-an-hour after lunch. I'll ask Hawla to come up and help you unpack, sort out your things. We'll then meet with Colin to discuss your timetable. You'll find everything here is organised and works to a strict routine. It comes from Colin's time in the navy,' she declared wrongly, because Joyce was as much a stickler for the timetable as her husband.

Jumapili said nothing. She held Joyce's arm as they again climbed the stairs to her new bedroom. Her white stick travelled before them. Joyce gave few instructions preferring Jumapili listened to the echo clicks from her tongue and the clacks of her shoes.

No sooner had Jumapili and Joyce tapped their way to the room than Hawla was by their side.

'Hawla will look after you now,' said Joyce. 'We'll meet in the study in say, forty-five minutes?' Joyce left, ignoring her own instructions of that morning of telling a blind person when you are leaving them.

Hawla had missed out on Joyce's lecture on the etiquette of helping Jumapili, so she took it upon herself to do the tasks which Jumapili wanted to do, in fact needed to do, herself. There followed a tussle between Hawla and Jumapili until, in frustration, Hawla realised the blind girl was going to have her own way.

'You obviously don't need me,' barked Hawla. 'You're expected in Mrs. Downsted's study next,' and with those few words she was gone.

It was an interesting victory because it was the first battle Jumapili ever remembered winning. It gave her a confidence she had rarely felt before.

To be left alone was precisely what Jumapili needed. To feel at home, she had to understand the space around her. Clicking fiercely, she explored her new bedroom, touching the windows, doors, curtains, beds, bedclothes, and cupboards. Time and time again, she allowed her fingers and ears to explore the room until she was confident that she knew where she was, and where everything was placed. Finally, with her possessions packed away, she took hold of her sensory blanket and mbugi, which had always been a part of her life, and placed them under her pillow. She lay down on her bed and for the first time she felt the smoothness of the pillowcase on which her head was to rest for many a day.

Jumapili slid her hand under her pillow and, holding her blanket, she listened to the silence. She found a quietude not found in the hospital, nor in Kibera, and she started to feel calm. She noticed the smell. It wasn't the smell of carbolic and disinfectant of the hospital or the rotten decay of Kibera, but the sweetness of polish and nature which, in turn, brought tranquillity to the room.

It was mid-afternoon by the time Jumapili made her way downstairs to Joyce and Downsted in their shared study. She had started off by herself and had successfully clicked and tapped her way down the stairs to the ground floor. It was only at the bottom that Jumapili had to appeal for help in getting to the right room.

'Mr. Downsted has prepared a timetable for you,' said Joyce once Jumapili was seated and holding a glass of water in both her hands. 'It's got three components, braille, music and some sport. Once you've mastered braille, we'll introduce other topics into the timetable. Those that you're going to need to pass exams.'

'Sport, music, exams,' repeated Jumapili in mild protest. 'Am I to do exams?' she asked clearly puzzled, and for the first time Joyce observed her deep frown.

'Exams - they're only tests,' answered Downsted. 'We have to prove, you have to prove, you're learning things. And music, as a blind girl, that's essential. If you can play an instrument, play music, you'll always be guaranteed an income, even if it's just as a street busker or as a pub piano player.'

'And sport?' questioned Jumapili.

'Of course,' insisted Downsted. 'Being blind doesn't stop you running. The blind have been playing cricket in Australia and football in Spain for the last sixty years.'

'Cricket, what's cricket? asked Jumapili.

Downsted started to explain the rules of cricket, which had far too many ins and outs for it to be comprehensible, until Joyce stepped in and stopped him.

'While learning Braille, you'll also have to do some basic maths and English classes,' said Joyce trying to take command of the conversation. 'You have so much catching-up to do.'

'But your main focus will be music,' interrupted Downsted. 'You'll learn the piano, of course. It's a basic instrument every musician must learn. But what's your choice for string and wind instruments? Do you want to stick with the violin you've started with?'

Jumapili didn't answer. She did not know what he was talking about.

'You already play the recorder. I've heard you,' said Downsted. 'That's a wind instrument.'

'Well, I'll play that,' answered Jumapili earnestly.

'That wouldn't be appropriate for an orchestra. It doesn't have the range. Break it down: do you want to learn a brass or wood instrument?' Although the words were harsh, his tone was one of encouragement.

'Colin,' protested Joyce, 'you're asking questions which Jumi will have no basis of answering. You need to find some music to demonstrate the possible choices.'

Joyce disappeared as Colin spent a delightful hour going through his record collection, playing his favourite pieces to Jumapili while getting emotionally immersed in the different sounds he had chosen to play her.

'I think the decisions the clarinet,' said Downsted when Joyce re-entered the room. 'Jumi's torn between the clarinet and saxophone. It's just, we have a spare clarinet, and we don't have a spare saxophone,' he explained.

'OK,' acknowledged Joyce. 'They're both reed instruments so once Jumi's mastered the mouthing technique of one she'll be able to play both. Of course, the fingering will be different. What has Jumi decided as her string instrument?'

'She likes the sound of the cello or double bass. Don't you Jumi?'

'Colin, for pete's sake!' rebuked Joyce. 'Be practical. It's absurd to suggest that Jumi can carry an instrument that big around as well as her stick. The choice is simple. It's between a voila and a violin and she's already started on the violin.'

The violin she's been using is in a dreadful condition. It was fine in hospital, but I couldn't bear to listen to it here.'

'But the violin produces a higher pitch and clearer note so it's a better solo instrument,' argued Joyce.

'I know but we don't have any spare violins. I'll find a viola from somewhere,' replied Downsted. He knew they didn't have a spare one of those either, but he was determined that there was not going to be another child scratching and scraping at a violin in Bottlesford Hall.

It was from that conversation that Jumapili's musical fortunes were set: she would learn to play the piano, the clarinet and viola. And neither said, because they had already decided, that Jumapili would have braille music lessons too, so she knew what she was playing and one day, through touch, would be able to learn new pieces.

'Look, it's teatime,' said Joyce, responding to the bell which was ringing in the hall. 'I think Jumi should join the others for tea and then she should go to her first braille lesson. Who's teaching her and where?'

Downsted gave the name of a teacher and classroom as Joyce moved to the door to ask a passing girl to accompany Jumapili into tea.

'Before you go,' said Joyce. 'I think when we're together, just the three of us, you should call us Colin and Joyce but when you are with our other pupils, your colleagues, you should refer to us as 'Mr. Downsted' or 'sir', and 'Mrs. Downsted' or 'miss'. Is that OK?'

Jumapili nodded.

'Are you alright? Is there anything else?' asked Joyce.

'There is one thing,' said Jumapili tentatively. 'Is there any chance someone could phone Rishi's house and speak to his mother? I'd like to have the toys my mother made for me. Knowing where they are – well, I'd like to have them back please.'

It was a request which was to have enormous consequences.

Chapter 41

I'VE SPOKEN TO Lakshmi about Jumapili's toys', said Joyce to Downsted, when they were alone that evening. All the children, in their school, including Jumapili, were tucked up in bed.

'Rishi's mother?' asked Downsted, although he knew exactly who Lakshmi was.

'Yes, apparently Graeme's gone to stay with his brother in Johannesburg.'

'But he's on bail. He's not allowed to leave the country!'

'I know,' said Joyce. 'Apparently the Nairobi police have already decided they should apply to have him extradited.'

'Jesus, that's not good. He's bound to end up in jail in South Africa and then here. At least until his trial,' commented Downsted.

'Apparently, the idea was to put him in a different environment to encourage him to stop drinking, but his brother told Lakshmi he's as bad as ever, if not worse.'

'It's hard to be worse than he was when he smashed into Jumapili, is it? I saw him, remember. He could hardly stand up.'

'Lakshmi's decided she wants a divorce. She asked me if I knew a lawyer who could help. I said you'd introduce her to ours, even take her to see him. You could pick up Jumapili's toys at the same time'.

Chapter 42

'IT'S CALLED A baby grand piano,' said Joyce as she guided Jumapili to the piano stool and helped her sit down. 'It's a Steinway, the very best. It came from my home in England after my father died. I'll take your stick. Now feel around you, feel the piano.'

Jumapili ran her fingers over the polished piano lid, allowing them to run from side to side.

'It's very wide,' she exclaimed.

'Get up and walk around it. Feel it's shape,' commanded Joyce. Jumapili did as she was told. Together they opened the lid and when it was propped up, Joyce encouraged Jumapili to run her fingers around the metal, heart-shaped frame and steel strings.

'It's effectively a harp on its side, placed on wood to make a sound board and then put in a box,' said Joyce. 'And rather than pluck the strings as you do with the harp to make the sound, they are hit with a small, padded hammer to make the strings vibrate, and it's the keys on the piano which operate the hammer.'

There followed a long conversation about sound being made by vibration which Joyce taught using a concert tuning fork which she struck and placed close to Jumapili's ear. Jumapili could feel the vibration in the air as Joyce held it close to her cheek, and at that moment Jumapili understood what Joyce was talking about.

Returning to sit on the stool, Joyce persuaded Jumapili to lift the piano lid. 'Gosh its heavy,' she protested.

'Yes, if it falls down it will break your fingers, so you must be very careful. Let me help you find the keys.'

Taking Jumapili's hand, Joyce guided her fingers over the keys encouraging Jumapili to press them to make different sounds. 'There are eighty-eight of them,' she said as she helped Jumapili differentiate between the lower white natural music keys and the higher black flat and sharp keys.

'As always, Jumapili took a long time to explore things with her hands because, after her burn, her instinct was never to fully trust where her hands were travelling. Caution was her subconscious byword.

'Why is everything in black and white?' asked Jumapili commenting on Joyce's description. 'It's the same in chess.'

'Well, we'll call them something different,' announced Joyce, noticing a slight discomfort in Jumapili's voice. 'The white keys, they'll be called ivory; the black keys, we'll call them ebony, as those are the materials the keys were first made from. Now let's find middle C as from there you can work out how to play every song ever written.'

By the end of the morning Jumapili had mastered *chop sticks*, *twinkle twinkle little star*, and Joyce had played for her *Für Elise*, telling her it was the tune she was going to learn next.

'I have my harmonica but do you know where my recorder or my whistle are?' asked Jumapili at the end of the lesson. 'I had them on the day of the crash, but now they're gone. I'd like to match the notes on those to the notes on the piano as that will help me know where I am.'

'Colin is seeing Mrs McGeown, Rishi's mother, next Monday afternoon to collect your mother's toys,' replied Joyce. 'I'll ask him to ask her if she knows where they are.'

Chapter 43

'DID YOU HEAR Jumi sing' said Joyce to Downsted as they were standing outside the newsagents and general store at Tayiania. The pupils from their school were lining up for sweets and ice creams after Sunday church. Good behaviour in church was rewarded with ice creams; bad behaviour meant the treat was forfeited.

'She sang at the McGeown funeral, didn't she,' said Joyce. 'Do you remember?'

Downsted nodded. 'I'd forgotten – exquisite, simply exquisite.'

'How did she know the words?'

'She used to busk on the street between the bakers and the coffee roaster's. Just there,' said Downsted, pointing to where Jumapili used to sit. 'She learnt the lyrics from overhearing their radios. I remember her singing *Somewhere Over the Rainbow* for the very first time. We were sitting outside the café opposite and we all stood up and clapped, we were so overtaken. Graeme McGeown was so smitten he rushed over and paid her to sing it again.

'Is that why she sang at his father's funeral?' asked Joyce.

'I guess so.'

'I think it was the best version of *The Lord is my Shepherd* I've ever heard. Her phrasing on that day was just perfect.'

'And *The Skye Boat Song*,' added Downsted. 'Do you remember? The way she blended the harmonica with her singing, the purity of the notes. We commented on it then.'

'I remember it all, even to the little black dress she was wearing.'

'You would. Only a woman would notice that kind of thing.'

'You didn't notice?' asked Joyce.

'No, sorry, why would I,' said Downsted, just as Jumapili was getting to the front of the queue.

'Jumapili, Jumapili,' shouted the shop assistant. 'How lovely to see you. How are you? You're lucky to be alive. Ya know that. How ya doin?'

Jumapili's new friends gathered around listening.

'I was here that morning of your crash. Gosh it were bad. You were bad,' continued the shop assistant. 'I thought yer's dead.'

'Well, I'm pretty much alive,' answered Jumapili modestly, as the group around her got closer to listen.

'Ya not coming back here to sing no more?'

'No, I don't think so, but you never know,' said Jumapili before doing as almost everyone else had done which was to order a choc ice.

'I hear you're now living at Bottlesford Hall,' continued the shop assistant.

Jumapili nodded and smiled as her initial excitement at being recognised evaporated on the worry that people were talking about her. 'How do you know?' she asked

'Absko told us. He was very pleased for you. He still comes here three or four times a day.'

'Thank you,' said Jumapili as, with ice cream in hand, she was pushed out of the way so others could be served.

The chaos and mess of eating a choc ice for the first time when no one tells you that you need to unwrap the paper, it melts rapidly and drips everywhere, might have distressed the most battle weary, but Jumapili could not care less. She was happy that, through this little shop, she would be able to send messages to her brother. She fought her way back to the shop counter and the shop assistant before asking, 'Would you say hi, to Absko for me. Tell 'im, all's good.'

Chapter 44

'MISS MWANGI!' SHOUTED Downsted from the edge of the sports field.

Jumapili came to an abrupt stop. It was Monday afternoon, and it was the first time Jumapili had been on the school's sports field with everyone else from the school.

Downsted stormed to where Jumapili was standing. 'I don't care if you're blind,' he shouted as he paced towards her. 'It's not an excuse. I'm not going to accept you running as if you're demented.'

'I've never run before,' shouted back Jumapili angrily. 'This is my first time.'

'Where are you running to?' demanded Downsted.

'Towards the whistle.'

'Good,' he retorted, 'but don't swing your arms like a windmill.'

'What's a windmill? How am I supposed to know what a windmill is?'

Downsted grabbed Jumapili's arms. 'This is how you're running – with your arms failing around everywhere,' he said as he waived them around in the air. 'It's not how you run. You run with your arms by your side, bending at the elbow. Like this,' at which point Downsted pushed Jumapili's arms backwards and forwards as though they were pistons on a train.

'Mrs. Valentine, would you please teach Miss Mwangi how to run,' he asked the school's sports teacher.

'And how do I do that?' asked Valentine.

'I don't know. I don't teach sport. But what I do know is that we're never going to accept second best from Jumapili because she's blind. She must perform to the best of her abilities like everyone else here or not at all.'

'Be reasonable,' demanded Valentine, upset at being rebuked in front of the whole school. 'She's just come from hospital having suffered two broken legs and a broken ankle.'

'I know that perfectly well.' The truth was that Downsted had forgotten. 'Jumapili, are your arms hurting?'

'No Sir.'

'Are your legs and ankles hurting?'

'No Sir.' Jumapili was now a little scared; she had never heard Downsted speak like that before.

Mrs. Valentine smarted at what other teachers in the school agreed was unfair treatment, but the message went round the staffroom and with it the terms were set for Jumapili's schooling. There were the same expectations on her to achieve, not necessarily in the same way as everyone else, but unquestionably to the best of her abilities. There was no second best for any pupil at Bottlesford Hall, and Jumapili was not to be an exception.

There was another thing that happened that afternoon. Jumapili had found her sport – running as fast as she could. With the dry grass prickling between her bare toes she would be reminded of the old days, before court shoes, when her feet were free. But it was, as she sought to go faster and faster, and endorphins stormed around her body, that Jumapili discovered an excitement and a freedom she had never felt before.

Chapter 45

THE CAUSES OF Downsted's appalling behaviour on the sports field were threefold. That morning he had been told that Mbua Aomba and Maunda Amwei were out of jail. It worried him because it was not good news. It was Downsted's evidence, when working for military intelligence, which had, in large part, put them there. President Kenyatta had, earlier that week, decided they should be paroled from their life-imprisonment sentence. The British Embassy in Nairobi were so certain that the release of these men presented a serious security risk that they took the effort to warn Downsted and suggested that he increase his security, but without any concrete proposals as to how he might do that.

The second reason was his annoyance at having to take Lakshmi McGeown to see his lawyer so she could get a divorce. Everything about the McGeown family frustrated Downsted. The friendship started because both Downsted and Graeme McGeown spoke Japanese, although their learning of this language came from two dramatically different experiences, because not once had Downsted visited Japan. It was because of this that Downsted listened patiently as Graeme told his horror stories time and time again in the hope that, in its retelling, his pain might abate, but to no avail. He had made exception after exception, for Graeme's appalling behaviour, regularly carting him home either violently drunk or unconscious from alcohol, but no more.

Finally, he was not looking forward to an afternoon with Lakshmi because he had never had a comfortable relationship with her. Although they would often meet at the same parties, Downsted always thought she carried an aloofness, a sense of superiority about her which made it difficult to have a conversation beyond the usual pleasantries. What annoyed him most, and he knew it was illogical, and every time he mentioned it, he would get berated by Joyce, but she always wore a saree, except not today.

To Downsted's amazement Lakshmi McGeown had dressed in western clothes to visit his lawyer. She was wearing tight fashionable jeans, trendy boots, and a tailored blouse. She had also changed her hair style to the point that Downsted nearly didn't recognise her. Her thick black wavy hair, which she always wore down, was now worn high on the back of her head in a French pleat. But the biggest change – she smiled. Never before had Colin Downsted seen Lakshmi McGeown smile.

At the lawyer's Office, Lakshmi told of McGeown's drunken and often violent behaviour towards both her and Rishi. Apparently, the only time McGeown found solace was in his garden shed, where he had built a model railway of the journey from Edinburgh's Waverley station to Glasgow's Queen station with replicas of three of the stations in between. His collection of locomotives and carriages would have been the envy of many a modeller if they had known about it. This shed was McGeown's private world where no one else was allowed in. He would spend hours, sometimes days, watching his numerous trains go round and round as he slowly drunk himself into oblivion.

The lawyer told Lakshmi that McGeown's drunkenness, violence and his forthcoming prison sentence were all sufficient grounds for her to get a divorce; no other reason was necessary. She would have to prepare a statement giving as many examples of his cruelty as possible and a *decree nisi* would be hers within months.

'As with all divorces, the problems start and end with the financial settlement,' said the lawyer. As the aggrieved spouse, you ask for everything and get half. In fact, you'll get more than half because there'll need to be financial provision for Rishi and for you while Rishi is growing up. Mr. McGowan will have no custody rights over your son, not even joint custody, because he won't be able to look after your son when he's in jail.'

'I want five thousand pounds – above half of what's left, plus something to look after Rishi,' said Lakshmi firmly.

'Why five thousand pounds?' asked the lawyer in surprise, taking time to glance at Downsted.

'I want my money back,' said Lakshmi. 'It's my money and I want it back. When I got married my father gave Graeme a dowry of five thousand pounds. It was paid in sterling. It was paid to Graeme to look after me.' Her sentences were clipped, precise.

Downsted whistled, amazed at the enormity of the sum. In 1948, when he had got married, this would have bought two large brand-new detached houses in one of the best suburbs of London.

'I had no idea how much money it was then,' said Lakshmi, 'But I know now. It would have been my parents' life savings, and probably more. My father thought he was buying me the security of an English officer and a gentleman. How wrong he was. We'd have all been better off if he'd saved his money and I'd stayed in India.'

'I'll do my best,' said the lawyer. 'Dowries are always complicated, but the courts are usually sympathetic to giving back to a wife whatever she brought into the marriage if it was substantially unequal. Of course, the longer the marriage continues, the less weight the courts will place on the original gift.'

'I also want the business,' said Lakshmi. 'Graeme has had nothing to do with it for years. It was run by Graeme's father and me until my father-in-law's death. Graeme's drinking got so bad he couldn't tell one tea blend from another. I've kept the business running as it's our only source of income, and Graeme won't be able to operate it when he's in jail, will he!'

Downsted studied Lakshmi carefully as she spoke about their tea tasting and exporting business, then about the future sale of both her deceased father-in-law's home and their matrimonial home, where she was going to live and how she was going to pay for Rishi's school fees. The fact that she had done a lot of thinking in advance of the meeting made Downsted realise that his perception of her as an arrogant, reserved, timid housewife was entirely wrong, a fact further confirmed when he took her home. The journey into Nairobi had been predominantly in silence. The return journey was one of relaxing chatter.

Was she shy? he wondered. Joyce once told him his mere presence could be intimidating. He pondered on whether he had that effect on Lakshmi.

'I need to collect Jumapili's toys,' said Downsted as he stopped in front of Lakshmi's house.

'Would you like to come in?'

'Yes, just for a moment, until you find them.'

Downsted waited patiently in the hall as Lakshmi rummaged around Rishi's bedroom looking for toys made from pipe cleaners and beads. 'You don't know where her recorder or tin whistle are, do you?' shouted Downsted up the stairs.

'Belonging to the blind girl?' asked Lakshmi, shouting down.

'Yes.' Downsted paused, mesmerised by the seductive way Lakshmi descended the staircase. 'Now she's living with us, I'm keen she learns music, to play an instrument.'

'She should sing,' said Lakshmi as she reached the bottom step and looked directly into Downsted's eyes. 'Her voice at the funeral had me in tears.'

'I think we all struggled,' agreed Downsted, as he too looked into Lakshmi's eyes.

They both smiled in embarrassment for something had happened between them which neither understood.

'Would you like to see Graeme's train set?' asked Lakshmi shyly. 'I'm told it's something rather special. Come on, follow me.'

It was dark when Lakshmi and Downsted made their way through the house and the garden to what Lakshmi had described as a shed but would have been better described as a small bungalow.

'I don't know how it operates,' said Lakshmi turning on the lights to reveal a complex network of Hornby rail track nailed into bespoke tables occupying three sides of the room.

'I know, it's switched on here,' she said just as Downsted turned the knob on one of the controllers. Immediately he heard a train on the track start to move so he instantly returned the controller to the neutral position.

'It's very impressive,' acknowledged Downsted with a little envy.

'Every time I come in here I swap the trains around, complete locomotives, carriages, everything' said Lakshmi. 'I do it just to annoy him, but most of the time he's too drunk to notice. I had to have my little victories, otherwise I'd have gone stark raving mad.'

She squatted down to reach into a fridge placed under one of the train tables. 'Drinking is *de rigueur* in here,' she said with a smile as she handed Downsted a cold bottle of white wine. 'I want to say thank you for today.'

'Oh, that's kind,' replied Downsted assuming the bottle of wine was to take home, but it was the presentation of a corkscrew and two glasses which indicated that Mrs. Lakshmi McGeown had something else in mind.

Chapter 46

DOWNSTED POURED JOYCE a belated sundowner gin and tonic as he told of his meeting with Lakshmi and their lawyer.

'I can't believe how different she was,' said Downsted as the tonic water slid over the ice cubes. 'She wasn't the woman we all know – or thought we knew. It's as though she's been playing a role, the one her husband expected her to play, and now he's gone, she's stopped. But I can't work out if this new her is real or not.'

'All married women do that,' said Joyce. 'We all play a role to please our husbands.'

'Like hell. No more than the role we husbands play to please our wives.'

'I hear she's lost a lot of weight.'

'Yes, perhaps. She was certainly very thin, but she's always been that. But giving up the saree and wearing western clothes, that gave her a strange *je ne sais quoi*.'

'So, you quite fancy our new divorcee, do you?' teased Joyce. 'I didn't think she'd be your type.'

'Who's my type?'

'Me normally,' said Joyce confidently, '... except when you've upset me, and then you can't bear me and, oh boy, have you upset me today.'

'Why, what have I done?' pleaded Downsted confused.

'Mrs. Valentine, she's really upset.'

'Good.'

'She told me she's resigning because you were rude to her on the games field this afternoon.'

'Yes,' chuckled Downsted. 'She's right. I was, but only because she's bloody useless and deserved it. She stands in the middle of the field like a lead balloon, blowing her bloody whistle giving orders and shouting out the rules. And have you noticed she never runs? It's because her bust falls to below her waist and then over her shoulder with each pace. It's as funny as its ridiculous.'

Joyce snorted with amusement because Downsted's description was true.

'She's quite hopeless,' he continued. 'If she's resigned, I hope you've accepted it.'

'We've agreed she'll leave at the end of this term.'

'Hang on,' said Downsted. 'You shouldn't be pissed off with me, you should be pleased; I've instigated a change which you know had to be made.'

'Except I now have a vacancy to fill which I didn't have before. No – I've a better idea: *you* have a vacancy to fill. You caused the problem; you solve it.' Joyce topped up her glass with ice.

'Good plan,' said Downsted, 'but I'm not hiring a sports teacher. I want a sports coach, someone who can lead, encourage, enthuse. Anyone can learn and teach the rules of netball or lacrosse, but to teach technique and inspire, that's different.'

'Well don't forget, they must be able to swim,' said Joyce. 'Remember, I hired Mrs. Valentine because the sports teacher you hired before her, who was supposed to teach swimming, couldn't swim!'

'Yeh, now that was a foul up,' admitted Downsted, amused at his own stupidity.

'Perhaps your new best buddy could do the job,' teased Joyce again. This time with a huge false smile on her face.

'My new best buddy?'

'Yes, Mrs Lakshmi McGeown.'

Downsted felt uncomfortable because he knew Joyce's smile was not genuine. Had he said something wrong? Was Joyce showing a jealousy she had never shown before?

Upstairs in her bedroom Jumapili was getting undressed for bed and feeling equally uncomfortable because she had noticed there were sniggering sounds around her. She was quite exhausted. Not only had she the exhilaration of running for the first time on the sports field, but then she had had two fifty-minute lessons of braille, interspersed with a fifty-minute piano lesson. Her fingers were aching from holding the braille stylus, her mind was overloaded with where to place the dots in each of the grids to write each letter, and for the first time she was having to learn how to spell words. To make matters worse she found that her fingers were incapable of doing what she expected them to do when seated at the piano.

'What's wrong?' snapped Jumapili as the giggling increased. It was clear from the sounds at the bedroom door that there were other pupils looking in who were obviously amused.

The room went deathly quiet.

'What's wrong,' snapped Jumapili again.

'You walk around naked, with nothing on,' said Catherine Delfont, one of her two roommates.

'So?' replied Jumapili, shaking her head confused. 'Am I not supposed to?'

'We don't,' continued Alison Kitchen, the other girl who shared Jumapili's bedroom. 'We always wear something.'

'Why?'

'Because it's not done. It's not polite.'

By now, those who had been at the door staring in had gone, scared of the contretemps which they felt was about to take place.

'I don't understand. Why?'

'It's just the way it is,' answered Catherine.

'Why?' repeated Jumapili. 'They didn't make me wear clothes in hospital when I went to have a shower.'

'Because we don't want to see you naked,' explained Alison.

'Why, what's wrong with me?'

'Nothing. It's just we don't want to see your bottom,' continued Alison, emphasising the word your.

'Be fair Alison,' said Catherine. 'We don't want to see anyone's bottom, not just Jumi's.'

'Have you stroked a dog or cat?' asked Jumapili completely bewildered.

There was no answer.

'They don't wear clothes, do they? They show their bottoms, don't they?'

'But we're not animals, Jumi,' said Alison. 'I know your lot from the bush go around bare breasted, but we're not from the bush. We're civilised. We don't do that. We cover our breasts. We wear bras.'

'What are those?'

'You don't know what a bra is?' asked Alison, guffawing with laughter.

Jumapili didn't reply.

'Look Jumi, let me help you,' said Catherine, feeling sorry at the way Alison had been speaking to her. 'This is what I do. Where's your dressing gown?'

'I don't have one.'

'Then Mrs Downsted will need to get you one. Borrow mine for the moment and I'll show you what I do.'

She then proceeded to show Jumapili how to get undressed and dress in a dressing gown.

'We also walk around like this when we've no clothes on,' continued Catherine, before wrapping Jumapili in a large bath towel.

Later, when Jumapili, Catherine and Alison were in bed, Joyce and Downsted toured the dormitories and bedrooms, as they did every night, to turn out the lights.

'Jumi,' called Joyce as they entered the bedroom. 'Mr. Downsted has got the beaded zebra, hippopotamus, and giraffe you asked him to get from Rishi McGeown's house. He's also got your musical instruments. Do you want him to put them in your cupboard?'

Jumapili shook her head. 'No, the animals, I'd like to hold those please. It's been a long time.'

Downsted bent over and placed the three animals in Jumapili's hand. She raised them to her lips and nose.

'Thank you,' she whispered and smiled.

When the lights were out Jumapili found she could not sleep. She lay awake for hours. Once again, she'd heard the smacks and yelps of girls at the bedtime beaming and wondered what the hell was going on but, as with so much that was strange to her, she was too scared to ask. The more she thought, the more frightened she became. She knew she could not stay. She would not survive, not with their rules and expectations of her. As Jumapili tossed and turned with nervous anxiety, she made a plan: she would leave a message for Absko at the village shop next Sunday after church when they bought ice creams. The message: to get her out. She was sure he would rescue her. He always had.

Chapter 47

'I'VE DRAFTED A reply,' said Joyce. 'It's taken me ages because every time I worked on it I got angrier and angrier. How dare they, how dare they!' she exploded as she handed Downsted her final draft.

Joyce was responding to a deluge of letters from parents complaining about Jumapili being in their school. It was clear from the letters that the parental protest had been orchestrated by some of the girls. Downsted took Joyce's letter and put on his spectacles:

Dear Parents

Colin and I have received many letters of concern about a blind Kikuyu girl from the slums of Kibera who has recently joined us. Your daughter may have been one of those who have written to tell you about our new pupil.

Firstly, I need to record our deep upset at the appalling language some parents have chosen to use in their letters of concern to us. To use terms to describe a young girl whom they have never met, and in words which are so offensive that I will not use them, is the height of bad manners.

In normal circumstances Colin and I would ask those parents who write in such racist terms to remove their child from this school immediately, but it does not solve the problem which is basically one of ignorance, intolerance, and fear.

When we first meet parents to discuss their daughter's future, Colin and I always say that we are not in the business of education but in the business of teaching our students to pass exams. Well, no more. It seems there is enormous learning required of some of our girls in the art of human decency, and that learning starts today.

Let me assure you that no harm will come to your daughter from the girl mentioned being a member of our school. In fact, it is the opposite. Our school and your daughters will benefit considerably from having in our midst one who is less fortunate than we. Not only will they see a young girl get through each day with determination and perspicacity, but a person with rare talent. It is now the development of talent which is the mission of this school.

Although our mission might change, our creed remains steadfast. It is found in the speech of Martin Luther King which was recently discussed in front of the whole school. Irrespective of colour or disability, we are all of the same race, the human race. No one in this school will judge a person on the basis of their race, skin colour or incapacity but on their strength of character and the memories they create.

If you are offended by this letter, then it is highly likely that we will have incompatible views on racism. In these circumstances, you should reconsider your daughter's educational plans with us.

Your sincerely

Joyce Downsted (Mrs)

'Bravo,' said Downsted. 'I'd like to read it to the whole school at the end of breakfast tomorrow, just before lessons start.'

Joyce nodded her agreement. She was pleased Downsted had liked her letter.

'We should have a phone around and make sure all the teachers are in school early,' he said. 'They should hear this too.'

'Are you sure it shouldn't be read by me?' asked Joyce.

'No,' said Downsted firmly. 'This is something I would like to do, I need to do.'

Chapter 48

JOYCE'S INSISTENCE THAT Jumapili use a fork and knife made eating breakfast an incredibly slow affair for her. Nevertheless, a routine had been developed where Catherine and Alison would, between them, assist Jumapili with cereals, tea and toast and explain to her what food was on her plate and where. Both her room mates had finished eating and Jumapili was struggling on when Downsted banged heavily on the table he was sitting at and stood up.

He waited until the room was silent and then, hearing one girl still talking, he impatiently banged the table again. Downsted shouted out the girl's name angrily, telling her to 'shut up.' The tone of Downsted's voice brought silence, but also a chill to the room as he started to talk.

'Just a few days ago Mrs. Downsted told you that this school is colour-blind. She told you we are racially agnostic. She told you we value the quality of a person's character, not their race, not their skin colour, not their ethnicity, not their disabilities. She told you this school not only expects but demands that you give the very best of your talents whatever they may be. Disgracefully, it seems that these lessons have not been learned because clearly some of you have written to your parents objecting to Jumapili being in our midst.

On hearing her name, Jumapili placed her hands on the table and froze like a statue.

'Jumapili. I am so sorry,' continued Downsted looking directly at her. 'I apologise for embarrassing you, but this is important to you, to every girl here, to this school. It must be said.'

Downsted stopped and watched as Joyce walked across the room, dragged a chair from a table close by, sat by Jumapili's side and held her hand which had been clenched into a fist.

'Several of your parents have written to Mrs. Downsted and me telling us that they do not want a blind Kikuyu girl from the slums of

Kibera in our school. This request can only have come from some of you, from students in this room. I'm going to read Mrs. Downsted's reply.'

Downsted slowly and clearly read Joyce's letter. He stopped after each paragraph to stare at the students sitting at each table before he continued.

'Let me say this,' he said after he had finished reading. 'If you're one of those girls who have written to your parents objecting to Jumapili being in this school then you're free to leave now. If you can't treat with dignity and respect another individual, then you must leave now. If you want to treat someone differently because of their race, their skin colour, their background, or their disability then you must leave now!' Every time Downsted repeated the word now, he heavily lent on it until he was almost shouting.

'If you cannot accept that this school is a diverse community then Mrs. Downsted and I don't want you here. This is because your ideas are small minded and ignorant. This school, this city, this country, this continent, this world will only survive ... will only thrive ... if we recognise that, foremost, we are members of the same race, the human race.'

Although Downsted's words were measured and carefully chosen, all those in the room could tell from the change in the tone of his voice, that he was getting angrier and angrier.

'The great benefit we have from being members of the human race is our differences. It's the diversity of the individual talents among us which gives us our strength. There might be some unique individuals like Mozart or Einstein who make a bold outstanding contribution, but even they don't operate alone. Mozart needed an orchestra to bring his work to life; Einstein needed the work of other former physicists and built on their work; Neil Armstrong didn't get to the moon on his own, it took engineers, physicists, chemists, mathematicians, dieticians, doctors all working together. It was achieved by a diverse group of talented people working to achieve a common goal, and that's what this school is about, helping you to be a talented, well-educated individual capable of contributing to the common good of society.'

'So be in no doubt, our ideas are better than the horrible ideas expressed in the letters we received. But our ideas require civil discourse for them to work. So, if you can't accept our better ideas, if you can't be polite as one human being to another, if you can't offer help and succour to another at their time of need then you need to get out of here, because you're not one of us.'

'There's something about parents writing to us to complain about Jumapili which makes the whole issue doubly, no, trebly offensive. Jumapili is in the minority in this school. She's in the minority because she's black; she's in the minority because she is blind; she's in the minority because she's an orphan.'

Downsted paused, sensing the tension in the room rise on the news that Jumapili had no parents.

'To pick on a person who's in a minority group is shameful. It's bullying, but when that person is in a minority group not once, not twice, but three times over, it's not only despicable, but shameful cowardice too. Your job, everyone's job is to protect the weak and look after the vulnerable. Too many of you have failed to do that, and you should be thoroughly, thoroughly ashamed.'

Downsted paused to look at Joyce who had her arms wrapped around Jumapili, who was leaning into her shoulder weeping in a mixture of shame and embarrassment. How could this be happening to her? she wondered in despair.

'As a result of this horrible debacle, this morning's first two lessons are cancelled,' continued Downsted to Joyce's surprise. 'You'll go to your classrooms where you're to write two essays, one on diversity, and why it is a good idea. The other is what history has taught you about bullies picking on the weak and vulnerable. Those who can't or won't accept our better ideas and want to go home, then they should go and see Mrs. Downsted straight away. She'll speak to your parents and arrange for you to be collected.'

Suddenly Downsted started to bellow. 'I will not have. I will not have,' he shouted, 'racism of any kind in the school, none at all! Is that clear?'

The room was silent.

'Is that clear?'

There were murmurs of yes around the room.

'You're dismissed. Go to your classes. Your class teachers will take in your essays at the end, ... and – this afternoon you'll all be doing a five-mile run.'

Immediately after they had been dismissed, several girls, including Catherine, went to Jumapili's side to say how sorry they were. Alison Kitchen was one of the two girls who left the school that afternoon.

The girls of parents who wrote letters and did not leave were not to get away scot-free. If they got more than two questions wrong in the morning test and were listed for a bedtime beaming, then Joyce got her revenge. She whacked their backsides as hard as she possibly could, creating a sting which the miscreant would never forget. But the phrase 'you now know why we don't sjambok the blacks,' was never heard in Bottlesford Hall ever again.

The events of that day also started to change Jumapili's thoughts about running away. Were Joyce and Colin really prepared to see every girl in the school leave but her? she wondered. If they were prepared to keep her over everyone else, didn't that mean she was rather special? It was a conundrum which was to perplex her over many years. It also turned out to be the day that Miss Jumapili Mwangi found conviction in herself.

Chapter 49

VERY QUICKLY, JUMAPILI'S life fell into a routine. She was so busy living and learning that she had little time for anything else. She quickly mastered writing in Braille, a task that Downsted and Joyce found difficult and painfully slow. Like many sighted people learning to read for the first time, Jumapili found reading Braille hard as she struggled with the phonetics of every word, but slowly the pattern of dots under her fingertips became familiar and there would be joy with each word she recognised, and disappointment with each word she didn't.

The dexterity and muscle memory of Jumapili's fingers developed as she learned to play the scales and arpeggios of the three instruments she was learning to play, with the pieces always the same on each. Slowly but surely her repertoire grew.

Downsted became anxious that Jumapili's ability to play any instrument at the top level was being hindered by the time she was giving to learning the other two. He wanted her to concentrate on one. He didn't mind which, but Joyce would not agree for the simple reason that she could not discern which was Jumapili's best instrument, other than her singing voice, which they both agreed was exceptional. It had a purity which Downsted proved time and time again as he got Jumapili to sing a single note for a prolonged period into an oscilloscope. The wave patterns did not modulate; they were as perfect as could be recorded anywhere.

Absko made a point of being at the newsagents and general store at Tayiania each Sunday after Church so he could have just a few moments to make sure his sister was OK. He looked forward to each meeting with excitement and always felt deflated when she was gone because he missed her so. It was only much later in his life that he realised Jumapili had given him a purpose. Without her he only had himself to look after, and what was the point in that? he would wonder.

After almost one year, and just at the start of Jumapili's first set of summer holidays at Bottlesford Hall, she was given her own bedroom but again at the top of the house so in term time she could be near everyone else. It was her haven. She had never had a room to herself before and it made her feel as though she were a princess. Although make-up had not gripped Jumapili as it had other girls of her age, scents, perfumes and soaps were her passion, as was the texture of material in the clothes she would wear. If you wanted to please Jumapili bring her anything with a pleasant smell, which is what Rishi did every time he returned from Scotland. It gave him the excuse he thought he needed to see her.

For their summer holidays, Downsted, Joyce and Jumapili would head off to the beach at Watamu, made famous by Ernest Hemingway after he wrote about the unspoilt wonders of its blue lagoon after two days of deep-sea fishing.

Downsted and Joyce loaded up their Land Rover with the camping gear he had travelled the country with when working for military intelligence, and with Hawla and her husband as their assistants and most importantly guards, they travel through the Tsavo West National Park, camping as they went. They would light fires at night and use all the skills of bushcraft Downsted had learnt in his previous country-wide travels.

As they journeyed, Joyce gave Jumapili a commentary of what was nearby and far away. Without sight, the sounds and the smells were more intoxicating for her than if she were a sighted person.

At the beach, they would pitch their tent and do nothing but swim, read, eat and drink. It would be an idyll of doing nothing until it was time to get back to the duty of running a school and, for Jumapili, the job of catching up on so much of what she should have learnt in her earlier life.

The bond between Jumapili and Joyce grew stronger and stronger. They would hold and cuddle as a mother and daughter would naturally do. Joyce would comb and stroke Jumapili's hair and they would laugh and play together as well as argue and tease. Downsted would look on in an amused, detached manner. He took delight at the way 'mother' and 'daughter', which was the way he thought of them, exuded a natural love for each other.

Chapter 50

IT WAS SHORTLY after Jumapili had returned from a magical summer holiday and was comfortably ensconced for a new school term that Absko had come screaming up the path calling for her to see the eye doctor. To Jumapili's shameful regret she did not go to him that evening as he called her from outside the school gates.

The next day Downsted and Joyce knocked and waited until Jumapili invited them into her bedroom.

'We'd like to talk about yesterday,' said Joyce taking a seat at the end of her bed.

Jumapili said nothing. She was still deeply upset at the way Absko had been dismissed. Joyce's threat of setting the dogs on him was, to her mind, unforgivable.

'It's just ... well, we know what they'll tell you,' continued Joyce. 'When you were in hospital, when your legs were broken, they also did tests to understand why you can't see.'

Jumapili sat up and turned toward Joyce to hear what she was saying.

'There's a retina in your eye. The retina has light-sensitive cells called photoreceptors. These transform light rays into electrical impulses. The electrical impulses travel down the optic nerve fibres and into the brain. The brain decodes the signals, and all sighted people get an image in their brain. The optic nerve is the connection between the eye and the brain.'

'Yes I know this,' said Jumapili. 'Rishi told me about it when I was in hospital.'

'The thing is ...' Joyce paused. 'The thing is ... you have no optic nerves. They're not there. They've never grown.'

'It means you'll never be able to see,' added Downsted. 'You are as you are.' Whereas there was sympathy in Joyce's voice there was none in his.

'But what we're going to do, just to make sure, is to make an appointment for you to see the best ophthalmic surgeon in Nairobi Hospital ...' added Joyce.

'Is that an eye doctor?' asked Jumapili interrupting.

'Yes, and we're going to get the tests done again, and they'll tell you directly to your face, what they've found. Not to us. We think it's important you hear it from them.'

'When?' asked Jumapili anxiously. 'I need to be able to tell Absko.'

'As soon as it can be arranged,' answered Downsted. 'But Jumapili, please, please take care about what you wish for. I don't think you understand what remarkable ears you have, and your voice, when it sings, it's unique. Believe me when I say this. You have the ability to be ranked as one of the best singing voices in the world. It is so pure, so pitch-perfect, everyone's spellbound when they hear you sing. It might be, if you were to get sight, that these senses of yours, which are heightened way beyond those of a sighted person, could be lost.'

'There's something else, Jumi,' said Joyce. 'You have this rare thing, this rare talent which the doctors in Nairobi called echolocation. Now we've watched you, seen how you get about. It's remarkable. How you acquired this skill, no one knows but its impressive. We really ought to see if it's a skill which can be taught. We worry that if you were to see, it's a skill which almost certainly will be lost, and then the opportunity would be gone forever.'

'Don't you think it's something you should strive to do for other blind people,' said Downstead, 'to teach them how to do what you do instinctively?' It was, as typical of him, posed as a command.

'It was why Colin was so fierce with Absko yesterday, wasn't it darling? He was frightened of the things you might lose. He wanted to protect the special things you have. That's right, isn't it Colin? said Joyce while failing to recognise her own officiousness.

Downsted reluctantly acknowledged the points Joyce was making, with a few well-placed grunts, but it was much simpler than that. The truth was that Downsted saw Jumapili as his protégé and he wasn't going to lose her.

Jumapili moved to kneel on her bed facing Joyce directly.

'Do I have any money?' she asked. 'Did I ever get paid any compensation for my accident?'

'Yes,' said Downsted, seeking to change the conversation away from his own feelings. 'I can't remember how much it was, but after the lawyers took their fees, it was still quite a lot, and I'm sure every shilling's still in your bank account. It's not been touched. There's no reason for it to have been.'

'It's just Absko and I talked about him buying a matatu with it. He would drive and I would take the money. It meant we could be together, as we were before ...'

'Can he drive?' asked Downsted quizzically.

'He can learn. He can learn to do anything!' replied Jumapili, ignoring the important issue that Absko hadn't got his High School Certificate.

'How much does a matatu cost?' asked Joyce. 'Does Jumi have enough money for that?'

'Oh yes,' replied Downsted, 'more than enough.'

'Then you need to make it work for him, for them, don't you Colin?' It was not a request, but a rare instruction, and an instruction from Joyce had to be obeyed.

'I think Jumi could lend him the money secured on the bus, but the loan would have to be repaid and interest would have to be charged.'

'So, you can make it work for both of them?'

'It can be made to work, but we'll need Miss Onyango's permission.'

'What, the woman from the council, she'll never give it,' said Jumapili. 'She's horrible.'

'She'll agree,' said Downsted. She's made the mistake of letting other people have the dropsy on her.'

'Colin please!' protested Joyce.

'What's dropsy?' asked Jumapili.

'It's an expression associated with the death penalty: you never let anyone have any incriminating evidence on you as they could use it to get you hung.'

'You have evidence on Miss Onyango which could see her hung?' asked Jumapili excitedly.

'No, no, not like that. But let's just say, we've good reason to believe she'll agree.'

Over the next few weeks Jumapili had a series of eye tests which confirmed the diagnosis and Downsted secured Miss Onyango's permission that Jumapili could use some of her compensation to buy Absko a brand new Matatu bus, but only after he had passed his test. His planned route was from Nairobi to Mombasa and back.

Chapter 51

JUMAPILI WOULD, MUCH later, reflect on the dreadful premonition she suffered as she lay in her bed that night. She would remember it as the first night that Downsted had slept away from Bottlesford Hall since she arrived, but that was not the reason for her nervousness. He had gone to Mombasa for a naval reunion and would be away for four nights. Joyce seemed very relaxed about him leaving, which had the effect of reassuring her.

Jumapili would remember how the birds in the trees and bushes were unsettled. Something threatening was keeping them in flight. Jumapili dismissed her concerns, assuming that whatever was happening involved the big game which wandered around outside the school compound, kept at bay by imposing gates which were always shut at night, together with an eight-foot-tall wire-mesh perimeter fence.

It was when Jumapili heard two matatu bus engines at the school gate that she took particular notice because she wondered whether Absko had come for her, but then they were switched off and she heard them no more. It was when she heard voices in the distance that she knew something was wrong. A group of men were gathering by the front gate talking quietly, but not so quietly that Jumapili, with her acute hearing, could not make out what was going on.

Then she heard the dogs bark furiously and whimper as though they were in pain, before they became silent. As she heard the men approach the house, she became certain they were about to be attacked by a raiding party. It had happened at other grand houses in the surrounding area, and she was convinced it was now their turn.

Picking up her white stick and tapping and clicking loudly, Jumapili made her way to her old bedroom where she woke up Catherine

Delfont, and her two new roommates, Florence Partaker and Diane Leander.

'Quick, quick,' shouted Jumapili. 'The schools about to be attacked. I've heard them coming. We've got to get everyone out.'

'What, what's happening?' asked the three girls 'What do you mean?'

'You need to get everyone out over the roof, through the back, like we've had at fire practice.'

'Jumi, stop,' instructed Flo. 'Say again, slowly.'

Jumapili told how she knew what was happening. She repeated her warning and the suggestion that they should all evacuate, a point that was quickly grasped by Catherine who started to take control.

'I'm sounding the alarm,' shouted Jumapili. 'It will warn everyone. It will warn the neighbours,' and with that she was gone into the corridor and then onto the landing. She scraped her hand along the wall, stopping when she felt the thick fire-resistant electric cable running vertically. She ran her hand down the wire, as she had been taught by Downsted, until she touched the alarm. She pressed the glass. It didn't break. She thumped it with her thumb harder and still nothing happened so, in desperation, Jumapili thumped her palm into the glass. It broke causing shards of glass to snap off and impale themselves deep in her hand, but she did not notice. The noise from the alarm was overwhelming and painfully deafening. It was so loud that it was almost impossible to think.

There was not a person inside Bottlesford Hall who, on hearing the alarm, did not know that they had to get out fast, very fast. Equally as important, the sound reverberated for miles around, waking those who were asleep. There was not a settler in a ten-mile radius who did not reach for his gun and car keys and in seconds was out following the sound.

Such was the noise that Catherine, Florence and Diane were prompted into acting faster. It was the adrenalin shot they needed.

'Shoes, shoes, put on your shoes!' commanded Catherine. 'You don't need anything else but your shoes.' Florence and Diana joined in, shouting the same instructions as they ran from room to room.

'We're being raided! We must get out, through the back, into the woods,' they screamed, almost forcefully moving every girl they came across in the direction of the stairs leading to the roof and then fire escape.

With her hand bleeding profusely and the alarm ringing in her ears, so that clicking was no use, Jumapili started to make her way downstairs yelling as she went. 'Joyce, Joyce we're under attack! We're under attack!' But there was no chance that Joyce would hear her under the noise of the alarm.

Jumapili reached the first-floor landing just as Joyce was coming out of her bedroom, Downsted's shotgun in her hand. She too had heard the men, their heavy boots crunching as they ran down the drive. There had been many similar raids throughout Kenya, and Downsted and she had talked about what they might do if they were raided. It was easy for them to agree that they had to fight. The drugged savagery of past attacks had shown that passive acquiescence did not work. Their plan – Downsted would defend, while Joyce would lead the girls out the back to the woods, where Catherine was now leading them.

'Where Jumi? Where are they?' shouted Joyce as she barged past, but at that moment the front doors of Bottlesford Hall were slammed open with a makeshift battering ram.

Joyce descended the stairs and shouted: 'Get out or I'll shoot! Get out or I'll shoot!' but little was heard under the wail of the siren and the attacking screams of the raiding men. And then there was a deafening silence as the alarm was disabled.

The two gang leaders paused. They were startled by the sudden silence and the sight of a woman holding a gun, but as other gang members rushed in behind them, they were forced forward towards Joyce who fired from her waist at point blank range into one, and then the other. They fell instantly on the stairs where they were to die screaming in agony from their wounds.

After that Joyce didn't stand a chance because, with her gun empty, she was defenceless. She was hacked to death in a frenzy of stabs and slashes with the machete knives of half a dozen of the marauders.

Just as Joyce was being hacked to death, Mawla and her husband appeared from the basement kitchen. He had a single bolt action rifle in his hand capable of firing only one shot at a time. She was carrying two long kitchen knives, one in each hand. Using the stairs as cover, her husband shot one of the gang dead as they were climbing the stairs. He reloaded and then shot and fatally wounded another who was rushing towards him. He was able to get off a third shot, which missed, before he too was stormed, overpowered and, with his wife, hacked to death. But it was not before they had both done serious harm to two of their attackers with the knives Mawla had brought with her.

Jumapili was stationary on the landing, listening intensely to what was happening. She didn't know where to move for the best. Suddenly she felt men rush past her, throwing open the doors around the first-floor landing.

'There are no girls here! No girls here!' they shouted as they came out of each room.

'There are no girls down here,' shouted a voice from the ground floor.'

'Where are the girls?' shouted one of the men as he returned from another search of the rooms on the first floor before grabbing Jumapili.

Sijui. Mimi ni kipofu, Siwezi Kuona[31],' she said in Swahili, causing her attacker to pause for a millisecond in surprise.

'You Kikuyu?'

'Ndiyo, Ndiyo, Yes, Yes. *Kutoka Kibera*.'

'You're from Kibera?' he asked with surprise.

Jumapili nodded.

'Where have they gone? Where are the girls?' she was asked with the point of a machete dug into her throat before it was moved more viciously to her stomach.

'Sijui. Mimi ni kipofu, Siwezi Kuona,' she repeated, at which point the man let go of her arm and, in anger slashed her thigh with a back slice of his machete. He then grabbed her hair and pulled her like a

---

[31] I don't know. I'm blind. I can't see.

rag doll down the stairs, her body thumping as it hit each step until she was at the bottom. There she deliberately lay still, lying next to Joyce's lifeless body, listening hard. She was determined to notice and remember everything she could about her attackers.

'They're not here. There's no one on the third floor,' shouted another voice. 'They've escaped, or the tip-off was wrong.'

Two buses and the tip off was wrong. The raiders had come to kidnap them, concluded Jumapili.

'Grab anything, grab everything,' shouted one of the voices. It was the same one who had slashed Jumapili's thigh.

She heard the attackers rampage throughout the house, swarming like locusts, picking up anything of value, and a lot which was not, before stuffing it into their pockets. So badly prepared had the men come that they started to make swag bags out of curtains and tablecloths.

'We must go. We must go,' shouted the man who had declared the top floor empty. The walowezi will be here soon, any moment.[32] That noise will have brought them.'

'Have we looked for the girls outside? Have we checked outside?' shouted a voice Jumapili hadn't noticed before.

'Teketeza mahali hapa' [33] commanded a man who had clearly stepped up to be the new gang leader. *'Hatupaswi kuacha ushahidi.'*[34]

Jumapili's heart thumped violently. They were going to set the place on fire to hide the evidence. She would be burned. Not again, not again, she thought, and her body started to tremble uncontrollably. But she knew she should stay still because she was all too aware of what had happened to Joyce.

In the silence, she could hear paper being rustled, matches struck and cigarette lighters being lit. This was followed by the smell of burning papers as flaming torches were carried from the hall into the east and west front sitting rooms on either side of the hall. There the raiders set light to the curtains and settees, holding their paper flares

---

[32] Settlers

[33] Set the place on fire.

[34] We must leave no evidence.

until they were certain that the flames had taken hold. Their final efforts were to throw lighted fire balls of paper to the back of the hall in a half-hearted attempt to set on fire a heavy antique table placed there.

Wafts of smoke percolated through Jumapili's nostrils adding to her fright, but she remained lock-still, afraid to move because she could sense the raiders were still in the house. It was only when she heard the front door slam shut that she thought it safe to move. She started to make her way to the front door but immediately she stood up and moved, she fell, and then again and again as she tripped over the bodies which lay between her and the front door.

So disoriented had she become by her falls that Jumapili lost all sense of her bearings. Suddenly she had no idea which way she should be going to get out. Clicking her tongue but hearing no echo, she crawled forward, feeling as she went, until she found a wall where she turned right. It was the wrong way as it took her further back into the hall. It was only when she reached the lowest step on the staircase that she realised her mistake. Remaining on her hands and knees, she turned around and, constantly touching the wall, she worked her way around the room not realising the trail of blood she was leaving behind from her machete wound. There was a horrible moment when she felt the wall, the architrave and then nothing. There was a gap. The door into the east sitting room was wide open. Jumapili could feel the heat from the fire, which was taking hold, and the fumes from the smoke started to make her cough more violently. Still, she crawled forward with her right-hand waiving in the air. Her hope was to find the wall on her right, but nothing was there.

Jumapili crawled forward and then forward some more, feeling nothing around her but the cold stone of the floor. Then, at last, bang. Her hand slammed into the rough stone threshold of the front door. The path she had taken had stopped being straight, as she had unconsciously turned away from the fire in the east front room.

At the door, Jumapili hauled herself up, the gash in her leg making it almost impossible to stand, but stand she did. Struggling with the broken lock and handle, she was able to force the door ajar until she crashed through it, falling unconscious onto the steps outside. She had finally succumbed to the toxic poisons being carried in the smoke.

Chapter 52

THE FIRST PEOPLE to respond to Bottlesford Hall's alarm were the former shepherd, Geteye Odhiambo and his son Gatimu. They lived close by in a small hamlet and with their sheep gone, they were employed to maintain the hall's gardens and grounds.

They were at the gates in less than two minutes, but immediately they saw the two parked matatu and some of the gang marauding outside the hall, they stopped and took cover. From the outside, they could not see the carnage within, but they heard the gunfire. Neither Geteye nor Gatimu were cowards, but both knew it would be suicidal madness to take on, without guns, a machete-waving gang high on khat, so they waited and watched.

When the second bus driver heard the gunshots inside, he became agitated. This was not in their plan. It was on the shouts that there were no girls inside that this driver decided enough was enough. He reversed his bus, bashing into the gates, and disappeared at great speed into the distance – but not before Gatimu had engraved the number plates of both buses into the hard earth with a stick.

Geteye and Gatimu continued to watch as they saw flames appear in the east and west front rooms. Then, as the fire took hold, they saw the gang run half-heartedly around the outside of the Hall looking for their victims, but it was obvious from the shouts that their mission had now changed. It was now one of robbery and escape.

The driver of the remaining matatu drove through the gates and parked on the drive outside the front door of the Hall with his engine still running. This made it easier to load everything that had been stolen. Immediately, the driver of the matatu saw the car lights of the first neighbour appear, he was off. Irrespective of who and what was on board, he had decided it was past time to depart. It meant a run, jump, and scramble for those whom the driver was more than willing to leave behind.

The first neighbour's arrival was very quickly joined by a second, third and fourth, each carrying a flashlight and rifle, and some had taken the precaution of wearing a side arm.

Seeing the flames, seeing Jumapili's body on the steps and knowing it was a girls' boarding school, the first three men on the scene, ignoring their own safety, ran straight into the building. Instinctively, but sensibly, they closed the doors to the east and west rooms as they went. It was this act that almost certainly saved their lives because the poisonous fumes would have killed them long before any flames got close.

'Hello,' they shouted furiously, 'anyone there?'

They continued to shout as they ran through the building, going into every room before retreating, taking Joyce's body with them in the hope she might still be alive.

Slowly but surely, the neighbours started to get organised. One left to drive to the nearest telephone to call the emergency services. Another used his Land Rover's citizen band radio to do the same thing. Jumapili was picked up and moved onto the lawn where her pulse and breathing were checked before she was placed into the recovery position.

As soon as they saw others arrive, Geteye and Gatimu appeared at the front of the house with an irrigation pump and hoses which they normally used to water the lawns. Using the swimming pool as a source of water, and after throwing rocks through the front window of the east room, father and son managed to get a strong stream of water into the fire. Another settler, having seen the fire at a distance, had turned around, collected his irrigation trailer and, in no time at all, his makeshift fire engine was also pouring water onto the flames, this time into the west room where Joyce's precious piano was startingto burn.

The Nairobi fire service took a long time to appear, but then they had a long way to travel. Within minutes of their arrival, men with breathing equipment were inside the house and with a fine spray from their powerful hoses the fire was brought quickly under control.

Likewise, within minutes of their arrival, an unconscious Jumapili and a semi-conscious but badly injured attacker, were masked up and put on oxygen.

With bodies in the hall, the Chief Fire Officer had no difficulty in declaring Bottlesford Hall a crime scene.

Chapter 53

CATHERINE, FLO AND Diane, together with thirty-eight other girls had made their way up an old staircase which gave access to the flat part of the outside roof, close to the brick balustrades. There they crossed the roof to a newly made gap in the wall where a vertical fire-escape ladder had been installed only a year before. It would have been a dangerous descent at the best of times, in the dark it was doubly dangerous and with nerves heightened by the sound of gunfire, it had the potential to be lethal. Nevertheless, every girl got to the bottom of the ladder safely.

In groups of threes and fours, the girls set off to run behind the former polo-pony stables, which had been turned into science classrooms. Then, crouching low, they ran around the edge of the perimeter fence, towards the woods until they came to the gate in the middle which would get them out of the school grounds.

Once through the gate, and before they could reach the safety of the woods, the Jatropha hedge had to be broken through. It was a painful job achieved with broken logs, sticks and their heavy court shoes. It wasn't the thought of the Jatropha hedge that had made Catherine shout to the girls to put on their shoes, but the memory of her feet hurting on the rungs of the escape ladder, but it turned out to have been the most useful bit of advice, for there would have been no escape into the woods without them. The girls were lucky in one respect: the gang of men were so high on khat and the battle they were in was so fierce that they did not hear the noise the girls were making in their fight against the vicious thorn leaves of the Jatropha plant.

In the woods, the girls gathered in small lots, mainly with their age groups.

'We wait here until we see a teacher arrive,' commanded Catherine. She was not the eldest by any means, but her leadership in getting everyone out of the school building and into the woods had confirmed her in that position.

When they saw the blue lights of the fire engines, ambulances and police cars there was a debate as to whether they should reveal themselves.

'We should wait until the first teacher arrives,' argued Catherine putting down any dissent.

When they saw the first teacher arrive for the early morning test, the girls agreed it was time to leave. With Flo and Diana at the front and with Catherine bringing up the rear, the girls of Bottlesford Hall walked purposefully across the sports field in their pyjamas, their heads held high, as though they were taking a Sunday walk.

Chapter 54

IN CHARGE OF the Bottlesford Hall crime scene was Assistant Superintendent Charter Ahenda, a man who rarely used his surname because it identified him as being from the minority Kamba tribe and, in a force where tribal allegiances influenced everything, he had long decided that he should be seen as tribally agnostic. However, nothing could have been further from the truth: A.S. Charter Ahenda had a passionate hatred for both Kikuyu gangs and White settlers. He did not know which he disliked more.

It was not that the Kikuyu gangs were more vicious or violent than any other gang; they were not. What Charter could not bear was the practice of oathings where the savagery used to bind the loyalty of one man to another was beyond extreme. The psychology was simple: this is the amount of pain you must bear to support your promise when you join your gang – just imagine the amount of intolerable pain that your gang will inflict on you if you break it. It was the binding force of the Mau Mau and it was why getting information required extraordinary efforts and techniques; techniques that Charter had, at first, found deeply unsettling but the more he used them in his interviews the more inured he became to their use – and the more often he used them.

Charter's loathing of White settlers had more justification because, in years gone by, his family had been forced off their highland homes. Price-fixing by European settlers had forced his family to abandon their farms to go and work for the settlers on their plantations in poorly paid jobs. Then mechanisation forced them out of work and into the slums of the cities. Later, when the Mau Mau rebellion took hold, they were moved lock, stock and barrel and dumped in designated areas. They were allowed to take only a few of their possessions.

And when Charter's father protested at their treatment, he was locked up in a British concentration camp. Whatever anger Charter felt at his father's illegal imprisonment, it was nothing to the anger he felt when he was released, thin, emaciated, and unwell. Charter concluded that the Whites were the most hypocritical people on this earth. His evidence: their Christian ethical preaching stood for naught in practice. He loathed them for it.

Consequently, Charter could not give a fig for the deaths of Joyce Downsted or the gang members who had been killed. If these had been the only victims, he would not have bothered to even open a file. However, the slashing with a machete of a young blind orphan Kikuyu girl from Kibera, and the death of a man and woman with Luo tribal surnames, were crimes which A.S. Charter Ahenda was more than prepared to invest his time.

Charter had been a member of the Kenyan Defence Force, but he had started to find the discipline and routine claustrophobic. He attended Nairobi's police training college for nine months, leaving with the rank of inspector, which was the equivalent in rank to his former position of sergeant major. A year later, he was a chief inspector and now his rank was the equivalent of a lieutenant in the Kenyan Defence Force.

Although Charter had been through police training, it had only taught him the very basics. Nothing but common sense and an addiction to British and American detective television series, true-crime books, and crime novels, had equipped him to deal with finding a gang of murderers and bringing them to justice. Now, as in most of Charter's cases, he was supremely confident that, on this occasion, justice would prevail, and quickly. The gang had behaved so savagely, he was certain they would have been high on khat. That meant that they would have made many silly mistakes, like leaving one of their gang behind, who was now in his custody. Charter only had to find and follow the clues and then, by fair means or foul, the others would soon be found.

Chapter 55

AS THE GIRLS walked across the sports field, all apparently unharmed, Charter beamed with delight. Until that moment, his working assumption had been that the girls had been kidnapped. He had already demanded the extra resources he thought he needed if the kidnappers were to be tracked and the girls found. It would have meant him losing control of the case, which he didn't want, but now that risk had gone. The only person still missing was Downsted, and, given the carnage in the house, Charter found it hard to believe he was the only kidnap victim. He was certain Downsted had to be somewhere; presumably dead.

The blast of questions the girls first asked when they got to the congregation of emergency service vehicles were all about Jumapili. They were certain, and said so in quite vocal terms, that if it had not been for her and her warning, they would have been captured.

The girls were briefed on Jumapili's situation in a straightforward, adult manner. Nothing was hidden. They were told she had been badly injured by a machete and had suffered toxic poisoning from the fumes of the fire but had not been burned. After being administered with a bag of plasma and a hefty supply of oxygen, Jumapili had regained consciousness by the time the ambulance left to take her to hospital.

The news of the death of Joyce, Mawla and her husband hit the girls badly and many wept in grief and shock before they were led away to the science rooms by their teachers. There was no debate among the adults: after such a trauma, the girls needed to be with their parents, and, with Joyce dead and Downsted missing and the main building gutted by fire, it was easy to decide that the school would have to close. It would be up to Downsted to decide when it might be reopened, but most teachers assumed that would be never.

The job now was to get the girls home, and since some parents lived a day's car-journey away, careful planning was required, not least they had to be found some clothes to travel in, a task made more difficult because no one was allowed in the building until it had been declared safe.

Chapter 56

CHARTER KNEW EXACTLY where he would start his investigation and it was not at Bottlesford Hall. It would be at the hospital where both Mbua Aomba, the injured gang member, and Jumapili had been taken. And Charter's inquiries would start at Aomba's bedside.

In a hospital side-room, handcuffed to the bed and with his mouth full of rags, Charter set about torturing Aomba with the words 'I'm about to cause you more pain than any oathing has ever involved. Do you understand?' The menace in his voice would have turned water into ice.

Aomba, his eyes wide, looked straight at Charter and said nothing.

'You can stop it at any moment by telling me everything I need to know,' said Charter. 'Do you understand?'

Aomba locked his eyes into Charter's and still said nothing.

Aomba held out for longer than Charter expected, but when he set to work on his eyes he got the name of every participant, including those who were dead and those who drove the matatu.

Charter didn't care his actions were unlawful and he certainly didn't care that Aomba's name meant he was from the same tribe as him. He only cared about putting at the end of the hangman's rope those who were so weak that they hunted, maimed and murdered in feral packs. Sometimes, when you've been the smallest kid in the school and bullied, the pain goes deep, with revenge the only comfort. There was no doubt that, in that tiny room, A.S. Charter Ahenda remembered how deep his pain ran.

With his notebook full of names and possible addresses, Charter went to see how Jumapili was doing. She was in a poorly state but anxious to talk. She needed to know what had happened. Charter told her all the girls were safe thanks to her warning, and then confirmed her worst fear by telling her that Joyce, Mawla and Mawla's husband had been killed. Charter thought that Jumapili took the news stoically, but he hadn't appreciated how long Jumapili had been lying alongside Joyce's body, and the time she'd had to absorb the fact.

Jumapili solved another of Charter's problems because she told him of Downsted's whereabouts. He was in Mombasa and would be back the next day.

'You know I can identify some of them,' said Jumapili confidently as he was writing her full name in his note book.

'You can?' replied Charter surprised. 'I thought you were blind.'

'I am, but I can still tell you who was there.'

'How?'

'I heard them when they called out to each other. I know some of their names.'

'What names? demanded Charter, as he pulled up a chair.

Jumapili weakly whispered the names she could remember while Charter wrote them down in his note book. In silence, he crossed referenced the names to those Mbua Aomba had given him.

'I think I may be able to do better than that,' said Jumapili breathlessly.

'How?'

'By their voice. Each voice is different. If I hear them again, I might be able to say if they were there or not.'

'You can? Come with me,' he commanded.

'Where?' protested Jumapili not wanting to leave her bed.

Within a few minutes Charter had Jumapili in a wheelchair storming towards Mbua Aomba's room.

'Say, where are the girls,' demanded Charter to one of the policemen guarding Aomba.

After some debate, the man did as he was told.

'Recognise him?' asked Charter.

Jumapili shook her head.

He asked the same of the second guard who, prewarned, quickly did as he was asked. Jumapili shook her head again.

'Aomba, say where are the girls,' ordered Charter.

Aomba did as he was asked.

'He was there. He was there!' shouted Jumapili, as she jumped up to try and get out of the wheelchair, and out of that room.

Chapter 57

SECONDS AFTER DESCENDING the steps of his matatu, Absko was grabbed from behind by two men. One took a stranglehold around his neck and the other viciously grabbed one of his arms. Under their weight Absko collapsed to the ground, smashing his head on the side of the bus, before crashing his face into its steps. He landed face-down in the dirt. Blood was pouring from gashes to both his lips and an eyebrow.

Absko fought hard against his two attackers. Having worked on the matatu bus service for years he was not beyond looking after himself. However, with the element of surprise and two against one, it was only a matter of time before he was eventually overcome – but only after he had acquitted himself reasonably well. It was his attackers' shouts of 'police, we're the fucking police,' that made him stop fighting.

'Absko Mwangi, I'm arresting you on suspicion of murder and attempted kidnapping' shouted a breathless policeman as his heavy body had Absko pinned down. 'Do you understand?' he was asked.

'Fuck, what are you talking about?' Absko shouted back.

The second policeman, equally as breathless, repeated the caution.

'I don't understand. Let me go! There must have been some kinda mistake.'

'We'll talk about that later. In the meantime, you're coming with us,' and with that Absko's hands were cuffed behind his back. He was jerked onto his feet and put into the back of an ordinary car.

The events leading up to Absko's arrest were straightforward. The detail of the number plates of the two matatu buses parked outside the gates of the school and carved in the earth by Gatimu Odhiambo led Charter to the bus compound where Absko worked. There he identified a matatu with the dents which had been made when the bus reversed into the gates of Bottlesford Hall. At the bus pound Charter saw the name Absko Mwangi on the staff roster and very quickly the drivers helped him make the connection with Jumapili Mwangi and Bottlesford Hall. In Charter's mind, even if Absko was not the driver of the bus, he was certain that he had been the informant, the inside man who had briefed and prepared the attack. He only needed to prove it.

Charter's methods for interviewing suspects would not be found in any policing manual. They involved the enhanced interrogation techniques he had been taught to resist when in the army. Every one of the names forced out of Mbua Aomba in his hospital bed were arrested. They were hooded and then in a small room smelling of stale urine, they were forced to lean with their hands against the wall and their legs apart. It meant that the whole weight of their body was forced onto just a few muscles. The pain would be intense, growing in agony until it became unbearable when they would collapse on the floor. After a series of kicks and thumps with heavy batons, the suspect would be hauled up and put back in the same position. For hours and hours Charter would allow this to go on until he had the information he needed.

If after a few hours Charter hadn't got the detailed confession he required, he would move to waterboarding them. Strapping his victim to a bench, he would place a cloth over their face and pour water onto it. This would give his victim the sensation of drowning. No one ever needed more than three waterboarding sessions before Charter had what he wanted.

Not one member of the gang who raided Bottlesford Hall got past being waterboarded just the once. By then each had made a confession incriminating every other person. Absko's name was not on the list.

Absko had said nothing because he had nothing to say. But this did not stop Charter taking him through his routine of stress torture, then waterboarding, before handcuffing his hands behind his back, attaching a rope to the handcuffs, and hauling Absko up, using a pulley fixed to an innocuous hook in the ceiling. Charter lifted Absko until he was resting just on the balls of his feet and there, he allowed him to stay, a pain so dreadful that Absko lost consciousness. In a final act of pique, and with the screams of hellalah piercing Charter's ears, he pulled Absko completely off the ground, tearing his muscles and dislocating his shoulders. In that moment Absko's ambition of being a matatu driver was destroyed. He would never have the strength to turn the heavy steering wheel and certainly not without excruciating pain.

It is impossible to say how long Charter would have kept torturing Absko. It was only when his assistants had gone through all the witness statements, cross-referencing every one of the gang members, that it became obvious that Absko was not the driver of either of the buses. As far as Charter was concerned that did not mean he wasn't the mastermind of the whole plan, but his colleagues did not agree. The gang were all from the Githurai Township whereas Absko was from Kibera. The gang were all from the Kamba Tribe whereas Absko's heritage was with the Kikuyu Tribe. The chances of Absko and them being connected, they argued, was remote.

'He stays there until he tells us something,' commanded Charter, but Absko had nothing to say. He only knew what he had been told. There had been murders and a kidnap attempt at Bottlesford Hall and this limited news left him petrified for his sister.

Chapter 58

DOWNSTED LEARNT OF the attack on Bottlesford Hall, the death of his wife, the two unnamed others, and the attempted kidnapping of 'his girls', as he referred to them, from a newspaper he had purchased on Mombasa railway station. He was on his way back to Nairobi. In a panic he phoned the school. There was no answer. Before the attack the attackers had cut its phone lines. He phoned Nairobi police. They couldn't or wouldn't tell him anything. He phoned the homes of his teachers. Their phones rang and rang. They were all at his school. In desperation he phoned Lakshmi McGeown. After expressing her condolences, she could only confirm what he had read in the newspaper. She knew nothing more.

Downsted felt sick and in despair. It was the not knowing and inability to influence events which drove him almost crazy with worry. Never had he felt so hopeless. He didn't sleep for a single moment on the journey from Mombasa to Nairobi. He spent his time either staring vacantly out of the window or pacing up and down like a caged tiger. Every time the train stopped for any reason, Downsted would curse out loud and demand, to the world at large, that it went faster.

Expecting to take a taxi from the station to Bottlesford Hall, Downsted was delighted to be met by Lakshmi. She had been up to the school and spoken to one or two of the teachers. She was able to brief him further. He knew Joyce was dead, but Lakshmi told him that Mawla and her husband were the other two who had died. On hearing this news Downsted said nothing; he simply shook his head in despair. Lakshmi told of Jumapili's machete injury, but not of her poisoning, said she was recovering well and was expected to leave hospital within the next couple of days. The most important news, which on its hearing allowed Downsted to visibly relax, was the fact that every girl was safe and had returned home to their parents.

Neither the newspaper nor Lakshmi had mentioned the fire, so Downsted was shocked to see Downsted Hall so badly burned. In fact, the building was not as badly damaged as he had first feared. Most of the damage was confined to the east and west front rooms, and the basement kitchen, sodden with the water used to put out the flames. Although scorched, the fire had not broken through to the rest of the building.

Downsted spoke to a couple of teachers who were working in the science classrooms. They were in the slow process of retrieving each girl's possessions, packaging them up and sending them home. Sitting down quietly with a cup of tea they gave him more information about the girls and what had happened that night. For the first time he heard about the warning given by Jumapili and learnt of the girls' agreement that, if it had not been for her, everything would have been worse, much worse.

It was as Downsted made his way to the study which he shared with Joyce, that he saw her blood soaked into the wooden steps of the staircase. It was intermingled with that of her attackers. Downsted could cope no more. He stopped, turned around, locked the broken door, and left.

He would never enter Bottlesford Hall again.

Chapter 59

CHARTER INTERVIEWED DOWNSTED at Lakshmi's house where she had kindly offered him a bedroom. It was the morning after he had closed the door on Bottlesford Hall. In the sumptuousness of a soft bed, he had had a good night's sleep, and although still shaken, he felt ready to face the world again.

Lakshmi's divorce had been finalised. Her matrimonial home had been sold. She now lived in what might be described as an English-cottage-style house. But it was only that in style, for it was as large as it was impressive, built at the beginning of the century on the edge of a tea plantation.

'We've got most of the gang in custody including the man who organised it,' said Charter to Downsted as his opening remarks.

'Who's that?' asked Downsted.

'Absko Mwangi,' answered Charter.

'What Jumapili's brother, don't be ridiculous!'

'One of the matatu used in the attack came from the depot Mwangi worked from,' answered Charter.

Downsted threw himself back onto a soft sofa seat and exhaled loudly before staring at the ceiling. 'Why? What for?' asked Downsted, but he knew his answer. To get Jumapili out of the school to have her blindness cured.

'Money. We think he did it for money,' answered Charter.

'That's nonsense. He didn't need to,' responded Downsted sharply. 'Jumapili was lending him the money to buy a matatu from the compensation she got from a car accident. I can assure you he won't have tried to kidnap his sister for money. The idea is ridiculous. If you knew the history of the boy, you'd know how absurd that is.'

'What do you know about the others, asked Charter defensively as he reached for his notebook and read out sixteen names selected from several pages.

'I know two of those,' said Downsted without emotion.

'How?' asked Charter sharply changing his manner to one which suggested he could have been about to handcuff Downsted.

Downsted reached for his jacket which was laying alongside the sofa he was sitting on, stood up, removed his wallet from an inside pocket. From the wallet he took an out-of-date identity card and handed it to Charter.

'Military intelligence?' said Charter, staring at the card.

Downsted nodded.

'Fucking British Military Intelligence,' continued Charter. 'I hate you fuckin lot. When your lot were responsible for running this country, my country, you fucked us up good and proper. Look what you did to Kenyatta at his trial. You lied and lied and lied! Mzee didn't stand a chance.'[35]

'I agree. It was wrong. It was stupid, but I wasn't there, and I wasn't involved!'

'So, which of these did you stitch up?' asked Charter waving his notebook with the gang's names in it angrily in the air.

'I didn't stitch them up. They stitched themselves up. I just found the evidence and presented it in court,' answered Downsted, knowing he wasn't telling the whole truth.

'Yeh, well tell me which ones?' asked Charter again.

'I know Mbua Aomba and Maunda Amwei. They were young men then; they must be a lot older now.'

Charter looked in his notebook for the names. 'We think Maunda Amwei's the one your wife shot dead,' he said after a pause. 'But we're still waiting for forensics to confirm. Mbua Aomba's in hospital. He's quite badly wounded.'

[35] Mzee means old man in Swahili. It was a term of affection used by people of Kenya towards their president Jomo Kenyatta.

'Good,' said Downsted using the same aggressive tone Charter had adopted towards him. 'The bastards should have been hung long ago. At least this time they have the certainty of being found guilty.'

'So, you admit it do you?' continued Charter picking up on the nuance in Downsted's voice. 'You're saying some of those your lot hung, imprisoned were innocent, were not guilty, are you?'

'Yes, sure,' said Downsted. 'With the benefit of hindsight, we made mistakes, but there are mistakes being made now, and it doesn't take hindsight to see that.'

'Yeh, but it didn't take hindsight then, did it? And it's not just one mistake, not ten mistakes, not even a hundred mistakes.' Charter was almost spitting. 'One-thousand-nine-hundred fucking mistakes – that's the number you bastards hung, you executed, during the Mau Mau wars!'

Chapter 60

WITH DOWNSTED BY her side, Jumapili was taken in a wheelchair from her hospital to the cells area of the main Nairobi police station where Charter was stationed. Her leg wound had gone septic, and she was not well enough to walk.

She had been told by Charter to listen to the men talk and tell him if she recognized any voices she had heard during the attack on Bottlesford Hall. She didn't recognise one. Charter was delighted. It was his testing chamber because, deliberately, there was no one in those cells who had been accused of being on the raid.

Jumapili was taken to another police station and another set of cells. She listened and quickly identified four voices, and where she had heard them. It was just as she was leaving the room, she thought she identified Absko's voice. It was very faint for he was both physically and mentally defeated.

'Absko is that you?' she shouted. 'Absko what are you doing here?'

'Jumi, Jumi,' shouted Absko. 'Is that you?' There was panic in his strained voice. 'You must get me out. You must get me out. They're killing me in here.'

'Shut the fuck up,' rang out a voice as the sound of a heavy truncheon banged against the bar.

'A.S. Charter thinks Absko ordered the attack on Bottlesford Hall,' interjected Downsted before Charter had any time to intervene. 'He thinks Absko pulled the gang together and organised it all, don't you, *assistant* superintendent?' Downsted placed emphasis on the word assistant causing Charter's antagonism to grow.

'That's absurd, ridiculous,' retorted Jumapili in a voice Downsted recognised immediately. It was said in the same headmistress tone with the same inflexions so often used by Joyce. It both warmed and chilled him at the same time.

Jumapili was badly rattled not only from learning that Absko was in jail, but from the desperation in his voice. It meant she was feeling far from happy when she was taken to another police station and another set of cells. There she identified three other voices including the voice of the matatu driver who had driven his bus to outside the Hall's front door.

With Jumapili's evidence the events of that night became clearer. There had been fourteen men in the raiding gang, including the two bus drivers. Four had been killed at the scene. Of those ten attackers still alive, Jumapili had identified eight of them, including one of the matatu drivers and one still laying in a hospital bed.

Jumapili and Downsted travelled from the last set of police cells back to her hospital in his Land Rover. There were long periods of silence between them. Both Downsted and Jumapili were pleased that the whole gang had been captured but they were very concerned for Absko.

'A.S. Charter wants me to give evidence, doesn't he?' asked Jumapili as they waited in one of the never-ending cues of traffic that dominates Nairobi at rush hour. 'He wants me to appear in court, doesn't he?'

'Yes.'

'It's going to be dangerous isn't it?' This gang's family, they're going to hate me, aren't they? They won't want me there, will they? 'They'll do everything they can to stop me, won't they?'

Downsted had been thinking the same thing.

'It's difficult Jumi. We all get frightened, but sometimes we just have to do our duty.'

'My duties to get killed, is that it?'

'No. Your duty is not to allow fear to stop you from doing the right thing. "The only thing necessary for the triumph of evil is for good men to do nothing."[36] We cannot let evil triumph, can we? I think we both owe it to Joyce to make sure they're locked up, don't you?'

'I have a duty to my brother, don't I?'

'Yes, you do, but you have a wider duty.'

---

[36] Attributed to Edmund Burke 1729-97.

'I need some sunglasses. People can see my eyes move and they don't like it. Mine are still in the school. Can we get some please?' Downsted thought it a strange, forced change in the conversation.

At the end of their short but fraught journey, they sat in the hospital car park, handbrake on and the engine off, enjoying the silence.

'You don't think Absko arranged this, do you? asked Jumapili.

'Charter does, but his two assistants working with him don't think he's involved. He first arrested him because he thought he was one of the bus drivers, but he now knows he wasn't.'

'What about you? What do you think? Do you think he organised it?'

'No, I don't think he's involved at all. In fact, I'm sure he's not.'

'Colin,' said Jumapili after a little while. 'I'll appear in court. You can tell Mr. Charter that, but there are two conditions. First, my brother's let out of jail, and he must be let go straight away. Second, the police hide both you and me. The attack on Bottlesford Hall was because of you, or that's what Mr. Charter says, and I'm the reason they going to be locked up for a long time, isn't it?'.

'Jumi,' said Downsted, his tone heavy. 'I think we must be realistic. If these men are found guilty then there's a high probability that they're going to be hung.'

'I don't want that, Colin. I don't want anyone else killed.'

'I don't want it either. It doesn't work. I learnt that during the Mau Mau war.'

'So, what do we do?'

'We give our evidence honestly. We tell the court we don't want them hanged, and we rely on the court to deliver justice. It's all we can do.'

Chapter 61

DOWNSTED NEGOTIATED THE release of Absko with Charter as Jumapili had asked. However, he decided it was better to wait until he knew Absko was free before negotiating her security arrangements. Not trusting Charter one inch, Downsted had insisted on a letter from him confirming the police had no evidence against Absko. Amazingly, Charter also agreed to confirm that Absko's arrest had been a mistake. Actually, Charter had no choice. Every member of the gang was claiming that they'd been framed and had been tortured into confessing. Jumapili's witness statement, and the fact that items stolen from Bottlesford Hall were recovered from some of the gangs' homes, provided the only untainted evidence on which Charter could be sure of securing a conviction.

Absko was released from custody after ten days of hell. Immediately he walked out of the police station he swore to himself that he would kill Charter. Absko was convinced that a man like that should not be allowed to walk on this earth, and certainly not be free to abuse his power.

Absko showered in the community showers and his hatred for Charter was renewed when he discovered he could not raise his arms to wash his hair. He used the money he had to purchase samosa, fruit, chocolate, and water before returning to his shack. For the first time in many years, Absko chained and locked himself inside. The fear that Charter would pick him up again did not leave him.

After a night's sleep Absko packed a bag and walked to the bus depot via the liquor store close to the Catholic Church. At the liquor store Absko rented out his shack to the liquor man for a fixed rent of fifty shillings a week on the basis that he would sub-let it. The rents in Kibera had risen significantly since Absko had hired the dog man to get his home back. It meant that the liquor man would make a super profit but, as Absko found, when one party is in a hurry and the other has all the time in the world their bargaining positions are different.

At Absko's matatu depot he collected the money owed to him and resigned. He described to his colleagues what Charter had done to him and warned them against this rogue policeman. There was not a man who heard Absko who didn't believe him because he had changed. He was no longer the caring, confident, happy man he had always been. It was obvious to all those who saw him that Absko had been physically destroyed. He was now a broken man.

Absko took a matatu from his bus depot to a stop a couple of miles beyond Tayiania Village. From there he walked to Bottlesford Hall in the hope of seeing Jumapili. He was shocked to see the school closed and the building boarded up. Walking back to the village he asked the newsagents what had happened. Like everyone who knew Absko, they were shocked to see such a changed man. After he had gone, they talked about how he had aged twenty years in as many days.

The newsagents told Absko of the gang's raid on Bottlesford Hall with the detail of a prosecuting lawyer. They emphasized, time and time again, Jumapili's heroism. They knew she was out of hospital but didn't know where she was staying. The rumour was that Jumapili was being hidden by the police because her evidence was vital to their prosecution.

'If you see her, will you give her a message?' asked Absko. 'Will you tell Jumi I've had to get out of Nairobi. It's not safe for me to be here. Tell her I've rented out our shack so she can't go there. If she wants me, the Matatu station will know how to get hold of me. Tell her I'm ok, but I must get out of here. Tell her I'm sorry.'

'Are you ok, really ok?' asked the shopkeeper concerned.

'No,' Absko replied sharply. 'No, I'm not!'

Chapter 62

ON LEAVING HOSPITAL Jumapili went to live with Downsted at Lakshmi McGeown's cottage. Lakshmi had taken time preparing the house for Jumapili's arrival, removing ornaments and objects that she might knock over or into. After a day of settling in, Lakshmi took Jumapili to Bottlesford Hall to collect her things.

'It sounds different in here,' said Jumapili just after Lakshmi had pulled her wheelchair up the front steps and they were resting in the hall. 'It sounds bare.'

'It's because there's no one here,' said Lakshmi.

'It's changed. It's got a chill about it. It also stinks. The smoke. Aagh, I can still smell the smoke.'

'It's the damp. There's no heating on to dry out the water used to put out the fire,' offered Lakshmi as she helped Jumapili out of her wheelchair ready to make the long painful climb to the top floor and her bedroom.

'Who's here? shouted Jumapili as she stopped suddenly halfway up the first flight of steps. 'There someone here. I know there is. Who's here?'

'There's only you and me. No one else,' said Lakshmi surprised at Jumapili's outburst.

Although Jumapili clicked and tapped with her white stick, she was pleased to be supported by Lakshmi to her bedroom on the top floor. To say Jumapili was relieved to find her sensory blanket was still under her pillow, and the toy animals her mother had made and her grandfather's mbugi were still in her cupboard, would be an understatement.

'I think you'd like these,' said Lakshmi as she placed Jumapili's sunglasses in her hand. She put them on immediately and suddenly felt whole again. The naked feeling that had worried her from the moment she had arrived at the hospital in the ambulance was over.

Lakshmi packed Jumapili's clothes and musical instruments into the bags they had brought with them, and then, when the bags were full, they stood at her bedroom door in silence.

'Why's it gone wrong?' asked Jumapili speaking to herself in a painful whisper. 'Why, why, why?' she asked as her head shook slowly from side to side. 'I was happy here. So happy.'

Lakshmi put her arm around her. 'Come on,' she said. 'It's time to take the first steps into your new life.'

As they were descending the final flight of stairs and halfway down, Jumapili suddenly stopped again. 'Who's there?' she called.' 'Who's there? – Lakshmi someone's here. I know there is.'

Lakshmi had stopped too. The hairs on the back of her head were tingling and she shivered involuntarily from a cold chill. 'There's no one here Jumi, but there's something ...'

'Can you feel that? Can you feel the cold breeze?' asked Jumapili.

'Er, yes.'

'It was here. I'm sure it was here that Joyce was killed,' said Jumapili.

'Come on, let's go,' said Lakshmi. 'There's something very strange here.' And she rushed Jumapili down the final steps, into her wheel chair, through the front door and out into the sunshine.

Chapter 63

DOWNSTED HAD BEEN thinking about Joyce's funeral service from the moment he learned of her death. He wanted it to be a statement of her life, an event all her mourners would remember. While Jumapili was collecting her things from Bottlesford Hall, Downsted meticulously prepared an order of service and wrote out a full service-sheet. Later in the afternoon, and sitting with Jumapili on Lakshmi's veranda, he shared with her his detailed proposals. Jumapili asked a series of questions which were more like suggestions, each of which Downsted was happy to accept.

'Would you like to sing at Joyce's funeral?' he asked. 'I think she'd have liked it. Why don't you sing *Somewhere over the Rainbow*? It's the first song you ever sang. I watched Rishi try and persuade you to sing it, do you remember?'.

'Yes, but most of all I remember Rishi's father paying me two shillings to sing it. It made me feel so rich. But I was thinking, if you wanted me to sing anything, I would like to sing *How great thou art.* It's what I'd like to say about her.'

'Do you know the words?'

'I think so. I'd do it as a solo without any accompaniment.'

'Jumi, would you, could you, sing it for me now?'

'Now?' Slowly Jumapili stood up from the wheel chair she was sitting in. Once again, her face grimaced involuntarily as her machete wound was so deep it was taking time to heel. She relaxed her hands by her side and pulled back her shoulders, as Joyce had taught her to do.

'Oh Lord, my God. When I, in awesome wonder,' she sang. By the time she was singing the first chorus, '*Then sings my soul, my Saviour God to Thee. How great Thou art, how great Thou art,'* tears were pouring from Downsted's eyes. The joy he felt from hearing the

beauty and clarity of Jumapili's voice contrasted sharply with the pain he was feeling from his well and truly broken heart.

Chapter 64

THE SMALL CHURCH built by missionaries, and where the girls of Bottlesford Hall had gathered every Sunday, was chosen by Downsted as the place of Joyce's funeral.

There had not been a Sunday when Downsted and Joyce had not discussed the need for the church stone walls to be whitewashed, and the tin roof painted with a coat of red paint. Without seeking anyone's permission he had commissioned it to be done. It would be her present to it, because Joyce loved that little church. With its arched windows and crude altar, lectern, and pulpit, it had reminded her of home.

'Its mere presence,' she once said, 'gave me a rock of hope.'

As might have been expected, Joyce's funeral was jam-packed. There were as many standing outside the church as were within it. Girls from the school, both past and present, had returned from far and wide. The news of the attack on Bottlesford Hall, the escape of the girls, and Joyce's death had become international news.

Friends, many of whom had not seen each other in years, hugged and sobbed in each other's arms. It is an indisputable fact that we each remember the teacher who was most influential in our lives and, for each girl who went through Bottlesford Hall, Joyce Downsted, née Haynes, would be the first person they would remember. The evidence of that – each girl had arrived for Joyce's funeral wearing white gloves which she had insisted be worn for Sunday church parade.

The settler community came out in force, including many who didn't know either Joyce or Downsted. They wanted to show their solidarity, as those who had seen the carnage at Bottlesford Hall on the night, or visited the site afterwards, were now far more worried about their own safety. They wondered out loud whether it was time to leave Africa.

Lakshmi arranged for Rishi to have an exeat from school as she thought it important he be at Joyce's funeral. It was a strange decision given that Joyce and Rishi had hardly known each other, until one appreciated Lakshmi's ambitions for a much closer relationship with Downsted. Subconsciously, she wanted her son to be there to give his approval.

Downsted's morning-coffee set had rallied around him to make sure he continued with their tradition of meeting at the small café in Tayiania, and it was this group of men who carried Joyce's coffin into the church.

Downsted gave Joyce's eulogy. He stood ramrod-straight as might befit a naval officer, and with his half-moon glasses resting on his nose, he carefully read what he had written. Remember the good times was the advice he had been given. Remember the funny times, but in the tragedy of Joyce's death the good times, the funny times, of which he spoke, appeared neither very good nor very funny.

Jumapili's slow and obviously painful steps from her wheelchair to the front of the sanctuary to sing her solo were watched with sympathy and respect by all those in the congregation, particularly by those girls who had managed to escape from the Hall that dreadful night. For many, it was the first time they had heard Jumapili click her tongue to navigate to exactly where she wanted to stand.

The little black dress which Jumapili had worn when she sang at the McGeown funeral no longer fitted, so Lakshmi, who had been sewing since sitting on her mother's knee, made her a new one in the same design. The thin gangly girl of then had turned into a perfectly shaped young woman. Nevertheless, however good Jumapili might have looked, it was her solo rendition of *How great thou art*, the purity of her voice and its resonance against the stone walls of the church which everyone would remember. Jumapili had created a sound which was as superb as it was unique.

Immediately after the service Catherine Delfont, ably assisted by Flo and Diane took charge of Jumapili's wheelchair and looking after her. There was a strange camaraderie among these three girls found only among combatants who had seen down a shared common foe, except among these combatants Jumapili was the celebrity who knew and could tell more than most.

The wake at the country club was a depressing affair. Girls who would normally have been excited to see each other at a school reunion bubbled at first sight, but then deflated when they started to talk about the reason they were there. It meant that, throughout, the tone was heavy and the mood depressing, except when Jumapili was among them. Her resilience lifted their spirits while Catherine, Flo and Diane bathed in Jumapili's transfer charisma.

At Joyce's request, her body was cremated. Leaving Jumapili, with Lakshmi, Downsted flew with her ashes to England to scatter them around the memorial stone in Oaston Road Cemetery as Joyce had stated in her Will. As he discreetly tipped Joyce's ashes where she had asked, Downsted had no idea of the connection between the memorial stone and Joyce's first fiancé, her very first love whom she never forgot.

Downsted went to see the house in Leamington Spa which had been Joyce's family home and was now his. As he walked through the rooms which had seen her formative teenage years, he began to realise how different her life had been compared to his. The building had an opulence, a grandeur and an oppression about it which must have influenced her upbringing as a single child. It all needed throwing open, he thought. He resolved to go and find his brothers whom he hadn't seen since his wedding day. They'd had such fun together growing up. He knew he needed to find them, find that fun, if he was going to survive.

Chapter 65

THE TRIAL OF the ten members of the Genge la Chupa,[37] as the press labelled them, started on a Monday in Nairobi's main courthouse. Jumapili, supported by Downsted, had moved into a nearby hotel the day before. They expected to stay there for the duration of the trial.

The Nairobi Police had agreed to pick up the hotel bill, and Jumapili was given police protection in the hotel, to and from the courthouse, and in the court itself.

The court was packed when it came to order. It was as though every member of the defendant's family was there, along with hundreds of people from the press.

The jury was sworn in and then they were sent home for legal argument. For the next three days ten lawyers, each representing their clients, argued that their signed admission of guilt was inadmissible because it had been obtained under torture. A story heard too often in the courts of Kenya.

'Are you expecting me to believe that ten men were tortured and that, by some mysterious co-incidence, they each named exactly the same thirteen other men; they each named the two bus drivers; and they each named the same four members of their gang who were killed?' asked the judge.

'Yes, that's precisely what we're asking you to believe,' said the most senior of the defence lawyers. 'We're asking this court to believe it because it's just that, too mysterious, too organised, too off-pat to be true.'

The judge decided to delay giving his decision on the admissibility of the admission statements until after he had heard the other evidence and so the trial started in earnest with Jumapili as the star witness.

---

[37] The Bottles Gang

At Downsted's request, Lakshmi helped Jumapili choose her clothes for her court appearances. They both knew how important first impressions were. Dresses, suits, trouser-suits, skirts and blouses were all chosen, and to Jumapili's delight a range of different sunglasses were purchased. Jumapili's hair was cut and styled. She would feel as good as Lakshmi and Downsted could possibly make her.

For two-and-a-half days, Jumapili appeared in the witness box. She was taken through her witness statement by the prosecution lawyer. This was then attacked fiercely by two of the defendants' lawyers. Each wanted to test and destroy Jumapili's statement, but the judge only allowed two of them to cross examine her on its substance because, as he said: 'If I allow anymore, it will be repetitious bullying and I'm not having that.'

It was Jumapili's ability to recognise and identify voices which had to be destroyed if the defendants were to go free. For this reason, the judge agreed that for ease of reference each of the defendants would have a number, chosen at random, which would be placed in front of them. They would be referred to by that number and not by their name, and each lawyer would have a right to cross-examine Jumapili on the specifics relating to their client's voice only.

'Stand up defendant number four,' ordered the first of the defending lawyers after which this defendant was ordered to repeat a few sentences.

'Now that's the voice you say you heard on the stairs,' said the defence lawyer to Jumapili.

Jumapili was shocked into a brain freeze for she was certain that was not what she had said.

'If I said that, I was wrong,' said Jumapili. 'I'm sorry, so sorry. That voice wasn't on the stairs. I should have said that voice was on the bus. He was the matatu driver.'

The defendant's lawyers glanced rapidly at each other, just as the judge started to intervene.

'Mr Ord-Smith according to my notes, defendant number four is the bus driver and was not on the stairs as you contend. It appears to me that, in respect of your clients, Miss Mwangi has just confirmed in this court her witness statement of several months ago, has she not?'

'Yes, Your Honour, that's right, Your Honour,' admitted Ord-Smith.

'You mustn't deliberately mislead the witness!'

'Yes, Your Honour. I'm sorry, Your Honour.'

Ord-Smith sat down.

Following the strategy agreed at a conference of the defence counsel, the next lawyer stood up to deliberately try and confuse Jumapili once again.

'Defendant number one is the person who you say grabbed you and pulled you downstairs, isn't it,' asked the second defence lawyer after his client had spoken.

'No, I didn't,' retorted Jumapili now sharply aware of the tactics being used against her. 'That's the voice of the man who told everyone to set the place on fire. This isn't fair, you're trying to confuse me. Just because I'm blind, you're trying to make fun of me. It's not fair!'she shouted.

The defendants laughed and jeered at her discomfort.

'Nyinyi wanaharamu, mnyongwe Nataka mfe'[38] shouted Jumapili angrily in response.

The judge banged on his hammer as he sought to bring order to the court. When silence had returned, he continued.

'Miss Mwangi, you are not to shout out. You're here to answer the questions put to you do you understand?'

Jumapili said nothing. She was quietly seething.

'Mr Reth,' continued the judge referring to the second defendant's lawyer. 'According to my notes, your client, defendant number one, is recorded in Miss Mwangi's statement as being the person who order Bottlesford Hall to be set on fire, not the man who you said pulled her down the stairs.'

'Yes, Your Honour. I'm sorry, Your Honour.' said Reth.

'Gentlemen,' said the judge, looking sternly at the front row of the court with all the lawyers dressed in their gowns. 'I appreciate your job is to test this witness's evidence, but it is not to mislead this court. Do I make myself clear?'

---

[38] Hang you bastards, hang. I want you dead,

There was a general murmur of agreement, but nothing changed as each defendant's lawyer sought to catch Jumapili out by confusing her evidence. When she was not caught out, which was every time, they merely apologised to the court afterwards for having made an unfortunate mistake.

Downsted, Lakshmi and Rishi watched Jumapili's performance with admiration because if there was one person who acquitted themselves well in the court room that day, it was the little blind orphan girl from the slums of Kibera. Joyce would have been so proud of her, thought Downsted; she had taken a wilted flower and raised a champion bloom. But this was to ignore Downsted's own influence because it was his sturdiness, his even temper and strength of character that Jumapili so wanted to emulate.

After Jumapili's second day in the witness stand, the court reporters and photographers followed Jumapili and Downsted back to their hotel. In the throng, her police security had become almost non-existent, so the idea of having tea in the residence lounge had to be abandoned. It wasn't until much later that Jumapili and Downsted felt able to come down to the hotel restaurant to eat. Rishi had been waiting for them since the court had risen three hours earlier.

After dinner, Downsted moved to the hotel's lonely piano sitting unloved in the corner where, with Jumapili and Rishi listening on, he played his way through a repertoire of Herb Alpert and the Tijuana Brass for no other reason than Joyce loved them so much. Later, when Downsted went up to bed, Jumapili took over, playing songs chosen by Rishi and the sole policemen making up her security detail.

'Miss Mwangi, would you like to tell your story?' asked a young man as she extemporised waiting to decide what else she might play. The young man had been ignoring his work colleagues because he had become mesmerised by Jumapili's piano playing. It was the lightness of her fingers as they stroked the keys which had fascinated him.

'Are you a journalist?' asked Rishi, bristling.

'No, I'm an assistant producer, what they call an AP, on the Evening Show. My colleagues ... we come here once the show's ended to wind down for a bit before we go home.'

'What? the TV show on KBC?'[39] asked Rishi. It was the most watched television programme in the whole of Kenya because its format was a relaxed magazine style that went out live in early evening every day immediately after the news.

Jumapili stopped playing.

'I think you'll be an interesting person to interview,' continued the young man.

'Why?' she asked not listening to the answer instead concentrating on the soft seductive nature of his voice.

'cause you've got an interesting story – to identify people from hearing, that's quite unique.'

'I'll think about it. But only when the trial's over. There's so much that can still go wrong.'

'You should get her to sing when she's on,' said Rishi to the young man, before turning to Jumapili. 'You should only do it Jumi if they agree you can sing, otherwise everyone will just see you as a victim.'

'Can she sing?' asked the assistant producer.

'Oh boy! Can she sing?' replied Rishi with a big beam on his face, before turning to her and adding anxiously: 'Come on. Let's go upstairs. I don't know where your security is, but it's not here.'

Unknown to Downsted, Jumapili's security detail went off duty at 11 pm. They would not return until the morning, when they made a note in their security log book: 8.05 am - Rishi McGeown left JM hotel bedroom.

---

[39] Kenya Broadcasting Corporation

Chapter 66

THE NEXT DAY the court started late. The judge was furious. He considered the report in Kenya's leading national newspaper, which described Jumapili's 'crushing and overpowering' evidence of the previous day, as a contempt of his court. The trial was delayed as the judge insisted both the editor and journalist came before him, where he fined them one thousand shillings each and warned them of a prison sentence if they reported on any one of his trials unfairly again. The simple fact was that the Genge la Chupa trials had reached deep into the Kenyan psyche, with opinions and tempers raised.

It was now the turn of the fifth defence lawyer to try and prove his client had not been at Bottlesford Hall.

'Stand up defendant number five, please' ordered his lawyer, 'and say after me the_*Mshenzi wa machafuko* poem which he then proceeded to say out loud.

Mshenzi wa machafuko,
Ana sura kiburi na kauko.
Vurugu vyake, bila uoga,
Na kupotea, peponi.
Anacheka na mbwembwe,
Matatizo akiyachochea.
Na kuyeyuka kama mvuke, [40]

[40] The troublemaker,
Wears pride from afar.
In chaos, no fear,
Then vanishes in the air.
With laughter and flair,
Stirs problems in the air.
And disappears like a haze,
In a playful, carefree daze.

But it was not defendant number five who stood up; it was another defendant who had been given a different number and had his voice identified the previous day.

The defendant repeated the words from the *Mshenzi wa machafuko* poem twice. 'Now Miss Mwangi, where is it you heard my client?'

'I didn't hear that voice,' replied Jumapili assuredly.

A wise lawyer would have left it there, but he sought to press home his advantage.

'So are you saying that you don't recognise my client's voice?'

'It's not your clients voice,' said Jumapili shaking her head slightly. 'He's trying to disguise it. Anyone can hear he's using the accent of the Kiswahili whereas the men arrested are all Kamba.'

The judge banged his hammer and looked straight at the ten men in the dock.

'I think it's time to remind each and every one of you that you're on trial for murder for which the penalty, if found guilty, is death by hanging. Now, note this well. This court has enormous discretion as to whether it imposes the death penalty or not. Please be assured that this court is likely to be far less lenient than it otherwise might be if its time is wasted in silly games. Now Mr. Mbingu,' said the judge addressing defendant number five's lawyer: 'Will you please ask your client to say the same words but this time in his normal accent.'

The lawyer did as he was asked. The defendant repeated the words and then Mr. Mbingu turned to Jumapili and asked: 'so where exactly did you hear this man?'

Jumapili took her hands off the top of the witness stand, removed her sunglasses, and buried her face deep into them. She heard her own heavy breathing as she wondered what was going on? Were her ears playing tricks on her? With her hands returning to the witness stand she started to click her tongue nervously,

'I heard him yesterday,' she said quietly. 'I told you yesterday. I heard that man attack Mawla and her husband,' she continued in a whisper. Then it dawned on her what had happened. 'They've swapped their numbers. They swapped their numbers!' she shouted. 'They're not being fair. They've swapped their numbers!'

'For chris' sake judge get a grip on this trial,' shouted Downsted angrily from the public gallery. 'This is just a bloody charade!'

Mbingu shot around to look at the dock, and as he did so, he realised that the defendant with the number five label in front of him was not his client. Someone else was speaking on his client's behalf. Not only had the defendants deliberately swapped numbers, but their jackets as well.

'I'm sorry, Your Honour,' started Mbingu, but he was cut off before he could say another word.

'Be quiet!' The judge banged his gavel several times. 'This court is adjourned for a thirty-minute recess. Gentlemen, we will meet in my chambers – now!'

The judge's chamber was not a large room so there was standing room only.

'This morning's newspapers have suggested that a fifteen-year-old blind girl has been making fools of you, and I cannot but help agree,' said the judge when everyone was assembled. 'This nonsense must stop. I'm going to take over. Every man will have his original number given back to him, so the jury isn't confused. Then, starting at defendant number one ...'

'But he's already spoken, Your Honour,' protested his lawyer.

'I know,' said the judge: 'but we're starting this part of the trial all over again. Now, I'm going to get each man to repeat the *Mshenzi wa machafuko* poem. I'm then going to ask Miss Mwangi where she heard that voice. After she's off the stand, we will each of us, you on behalf of your clients, you Mr Odhiambo on behalf of the prosecution, and me on behalf of the Court and a fair trial, we'll all then compare Miss Mwangi's statements in court with her written statement. Are there any objections?'

Two-and-a-half hours later, just before the court adjourned for lunch, Jumapili was released from the witness stand. The eight defendants whose role she had described in her witness statement were reconfirmed in fuller detail by her oral evidence from the witness box.

There were two men sitting in the dock who, after hearing Jumapili's evidence, considered themselves fortunate. They were the ones whom Jumapili had not heard speak and that included the matatu driver who had borrowed the bus from Absko's depot and had been the first to drive off.

After Jumapili had given her evidence, Downsted looked around for her close-protection police officer to take them back to their hotel and then on to Lakshmi's cottage, but he had gone. Jumapili had given her evidence, so Charter didn't need her anymore and he had ordered her security detail withdrawn. It was down to the court staff, Downsted and Rishi to wrestle Jumapili through a mob made up of the defendants' families and their supporters, who kicked, punched, and spat at her, as well as a throng of photographers wanting their front-page photograph.

To be besieged by a horde is frightening for any sighted person but when you are blind, and your senses are being drowned out by an angry noise with no idea of how to escape, the sensation is truly terrifying.

Downsted had had the foresight to organise a taxi to wait outside the courthouse. When the mob saw Jumapili's escape route they surrounded the cab just as she was being physically pushed onto its back seat by Rishi, who picked up her limbs and roughly folded them inside, turning her over onto her back in the process. He was then shoved violently and fell in on top of her, but not before a couple of fists covered with knuckle dusters had thumped him hard in the kidneys.

'Drive, for God's sake drive,' yelled Downsted immediately he was in the front passenger seat. He looked round and shouted into the back. 'Are you two alright?'

'This isn't fair mate!' protested the cab driver. 'I don't get paid enough for this, Gov.'

'Drive, just drive,' shouted Downsted.

'Where?'

'Anywhere, just get out of here!'

'They're people in front. I'll run 'em over!'

'Run 'em over. They'll get out of the way. For God's sake just go!' Downsted pulled on the car door to stop it from being opened.

Cautiously the cab driver moved forward and as he did so, the crowd parted and made a path for him to drive through. As soon as there was no one in front of him, he accelerated away.

'Fuck me,' said the driver. 'My misses's never gonna believe this when I tell her.'

Downsted ordered the cab driver to make a series of small journeys comprising several figures of eight throughout the city until he was certain they weren't being followed. They then made their way back to the hotel where they packed up their rooms before loading their bags into Downsted's Land Rover and heading back to Lakshmi McGeown's house.

Chapter 67

AFTER DOWNSTED AND Jumapili had showered and changed they regrouped on the veranda to discuss the day. Lakshmi had taken Rishi to hospital to get him checked over, as his beating had left not insubstantial wounds.

'I think the judge knows they're guilty, don't you?' said Jumapili.

'It's not the judge, it's the jury that'll decide, and I've been watching them carefully,' said Downsted. 'I'd say the eight men you identified will be found guilty. The matatu driver will be found not guilty and the last of them will be found guilty of possessing stolen property.'

'I think that's right,' said Jumapili. There was a long pause before she asked. 'Do you know what Joyce thought about the death penalty?'

'I'm sorry. I don't. It wasn't anything we ever discussed.'

'You said we could write to the judge if we didn't want the death penalty. Are you going to write?' asked Jumapili.

'Yes. I'll write asking for leniency. So many mistakes, so many stupid horrendous mistakes were made under British rule. Too many people, too many wrong people were hanged. I couldn't abide that happening again.'

'But these men are definitely guilty aren't they? There's no mistake.'

'But what's the purpose, Jumi?' asked Downsted. 'Perhaps the price of past miscarriages is that we save the lives of these men.'

'It stops other people doing the same thing, doesn't it?'

'*Pour decourager les autres*?' said Downsted quoting the French maxime. 'The question is – does it?'

'What about other people. What do they think? What do they think of this case, this gang?'

'Jumi, this is not a subject you can take a poll on and follow that. You must take responsibility for your own thinking.'

'It's just, I don't think I could go to bed every night thinking I caused someone to die when I might have acted and been able to save them. How would I live with myself?'

'How would you live with yourself if they killed someone else some day in the future? It could happen.'

'What happens in the UK?' asked Jumapili. 'Do they have the death penalty there?'

'No – it's been abolished in favour of life in prison.'

'Then they're lucky as it means people like you and me don't have to write to the courts to let them know what we think.'

'Jumi, can we change the subject?' asked Downsted. 'It's just, I have a present for you. I want to say thank you for singing at Joyce's funeral. I also want to thank you for everything you've done at the trial over the last few days. It's been really tough, but you've been magnificent. Joyce would have been so proud, so this is from her too.'

Downsted picked up Jumapili's hand and placed a long, thin, oblong box in it.'

'What is it?'

'Open it and see,' he said with a chuckle.

Jumapili tore open the wrapping paper, opened the box with its sprung lid and felt inside. 'What is it?' she asked excitedly. She had never felt anything like it before. 'She ran her finger tips down its length.

'It's a braille watch,' answered Downsted. 'You'll be able to tell the time. The watch face has a lid. Lift up the lid and you'll be able to feel the position of the hands against the dots on the clock face. The dots stay still but the hands move around as the day passes. For the first time you'll be able to know whether it's day or nighttime without asking.'

'A watch,' said Jumapili breathlessly. 'I have a watch! I can't believe it. Thank you, thank you so much.'

'Jumi, it's my pleasure. You more than deserve it.'

For the first time in her life, she gave Downsted a heartfelt hug.

That night when the house was quiet, Rishi knocked on Jumapili's bedroom door. He didn't wait for an answer before entering.

'Would you like me to teach you to tell the time?' he whispered before tip toeing across the room to her bed.

Oblivious to the gentle rhythmical rocking coming from above his head, Downsted was sitting at the dining room table concentrating hard. He had a difficult letter to write to the trial judge. It had to be carefully penned because to stray one way and he would be in breach of the Official Secrets Act; move too far in another direction and he risked being charged with perjury and perverting the course of justice.

Unscrewing the cap on his Parker Dufold fountain pen, he thought of Joyce. She had given it to him as a present just after he had been dismissed from the Navy.

'It's to write your book on Kenya,' she said, before handing him her beautifully wrapped gift.

With a criminal record for 'terrorism offences' during the Mau Mau war, accompanied by a long prison sentence, it was almost certain that, of all the members of Genge la Chupa, Mbua Aomba was the most likely to be sentenced to death. Downsted didn't want that. With Joyce's pen in his hand, he knew he was writing this letter for her too.

Dear Judge he wrote, and as those two words flowed from his pen he realised he didn't know the form of address for the trial judge and thus, whatever he penned now, it could only be a draft:

> *My wife is Mrs. Joyce Downsted whose murder is, inter alia, one of the three murders which is the subject of the trial currently before your Court.*
>
> *I am in no doubt that the jury will find most of, if not all, the men guilty of murdering Mrs. Downsted.*
>
> *The proscribed penalty for murder is the death penalty. I would like to inform the court that Mrs. Downsted would not want this, and neither do I.*
>
> *Kenya's harrowing history under colonial rule proves that the death penalty served little purpose in the past, and I do not think that more people hung will serve any purpose now. I am sure my deceased wife's opinion would have been the same as mine. For this reason, my plea to the court is that it treats all the men found guilty with leniency.*

The court does not yet know, but it will do when it comes to sentencing, that Mr. Mbua Aomba has a previous conviction for terrorism. I know this because I was employed by British military intelligence in Kenya's former Colonial Office. In this role I was able to review the evidence which saw him found guilty.

I have strong reason to believe that certain key facts which would have been important to Mr. Mbua Aomba's trial defence were withheld from him and his defence lawyers. If this information had been put before the court, it is almost certain he would never have been convicted, and it is highly likely that the matter would never have come to trial in the first place.

If Mr. Mbua Aomba were to launch an appeal against his terrorism offence and were the full evidence to come before the court and a new jury, I am in no doubt he would be found not guilty.

Downsted thought of Miss Eucabeth Mutinda, his assistant in the Colonial Office, who had arranged for him to see many of the secret files from the Mau Mau war years for the book he was writing. It was from these papers he knew of Aomba's innocence. He also knew the British Colonial Office knew, and it had deliberately misled him in the evidence he had put before Aomba's trial.

Once again, it made him realise how important it was to finish his book. Lives had been destroyed through the "good cause" corrupt practices[41] of the British Government and its determination to destroy the Mau Mau by fair means or foul.

Downsted knew he must write more if his plea for clemency was to be effective, but he suddenly felt exhausted. Carefully, he put the lid back on his pen, re-read what he had written and sat back in his chair.

---

[41] Good cause or noble cause corruption involves lying, and / or the planting or fabricating of evidence, and / or the dishonest manipulation of facts in a report for the purposes of deliberately misleading a court. Generally, it involves the state and / or police authority abusing their authority for the purposes of achieving a conviction when, in all likelihood, no conviction would be obtained without such wrong evidence being produced in court. It is done in the false belief that getting a conviction is more important than achieving justice.

‘It’s a good start,’ he thought, before he stood up and headed to Lakshmi’s bed.

Chapter 68

JUMAPILI SAT AT the baby grand piano which had been brought into the TV studios especially for her. She was listening attentively to everything going on around her. There was a confusion of smells and noises: the smell of perfumes, aftershaves, burning studio-lamps and the dust, which swirled around her as items and people moved, doing what she could not say but they all seemed busy and acting with a purpose.

The one thing Jumapili knew and that was her feet were hurting her. Lakshmi had dressed her in a white, tightly fitted trouser suit with extra length in the leg specifically designed for wearing with high heel shoes. She originally had it made for herself, so it was not the most practical attire for someone blind. But it was only after the judge had passed sentence that Jumapili was prepared to go on television, and the borrowed trouser suit was the best available. The negotiations between the lender and wearer ended with Jumapili agreeing to wear the shoes on stage, but she would kick them off the moment she came to play the piano.

The longer she sat in the studio, the more relaxed she became. She rehearsed the song they agreed she should play, and words of encouragement calmed her down. A floor assistant lifted her hand to show her where the microphone was placed so that she had an idea where to sing, but he told her not to worry too much as there would be a boom mic overhead which would pick up her voice wherever she went.

'Our final guest after the break, is Miss Jumapili Mwangi,' said Murade Ngesan, the anchor-man who held the evening show together. 'She was the star witness in the Genge la Chupa trials. We'll see what she has to say about today's verdict and the gang's sentences.'

As soon as the camera was off, Ngesan moved to sit on a matching swivel piano stool next to Jumapili.

'Are you okay?' he asked.

'Yes, it's fun, isn't it?' she answered, as the floor manager shouted: 'three, two, one, on air.' The break had seemed like milliseconds.

'My next guest is Jumapili Mwangi,' said Ngesan, before reading from the autocue almost the same words he'd used to close the programme before the adverts.

'I think everyone calls you Jumi, is that right?' asked Ngesan.

'Yes,' Jumapili replied softly.

'So Jumi, how are you feeling today now you know the verdict and sentence?'

'Relieved,' answered Jumapili.

'Relieved,' repeated Ngesan.

'I knew they would be found guilty. Well, they were, weren't they? There was no doubt. I'm just glad that there'll be no hangings.'

'They killed your teacher; didn't you want them hung for that?'

'Not just my teacher, my best friend too. Joyce was like a mother to me.'

'Aren't you angry at her death?'

'Yes, very angry, but that doesn't mean I wanted them hung – so I wrote to the judge telling him that.'

'You wrote to the Judge?'

'Yes, but only after I thought about it for a long time. We all know the expression "an eye for and eye, a tooth for a tooth" but Jesus also went on to say "whoever shall smite thee on the right cheek, turn him the other". The Bible teaches us not to treat evil with evil, but rather with love. It makes it very clear that only God can judge a person, and I don't think he made it my job to bring him to make an early judgement, do you?' she asked.

'Are you religious?' asked Ngesan.

'No, not at all, but I've been to church, and I listen. For example, did you know Mahatma Gandhi said, "an eye for an eye makes the whole world blind", and I think there's a lot to be said for that.'

Ngesan said nothing, playing the interviewer's trick of silence, knowing that the other person will feel compelled to speak to fill the gap, which is exactly what Jumapili did.

'It takes time to truly repent, and I don't think those men were inherently evil. They were all high on khat. You could hear it in their voices. They didn't set out to kill that night. The evil men are those who make and supply that wretched drug. If there had been no khat, they'd have been no deaths, I'm sure of it.'

Ngesan saw the floor manager signal ninety seconds to the end of the programme. I'm told you're a bit of a musician and you're going to play us out this evening. What are you going to play?

'I've chosen *Somewhere Over the Rainbow*,' said Jumapili. I've chosen it not only in Joyce's memory, but for all those who died that night, because that's where their souls are - somewhere over the rainbow.'

'Off you go,' said a Ngesan tapping her on the leg.

'Jumapili swung round on the piano stool, found her bearings, allowed her fingers to settle calmly, and she started to play. On key she came in with '*Somewhere over the rainbow. Way up high There's a land that I heard of, once in a lullaby*.'

Usually, at this point in the show, the credits start running and, in the studio, off-sight of camera, people start packing up but not that evening. They stopped and listened to a remarkable voice. They had heard her practice earlier on, but the raw emotion in the song, which had not touched them then, now surrounded the studio, radiated through the television screen and into the homes of the families of the Genge la Chupa, and every member of the Kamba tribe.

Jumapili would be able to walk the streets of Nairobi without fear because every family member of Genge la Chupa was convinced that it was Jumapili's appeal to the Judge that had saved their family member from an early death.

'You were great, kid,' said Ngesan when the red light on the camera had gone off. 'Wanna come back again? Wanna come back next week, play us out then?'

Jumapili nodded her head furiously.

Chapter 69

JUMAPILI, DOWNSTED, LAKSHMI and Rishi walked to the hotel and then to the bar where the Assistant Producer had first suggested that Jumapili appear on the Evening Show. He was already at the bar.

The AP watched as Jumapili, with her trouser hems turned up and in a comfortable pair of trainers, clicked and tapped her way across the room, without any help. When her white cane touched a bar stool, she tapped around its edge before both hearing and feeling it stop abruptly as it hit the bar panel. Clicking loudly, she cautiously put out her hand and felt for the bar edge.

'How blind are you?' asked the AP, once Jumapili had folded up her white stick and placed it on the bar.

'An interesting question not usually asked?' answered Jumapili abruptly.

'I've got a blind aunt, so I have an interest in theses things.'

'Not a single thing, not day nor night,' she replied as she had done many times before.

'But I've just seen you navigate your way through here without any problem. You tapped your away around some furniture, but it seems as though you already know it's there.'

'She uses a technique called echolocation,' said Rishi. 'She clicks and taps, a bit like a screeching bat, and from the echo she makes a mental map of the world around her.'

'Is that right?' asked the AP.

'So they say,' replied Jumapili.

'We must have you on again, next week, to talk about this. It will make such a good story. Would you be happy to sing us out again, like you did tonight?'

Jumapili was non-committal. She found talking about her blindness both embarrassing and boring. How do you answer the interminable question, what's it like being blind when you have no other experience. She signalled to the barman indicating she wanted to order a drink.

'What would you sing for us next time?' asked the AP, responding quickly to her reticence.

Jumapili thought.

'*You'll never walk alone*,' she answered.

'Are you a Liverpool fan?'

'What's that. Who are they?'

'It's the song of Liverpool Football Club.

'Oh, no, sorry.'

'What about Gerry and the Pacemakers?' asked the AP. 'They made the song famous.'

'No, they didn't,' said Jumapili in a tone which suggested that she was not going to debate the subject. 'The song's from the film *Carousel* written by Rodgers and Hammerstein. It's one of the best musicals ever written.'

'Never heard of it,' said the AP man, 'but I guess we can buy the rights.'

Thus, the following week Jumapili was back in the same studio. This time she was in a white dress, tailored purposely for her by Lakshmi, a pair of comfortable shoes and brand-new sunglasses. In response to questions from Murade Ngesan, she talked about being blind, being badly burned as a child, the death of her father and mother – and praised her brother.

'I'm told you're going to sing for us. What have you chosen?' asked Ngesan.

'*You'll never walk alone* from Carousel,' said Jumapili. 'It's for my brother because he always made sure I never walked alone.' She turned to face the piano keys.

Sitting in the staff changing-rooms of Kisumu Airport, on the shore line of Lake Victoria, was Absko. He had been getting ready to go home after working the day in the restaurant's kitchens, when he heard Jumapili's voice. He stopped what he was doing to stare at the television.

'That's my sister,' he said proudly. 'She says that song's for me.'

Everyone stopped and listened.

'She was on last week. She was brilliant then,' said a colleague.

'I didn't see it,' admitted Absko

'She identified the Genge la Chupa from their voices.'

'Yeh, I know.'

'And she stopped them being hanged,'

'The man they should have hanged was the policeman who arrested them,' said Absko. 'He's as corrupt and dangerous as hell.'

'What Charter Ahenda? He's been shot dead. He was leaving the house of his mistress when he got whacked. It's in today's papers. It says he was expecting a promotion after the trial but got topped instead.'

'Good,' said Absko with a cold smile. 'It couldn't have happened to a nicer person.'

'Here's the paper with his picture in it,' said his colleague as he threw over an assortment of readily thumbed pages.

Absko looked at the newsprint, but he found it difficult to read all the words. Instead, he studied Charter's eyes and saw there was no connection to this man's soul. Absko shuddered because he remembered those merciless eyes. They were evil personified.

Chapter 70

AFTER THE RAID on Bottlesford Hall, the trial, the guilty verdict, and Jumapili's appearance on television, both she and Downsted found it hard to settle down to a routine. Several times Downsted spoke to Lakshmi about moving out, but each time she persuaded him to stay, and in the end a compromise was reached with Downsted contributing to her household's running costs. The fact was that Lakshmi McGeown wanted Downsted in her life. She found his companionship gave her renewed status in their small ex-pat community.

Jumapili resumed her music lessons but, because Lakshmi didn't own a piano, they took place in the little church where Joyce had her funeral. The piano was retuned, and her music tutors would, each morning, take her through three fifty-minute lessons, piano first, then the viola and finally the clarinet. The one instrument that Downsted might have wanted Jumapili trained in, her voice, never entered his mind, probably for the simple reason that she was a natural singer.

In the afternoon Jumapili was taught English, French, geography and history through a series of tutors arranged by Downsted. Most of them had taught at Bottlesford Hall and were familiar with its demanding teaching methods.

Downsted taught her maths and physics, as he had done before, and was about to agree that Jumapili need not learn chemistry when he suddenly changed his mind. It was his realisation that no one sees molecules or atoms which made him realise they did not need to do experiments. It was, he told her, a cerebral subject because, while matter might change its form through physical and chemical forces, the same amount of matter exists before and after the change – none is created or destroyed. All she had to do, he told her, too simply, was to be able to count atoms. But perhaps the real reason was that

Downsted wanted an excuse to return to a subject he once loved and gave up when he went to university.

To Jumapili's chagrin Downsted returned to playing the Jekyll and Hyde character he displayed at Bottlesford Hall and which she had got to know so well. When he was in his adoptive-father mood he was kind, caring and considerate, but when he was teaching, he turned into a complete tyrant, an ogre, whose demand for excellence knew no bounds. It was only much later in life that Jumapili recognised the work-ethic he had instilled into her and was grateful for it.

In mid-September, just before Rishi returned to England to go to university, Downsted, Lakshmi, Jumapili and Rishi went on holiday. They chose to head towards Lake Victoria so there would be few reminiscences of Joyce. Nevertheless, they still chose to camp which made it difficult not to make comparisons.

Normally Mawla and her husband would have come with them, but they were now resting in their graves. Downsted didn't want to train and trust anyone else and so his hope was that Lakshmi and Rishi would pull their weight and they would be able to manage just as well.

Nothing had prepared Downsted for Lakshmi's complete inability to take to the art of camping. As far as she was concerned it was a discomfort too far, and her constant complaining really irritated both Jumapili and him. The fact was that Lakshmi saw her purpose in life as being sexually attractive and desirable, and her job was to order everyone else around her to do what she wanted, so she could maintain a meticulous lifestyle.

Rishi kept Jumapili amused, but there was no swimming from the shores of Lake Victoria as they had hoped. They were warned against it because the water was badly polluted. Instead, temporary membership of a local country club gave them access to a swimming pool, tennis courts and a restaurant which met Lakshmi's standard. Sadly for Downsted, camp-side cooking, which he always saw as a holiday treat, was soundly frowned upon by her.

Downsted returned to Lakshmi's Cottage exhausted. He hadn't realised how easy and low-maintenance Joyce had been as, in every respect, Mrs Lakshmi McGeown was different. No wonder Graeme had resorted to booze, Downsted told himself as he single-handedly unpacked his Land Rover.

Their return from holiday was greeted by an officious letter from Miss Gasira Onyango of the Nairobi Child Services giving them an unequivocal date and time for an appointment to see her. It was, the letter said, to review Jumapili's development. The fact was that Miss Onyango had hardly thought about Jumapili at all since the meeting to discharge her from hospital, but her appearance on the Evening Show had prompted Miss Onyango to recall the file.

There was a minor explosion in the Lakshmi household when the letter from Miss Onyango arrived, not least because Downsted wanted to know how she had got hold of their address. He remaind sure that Jumapili's life was threatened by the Genge la Chupa. But of course, a phone call to Nairobi police from Nairobi's child services department proved as simple as a magician saying 'open sesame' to a locked box.

Downsted and Jumapili presented a united front when it came to dealing with Miss Onyango. Each line of attack she had prepared to interfere in their lives was shut down at every opportunity because neither liked her. In the end, the only criticism Miss Onyango could make was that Jumapili had not had her annual medical check-up for over two years, and she lectured on it to the point of tedium.

'For God's sake,' exploded Downsted. 'She's just come out of hospital having been poisoned by fumes from a fire and nearly bled to death from a machete attack. You don't think they'd have discharged her if she was unwell, do you?'

Miss Onyango didn't like people challenging her. 'Mr. Downsted.' she said firmly. 'It's a condition of Jumapili living with you that she has an annual medical report. You're in clear breach of those rules. I'm giving you two weeks to rectify matters.'

Miss Onyango's unspoken message was clear, 'you British are no longer in charge of my country'.

Chapter 71

'DO YOU WANT me to tell your father?' asked the doctor.

'What, Colin? He is not my father,' said Jumapili sharply for she was in a state of shock.

'Yes, sorry,' said the doctor. 'The nurse told me. Do you want me to tell Mr. Downsted?' she asked again.

Jumapili nodded.

Downsted was summoned into the small consulting room in the local clinic where he was expecting to hear Jumapili had an A1 medical report. He thought she had never looked healthier.

'And?' said Downsted, sitting down and raising his eyebrows as an indication that he was ready to start the conversation.

'Good afternoon,' Mr. Downsted.

'Good afternoon, Doctor.'

'I've been asked to share some news with you.' There was a very slight hesitance in the doctor's voice, 'Jumapili's pregnant.'

'Ah, I wasn't expecting that,' said Downsted after a paused but with the characteristic reserve for which the English are famous. 'That'll take some thinking about.'

All three sat in silence for what Jumapili thought was an eternity.

'Who's the father?' asked Downsted.

'Jumapili's not sure. She thinks it's a boy called ....' The doctor paused to read her notes – 'Rishi.'

'She's not sure. What do you mean, not sure?' asked Downsted confused. 'There's more than one candidate? Rishi makes sense, but others?'

Mr. Downsted, I'm afraid Jumapili's education has been missing in one important aspect, sex education. Apparently, that's not on your school's agenda.'

'Didn't Joyce talk to you about this when you started ....?' asked Downsted, as he waved his hand around in the air using it to fill the gap for a word he was too embarrassed to say.'

It was his only response before he stood up. 'Doctor, I think you two need to have a serious conversation on the birds and the bees. It's pretty darn important if we're going to tell a young man he's going to be a father. And don't anyone tell me that it was an immaculate conception. We learned that was nonsense in 1875.'

'1875? What are you talking about?' asked the doctor confused.

'We've known where babies come from forever, but amazingly that's the year mankind worked out how sex causes babies. It's worth remembering that the next time someone preaches to you from the bible.'

On those pearls of wisdom, Downsted left the room and closed the door behind him.

Chapter 72

'WELL, YOUNG LADY, you throw up some challenges, don't you,' said Downsted in a head-masterly tone. Jumapili had just made her way back from the clinic to his car unaided and had climbed into the passenger seat.

'What do you think Miss Onyango will say?' asked Jumapili.

'Fuck Miss Onyango,' said Downsted, breaking one of his rules not to swear, particularly in front of children. 'Is Rishi the father?' he asked.

'Yes, only him. But I don't understand it. We were only doing what Lakshmi and you were doing.'

'Lakshmi and me?' Downsted almost choked with surprised.

'Yeah, we heard you were having fun, so Rishi thought we should have some fun too.'

Downsted swallowed hard to try and overcome his embarrassment.

'Colin, what am I going to do?' Jumapili asked.

'You're going to have a baby, that's what you're doing, but before that, you've got to tell Rishi, because like you, he's now facing a whole host of problems.'

'Like?'

'Well, you're under age, so he's committed a criminal offence and, given Miss Onyango's involvement in your care, I'd say it's highly likely he's going to get prosecuted.'

'What do you mean, under age?'

'You're not allowed to have sex under the age of sixteen in this country. You're fifteen, he's eighteen, so he's on a go-to-jail ticket.'

'Under age, how can there be an age limit on that kind of thing. It's nature for God's sake. In any case, no one told me I wasn't to ...' Jumapili paused. 'How can I break a law I didn't know about?'

'You might not have known, but Rishi will certainly have,' said Downsted sharply. 'It's a complete snafu.'

'Snafu?'

'It's an acronym for "Situation Normal, All Fouled Up", but most people change the F to a rude word.'

'Yeh, well, it's me who's well and truly fucked up, isn't it!'

'Yeh, you, and Rishi too.'

There was a pause in the conversation as Downsted started the car and reversed out of the parking spot.

'I want to see Absko. I need to see Absko,' said Jumapili beginning to cry. 'He'd know what to do. I promise you, he's always the best person to go to in a crisis.'

Downsted reached across and placed a clean handkerchief into her hand.

'Colin,' said Jumapili, taking control of her voice. 'Do you think my baby will be born blind? Will what's happened to me happen to her?'

'Her?' repeated Downsted.

'Him, her, whichever.'

'I don't know Jumi. I've been wondering the same thing too. We just don't know whether you not being able to see is genetic or an accident of birth, but given your parents and grandparents weren't blind, my guess is your baby will be able to see perfectly well. But being honest, I just don't know, and I don't think anyone will, not until the baby's born and a few months old.'

Chapter 73

JUMAPILI AND DOWNSTED sat in silence for the rest of the journey to Lakshmi's cottage. Once parked, they tarried a little longer, because neither wanted to break the news to Lakshmi that she was going to be a grandmother.

'Jumi, I need to say something,' said Downsted very gently.

Jumapili turned her head, scared stiff about what he was going to say.

'I'm with you, okay? I'll look after you and your baby the best I can. Joyce would have wanted me to, but that's not the reason. I've been thinking as we drove here. I couldn't imagine my life with you and your baby out there, not with me. If I didn't know you were safe, I know I'd go out of my mind with worry. So, for purely selfish reasons, I'm conscripted into Team Jumi. I just have to be.'

'You'll look after me. Look after us?'

'Yes, Jumi, as I said, as best I can.'

Chapter 74

LAKSHMI WAS ON the veranda arranging flowers in a series of glass vases in preparation for dressing the church for harvest festival. Although she was brought up as a Sikh and had never been baptised, she said she found it easy to accept Christianity because it believed in one God as compared to the many gods of Hinduism. But if the truth were known, her key reason for supporting the church was the access it gave her to the ex-pat community and what she thought was higher societal status.

Immediately Lakshmi saw Downsted and Jumapili walk through the lounge towards her, she reached for the bell to summon her white-gloved houseboy.

'Would you like something to drink?' she asked. 'How did you get on?'

We have some exciting news, don't we Jumi,' said Downsted trying to put a positive spin on the situation.

Jumapili, who was now standing on the veranda, said nothing. Instead, she fidgeted uncomfortably picking at the top of her white cane, before directly facing Downsted, who took this as his cue to speak. 'You're going to be a grandmother. Rishi's going to be a father. Jumi's pregnant. Isn't that excellent news?'

Lakshmi looked at Downsted and then Jumapili, her eyes moved rapidly between them thinking for a moment it was some kind of prank, but the lack of fun in their eyes told her it was not.

'I'm a grandmother, Rishi's a father and Jumapili is *pregnant*?' said Lakshmi slowly before picking up one of her flower arrangements and hurling it at Jumapili, missing her by only a few inches.

'Get out, get out, get out of my house!' shouted Lakshmi before throwing a second, and then a third, glass vase straight at Jumapili.

'Jumi, stay still! There's broken glass everywhere,' commanded Downsted before shouting 'Lakshmi shut up,' and rushing towards her to stop her throwing any more vases.

'Get her out of my house. My son's not having a kid with a blind peasant from the Kibera slums!' she screamed. 'She's the runt of the litter. Kids like that need to be put down at birth. She should have been put down.'

'Lakshmi, for God's sake shut up. You can't say things like that.'

'My family is Khatri. My husband's Scottish, my son has the best blood. It's not going to be diluted by a Kikuyu whore.'

'Lakshmi, that's nonsense,' shouted Downsted. 'Don't be ridiculous.'

'Don't you tell me I'm being ridiculous. How can a man hold his head high, get a good job with a black tart as a wife? How can he? He can't.'

'Lakshmi stop it, just stop it, be reasonable,' pleaded Downsted but to no avail for in an instant she had her hands shaped as talons, ready to tear Jumapili apart.

Downsted grabbed Lakshmi's wrists and pushed her away before she could do any harm.

'Get out, get out!' yelled Lakshmi to Jumapili who was quivering with fear. 'Get the girl out of here!'

Downsted moved to Jumapili's side.

'Jumi, come with me I'll take you back to the car,' he said as he kicked the broken glass out of the way. He took her arm and carefully led her back through the lounge.

'Don't worry, Jumi,' said Downsted when she was sitting safely in the front seat of his Land Rover. 'This is madness. I'll sort it out.'

Lakshmi was in no better mood when Downsted reappeared in the lounge where she had taken to pacing up and down like a tiger.

'You're going to tell Rishi he's going to be a father. He's going to have to stop poncing around at university and get a job. He's now got a family to keep,' said Downsted.

'No, the witch 'll get nothing from him, not a shilling, nothing. She's worthless don't you see.'

'For Christ's sake! What do you mean, "worthless"? No one's worthless. Look, get real. Rishi's got a serious problem: Jumi's fifteen; Rishi's nineteen. She's below the age of consent. He's broken the law. Having sex with a minor is illegal and with Nairobi child services involved you don't think it's an issue which is going to just go away, do you?'

Lakshmi stopped pacing as she absorbed the news, before retorting, 'put my son in jail for screwing that black witch? Don't be stupid!'.

'Yes, you need to face up to it. It's a real possibility.'

'No, no, no!' shouted Lakshmi. 'We'll say it's yours. Rishi and I will both say it's yours.'

'That's absurd. Can't you see how silly that is.'

'It's yours. It's yours,' repeated Lakshmi loudly in the childish hope that continually repeating something might make it true.

'I'm not arguing anymore,' said Downsted. He turned abruptly and returned to his car. There he found Jumapili sitting calmly. Her head was held high, and she was looking straight ahead. She had a serenity about her that took Downsted completely by surprise.

'Jumi, you need to come inside and pack. We're leaving,' he said.

'We're leaving. Where to?'

'Anywhere but here.'

'Are you coming? she asked, now confused.

'Oh yes. I'm most definitely not staying here.'

Downsted didn't say goodbye to Lakshmi before he closed the front door and drove away. She was sitting alone in her garden watching a small Victorian fountain spray water in the breeze. She had calmed down and was in quiet contemplation. She too had some news which she had planned to share with Downsted at church on Sunday just before the harvest festival. It was why she had been working so hard on decorating the church. He was going to be a father.

Lakshmi McGeown was carrying Downsted's baby.

Chapter 75

IT TOOK A week for Jumapili and Downsted to get organised. They spent the first few nights in the hotel they had stayed at during the trial before he was able to rent a modern open-plan furnished bungalow in a new development on the Tayinia side of Nairobi.

The only part of their lives that remained uninterrupted were Jumapili's music lessons, which continued every weekday morning at the little church. Neither Jumapili nor Downsted had the inclination to continue her academic studies. Instead, they treated their time as though it were a sabbatical.

Joyce had started to teach Jumapili to cook but only in holiday times. The problem was that the Bottlesford Hall kitchen was ill-suited to the needs of a blind person. The bungalow's kitchen was very different. It was not only compact but efficiently organised, an essential ingredient if it is to be used by a blind person.

After each shopping trip Downsted would hand Jumapili every item telling her what it was before she put it away. She needed the same kind of things to be put in the same place if she was ever to find them again. She used six rubber bands in a combination, with up to three placed around the top of the tin and three placed around its bottom, to identify its contents. That way she could identify a tin of soup from a tin of baked beans from a tin of fruit. Meats, cheese, fruits, and vegetables were all easy to differentiate by touch and smell.

Jumapili's fear of boiling water never left her. However, with Downsted slowly explaining what he was doing, then carefully showing her by guiding her hands, and then by watching, simply acting as a guardian to make sure she didn't hurt herself, Jumapili became a competent cook. Dishes like toad-in-the-hole, home-made lasagne and spaghetti Bolognese all came into her kitchen repertoire, as did sausages, fishfingers, mash potatoes and chips. Although Jumapili's inability to peel potatoes, to Downsted's satisfaction, meant mashed and roasted potatoes were never fully mastered. However, it was as a baker that Jumapili excelled. There was not a bread or cake baker as good as her for miles around.

Jumapili's biggest failing in the kitchen was the mess she would make. She would rarely reuse a cooking implement. In the pressure of the moment, she would choose not to remember where she had placed something, preferring to take a clean item instead. It meant that there was always double or treble the washing-up and the surface areas were an indescribable mess. No matter, Downsted, who was normally impatient and meticulous, would clear up after her with the rarest of complaints because he knew, if the tables were reversed and he were blind, he would never be able to do as well.

Downsted arranged for his things at Bottlesford Hall to be collected by a removal company. Time and time again he thought he should do the job himself. Several times he drove there and parked outside the front door. There both happy and sad memories streamed through his mind, but he could never bring himself to go inside.

Slowly he sifted through his possessions throwing much away. He was surprised at how few of the material things he possessed truely represented him and his life. Nothing, it seemed, was indelibly him – and it worried him.

Downsted re-read the draft of his book on the Mau Mau which was almost complete. He thought it passably good until he started to delve into his source material and notes, after which he concluded it needed much more work. With a long list of questions, he met up with Miss Mutinda who was delighted to see him again. As indispensable as ever, she was now working in the British Embassy. Like everyone else, she had followed the Genge la Chupa trials, but to have the inside story told by someone involved made her feel special. Once again, she became an invaluable source of information who enabled Downsted to start redrafting his book. The trouble was that the information Miss Mutinda revealed continued to show that Britain had a much darker involvement in Kenya than that portrayed in the official history.

Jumapili and Downsted's time in the bungalow might have been delightful except for the shadow cast over them by Nairobi's children's welfare services and Miss Onyango. Those matters were always left until evening. Downsted would light a kadia fire bowl outside. They would sit around it, throw on the occasional log and watch the flames until bedtime with plenty of time to discuss the issues. Downsted would have a glass of scotch whisky and Jumapili a bottle of Guinness. The latter to satisfy Downsted's insistence that the iron in the Irish brew would do Jumapili and her baby good.

Downsted raised the difficult question of whether Jumapili wanted to go to London to have an abortion where, only a few years earlier, it had been made legal. Jumapili refused, saying she needn't go to London because she was certain she could get the same thing in Kibera, although abortion remained illegal in Kenya. There would also be the question of money, and Jumapili didn't dare ask Downsted for money for something which, through his tone, she knew would make him unhappy.

For Downsted there was no drama, no crisis in Jumapili being pregnant. He thought it a matter of joy, not sadness. He saw the situation in simple terms: Jumapili would have her baby and all three would live quietly together with no one interfering.

Miss Onyango learned about Jumapili's pregnancy from the medical report, which had been independently sent to her. As there was no mention of a father's name in the medical report, Miss Onyango was immediately suspicious that Downsted was to blame.

Once again Jumapili was the star witness, convincing Miss Onyango that Downsted wasn't the father while at the same time refusing to name Rishi because of the implications for him.

Downsted offered to adopt Jumapili's baby and, if it helped, Jumapili herself, but Miss Onyango refused to consider it on the grounds that he was too old and was not married. As far as Miss Onyango was concerned, Jumapili's baby was going to be put up for adoption. She would brook no debate.

'I was thinking I should try and find Absko,' said Jumapili at breakfast one morning. 'I'm sure he could find me someone to marry. If I was married, I'd be able to keep the baby.'

'Jumi, it's not a matter of married or not. It's not a matter of finding someone to marry you. I'd find somebody if that would work. For God's sake, I'd marry you myself. But it won't work. You're a ward of the court or as near as dam it, and Onyango's not going to allow it.'

Being told that your child is going to be adopted is distressing enough, but when Jumapili learned that the adoption was being arranged through the Catholic Church, she was beside herself with worry. She remembered only too well how Absko had shared with her their mother's views on the Church's immorality. It was an opinion well held because the Kenyan Catholic Church charged large adoption fees to adopting parents which they dressed up as donations. For them it was a lucrative business.

One might have thought that keeping a mother and child together would have been a priority for Nairobi's children's welfare services, but when the Catholic Church pays council officials a finder's fee for each baby adopted, no such considerations come into play. Miss Onyango was determined in her course of action. If an 'unwanted' baby was going to a good catholic home and she could make money out of it for herself, then that is what is going to happen. She did not see her behaviour as harmful, unethical or corrupt. Every one of her colleagues knew what she was doing and said nothing. They were all happy to share in the cakes that went around the department when another adoption was successfully completed.

Chapter 76

'YOU'RE GOING TO have to sign away all your rights to your baby,' said Downsted when they were sitting around the kadia fire bowl one balmy evening. They had both resigned themselves to the fact that her baby was going to be adopted within days of its birth.

'I won't.'

You'll sign,' said Downsted wearily. 'You're going to have to agree never to try and find your baby again. They'll want your loss to be permanent. We must plan on making it temporary.'

'What do you mean?' asked Jumapili.

'If you have a daughter, as you think you will, I promise you she will come looking for you. She won't be able to help herself. It might happen when she starts to have you know ...' Once again Downsted waived his hands in the air until he embarrassingly continued ... 'her periods, but it will certainly happen when she has children of her own. She'll need to know her baby's genetic make-up. She'll want to know which bits will have come from you.'

'And if I have a son?' asked Jumapili.

'I'm not so sure. Maybe they will, maybe they won't. I just don't know.'

'How do we make sure she finds me again?' asked Jumapili.

Downsted had suddenly given her a glimmer of hope. A tiny light at the end of a long tunnel.

'We must give your baby something which they can use to trace back to you. It must be something which we can hand over when they're taken away. It could be concealed inside the baby's clothing. It will have to be something which will travel with them through life,' said Downsted.

'Can it have my name on it? Can it say who I am?' asked Jumapili.

'No, if it's got your name on, you can guarantee it will get taken away – unless it's written in code, in which case it will have to be something which is very clever.

'I was thinking of making her something like the sensory blanket and the wire animals which my mother made for me, but I don't know what.'

'We have to accept she might go abroad,' said Downsted.

'What do you mean "abroad"?'

'I was talking to my little group at the Tayiania village coffee shop the other day.'

'Have they heard from Absko?' interjected Jumapili. She was certain that he would leave any message he had for her there.

'No, no. I was talking to them about adoption. I wanted to see if I could find someone to adopt your baby, so we didn't lose touch. They mentioned that most adopted Kenyan babies go to the US. Apparently, it's a status symbol among the very rich there to have an adopted Black baby.'

'She'd go to a rich American family?'

'It's a possibility,' answered Downsted before rising to throw an extra log on to the fire bowl and pour himself another small scotch and water. 'Whatever we give your baby, it must bring them back here. It must have something about Nairobi. It must have ...'

'But won't the adoption papers say Nairobi or Kenya. Won't the baby know from that?'

'Good point,' acknowledged Downsted. 'Look Jumapili, I think when all this is over we should go to England. There's nothing for me here. I'm just haunted by sad memories, and this country doesn't want the likes of me, an old colonial.'

'You want me to come too?'

'Of course.'

'But how would my baby find me if I'm not here?'

'They won't come looking for ten or fifteen years. You can be back here for then.'

'What would I do? Where would we live?' asked Jumapili.

'We'd live in Joyce's house in Leamington Spa. It's a nice town and you can go to school there.'

'Won't I need a passport?'

'Yes, but you already have an identity card. The leap from one to another is not too hard, especially if we do it in person and bucksheesh's involved.'

'You don't think Miss Onyango will try and stop me, do you?'

'Of course she will – but if she doesn't know...'

Chapter 77

'I WANT TO give her this,' announced Jumapili shortly after they had returned home from the morning music lessons. She had gone to her bedroom and retrieved a metal sleeve with ancient bale twine around it. It was three or four days after they had discussed her baby being adopted by Americans.

'What is it?' asked Downsted.

'It's my grandfather's mbugi. I have one from one grandfather and Absko has the other.'

Downsted pulled a face, which Jumapili didn't see, for while he was familiar with the mbugi he thought it hardly an appropriate present for a new-born baby.

'I have a code,' said Jumapili. 'Joyce told me I have a code – braille is a code. If you can read braille then you can break its code.'

'That's good,' acknowledged Downsted.

'I thought,' continued Jumapili, 'what if she's blind like me and can't see to read. How would she read anything we write? So I thought, if I make braille indents on the mbugi small enough to make it look like a design but it's my message then, if she touches or sees it, she'll be able to read what is says.'

'Genius, you're a genius. You write what you want to say in braille. I'll get a jeweller to tap the dots into it and then we'll get it silver-plated. That way it'll look expensive, and people will take much more care of it.'

'You like the idea? You like the idea?' said Jumapili becoming breathless from the emotion she felt from Downsted's approval.

'Yep,' said Downsted, understating what he really thought. 'But I think we need to make a cloth case, something in silk, something which is soft, something we can safely smuggle into her clothes.'

Chapter 78

'From the slums of Kibera
To Bottlesford Hall,
The blind girl saw nothing,
But learned to tell all.

A gang came to kidnap,
The girls late at night,
The blind girl could hear them,
She didn't need sight.

Tapping and clicking
With echolocation
She raised the alarm.
To bring them salvation.

The gang, they were evil,
They murdered and maimed,
The girl heard their voices,
And what they were named

All were found guilty,
And sentenced to hang,
But the blind girl's appeal
Led to life for the gang.

The blind girl now sings.
Her voice, her vocation.
Seek a singer of songs,
To find her location.'

'What's this for?' asked Downsted after Jumapili had read him her doggerel.

'I thought it could be the braille message.'

'Why like this? Why not just your name, a date and a few things like that?'

'We'll put those of course, but I want her to find what I look like. That way she'll go to the old newspapers where there are photographs of me from the trial, and when I was on TV. You told me they were there. I want her to find a picture of me. I want her to know what she's looking for. I can't give her a photograph, but surely this should help her find one of me.'

'You have this in braille?' asked Downsted.

Jumapili nodded.

'The words "the blind girl now sings." What's that about?'

It's what I'm going to do; I'm going to be a professional singer. People have paid me to sing, haven't they? When they heard me on TV they said so. Even the people in the studio said I was good. If I can become a famous singer then she'll find me, know me, won't she?'

Downsted smiled at her naivety but said nothing. He didn't want to destroy hope.

'Won't she?' repeated Jumapili.

'You have a voice in a million, Jumi. Your baby will find you. Keep hope. Keep strong. and everything will be OK,' he replied, not realising that Jumapili had given herself a purpose – to become a famous singer.

'We talked about going to London. Is that still your plan?' asked Jumapili.

'To England. Yes, why?'

'I think it's a good idea. I'd like to come too.'

Her reason: she had heard that the UK had recently become the music capital of the world.

Chapter 79

'SHE'S BEAUTIFUL, JUMI, she's just beautiful,' said Downsted staring at a tiny little face with its eyes closed. Jumapili's baby was sleeping peacefully in her cot by the side of her bed. 'How are you?' he asked, taking hold of her hand. 'How did you get on?'

'It wasn't good. It was bad. Nothing prepares you for how bad, but I was lucky. It was quick. Much quicker than I was told,' replied Jumapili, her face turned away towards the cot to listen to her baby's breathing and every movement.

'Just over an hour,' said Downsted, who had driven Jumapili to the hospital. 'How heavy is she?'

'She's small, five pounds, eleven ounces. Colin, can you tell me what you see? Everything, every bit of her. I need to know, ... is she perfect? Truly perfect?'

Downsted leaned across and studied the baby girl.

'She's got the tiniest of fingernails,' he said as he started to describe Jumapili's daughter in painstaking detail.

'She's got fingernails?'

'She's got tiny eyelashes and eyebrows, and just an inkling of hair, black hair, I think, and a squidgy little nose.'

'I counted her fingers and toes. They're all there aren't they?'

'You want me to look?'

Jumapili nodded vigorously. 'Can you see her eyes?' she asked as he was gently removing tiny mittens and booties.

'She's asleep, so they're closed, but I'm sure when she's awake, we'll be able to see them and the colour, but we won't know whether she can see for two or three months because baby's eyes don't focus well until then.'

'I know,' said Jumapili, 'but I'd really like to know if she can see before she's taken away.'

Downsted knew they didn't have that amount of time, so he changed the subject.

'Have you thought of a name for her?' he asked. 'I know you had a long list of girls' names.'

'I'm calling her "Kaweira". In Swahili, it means" the loving one" or "the one who is loved." '

'Kaweira,' repeated Downsted. 'It's a lovely name.'

'It's the way I can tell her I love her,' said Jumapili, her voice breaking. 'She'll know from her name.'

Downsted didn't dare tell Jumapili that it was highly likely Kaweira's name would be changed by her adopted parents.

There followed days of joy as, in her own private room, paid for by Downsted, Jumapili nursed her baby in peace and calm. The only disturbances were created by the daily visits of Miss Onyango who made cursory glances in the direction of Kaweira in what appeared to be nothing more than a check to make sure her quarry had not gone astray.

Chapter 80

JUMI, I THINK it's happening. I think it's happening today!' exclaimed Downsted as he rushed through the door into her room. 'I think they've come for her.'

He reached into the cot, picked up Kaweira and placed her onto Jumapili's breast and into her arms.

'This might be the last time you can cuddle her, feed her, hold her.' His voice sounded alarmed.

'What, why?'

'I've just seen a priest and a nun waiting in the lobby. I've never seen them there before.'

Jumapili released a breast and, finding her baby's head, she placed its mouth close to her nipple, but the baby was still too sleepy to feed.

'Feed, please feed,' wailed Jumapili. 'Oh God, she isn't feeding. She won't feed.'

'Jumi, Jumi relax,' said Downsted. 'We've still got some time. Let's not panic.' The calmness in his voice did not reflect the huge amount of adrenalin now surging through his body.

'They can't take her! She's so small. She's not fed. Oh God, no! Please God, no! Colin, please stop them!'

'Jumi, I'm sorry, I'm so sorry,' said Downsted, tears starting to pour from his eyes.

'Colin please, please. I beg you. Please, please...'

The door barged open, but Downsted was on it like a light-sabre.

'Get out, get out,' he yelled as he lunged at them. 'Get out, get out!'

It was, as he had foretold, the party from the Catholic adoption agency.

'You're not coming in; I will bring the baby out,' he told them.

'We've come to collect ...' started Miss Onyango, but Downsted didn't allow her to finish. He pushed her and the crowd back into the corridor.

'Yes, yes,' he shouted, 'but you're not coming in. The baby's feeding. I'll bring her out. You're not coming in. Do I make myself clear?'

'The priest stepped forward to try to calm matters, but he was dealt with equally firmly, although perhaps more politely.

'As I've said, I'll bring the baby to you,' said Downsted. Tears were pouring from his eyes, but the grimace of determination on his face told those who were watching that he would murder anyone who did not do as they were told.

'Twelve-thirty, Mr. Downsted,' said Onyango. 'Bring the baby to me by twelve-thirty or I'll get the police.'

Downsted looked at his watch. They had twenty minutes.

'I'll bring the baby to you at twelve-thirty, but don't think for one minute you're coming in, 'cause you're not.'

He returned to Jumapili, where he found there was an air of tranquillity in the room. Kaweira was lying peacefully at her mother's breast. Jumapili's hands were moving gently over her baby's face, feeling every part of her: her ears, her mouth, her nose, her arms and legs, her fingers and toes. There was not a part of her which Jumapili did not stroke for the last time.

Downsted didn't trust Onyango not to disturb them, so he took the chord from Jumapili's dressing gown and wrapped it around the door handles to make sure the doors could not be forcibly opened.

'Please, Colin stop them,' sobbed Jumapili, no longer calm. 'Please, please stop 'em. I'll do anything.' Her voice was hoarse, cracking under the strain.

'I can't Jumi,' said Downsted. 'If I could, I would, but then they'll just bring the police and then what do we do?' He took some tissues and dabbed Jumapili's eyes before he blew his nose and dried his own eyes too.

'I love her too, Jumi. I really do. I don't want her to go. I really don't want her to go. She makes us feel like a family.' Downsted shook his head from side to side in despair as his eyes focused on the heaves of Jumapili's chest.

The clock on the wall ticked methodically on. Jumapili and Downsted no longer spoke. Instead, they both stared waiting for the final click of the minute hand and the axe to fall.

Through all the stress Kaweira slept soundly, unaware that her life's path was about to be irrevocably changed.

'It's nearly time,' said Downsted. 'I'll take her things first, and then come back for her. Let's not fight, Jumi. I couldn't bear it.' His voice was breaking, and his eyes were streaming once again.

Entering the sister's room, Downsted ignored Onyango, walked past the priest, and spoke directly to the nun.

'These are Kaweira's,' he said, handing over a bag of newly purchased clothes. 'This is her's too,' and he handed the mbugi to the priest. 'It's a family heirloom, Jumapili would like Kaweira to have it.'

The priest removed the silver box from its padded silk purse, now supported by a new colourful chord, which had been spool knitted by Jumapili. He examined the mbugi carefully, before he handed it to the Nun who only held it for a few seconds, until Onyango grabbed it, gave it a cursory glance, before shoving it into the bag of Kaweira's things.

'You know Miss Mwangi has given up all rights to her child, don't you,' said Onyango. 'She's not to come looking for the baby. You understand that don't you?'

'Yes, she understands that – but I haven't agreed to anything.'

'You have no rights Mr. Downsted. You have no rights at all,' insisted Onyango.

'I have moral rights, the right of every adult to make sure a child is cared for.'

'Yes, Mr. Downsted you do. However, I have the legal rights. So, I'm telling you, should you interfere in anyway, be assured I'll use all my powers to get the police and the courts to lock you away for a very long time.'

This was no longer about the well-being of a little baby. As far as Onyango was concerned Downsted was a White colonialist who had occupied and stolen the best parts of her country. She detested him, and his class, with every fibre of her being. They had ruled her country and her people for too long. Under no circumstances was she going to allow him, or them, to have their way now or ever again.

'I don't think you understand,' interjected the nun. 'This child is going to a better life. She's going to a good family. She'll be loved...'

'No, don't you dare say that, don't you dare!' shouted Downsted, cutting the nun off. 'You're damn hypocrites, all of you, damn hypocrites. I could have provided for this child and her mother with everything, don't kid yourselves. You're stealing her for a reason I don't know. Let's not try and dress this up as anything but the theft of a baby!'

Downsted turned and left the room. He couldn't bear to be among them a moment longer. Once in the corridor and on his own, he stood motionless, trying to regain his composure. He walked slowly to Jumapili's room where he found her remarkably calm. The baby was beautifully wrapped with the amazing care that only blind fingers can manage.

'Here Colin,' said Jumapili, lifting Kaweira and holding her high in the air in his direction. 'Please take her. It's best if ...' she choked on her words. 'Please, Colin, please, do this for me, please.'

Downsted took hold of Kaweira and held her tightly to his chest. He paused to look into her tiny, oh-so-beautiful face. It was an image he would remember forever. He looked back at Jumapili who had collapsed. She was burying her head deep into her pillow and moving to curl herself tightly into the foetal position. She wanted to die.

With tears streaming from his eyes, down his face and onto his crisp white shirt, Downsted opened the door and walked along the corridor for a second time.

'... and we can bring her back in three months if she can't see,' said a voice in a deep African-American accent.'

'It stopped Downsted in his tracks. He was still processing what was happening, when the priest snatched Kaweira out of his arms and placed her straight into those of the nun.

Downsted turned rapidly, determined to get back to Jumapili, but at the last minute he changed his mind. He went to the foyer and sat down in one of the waiting chairs, his heart thumping unmercifully in his chest. His intention was to watch them leave.

Eventually, the priest and the nun came out of the sister's room, followed by a man and a woman. The man was carrying a brand-new carrycot, obviously heavy with the weight of a baby. Downsted studied them carefully. They were both Black and tall. He was well-built; she was slim. The clothes, the shoes, the watches, the jewellery exuded money – but money, Downsted thought to himself, did not mean love.

He watched as they climbed into the car. The nun and priest sat in the front and their two clients in the rear. The adoptive mother was clutching her new possession. Downsted moved onto the front steps of the hospital and stood there watching until the car was out of sight. Had they just purchased another trinket or was Kaweira going to be truly loved? he wondered. From what he had seen, he had no idea.

'I hope you're satisfied,' shouted Downsted to Onyango as he stormed back in to the sister's room. 'You Judas. You damn Judas. How many pieces of silver did you get this time? And how can you have agreed that Kaweira can be given back in three months if she's blind? She's not a piece of meat to be traded. Why didn't you let her stay with us until we knew she could see or not?'

Downsted stopped speaking because there, on the table, were three fragments from torn photographs. They were each of Jumapili smiling. Downsted recognised them immediately. They were torn from the pictures he had taken of Jumapili cuddling and nursing Kaweira the day after she was born.

'You didn't think you'd get those past me, did you?' spat Onyango, referring to the photographs Downsted had placed in Kaweira's things.

'Some days you don't have to go far to see evil,' replied Downsted, shocked into a threatening calm. 'Believe me when I say this, looking at you today, I've seen evil, real evil!

Chapter 81

DOWNSTED RETURNED TO Jumapili's room trembling. She was still curled tightly as a ball. Downsted climbed on to her bed and lay on his back beside her. They did not touch. Nothing was said between them; there was nothing which could be said.

Eventually Jumapili uncurled herself and lay on her back too. Still, they didn't touch, but each noticed the other's breathing. Jumapili was conscious of Downsted's racing heart as it thumped loudly in his chest. They were both emotionally exhausted and while Downsted drifted in and out of semi-consciousness, Jumapili was certain she would never sleep again.

'This wouldn't have happened if Joyce had been here, would it? If she were here, you would have adopted Kaweira, wouldn't you?' said Jumapili quietly.

'Everything would be different if Joyce were here.'

There was a long pause.

'Perhaps I shouldn't have asked for clemency for the men who killed her,' said Jumapili.

'Why do you say that?'

'Because then their families would know how I feel. Those men not only killed Joyce, but they've killed my baby too. Having her taken away is just the same as killing her.'

'But you have hope, Jumapili,' said Downsted, speaking softly. 'You have hope that you'll find each other again. Those families, if those men had been hung, what hope would they have? None.'

'A blind girl from Kibera, what hope has she got, Mr Downsted?' It was the first time since Joyce had died that Jumapili had not called him Colin, but she did so as a point of emphasis. 'You're White, you have money, you have power, you have what you English call "class". What have I got?'

'You've got me,' said Downsted, hurt.

'I'm sorry, I'm really sorry. I couldn't manage without you. You know that.' For the first time she reached across to touch him.

'You have something else, Jumi. You have talent. You only have to harness that talent and then you'll have everything you need. Class, it's a thing of the past. Colour is a thing of the past. Do you remember what I said in the Hall after we had those horrible letters from some parents about you?'

Jumapili squeezed Colin's arm to say she did.

'I said it's character that's important. It's strength of character, and you have more guts, more determination, more courage than anyone else I know.'

'She squeezed his arm again and they allowed the room to go silent.

'I think I saw Kaweira's adoptive parents,' said Downsted. 'I think they're African-American. They certainly appear to have money, so they'll be able to look after her. I think she's probably gone to a good home, and for that we must say our prayers.'

'I've been thinking about this a lot: there is no God. No God could be that capricious. To give me a baby and then take her away. To give such joy and then create such pain. That's not the behaviour of any God I want to pray to.'

'Capricious', thought Downsted, once again amazed at the depth and breadth of Jumapili's vocabulary.

It was late afternoon when, still laying on his back, Downsted announced: 'There's nothing for us here. We'd better go home.'

It was a long time since they had spoken, just to share a drink. In their distress, each had placed a crisp defensive shell around themselves, and they no longer touched. It took some time for Jumapili to respond.

'I think we'd better go to London,' she said.

'I think so too. It's time to go.'

When the car was packed, and it was time for Jumapili to leave her room, Downsted took her hand and placed it on his arm to be her guide. As her voice clicked, and her shoes and cane tapped, Jumapili was back doing what she did naturally, making a mental navigational map of the world around her.

Chapter 82

FOR THE FIRST two days after Jumapili had discharged herself from hospital, Downsted left their bungalow early in the morning on his own, without saying where he was going. If Jumapili had known he was going to Nairobi airport to try and find Kaweira's adoptive parents before they left the country, she would have wanted to come with him, and he didn't want that. His intention was to give them his address in Leamington Spa and tell them that, if Kaweira was blind and they didn't want her anymore, he would take care of her. But he never saw them, and his message was never passed on.

On the third day, after the last day time international flights to Europe and the United States had left Nairobi Airport, Downsted drove to Lakshmi's cottage with the intention of giving Rishi a copy of the photograph he had taken of Kaweira being nursed by Jumapili. It was as happy a picture of mother and child as might be found anywhere. The smile Jumapili radiated hid any of the sadness she must otherwise have been feeling.

Downsted steeled himself for an argument with Lakshmi. He was relieved when he was told by the houseboy that she wasn't there and had gone to India. He handed the houseboy the envelope with the photograph he had in it for Rishi and asked him to make sure he got it. The news that Lakshmi had left didn't surprise him because she had spoken many times of going home to see her family.

The next day Downsted took Jumapili to the church outside Tayiania so she could play the piano and viola with her tutors. He then drove to the coffee shop to meet up with those with whom he had shared many a discussion over the years. After months of turmoil, he had begun to miss their company. However, his main purpose was to see the newsagents to enquire whether they'd heard from Absko. He was keen to organise a reunion between Jumapili and her brother.

It was well over a year since they had last swapped messages, let alone seen each other, and there was much they needed to share, not least the fact that Jumapili was going to live in Britain.

The newsagents had no news of Absko's whereabouts so Downsted bought writing paper, envelopes and pen and went to sit in the same seat, at the same table, he used to sit on the pavement outside the café. He was glad to be alone because there was much he wanted to write.

He wrote *'Dear Absko'* then he sighed heavily because he knew he had to either start or end the letter with an apology.

'I have some happy and distressing news.

Jumapili is well. She is in good health. The happy news is she has had a beautiful baby daughter whom she has called Kaweira. The sad news is that she has been forced to give up her baby for adoption. It was not her or my decision, but that of Nairobi Children's Welfare Services. They used Jumapili's age and blindness as an excuse to make the decision for her. We think her baby has gone to a good home in the USA, but we are not sure. As you can imagine, this has left Jumapili feeling quite depressed.

You are aware of the Genge la Chupa raid on Bottlesford Hall and Jumapili's heroic bravery during the attack. I imagine you are also aware how well she did in the subsequent trial, as it was all in the newspapers and on television.

The result of that experience has convinced me that I can no longer stay in Kenya. I have nothing to offer this country and it is time for me to leave. Jumapili has asked to come with me and I'm happy to keep my promise to look after her, which Joyce and I made when we took her into our care after her car accident.

Kaweira's father is Rishi McGeown, but I'm afraid he has washed his hands of all his responsibilities. Jumapili met him while she was busking on the pavement of Tayiania and then sang at his grandfather's funeral.

Rishi McGeown was born with all the advantages that life could give, and yet, when his test came, he was found wanting. He refused to take responsibility for his child and ran away. He lacked the moral fibre to do what was right. Forever he will be judged and shamed as a coward.

It is the contrast between Rishi's behaviour and your own which has been at the forefront of my mind over the last few months. You didn't run away when Jumapili needed you. Instead, you struggled and sacrificed so much, for so very long, to look after her. The mere thought of what you did, I find very humbling.

Time and time again, it has been proven to me how very hard you must have worked to look after Jumapili, to protect her, and help her to develop into the amazing young woman she is today.

Working with Jumapili has taught me something else which is equally as humbling. I remember clearly you coming to Bottlesford Hall asking, pleading for Jumapili to go with you to see the visiting blind doctor for you were certain they would be able to cure her blindness. I remember how young you looked, how thin you were, the poor state of your clothes and your worn-out sandals.

I remember dismissing you rudely because I was certain that I had better information, as from the tests made on Jumapili after her car accident, Joyce and I already knew that Jumapili had no optic nerve. Her blindness could not be ended by a simple operation. I arrogantly thought I had better information but, of course, in hindsight, I can see I didn't have this. I simply had more information, and it was my duty to share this with you rather than dismiss you as I did.

I arrogantly made a judgment not on who you were but on the way you looked. It was so wrong; I am so sorry. I do hope you will accept my apology, forgive me and trust that I have learnt from my mistake.

Another relevant moment has recently come back to me. I have recently been mesmerised by a black and white photograph taken during the Mau Mau wars of two pairs of men's legs. One pair, thick, muscular, and white, wearing woollen socks held up with garters and with shiny black military boots. The other pair of legs were thin, black, and bare, with worn dusty sandals on their feet. One man, with all the weapons of modern warfare considered himself so superior because he had the power and the might – but he did not see the courage of the man standing before him with no greater weapon than his ceremonial spear and the right.

The story of the photograph is already written because it tells of the defeat of the man with modern weapons, because Britain is no longer in charge of Kenya. The winning has gone to those with courage and fairness on their side, and so it will be between you and the likes of Rishi McGeown. He might wear polished shoes, but you have courage and righteousness. Believe me when I say he is not worthy enough to polish any shoes you might choose to wear. For my part, it would be a privilege to shine them, if you would so allow.

With deep respect and admiration.

Colin Downsted

Downsted's companions arrived just as he was putting the finishing touches to his note to Absko. Their conversation turned to his decision to leave Kenya and return home. They asked him what he intended to do about Bottlesford Hall. It would be sold, he told them, but unable to envisage who might want to buy such a house, they all agreed that his timetable would be uncertain.

It was from his colleagues that he heard that Graham McGeown had died shortly after coming out of jail.

'He was defeated by alcoholism and cirrhosis of the liver,' said a colleague.

'He was killed by the Japanese,' retorted Downsted. 'No one lives again after having been one of their prisoners of war.'

It was then that Downsted was told that Lakshmi had returned to India permanently and put her cottage on the market. His friends also shared the rumour that Lakshmi was pregnant. He dismissed the idea. His assumption was that the reference was to Jumapili being pregnant and Rishi having to leave Kenya permanently so as not to be arrested.

After many a laugh and joke, he said goodbye to his colleagues and went to the newsagents where he left his note for Absko should he ever turn up and enquire about his sister. After that he collected Jumapili from the church and drove to see Geteye and Gatimu Odhiambo. He explained he was leaving and charged them with keeping Bottlesford

Hall safe and secure. He explained how he would pay them money from England but, either they didn't trust him or understand, because they were insistent that, if they were to look after the hall, they be allowed to bring their flock of Red Massai sheep back onto the playing fields.

Downsted's final act was to drive, with Jumapili, to the gates of Bottlesford Hall but he would go no further. It no longer felt his. The insurance company had completed the repair work. He described in detail to Jumapili how the soot and scorch marks from the fire were no longer visible, and how the sun glistened on the new paintwork and the white window shutters, which were now firmly shut. From the outside, no one would have been able to tell the harm that had befallen within.

'Come on, Jumi,' said Downsted, rattling the gear stick of his Land Rover and starting its engine. 'Let's go. Let's go to England. Let's find Leamington Spa.'

Chapter 83

JUMAPILI FELT UNCOMFORTABLE as she listened to Downsted struggle to carry their suitcases from the taxi to the front door of Joyce's house in Leamington Spa. It had been a long tiring journey and a hot cup of tea, and a warm bath were their top priorities.

'It won't do. It won't do at all!' exclaimed Downsted as he walked around the large downstairs rooms before skipping upstairs to look around there too. It was not as he had last seen the house. Now vacated by students, it was uninhabitable. Jumapili could smell the mould, damp and dirt. It was certainly not a place they could stay in.

They decamped to a hotel where they spent three nights while Downsted got cleaners in to give the place a thorough overhaul. Very quickly he had two skips filled with filthy beds, broken furniture, destroyed carpets and all kinds of detritus. With the house stripped, it became obvious that major renovation work was required: the place needed rewiring, the central heating system had to be replaced, as did the kitchens and bathrooms.

While Downsted was talking to builders to get estimates for the basic work, it became obvious that he should also remodel and modernise the house by knocking down walls, making the kitchen much bigger and installing ensuite bathrooms in three of the five bedrooms. It would make it much easier for Jumapili to live safely.

Downsted was told the work would be completed in four months, so they moved from the hotel into dinner-bed-and-breakfast lodgings. They were there for nearly nine months.

Downsted found a specialist school in nearby Coventry which was supposed to cater for blind children. He drove Jumapili there in the morning and picked her up after school. But Jumapili hated it. She was treated as a simpleton and learnt nothing. She protested to Downsted who spoke with the school, but nothing changed. Four weeks later she went on strike and refused to get in the car.

In the meantime, Downsted had got a part-time job as a supply teacher, teaching maths, physics and chemistry at Kingsley School, an independent girls' day school situated close to where they lived. So as not to miss the lessons he had been booked to teach, he took Jumapili into school with him, asking her to sit quietly in his class.

At lunch time, when he went to see the headmistress to explain why Jumapili was in school, he left Jumapili at the piano in the assembly hall and ordered her to practice.

The headmistress found Jumapili before Downsted found the headmistress.

'You're playing Beethoven,' stated the headmistress, surprised.

'Yes,' answered Jumapili, 'his Piano Sonata Number 29.'

'It's a hard piece to learn,' commented the Headmistress before demanding, why aren't you in uniform? Why aren't you at lunch?' Without giving Jumapili a chance to answer, she noticed her white cane, so asked abruptly, 'are you blind?'

There then proceeded to be a fifteen-minute admission interview between Jumapili and the headmistress while Downsted waited anxiously in her study for her to appear.

'It looks as though we have a new pupil in the school, Mr. Downsted,' said the headmistress as she led Jumapili to her study. 'She tells me when she was at your school in Kenya she attended normal classes like everyone else.'

'Yes, that's right.'

'And she says the school she's at in Coventry is a waste of her time.'

'And she's right there too.'

'And you can't teach the first lesson in the morning nor the last lesson in the afternoon because you must take her to and from school?'

'Yes, that's right.'

'So, it would make a lot of sense if Jumapili came to school here and then you could teach those lessons too, couldn't you?'

'But the fees!' protested Downsted.

'There's a discount for children of staff, and I've just heard Jumapili play the piano,' responded the headmistress.

'She's good, isn't she?' said Downsted proudly.

'From the little I've heard, I'd say Miss Jumapili is better than good. I'm sure the Governors can arrange some kind of music scholarship. Let's worry about that after we know how Jumapili settles in.'

The school bell sounded, indicating the start of afternoon lessons.

'Come on, young lady,' said the headmistress 'Let's find you your class. Mr Downsted must go and teach.'

With those words Jumapili was introduced to her new school, in which she was going to thrive.

With nothing to do in their digs, Jumapili and Downsted did nothing but work, so determined were they that she would do well in her 'O' Levels.

In fact, her exam results were better than expected because Downsted brought to Kingsley School and their digs the cramming methods of teaching Joyce and he had developed at Bottlesford Hall. They celebrated her achievements by moving into their completely refurbished home. To be settled in after so long was a joy for both.

Jumapili's reward for getting the top grade in music was an upright white Bentley piano and a scholarship place at Kingsley School to do her 'A' Levels. It was, she thought, only fair reward for being permanently cold and having nowhere to run.

But nothing could remove Jumapili's pain at not knowing where her baby daughter Kaweira and her brother Absko were, or how they were doing.

Chapter 84

APART FROM GETTING to her platform and on the train to Warwick, Catherine Delfont's mind was on little else as she strode through Marylebone Railway Station. With the sound of boogie-woogie filling the concourse, she glanced in the direction of the piano before coming to a dramatic halt.

'Jumapili! Jumapili Mwangi!' she said to herself quietly. Tears filled her eyes and she started to shake. The last time they had seen each other was at Joyce Downsted's funeral.

Along with many others, Catherine stood and watched Jumapili's performance, mesmerised. She remembered marveling at Jumapili's piano playing at Bottlesford Hall all those years ago, and she was standing in awe once again.

Without a break in the music, Jumapili moved seamlessly to play Scott Joplin's ragtime, at which point Catherine went to sit on the edge of the piano stool and started ham-handily to join in, turning a solo performance into a duet. It was a bad mash up of the way they used to play together on the baby grand piano in the west front room of Bottlesford Hall.

Jumapili stopped playing. She had a premonition about the person sitting next to her. Catherine stopped too.

'How's the Bat Girl?' she asked, using Jumapili's Bottlesford Hall nickname.

'Catherine, Catherine Delfont!' said Jumapili immediately recognising the voice. She turned to grasp her re-found friend on the shoulders.

'Jumapili Mwangi,' said Catherine mirroring the form of address before they reached across and hugged each other with tears of happiness pouring down their cheeks.

'I've wondered about you so many times,' the two of them said in unison.

'What are you doing here?'

'I'm waiting for Colin, but he's late, very late.'

'What Mr. Downsted?' asked Catherine dismayed.

'Yes, we live together. In Mrs. Downsted's old home in Leamington Spa.'

'You live together?' repeated Catherine emphasising the word "live" in shock.

'No! not like that!'

'Would you like to get a coffee? asked Catherine. 'There's not much around here but I could get us a takeaway. It would be good to catch up.'

'I can't leave here: I always meet Colin by the piano and then he accompanies me home.'

'What are you doing?'

'I got into the Royal College of Music. It's my second year and I'm loving it,' answered Jumapili. 'I'm on my way home for the weekend. And you? What are you doing? What happened after Bottlesford Hall?'

'God! My parents sent me to an all-girls boarding school in England, a complete prison. All the girls there were as horny as hell so, of course, men were kept well away. I then went to King's, London, where I read anthropology. What a waste of a subject that is. Then on the last day of my last term I married a RADA drama student.'

'Ooo,' said Jumapili excitedly. 'How did you meet?'

'It was during our first term at uni, our digs were on the same street, and we happened to share the same pusher.'

'What drugs?' asked Jumapili shocked

'No, nothing heavy, just grass, marijuana. Well, my RADA husband turned out to have a major secret, didn't he.'

'A secret?'

'Well, more than one. He was a haemophiliac, so that would have been carried into any daughter we had –and his mother was stark raving bonkers. I mean *completely* bonkers, running around outside at night with nothing on – and to cap it all his father's a rapist.'

‘A rapist?’

‘Yeh, he bloody attacked me but got nowhere. In fact, he came off a darn sight worse. On our wedding day, a couple of Pete’s sisters’ friends’ kind-of warned me by asking whether I’d had ‘the pleasure of a visit from his father. So bloody euphemistic. I soon discovered what they meant, and bang, after that it was straight to the divorce courts.’

‘I’m so sorry.’

‘Don’t be. Although I wasted four years of my life on that prick, his family bought me off with a decent divorce settlement. There had been a few police reports about Pete’s father before, and he’d been interviewed under caution. They were all scared stiff that I’d complain and this time it would be different.’

What are you doing now?’

‘I’m doing an MBA at Warwick and it’s great. At least, I’m learning something which might be useful one day,’ answered Catherine, upon which they started a long conversation on the whereabouts of old Bottlesfordians. It resulted in both missing several trains.

‘Catherine,’ said Jumapili at a pause in their conversation. ‘Would you be so kind as to help me find the Leamington Spa train? I think something’s gone wrong meeting Colin and I should make my own way home.’

‘Sure,’ answered Catherine. ‘It’s on my way. We can catch the same train.’

Chapter 85

'I'M HOME!' SHOUTED Downsted as he pushed open the front door. 'Sorry I'm late. It took longer than I'd expected, and the darn tube broke down again. Are you okay?' He walked into the kitchen then stopped abruptly.

'Goodness me – Miss Delfont. How lovely to see you.'

'And you, sir,' responded Catherine.

'Would you like a drink?' asked Jumapili holding up the bottle of red wine that she and Catherine were sharing.

'I need a cup of tea first,' said Downsted as he moved across the kitchen to fill up the kettle from the kitchen sink, 'and then probably a large G&T'. What brings you here Miss Delfont?' he asked once the kettle was full.

'We met at Marylebone Station, and she helped me get home,' replied Jumapili.

'Oh good, thank you. And so, what are you up to Miss Delfont?' asked Downsted adopting his old headmaster's tone.

'She's married,' announced Jumapili.

'*Was* married,' corrected Catherine.

'You should call her "Catherine",' instructed Jumapili, demonstrating the strange equality that had developed in their relationship over the years.

'I'll call her "Catherine" with pleasure, but only if she calls me "Colin" and I'll bet you both a bottle of wine she can't. Whatever happens she'll still call me "sir". If my teachers were still alive and I met them today, I'd be calling them "sir". It's just the way it's ever been.'

Catherine gave Downsted the longer less gossipy version of what she had been up to since she left Bottlesford Hall, without the theatrics and swear words which were involved in its earlier telling.

'And you sir, what are you doing?' ask Catherine.

'Told you I'd win,' teased Downsted. 'I'm teaching again at a girls' independent school, which I enjoy. It's good. Keeps me out of mischief.'

'They love you and hate you, don't they,' interrupted Jumapili.

'Jumi,' protested Catherine. 'You can't say that!'

'It's true,' argued Jumapili. 'It's like Bottlesford Hall. Everyone was petrified of him there and yet they loved him at the same time. His lessons are the most interesting, even the boring bits. He teaches the best and he expects the best.'

'I get good exam results,' agreed Downsted modestly and then, keen to change the subject, 'I'm finishing my book on the history of Kenya and the Mau Mau wars. It was why I was in London – seeing the editor the publishers have appointed to check my manuscript.'

'It's very good,' said Jumapili. 'Colin's read it to me. I can't believe how atrociously the British behaved in my country. He's been through the records, even the secret ones, and is now exposing it.'

'Bit of an historian are you sir?' asked Catherine.

'I'd say it's more like intelligence gathering and code breaking, which I did in the war. Spies call it "gap analysis", spotting when something is missing from the official narrative and looking for the answers. I started work on the book in about 1960 so I think it's more a labour of love.'

'When do you think it will be out?' asked Catherine.

'I don't know. There are several legal issues which must be dealt with first, but if you think my pupils don't like me, you wait and see how the British government reacts. There are going to be some who are none too pleased.

'Yeh, and every Kenyan will love you for it,' added Jumapili forcefully.

'It seems to be another story of love and hate,' commented Catherine, who then looked at the clock. 'It's late. I need to head for home. May I use your phone to call a cab?'

No phone call was made. Downsted, accompanied by Jumapili, took Catherine to her student accommodation, which was in a dingy, unappealing mid-terrace house on a road with poor street lighting, close to the university campus.

'Do you think we could invite her to come and stay with us?' asked Jumapili as soon as Catherine was out of the car, and they were heading home. 'You could rent her the guest room. I'm sure she'd pay. It's just she doesn't like living where she is.'

'I'm not surprised,' answered Downsted, before adding: 'That girl has something about her, doesn't she? 'Joyce always thought so. She marked her out as a doer, an achiever.'

'She's right. It was Catherine who organised everyone's escape from the hall when it was raided. If it wasn't for her, who knows ...'

A week later, Catherine left her digs and moved to live with Downsted and Jumapili in the large guest room with its luxurious ensuite bathroom.

Chapter 86

JUMAPILI'S JAW DROPPED, and her eyes popped wide open. She was overcome by a thumping heart and gasps for air. Through shortness of breath, she was incapable of crying out, although tears streamed from her eyes. Her legs collapsed and she flopped involuntarily onto her settee, and there she sobbed.

Catherine had just read her the opening sentence of a letter from Lakshmi McGeown:

'My dear Jumapili

I have some bad news to share. Colin died last week.

'He's dead!' mouthed Jumapili unable to speak. 'How does she know?'

Catherine continued.

I am sure you know Mr. Downsted has been in India for the past few months, but I don't think he shared with you that he was staying with me and our daughter.'

'*Our* daughter!' Jumapili sat hurriedly up before collapsing back on to a heavy cushion, unable to say more.

'Did you know they shared a daughter?' asked Catherine. 'I knew he'd gone to India, but he said nothing to me about seeing Lakshmi and a daughter.'

Jumapili shook her hand to indicate her ignorance.

Catherine read on:

'I'm so sorry. I know how fond you were of each other.

He had a stroke, from which he never recovered. Thankfully, everything was quick and peaceful for him.

'I think you know Mr. Downsted wanted to be buried at Bottlesford Hall. He said that although everything ended in great sadness, his time there with Joyce was the happiest in his life.'

Jumapili waved to Catherine to stop reading. She was trying to compute the idea of Downsted having a daughter with Lakshmi and yet wanting to be buried at Bottlesford Hall rather than with Joyce's ashes in his precious England. Then she nodded to Catherine, urging her to continue.

This is not something I can do. My life is here in India. I cannot return to Kenya as my time there is not one I look back on with pleasure.

'Frigging right!' interjected Jumapili.

If I ship Mr. Downsted's body to Nairobi airport, will you please arrange his burial? I think it's the least you can do for a man who has been so demonstrably kind over the years and given you so much.

I look forward to hearing from you.

Yours.

Lakshmi McGeown

'What does she say about their daughter? He never said anything to me about a daughter. Read the whole letter again,' commanded Jumapili ungraciously.

Catherine did as she asked.

'Why is she referring to him as Mr. Downsted and not Colin? She knew I called him Colin,' protested Jumapili. 'Also, there's no mention of Rishi. There's no mention of him in the letter, is there?' Her face reflected the grip of pain in her breasts and in her stomach on the mention of Rishi's name.

Catherine shook her head gently.

'Why did she have to play the duty card?' asked Jumapili. 'She knew that I would go to the ends of the earth for him if he'd asked.'

'You've got another letter here. Much bigger, more official looking. 'Would you like me to open it'?'

Jumapili pursed her lips and shook her head vigorously before falling into despair. From then on, she did nothing. She didn't wash or eat and only sipped at the cups of tea Catherine brought her. She moved between her settee and her bed and back again, never going outside into her garden. She answered the phone, telling every caller she couldn't talk before abruptly putting the receiver down.

Eventually, she jerked the phone wires away from the junction box in the hall. There was no radio, no television, no sound, nothing.

Jumapili was in as deep a depression as any human has ever been in. Nothing could control her grief, her anger, her feeling of despair. Colin Downsted meant everything to her. She loved him, genuinely loved him, and wished, nay prayed, that it was her who was dead and not him. In a never-ending mind-loop she was convincing herself that there was no point in going on, telling herself time and time again that she would be better off dead.

'I think we should read the other letters,' announced Catherine after Jumapili came downstairs following a night's disturbed sleep. It was three days after Lakshmi's letter had been read. Jumapili was in an even greater dishevelled state having been up half the night, wandering around aimlessly in a fog of self-pity.

'But first you need to shower, wash your hair, and clean your teeth,' ordered Catherine.

'You don't understand. You don't understand,' wailed Jumapili.

'I understand perfectly well that you're beginning to smell, and a shower will make you feel a darn sight better,' retorted Catherine before forcibly leading Jumapili upstairs and into her bathroom. There she coaxed her into the shower and began placing shampoo and then soap in Jumapili's limp unresponsive hand. After a half-hearted attempt at washing, she switched off the water before wrapping Jumapili's body in a towel as though she were attending a small child.

'I've laid out your clothes on the bed,' said Catherine. 'The blue dress. The one with the white polka dots. You look nice in that, as one of the things we're doing today is going for a walk.'

Jumapili said nothing. It was as though she did not hear. For her own self-protection her brain had disengaged. She was exhausted from a lack of sleep.

'I'm putting the coffee on and making toast. We'll have breakfast on the patio. The morning sun will be good for us,' shouted Catherine as she descended the stairs.

It took Jumapili a long time to come down and join Catherine. She had dressed as Catherine had suggested but made no attempt to brush her long-braided hair, leaving it damp and in knots, and nothing was on her feet.

Once Jumapili was seated on the patio and had started to bathe her face in the warmth of the morning sun, Catherine made the coffee and toast she had promised, except she laced Jumapili's coffee mug with two large measures of Fernet Branca. She was hopeful that its bitterness, together with that of the coffee, would hide the alcohol content. Catherine was certain that Jumapili would not start to recover without a long sleep, and traditionally alcohol made Jumapili sleepy.

'I think we should tackle the outstanding post,' said Catherine. 'There's the large letter with a London postmark we haven't opened and there's masses of other mail, mostly bills I imagine.'

Jumapili said nothing.

'The big letter's from Colin's solicitors,' shouted Catherine as she returned to the patio, having gathered the post and found her glasses. 'I'll read it.' She sat down.

'Is it not in braille?'

'No.'

'They'll know I'm blind. Don't you think its bad manners, discourteous of them not to write to me in braille?'

'Catherine agreed and started to read out loud the letter in front of her.

Dear Miss Mwangi.

It is my sad duty to inform you of the death of Mr. Colin Downsted in India on 14th June 1982. I extend my deepest condolences.

'Do you know that's the day the Falklands War ended,' said Catherine lifting her head up from the letter. I'll never forget that date. The unbelievable relief knowing my brother would be safe. It was fantastic. Did I tell you his boat's due back around 10th July, maybe the 11th?'

Jumapili said nothing but nodded her appreciation. Catherine returned to reading the letter.

Mr. Downsted's death certificate records an Ischemic stroke as his cause of death.

I have been appointed an executor under Mr. Downsted's Will to manage the winding up of his estate. You are a named beneficiary under his Will and for this reason I enclose a copy.

Mr. Downsted has bequeathed to you his home in Leamington Spa, where I understand you currently live, and the property known as Bottlesford Hall in Nairobi, Kenya, together with all their contents and possessions.

'Oh Jumi, that's good. That's marvellous. It means you can stay here,' interrupted Catherine.

Jumapili gave no indication she understood what she was being told. Catherine continued.

'I understand Bottlesford Hall is known to you, and is presently unoccupied having been badly damaged in a fire. I am told that the building has been completely refurbished by the insurance company and that the proceeds from the loss-of-profits insurance claim arising from the subsequent closure of the school, are still sitting in a separate bank account which is bequeathed to you too. It is Mr. Downsted's hope, but without obligation, that you use this money to return Bottlesford Hall to its former glory'.

My understanding is that the Leamington Spa and Bottlesford Hall properties were the inheritance of Mrs. Joyce Downsted from her late father. I am asked to inform you that it was her wish, as it was Mr Downsted's, that these properties be bequeathed to you.'

'I bet this lawyer is another one who thinks I was fucking him for his money!' said Jumapili starkly.

'Jumi!' protested Catherine. 'Don't say that, and don't use that word.'

'Well, it's true. Isn't it? I've heard it said.'

'Who said?'

'The police in Nairobi for a starter. When we were hiding at Lakshmi's house before the trial. They thought he was shagging me, but he wasn't; he was fucking that bitch, wasn't he. Then there were those at the RCM who called Colin my "sugar daddy" with all the inferences that meant.'

'But it wasn't true ... was it?'

'Catherine please – no! Not once, not never.'

Catherine returned to reading the letter.

Mr. Downsted has also bequeathed to you his manuscript on the History of Kenya and the Mau Mau War. When or whether it is published he leaves to your sole discretion.

The residue of Mr. Downsted's estate, which after inheritance tax is likely to be substantial, is to be divided as follows:

a. *45% to Miss Chandni Downsted to be held in trust until she reaches the age of 21.*
b. *25% to Mrs Lakshmi McGeown to be held in a lifetime trust after which the residue of the trust funds are to be passed to Miss Chandni Downsted absolutely, but provided only that she has reached the age of 21.*
c. *30% to you absolutely.*

'It looks as though you're getting some cash too, Jumi,' commented Catherine.

'Is that her name? Is Chandni his daughter's name?'

Catherine scanned the letter and reread the appropriate section. 'Yes, Chandni, it's a nice name don't you think.' She read on:

It is Mr. Downsted's wish that he be buried at Bottlesford Hall. Mrs. McGeown has agreed to organise the expatriation of Mr. Downsted's body to Nairobi and she has suggested to me that you make the arrangements for his interment. This does seem sensible since Bottlesford Hall is now yours. Naturally, Mr Downsted's estate will pay for all his transportation and burial costs.

'How do you feel about going back?' asked Catherine.

'I miss Absko. I would like to see Absko,' replied Jumapili lamely.

'Do you know where he is?'

'No.'

'The lawyer's asked you to phone him because he wants to make arrangements for a surveyor to visit,' said Catherine, skim-reading to the end of the letter. Apparently, he needs to have the place valued for probate purposes, whatever that is, and, oh, he wants to talk about getting Colin's body from India to Kenya.'

Jumapili stretched and then started to stroke her eyes with the fleshy Metacarpals of her hands. It was the first sign that she was coming out from her semi-zombie state.

'Do you want me to read Colin's Will?' asked Catherine.

Jumapili nodded. Catherine took a deep breath as she prepared for an ordeal of legalese.

'Read that again,' demanded Jumapili, suddenly alert. Catherine was just a couple of pages into reading Mr Downsted's Will.

'Which bit?' asked Catherine.

'The bit which give Chandni's date of birth. You notice, she has his surname?'

Catherine nodded before scanning the Will and announcing: '10th March 1973. It says here Miss Chandni Downsted's date of birth is 10th March 1973.'

'That's two months before Kaweira was born – you know what that means?' said Jumapili excitedly. 'It means she was pregnant in October 1972, ... when she threw me out!'

'Who?' asked Catherine now confused.

'Mrs. bloody Lakshmi McGeown.'

'And Lakshmi's son is Kaweira's father, isn't he?' said Catherine making sure she fully understood.

Jumapili didn't answer.

'There's no mention of Rishi in the lawyer's letter is there?' she asked, before adding, 'and there's no mention of him in the Will either, is there?'

Catherine scanned the Will, carefully turning each of the pages several times before announcing. 'He's not there. There's no mention of him.'

'So, he inherits nothing.'

'Yes, I think so.'

'Good, thank God for that! Colin was furious about Rishi leaving me like that.'

'Why did he abandon you?' asked Catherine.

'His bitch mother made him.'

'Why? Did Colin know that?'

'She told me to my face and Colin heard. She said that under no circumstances was her son, of Scottish heritage, going to have anything to do with a blind, Black Kikuyu girl from Kibera. She was so proud her son had a Scottish father. Do you know what she told me: she said, "we don't breed with the runt of the litter". Those were her exact words – "runt of the litter." '

'What a nasty woman. What a horrible thing to say.'

'I think about it often. What she said. I think it's the most racially prejudiced moment I've ever suffered. I've been discriminated against for my disability many times. Countless times, but never because I'm Black, never. I'll be kind and think she was worried that I might have blind children, that my sight problem's genetic, but deep down I know it wasn't that; she considered herself better than me because she was Brown and I was Black.'

'But you can't see colour Jumi. You've made that point to me many, many times.'

'I know I can't, but I can hear the different accents and the different way people speak to those who speak differently. If only people listened more, they would all be so much wiser.'

There was a long pause as Jumapili thought about Rishi and her daughter. Meanwhile, Catherine thought about what Lakshmi McGeown had said. Was Jumapili's problem genetic? she wondered. Was Jumapili's adopted daughter blind?

'The hypocrite. The bloody hypocrite. I've just realised!' shouted Jumapili. 'She didn't take Rishi to India to stop me from seeing him and to stop him from seeing his daughter; she ran away from the shame of having Colin's child. Divorced, pregnant, no husband. She'd have been cut out from all her English friends. She was always on the edge, but she'd have been completely expelled.'

'Are you saying she went to India to hide the fact that she was pregnant, not to get Rishi away from you? I thought you said he would have been arrested for rape and having sex with a minor?'

'It was for all those reasons! Do you know what else she called me. I've just remembered it. She called me a "Kikuyu whore" and yet she was the whoring one. She was at it all the time. I heard them! It was almost as though she set out to trap him.'

'When did Colin learn about Chandni?' asked Catherine.

Jumapili shook her head. 'I don't know.'

'Do you know the interesting thing about this Will?' asked Catherine.

Jumapili shook her head again.

'It's an English Will all right, and it's signed by Colin, but the interesting bit is that it's been validated in front of an Indian notary public. Colin signed his Will when he was away in India.' Catherine looked at the date. 'He signed it just one, no, two months before he died.'

Jumapili and Catherine faced each other and said nothing but their thoughts were identical.

Chapter 87

JUMAPILI RAN HER hand anxiously over the front door of Bottlesford Hall looking for the keyhole. She already had the key ready to hand, so it was just a matter of marrying one with the other. As soon as the door opened and she was through, she stood still and clicked her tongue. The map she had once created in her mind was rapidly coming back to her. She walked forward slowly tapping with her cane until she found the first step of the staircase. There she reached out for the banister.

'Do you know where the light switches are?' asked Catherine who had agreed to accompany Jumapili to Bottlesford Hall because to have made the journey on her own would have been too challenging. 'I can't remember. In fact, I don't think I ever knew where they were.'

Jumapili did not answer. She had climbed the stairs and had stopped at the fifth step just as she had planned. That was where Joyce had been hacked to death and she needed to know if she would feel the same chill and tingle in her spine she had felt the last time she was in the house.

'Can you sense it, Catherine? Can you sense someone being here?' she asked but Catherine did not answer. She was calling Jumapili to come to her.

'Look, it's Mrs. Downsted's piano! I thought it had been destroyed in the fire.'

'No, that's not possible,' said Jumapili breathlessly as she tapped and clicked her way towards the west front drawing room. At the door she stopped and clicked some more. The sound before her was hollower than she had remembered as all the furniture was missing. However, the echo from the piano was as consistent as any she could recognise.

Jumapili moved to the piano, pulled aside the cover and ran her hands over its polished top. She felt her way around it, caressing its curves and tapping her cane until she found the piano stool and was able to sit down. Her hands lifted the lid to the keys, and she ran her fingers along its length.

'It's the same one,' she announced. 'It's definitely the same one.'

'It can't be. I saw the flames – I saw the flames,' repeated Catherine in an effort to convince herself that it couldn't have survived.

'Here, this key sticks,' said Jumapili, pressing the last key of c, 'and this one, you can feel a nick in it. It was made by Colin when he used a knife to get some Sellotape off.'

But Catherine was no longer interested. She was opening the windows and shutters, allowing the light to pour into the room while Jumapili started to rattle through her repertoire of scales and songs. It felt to Jumapili as though Downsted was still there, overseeing her as he used to do, ready to pounce if she made a mistake.

For over an hour the two of them toured their old school, opening windows, shutters and doors. Apart from the hall, the east and west front-rooms, the two conservatories attached to them, and the kitchen below, the building was a museum to the night of the raid. Catherine painstakingly described every room to Jumapili. She told how the library had the morning newspapers of the day of the raid still lying on the table. In Joyce and Colin's study there was evidence of heavy looting, and except for the books and papers Downsted had ordered to be collected and then taken to England, it had remained virtually the same. The girl's textbooks remained piled up, some marked, others waiting to be marked.

Colin and Joyce's bedroom was at the back of the house, on the other side from where the fire had started. It too had evidence of mindless looting, with drawers and wardrobes thrown open and things scattered around the floor. Joyce's clothes were still lying on the bed where she had left them when she responded to the fire alarm set off by Jumapili. However, it was when Catherine described how the top was off Joyce's make-up-cleaning cream, with the dirty used cleansing pads still lying around, that the tears came because the scene she described to Jumapili was so evocative that it would be a long-held memory by both.

'I don't get it,' said Catherine when they were back in the hall. 'How come none of this has been stolen? All these years and not a thing's been touched. All the workmen and other people visiting, and nothings gone.'

'Geteye and Gatimu will have stopped that.'

'What – the gardeners?' asked Catherine.

'Yes, you can guarantee it. Their honesty ethic is so strong that they wouldn't allow one of their sheep to eat a blade of grass not belonging to them, unless they had permission. It will be them, and Joyce's ghost, that's protected this place.'

'Joyce's ghost?'

'Yes, she still here. I know she is. I can sense her. She's not at rest, not yet.'

'Jumi, you're being silly,' protested Catherine as she moved through the front door into the sun, not wanting to be in the house a moment longer.

'You wait. When we bury Colin here in the grounds, then she'll be ready to rest,' continued Jumapili as she followed Catherine through the door. 'I'm sure of it.'

'Jumi, you're freaking me out,' said Catherine. 'In any case, I thought Joyce was buried in Leamington.'

'No, she was cremated here in Nairobi. Her ashes were spread near her fiancé's memorial stone in Nuneaton.'

'Her fiancé?'

The two were now sitting on the lawn, laying back enjoying the sunshine just as they had when they had been at school there.

'Yes, Colin was very upset when he discovered she'd been engaged before. When he was clearing out the house in Leamington, he found letters from her fiancé which she'd left behind in a chest in the loft. He left them out and the cleaner saw them. She wouldn't read them to me word for word as she said they were too fruity, but then she told me I had to understand that things happened then because it was war time.'

'What, Mrs. Downsted had an affair before she married Mr. Downsted? Is that what you were told?'

'That's what the letters suggested.'

'We should see if we can find them when we get back,' said Catherine. 'What happened to him?'

'Her fiancé? He was killed in a bombing raid on Nuneaton. He has no grave, just a memorial stone which is to all those that died.'

'Just think, Jumi: if that bomb hadn't fallen where it did, how different our lives would have been. We wouldn't be here right now, would we?'

Chapter 88

'NOW YOU'VE SEEN it, what are you going to do with it?' asked Catherine.

She and Jumapili had sat down to dinner in the restaurant in the Norfolk Hotel, Nairobi where they were staying. They had ordered and were enjoying their second glass of wine.

Most of their earlier conversation had been on the arrangements for Downsted's funeral, making sure that his friends and all Old Bottlesfordians were aware of the time and date.

'What am I going to do with Bottlesford Hall?' asked Jumapili, making sure she was on the right subject.

Through a sip of wine Catherine grunted her agreement.

'You know I went to a special school for the blind in Coventry, don't you? I hated it. It wasn't my thing at all. They tried to cater for so many different types of children and their needs, that in the end they catered for none of us properly. There were three others there, two girls and a boy who were blind, but I was the only one who couldn't see anything at all. I think the others were described as visually impaired. The boy was mentally handicapped as well, but the two girls, they were as capable as me. Except, I found my way around the school much better than either of them. Colin would drop me off in the morning and I would find my own way around, into the classroom, dining rooms, toilets, everything, whereas they needed help. Once I'd been introduced to the route, to the area, I could manage quite well. The difference between us was that I clicked and tapped everywhere I went, and this told me almost everything I needed to know. They didn't have that skill. They couldn't do it. One day we put a blindfold on them, and they practised clicking and listening and still they couldn't do it. I have this theory that partially sighted people's brains are struggling so hard to see and create an image whereas my brain doesn't have that struggle. It has no image to try and process and therefore that part of the brain normally used for sight is available for me to use in another way.'

'Does anyone else do what you do? Have your skill?'

'There's a man in America who seems to navigate his way around like me. As a young boy he would cycle his bike down the street clicking away, missing cars. I've heard of another one in East Germany and I'm sure there are more. The one in America has become quite famous. He's teaching other blind people, and it's him which has given me an idea for Bottlesford Hall.'

Just as Jumapili was about to share her idea, they were disturbed as their main courses were served.

'Would you please describe to me what is on my plate and where?' said Jumapili to the waiter, who immediately described the dish on the menu.

'Thank you,' said Jumapili patiently, 'but you've described *what's* there, not where. Could you describe where on the plate each item is, please?'

The waiter, flustered, tried again but his second attempt was little better.

'Don't worry,' said Jumapili sympathetically as her hands worked their way around the edge of her plate. 'I'll use the lucky dip method.'

'You were saying?' prompted Catherine after she had described to Jumapili what was on her plate using the clock method.

'I'd like to open a boarding school for the blind, and I mean those who are really blind. I want it to have the same attitude Colin and Joyce had. They refused to accept second best from any of us, and I want to do the same thing.'

'Yeh, and because of it we somehow rose to the occasion,' acknowledged Catherine.

'Do you remember how, on my very first day on the games field, Colin yelled at me?'

'Oh God, yes. He was livid. And poor Mrs. Valentine, he really had a go at her.'

'Well, if it hadn't been for him, I'd have never learnt to run and I think I was best at running,' said Jumapili modestly. 'All the time

I was there no one could beat me in the straight-line race, but I was hopeless if I had to turn a corner. Do you know a blind person walking across a field, like our games field, will not be able to follow a true line unless the path has already been made, or they can hear a directional noise, whereas someone with echolocation skills like me can do pretty well by themselves.'

'So, you want to turn Bottlesford Hall into a blind boarding school teaching echolocation, is that it?'

'Not just echolocation but all the subjects, just like Joyce and Colin did, but with perhaps a greater concentration on music than sport. And we'll teach everything for daily living. Did you know Joyce taught me to polish my own shoes?'

'No, why?'

' 'cause they were dirty and she said it was no one's job but mine to make sure they were clean. Do you not remember her saying it was the height of bad manners not to be clean and tidy.'

'Oh God, yes,' agreed Catherine, 'Do you know, I think I learnt more from my time at Bottlesford Hall than any time since.'

'Did you know I got chemistry 'O' level?'

'No, how did you do that? How did you do the practical?'

'I didn't. Colin argued with the exam board that it was a cerebral subject, and I shouldn't have to write up the results of what I saw from an experiment, but just the chemical formulae. They agreed I could write in braille and because of that I got some extra time too. When they gave me a 'B' grade he was furious. I think he saw it as a slight on his teaching, so he got it re-marked, and I ended up with an 'A'.'

'It wasn't as though we were being taught at Bottlesford, was it? It was more like we were being crammed with knowledge,' commented Catherine.

'Yes, and that's what I want for my school. I can teach echolocation. I'm sure I can. But the thing that makes me want to have a go is that ...' Jumapili paused, 'Joyce and Colin have left me the perfect building.'

'Because its already configured as a boarding school?'

'No, yes that too,' said Jumapili correcting herself, 'but the rooms, the hall, the stairs. They're all perfect. You couldn't have a better training place because they each speak to you. Each is different. Each one tells you everything you need to know if only you'll listen, and it seems to me that blind people, like me, need to be trained to listen if they can't already.'

'Whew, it's a big project. Where are you going to get your pupils from?'

'I don't know.'

'Who's going to pay for it?'

'I don't know.'

'Are you charging fees?'

'I don't know.'

'Where are your teachers coming from?'

'I don't know.'

'You don't know much, do you?' said Catherine.

'What I do know is that I'll need someone else who knew Bottlesford Hall from Joyce and Colin's time. They'll understand the culture. They'll know exactly what I'm trying to achieve, 'cause what I want is what they made, plus echolocation and independent living on top.'

'For Christ's sake, Jumi, you're asking one hell of a lot, aren't you?' said Catherine, well aware that Jumapili's last remarks were an attempt to conscript her into her plan.

'Yes, but it will be worth it, won't it?'

'Maybe, but what are you going to do about your singing and performing career? It's just starting to take off.'

'I'll do both. I'll ... we'll have to do both. The singing and the music will help pay for the school, until it gets going.'

'Jesus, Jumi, let me think about this,' said Catherine. 'There are crazy ideas and there's this one. It needs a lot of thinking about.'

'I've never thought about anything like this, ever,' said Jumapili. 'I've only ever gone with life's flow. I'm sure this is the way my life must now go. Joyce and Colin wouldn't have given me the Hall unless they expected me to use it.'

Chapter 89

DOWNSTED'S FUNERAL SERVICE was in the same small church as Joyce's had been but there were far fewer people. Most of Downsted's coffee-shop friends, former neighbours and teachers attended but only a handful of former pupils. Most, being descendants of the original settlers, were now spread far and wide. Individually they had come to the same conclusion: there was no future for them in Kenya. It could no longer be their home.

Jumapili spent a long time selecting the music which she would play and sing herself. There was so much Downsted had liked she found it difficult to choose, except for the song which would accompany his body as it left the church. With hi-hat cymbals tapping under her foot, she played Bert Kaempfert's *Swingin' Safari*. It was a song Joyce and Downsted would dance to most often when the school was closed and the three of them were on their own. It was a beat which raised the feet of everyone as they left the church.

Downsted's two brothers shared the eulogy, giving an insight into Downsted's time in England before the war: his service in military intelligence and then afterwards working in the Colonial Office in Nairobi. Given how long they had sat together, Downsted's café friends found it strange how little they knew of him before he arrived at Bottlesford Hall.

Downsted was buried in a grave dug by Geteye and Gatimu in the precise spot specified in his Will. He didn't want a headstone. Instead, he asked that a meru oak tree, a species native to Kenya, be planted where a headstone might have gone.

The wake was held in a marquee erected on the lawn by the side of the swimming pool. It was a lovely balmy afternoon with no one wanting to leave. They were enjoying the comfort of old friends.

'I haven't heard Lakshmi or Rishi's voice,' said Jumapili.

'They're not here. Are you surprised?' answered Catherine.

'No, I suppose not. She was so horrible to him. I think Colin would have climbed out of his coffin and shooed her away if she'd turned up.'

Catherine giggled. 'Except he spent the last few months of his life with her,' she added.

'No, I don't believe that. He went to meet his daughter, not her. I'm sure of it,' said Jumapili just before she left to talk to Downsted's brothers.

They spoke for a long time and as they did so, it seemed to her as though they were adopting her into their family too. She told them of the book Downsted had written on the history of the British in Kenya and the Mau Mau wars. It was finished, she said, while acknowledging that, perhaps, it wasn't as finished as Downsted might have liked because he had never got round to solving the legal problems set by its publisher. The brothers asked to see the manuscript because they didn't want to see their brother's work wasted and Jumapili promised to send it to them. What they didn't expect was all Downsted's notes and research materials which she sent too. It seemed to her that they belonged together.

It was not until sundown that people finally began to drift away.

'She's gone. She's at rest,' said Jumapili to Catherine as they watched the last guest car drive through the gates before they moved to sit on the lawn in front of the house, by the side of its drive.

Instinctively Catherine knew what Jumapili was talking about.

'What, you've been inside and checked?'

'Yes, she's not there anymore.

'Her spirit?' asked Catherine. 'You'll have me believing in voodoo next.'

'Yes, her spirit. Ahhh, your lot are too long from the land. Your people haven't touched the land with the soles of their feet for generations. You don't have a clue that trees talk to each other, but they do, and this sensing of the dead until they are at rest is all part of a greater understanding.'

'Look Jumi, let's be serious,' said Catherine. 'You asked me a couple of days ago whether I'd be interested in helping you establish Bottlesford as a specialist school for the blind, didn't you.'

Jumapili turned her head towards Catherine.

'And, and?' she asked anxiously.

'The answer's yes, but there are some conditions and I'm not sure you'll like them. I talked to those who've just been here about the idea. They think to make it just a school for the blind would be a mistake. They don't think there'll be enough pupils who will be able to pay the fees to make it financially viable, certainly not in Kenya or Africa. Also, they think it'll be divisive. The whole point of you being in the school was that you had to do everything we did. There were two curricula, but otherwise everything else was the same. Look at how Downsted yelled at you when you didn't run properly. And do you remember how he expected you to contribute fully to his scavenger hunts? He wasn't prepared to accept your blindness as an excuse. He was insistent that you behave as everyone else. I think we must do the same. The school must take both blind and fully sighted children.'

Jumapili raised her hand as an indication she'd like Catherine to stop talking so she could think.

'I agree,' she said after a little while. 'It's a good idea, and the other conditions are..?'

'You're not going to like this one, but you're going to have to sell the house in Leamington and move to London,' said Catherine.

'No! Why?' protested Jumapili.

' 'cause you're going to have to become "celebrity blind" and you can't do that from Leamington.'

'What the hell is "celebrity blind"?'

'What are you really good at?' asked Catherine. 'Singing,' she said, answering her own question. 'But there are hundreds, thousands of good singers in the world so you need something which sets you apart, which makes you unique, and you already have it – you're blind.'

'But what's that got to do with Bottlesford Hall and moving to London?'

'Number one – if you become famous; we can make Bottlesford Hall Blind School famous too. That way we find the blind pupils the school needs. Secondly, a blind school is never going to make money. The pupil-teacher ratio will bankrupt it.'

'But that's why I thought we were taking sighted kids as well.'.

'Yes, it'll help,' responded Catherine, 'but if you become a blind celebrity then you'll get paid for TV shows, concerts, radios, masses of things, and that will help subsidise the school – and you forget you're an interviewer's dream because you've got a great back story.'

'Back story? What's that?'

'Kibera slums, orphan, street musician, the Genge la Chupa trial, the adoption ... they all give journalists and interviewers a reason to talk about you.'

'Yes, I agree,' interrupted Jumapili again, her heart jumping out of her mouth as she spoke, but it was not for the reasons Catherine gave – if she was famous, if she was celebrity blind then her daughter Kaweira, would be able to find her more easily.

'Look, Jumi, I'm serious,' said Catherine. 'At the moment, you've got a bit-part career as a session musician, occasionally getting some orchestral work. It's a living but it's not enough. You're going to have to come out from the back and into the front.'

'Why London?' asked Jumapili.

'Because London's the centre of the world music industry. From there you can travel the globe. You can't go anywhere from Leamington without adding two days to your trip.'

'Do you think this is what Colin and Joyce would want?' Jumapili asked.

'Fucking certain of it,' answered Catherine, who very rarely swore. 'They gave you the means to own a home. No one said it had to be in Leamington. Look at Joyce, she moved away, didn't she?'

'D'you know, I've just realised why Colin wanted to be buried here. It was his way of making me visit the Hall again, of telling me to bring it alive. I'm sure of it.'

There was a long pause as they both thought about what had been said.

'Come on Catherine,' said Jumapili jumping up. 'I'm getting chilly. Let's go inside, get our things, lock up and go.'

'You're sure she's gone, aren't you?'

'Yes, she's gone, said Jumapili wearily. 'Go and stand on the fifth step of the stairs, close your eyes, and see what you can sense. There'll be nothing, I assure you.'

'And my conditions, do you agree?'
'I agree. I emphatically agree!'

Chapter 90

THERE WAS A reason Joyce had made Catherine Delfont, Jumapili's first Bottlesford Hall roommate. At a young age, Catherine had proved herself to be an organisational express train. Once set on rails, with her destination flagged, she was unstoppable. The mission set by Jumapili became Catherine's too. With a project book and numerous job lists, she set to work guiding, leading, cajoling Jumapili.

Stage one was to get Jumapili's house in Leamington Spa sold. In its place Jumapili purchased a three-bedroom duplex apartment occupying the basement, ground floor and first floor in a refurbished Georgian townhouse in central London, with access to its own private garden in the square, around which all the houses had been built.

There was a problem of downsizing from a large Victorian house as much of the furniture inherited by Jumapili was not suitable for a more modern apartment. However, both Jumapili and Catherine were ruthless in their clear-out, not least because Jumapili found a minimalist life much simpler to manage. However, Jumapili's real joy came when her Bentley piano, gifted by Downsted, was moved into the basement, and she had her very own music room to practice in.

Once they were fully settled in their London flat, Jumapili and Catherine opened up Bottlesford Hall and moved in. They were equally as ruthless in clearing the rooms occupied by Joyce and Downsted. Almost everything personal was sold to a clearing firm with Jumapili and Catherine keeping only a few selected items.

Catherine was insistent that the dreaded 'beam' be burnt. Jumapili, who had never felt its effects, thought it part of Bottlesford Hall's culture, so they compromised and agreed it would be bolted to a wall in the entrance hall so firmly that there was no risk it could ever be used again.

As they were touring their old bedrooms and dormitory, it dawned on them that there would be one major difference between Joyce and Downsted's time running Bottlesford Hall and their own. Back then, it had been an all-girls' school. If they were to attract blind children, Downsted Hall would have to be co-educational. It would mean a reconfiguration of bedrooms, toilets and shower blocks throughout the whole school.

Using the hall's insurance money, which Downsted had left Jumapili, the school was reconfigured to make it both co-educational and more blind-friendly. They had the place painted inside and out, but nothing they did removed the stain of the widely broadcast kidnap attempt as far as the public were concerned.

Despite both Jumapili and Catherine having been in the school at the time of the raid and feeling it was safe enough to return, this was not enough to instill confidence in parents to enroll their children. The sad fact was that, while kidnapping was, in the main, limited to those Americans and Europeans who were foolish enough to wander into the slum areas, large, isolated houses had become an ever more popular target for violent robbery.

Jumapili hired a security company, and their recommendations were followed almost to the letter. Another perimeter fence was installed, this time with razor wire. Perimeter alarms and video cameras, both on the fences and on the outside of the buildings, were installed. Double gates and ram bollards were put at the entrance to the drive. Bars were put around all ground-floor windows, and steel gates were installed on the inside of every exit door and around every door of the main hall, so that in an emergency, they could rapidly lock themselves in. The only advice from the security consultants they did not accept, because it was too expensive, was to install a sprinkler system to put out any fire that might be deliberately started in an attack. Instead, they hired security guards to patrol the grounds 24/7 on the basis that this was a more obvious deterrent.

In an attempt to recruit pupils, they advertised Bottlesford Hall's reopening in the major Kenyan newspapers. They supported this advertising with a professional public-relations campaign because there remained enormous public interest in the singing blind girl who had identified the Genge la Chupa. However, despite good national coverage, and the fact that Jumapili and Catherine had a security system which was much better than most people had at home, not one parent enquired about sending their child to the school.

Jumapili's degree in music, Catherine's MBA and her degree in anthropology, and their complete lack of any teaching qualification or experience, were other detractors to pupil recruitment. They knew they had to recruit experienced teachers, but they had a chicken-and-egg problem because no teacher was prepared to work for a school with no pupils, and no parent was prepared to enroll their child into a school with no teachers.

The sad fact was that rebuilding Bottlesford Hall as a school with the culture and ethos instilled into Jumapili and Catherine by Joyce and Downsted was close to failure because they had spent every penny Jumapili had been given, and they were fast running out of money.

The bitter reality was that the name 'Bottlesford Hall' had been irrevocably tainted. It was with a mixture of pleasure and sadness that Jumapili decided that Bottlesford Hall should be renamed 'Downsted Hall'. The two stones in the gate pillars on either side of the drive, with the name 'Bottlesford' carved into them, were removed. The reverse of each stone was cleaned up, the name 'Downsted' carved into them, and they were put back. As Jumapili ran her hands across the stone carving she knew immediately what she wanted as the logo for her school: it was the initials of D and H in braille.[42]

It was sheer pragmatism, or more precisely a lack of any alternative, which resulted in Jumapili and Catherine building their school in the same manner as Joyce had originally built hers. They found they had to start, just as she had done, as a tutorial school. It was only when a parent was confident in the quality of the tutorials and discipline at Downsted Hall would they be comfortable committing their child's full-time education to the school.

Catherine had set herself a timetable of twelve months to have Jumapili moved to London and Bottlesford Hall re-opened. It took

42 ⠙ ⠓

eighteen months before their first tutorial pupil walked through the door of the newly named 'Downsted Hall'.

Jumapili might have given up her ambition long before the first pupil arrived, except for one thing. On her first day back at Bottlesford Hall she had asked Geteye and Gatimu to remove their sheep from the games field and to roll and mow its lawn. Very early in the morning, two weeks later, she tapped and clicked her way to the sports field. Once there, she headed to a point about five yards from the boundary. She kicked off her shoes and set off the klaxon on her personal alarm. Then, she deliberately walked away tapping her cane as she went. After she had strode out six-hundred long paces, she turned, folded up her cane and listened for the sound. Then, like a greyhound out of a trap, she sprang off, running as fast as she could. As she reached the alarm she stopped and bent over. Her heart was thumping and her chest heaving. She felt ecstatic but knew she had not been fast enough. She knew she could do it faster, so she undid her cane and tapped her way back down the field to do it all over again, and then again.

After the third run, Jumapili switched off the alarm and simply started to jump and dance for joy. The freedom she felt was intoxicating. Nowhere had she ever felt like this. Through jumping and dancing she completely lost her bearings, only recovering her shoes by crawling around, sweeping her cane in a huge semi-circle until she felt them. Then she, as she always did: immediately learnt from her mistake. The next day, and every day she was at Bottlesford Hall after that, she came with a tape recorder loaded with dance music. It was thus towards the sound of music she would run and then dance afterwards, always lining up the edge of the tape machine in the direction she knew she had to return if she was to get back to the Hall.

Chapter 91

IMMEDIATELY DOWNSTED HALL had its first pupil, albeit only part-time, Catherine moved to stage three of their agreed plan – to make Jumapili a blind celebrity.

Catherine was very conscious that she could be accused of cynically exploiting Jumapili's disability, but she passionately believed that Jumapili's echolocation skills were unique and the lives of those who were totally blind could be fundamentally improved, if they could be found young enough and taught to do what Jumapili did instinctively.

The fact that Jumapili was already a minor celebrity in Kenya was of no benefit in busy bustling London where musical talent was picked, devoured, and discarded as fast as an apple can be turned into an apple core.

It was Catherine's decision to use a TV-talent competition to get Jumapili's career launched. Jumapili auditioned and won a slot on the last series of *Reach for the Stars*. Although she performed well, she didn't win – it was clear that her more classical genre of song didn't catch the mood of the day. She was unfavourably compared to Peters and Lee, a successful British folk and pop duo of the previous decade, one of whom was blind. The criticism hurt her and dented her confidence.

Catherine hired a small recording studio in Kensington, not far from Jumapili's former stamping ground of the Royal College of Music. With the support of an outstanding technician, Jumapili recorded a demonstration tape of half a dozen songs, all made famous by other artists. Those who heard her tape acknowledged that her singing was divine, and the backing track on which she played all the instruments was technically perfect. However, her voice was thought to be insufficiently original to make her star material. Catherine couldn't believe this. Like Joyce and Downsted before her, she was certain that Jumapili had one of the purest, pitch-perfect voices ever heard, which made it unquestionably unique.

Not giving up hope, Jumapili and Catherine toured the record companies talking to their A&R reps and talent scouts, the main musicians, their band managers, and show impresarios. The area of Soho and between Regent's Street and Charing Cross Road was the centre of the UK's burgeoning pop industry with original talent pouring through every doorway. Jumapili and Catherine got to know the area well, but no one was prepared to place her under contract because she lacked her own original music.

The usual practice of a performer buying an original music score from a song writer was not available to Jumapili because she could not read musical notation in any form other than braille. If she heard a song played, she could quickly learn to repeat it, but the alternative of writing her own music was not something she had the confidence to do.

Jumapili's best offer came from a booking agency who offered her *ad hoc* gigs on the tour circuit of pubs, clubs, universities, and colleges which she accepted to earn money. However, this was far from ideal because her performance fees were hardly enough to pay for the travel and living costs for the two of them. To make matters worse, the pianos at most places were not fit to be given that name, so a keyboard and sound and mixing equipment was purchased, which had to be carted around.

There was relief when Jumapili was contracted to do a one-woman show for the summer season at the Butlin's holiday camps in Bognor Regis, Minehead and Skegness, playing one week at each place before moving on, circulating around all three. It was during this time that Jumapili learnt to put power into her singing. She remained true to the purity of each note she sang but, gaining confidence, she started to be more forceful, more passionate in her performances, and her audience responded enthusiastically.

Everywhere they went, they searched the yellow pages, and phoned the local authorities to get the names of the local blind and SEN[43]

[43] Special Educational Needs

schools. They would call in at each one and explain what their school in Kenya was offering but each time their message fell on deaf ears because each school was in competition for pupils so they could remain economically viable.

Jumapili did not know this but Catherine's last punt, because she was ready to give up and admit defeat, was to take Jumapili to perform at the Edinburgh Fringe. Maxing out on her credit card, she hired The Blue Room at George Square Theatre for the first two weeks of the festival.

It was through sheer luck that they teamed up with an established quartet of musicians whom Jumapili had met when working as a fellow session musician at a recording studio. Although younger than Jumapili, they were either former Royal College of Music or Royal Academy of Music graduates like her. This gave them an immediate 'band of brothers' bond. They too had planned on going to Edinburgh but had made no arrangements. It made sense to see if they could work something out together.

Catherine was certain that Jumapili's talent would fill the one-hundred-and-thirty-seat theatre, but as the five musicians practiced together in Jumapili's basement they created a distinctive and exciting sound with a repertoire of orchestral television adverts and hits from films and musicals. What made them unique was their ability to play from memory almost any item of music requested by a member of the audience through slips they completed and were collected as they came in. However, once again they lacked any original music of their own.

From her early days of touring and playing at pubs and clubs and at Butlins, Jumapili had ended her concerts with the song *Somewhere, my love*, the theme tune from the film *Dr Zhivago*. She insisted her concerts in Edinburgh should end with the same song. It was not a popular choice with her colleagues. She was pressurised to agree to an ending that was more upbeat, and yet if they agreed that the last song should be different, Jumapili would ignore them and start singing *Somewhere, my love* on her own until the others joined in. Only once did her fellow musicians have a mini strike forcing her to sing unaccompanied through to the end, but mostly they would join in after a few bars.

It was eventually accepted as Jumapili's closing signature song, but it caused a small fission in the quintette which was to last. Jumapili's view was that if it's your name on the top of the billboard then it comes with certain privileges. Catherine's view was much simpler. Everyone except Jumapili was getting a guaranteed fee for playing in the Blue Room; Jumapili was taking the economic risk, only getting whatever was left after everyone and all expenses had been paid. She thought the motto 'she who pays the piper calls the tune' most apposite.

It was a request slip from one of the co-producers of *The Week Ending*, a BBC satirical current affairs sketch show for Radio 4, that saw Jumapili's quintette being hired as one of the resident bands for the show. The co-producer's request was for the Chaconne in D Minor by Bach. It was acknowledged as a difficult piece to play and definitely not something which a quintette might tackle on the spur of the moment. Further, it was not in keeping with the rest of their programme. In ordinary circumstances it would have been rejected into the 'too difficult' pile. It was Catherine who first recognised it as a test.

'Jumi, can you play Chaconne from Partita No 2 in D Minor,' shouted Catherine across the Green Room at the back of the theatre.

'What, Bach? Which one?' Jumapili shouted back. 'There are six of them.'

'It says here BWV 1004.'

'They're being silly – that's the longest one. I could once, but I'm not sure I can remember it now.' But as Jumapili answered, she remembered how strict Downsted had been in making sure she got it note perfect, stamping his feet or banging his hand hard on something, making her go back a few bars and start again if she made a mistake.

One of the quintette started to play the piece from memory. Another joined, and then another until all of them, excluding their wind-cum-percussion player, were playing in harmony. It was an unprompted jamming session which took on a life of its own.

'Yeh, yeh I can do it, I remember now.' said Jumapili. 'In any case, if we mess it up we can always fumble through.'

'Yeh, but we can't do the whole thing. It's about fifteen minutes long, and I'm sure none of us will remember that. I certainly can't,' argued one of them.

'But we could do a couple of minutes, just as we've done now, to show the bastard,' said another. 'It's a test. I'm telling you, it's a fucking test.'

'Who wants a wager he's from the RCM?' said the violin player.[44] 'It's the kind of bastard thing they'd do.'

'Or the RAM,' added the cello player.[45]

'Look, I'll get Jumi's spare keyboard in here so you can rehearse a bit in the break and if its good, you can do it as the first song of the second half,' said Catherine.

In fact, the actual performance of the Chaconne was better than good. This was because the percussionist had not been prepared to sit at the back and do nothing because she hated Bach; her view was that it was only good for funeral services. She started to create a rhythm that meant that, intuitively and unrehearsed, the Jumapili Quintette rearranged one of the toughest pieces of music that anyone can be asked to play, to make it appealing to pop culture. Any purist would have hated it, but their audience loved it, especially the radio producer from the BBC.

After the show, he gave Jumapili his card and told her that their agent should contact him as soon as possible.

He had a problem to solve and fast. There was a government edict that a certain percentage of music played on BBC radio had to be performed live. They had their big showcase performances such as the proms, but the reality was that the BBC was way off their target, and this was to be Jumapili's blessing. It led to her, and her band, being commissioned as one of the resident bands for many prime-time family shows on all the main radio and TV channels.

---

[44] Royal College of Music

[45] Royal Academy of Music

However, it was Catherine who was Jumapili's secret weapon. She was the fixer. Her efficiency made it very easy for producers to hire Jumapili and her band.

Chapter 92

'HI JUMI,' SHOUTED a voice.

'Absko, is that you?' cried out Jumapili.

'Hi Jumi.' Absko jogged closer to his sister. 'I was told I'd find you here.'

It was almost three years to the day since Downsted Hall had admitted its first pupil. Jumapili and Catherine were leaving the little church outside Tayiania Village where Jumapili had played the piano at its morning communion service.

'Where have you been?' screeched Jumapili. 'Where did you go? I've been worried sick about you.'

Absko walked up to his sister and took her in his arms and held her tight. She was no longer the skinny undernourished little girl he held long ago because her figure was now fully developed.

'Oh God, Jumi,' he said. 'It's so good to see you.'

'Are you okay?' asked Jumapili. Her brother seemed very thin.

'Now, I've got you, found you,' he replied, standing away from his sister, embarrassed by his tears.

'How did you know where to find me?'

'I went to the village shop. I thought they'd know. They read me a very nice letter from Mr. Downsted. It said you'd gone abroad, but they then told me that was wrong, and you'd come back. They said I'd find you, either here or up at the Hall.

'What happened? Where did you go? You suddenly disappeared.' said Jumapili. There was a hint of criticism, resentment, even hurt in her voice.

Absko stopped walking down the Church path. He took Jumapili's hand into his own and ran her fingers over the scars cut deep into his wrists.

'What's that?' asked Jumapili pulling her hand away in shock.

'It's where Charter - you know, the policeman - it's where he hung me up with my hands behind my back to get me to confess to organising the Genge la Chupa kidnapping.'

'Aaghow,' wailed Jumapili 'He did that?'

'Yes.'

'But you didn't do it, did you?'

'Of course not. Why would I! I didn't even know what had happened exactly until I was out of the police station and long gone. All the way through there were just hints. It was awful!'

Jumapili reached out for her brother and finding his arm, she squeezed it gently. It was all she needed to do for him to know she was saying sorry.

'Where did you go?' she asked.

'As far away from here as I could. After what Charter had done to me, I needed to get away. I couldn't risk getting arrested again. I couldn't go through that ...' His voice started to tremble as the memories of those dreadful ten days in captivity returned. 'I guess, I hoped Mr. Downsted would look after you. I'm sorry, really sorry, but I was so bad, so broken up, I couldn't even look after myself.'

'I'm so sorry Absko,' said Jumapili. 'I'm so sorry.'

'I'm sorry about your baby too.'

'How do you know about that?'

It was in Mr. Downsted's letter the shop read to me. It's just, if I'd known, if I'd been here, it might have been different.'

Jumapili said nothing more, instead she clicked and tapped her way down the church path unaided. Her daughter was far too sensitive a subject to be discussed, even with her brother.

'You never bought a matatu?' she asked. 'You know Colin organised the money for you?'

'Not after what Charter did to me. I can't turn the steering wheel. It's too heavy and hurts. However, I might be able to drive one of the new ones as they have power-steering!' Jumapili's heart lifted slightly as in that one phrase she could sense the return of the optimism he used to start each day when they lived together.

'You have a job?' she asked.

'I had a good job as a taxi driver in Mombasa until I got stabbed and couldn't work anymore.'

'No, no, where? That can't be. How much more ...?' protested Jumapili.

'In my shoulder, side and back. It weren't good Jumi. It's why I've come back to Nairobi. I must get the rent money owed to me by the liquor man for renting out our shack.'

'Renting our shack? ' asked Jumapili. 'What do you mean ?'

'Didn't you get the message I left at the Tayiania newsagent? 'cause I left one. It said about our shack, and the bwana at the matatu station would know where I was.'

Jumapili thought hard. 'After the Genge la Chupa raid, I was in hospital. Then I was at Lakshmi McGeown's house and not allowed out 'cause I was a special witness for the court case. After that, Colin and I lived in a bungalow, and we didn't go out much 'cause I was pregnant, then we went to England. No, I didn't get a message. I got nothing, but then I didn't go to the newsagents, only Colin did. I only came here, to the church for music practice.'

'I'm thinking I might return and live here. I don't like Mombasa,' he said.

'I like the sea,' said Jumapili. 'You know Charter died years ago, soon after the gang trial.'

'I know, but his soul was so evil it would have taken a long time for him to go for good.'

For the last few steps, Catherine had been by Jumapili's side helping lead her to their car. She had listened to the conversation between brother and sister as to the survivability of souls on earth after death. She was interested in the easy, natural way the manifestation of spirits was discussed between these two firm believers. She knew that one day she would need to ask, to understand more.

Jumapili was insistent that Absko should stay with her at Downsted Hall. He was pleased to have the invitation because he had nowhere to stay.

Equally as insistent, and with a lot less tact, Catherine was adamant that Absko had a bath, wet-shave properly and wash his hair. The only thing she did not tell him to do was to clean his teeth because, just like Jumapili's, they were white, sparkling and naturally perfect.

No sooner was Absko in the bath, than Catherine had all the clothes he was wearing, together with those in his bag, in the wash. Tomorrow, Catherine vowed, Jumapili would be taking her brother shopping for some new clothes and sandals.

That evening, Absko, Jumapili and Catherine sat around the kadia fire bowl that Jumapili had installed on the patio on the southeast corner of the Hall. She had cherished her fireside conversations with Downsted and particularly his descriptions of the white glow of the stars and the red glow of the logs. When interspersed with unintended lessons in physics and chemistry, he had kept her enthralled for hours.

As the fire bowl was fading, Absko asked Catherine to read to him again the letter Downsted had written. It had been read to him in the newsagents, but when he came to read it himself, he struggled with the words.

'Isn't that nice,' said Jumapili after Catherine had finished speaking. 'It's a lovely letter.'

'It's remarkable,' said Catherine, 'but he always did write such nice letters to parents.' However, this remark was to underplay the influence the letter had on Catherine. She had seen Absko in the same dishevelled and dirty state as Downsted had done. Had it not been for that letter, she would have made the same mistake as him in his assessment of Absko.

As Absko consumed glass after glass of rum and coke, it became clear exactly what Charter had done to him and the truly horrendous time he had had on the road after that. As he spoke, Catherine was noticeably revising her opinion of him until, like Downsted, it had become one of admiration.

Over the next few days, Absko and Jumapili were to spend long evenings on the patio sharing their stories, not only of the years since they had been separated after the Bottlesford Hall attack but from their earliest childhood. They repeated the memories of their mother and father they had shared over many a nighttime in their shack. On these occasions, Absko studied Jumapili carefully as she spoke. At different moments he could see traces of their mother and father's mannerism and characteristics writ in Jumapili's behaviour in a confusing mélange which fascinated and disturbed him in equal proportions

'So you have a blind school but no blind pupils to teach in it?' said Absko as they sat around the kadia fire bowl a week after he had started staying at Bottlesford Hall. He had neatly summarized Jumapili and Catherine's problem after they had outlined their ambition. 'That ain't good is it. Bit pointless that.'

'Er yes,' acknowledged Catherine in her plumiest private school educated voice.

'I'll find 'em,' said Absko confidently. 'They're everywhere.'

'They must be fully blind, not partially blind, and aged over seven,' insisted Catherine. 'We must test the hypothesis that echolocation can be taught to totally blind people first. We must prove whether it works. Only after that will we try it on partially sighted people too.'

I'll find 'em. Fully blind, over the age of seven,' repeated Absko. 'And you don't want paying?'

'No, we don't want paying,' said Jumapili, just as Catherine started speaking over the top of her.

'And under thirteen,' Catherine added. 'They must be under thirteen.'

Chapter 93

ABSKO WAS AS good as his word. Within twenty-four hours, using his network of matatu drivers, he found three children who met Catherine's specifications. Within forty-eight hours he had negotiated with the children's parents that they could come to Downsted Hall to study. The day after that, they were driven to the front door where they received a grand welcome, reminiscent of the welcome Jumapili had received on her first day at the Hall.

In any other circumstance, the expression 'the blind leading the blind' might have been an inappropriate way to describe Jumapili's teaching of echolocation because it's a parody phrase. It describes someone ignorant of the subject getting advice from someone equally as ignorant. However, in the case of Jumapili the phrase was appropriate: while she was a past-master in the practice of echo location, she could not teach it. Everything involved in the technique was intuitive to her such that she found it hard to explain what was required above the basic click of her tongue.

It is a fact that Downsted Hall would have failed spectacularly as a specialist school for the blind if it had not been for Absko. He knew how Jumapili had developed her craft, how she used the taps of her cane to judge what was ahead of her. What he wasn't aware of was how the echo of every step made in her court shoes endorsed or challenged the image she had created in her own mind. He therefore found it most odd for Jumapili to insist that this form of shoe be worn by everyone at her school. To Absko, it was anathema to put something so hard, heavy and obviously uncomfortable on someone's feet – until she explained their purpose.

Absko's big advantage was that he knew the tricks used by Jumapili to organise her day, her affairs, and her property. He was insistent, as he and his mother had been with her, that the three children had to sort out and find their own things. Catherine argued that they were too young, but Absko was a great believer in tough love, which ran contrary to the tenderness, kindness and patience he showed when dealing with the children in his charge.

The fact was that it was easier and quicker for a parent to do something for their blind child rather than expect them to do it for themselves. Equipping every child with small safety pins, lengths of tape and string, Absko taught them the basics of sorting and identifying their clothes. He made several large sensory boards with all the different types of cloths, fabrics, and fasteners, much like Jumapili's sensory blanket, but adding different types of metals, glass, and plastics. He taught how the different types of metal warmed up at different rates under the touch. He knew nothing about the science of thermal conductivity; he had simply observed and passed on his knowledge.

Catherine watched, almost mouth open, as Absko taught his pupils their colours by relating it to their other senses. She had often wondered how Jumapili would automatically know what she meant when she described something as being green, yellow or any other colour, but by observing Absko she soon learnt.

Green was taught by reference to growing grass, its smell when newly cut, and leaves while on the tree. Brown was taught by reference to soil, tree trunks and fallen leaves. Blue was taught by his pupils touching cold running-water and white was taught by ice which they held as it melted, leaving what Absko would describe as a pure and clean substance. Red was naturally associated with fire, but Absko would also link it to hot chillies and spicy peppers. Purple would be described as a mix between blue and red, and he likened it to nobility and power, an explanation supported by the smell of lavender and lilac.

The regimented routine of Downsted Hall, adopted and adapted from that used at Bottlesford Hall, came as a huge shock to the three children, as it did to Absko. He thought he had worked hard in the past, but he came to realise that he had just worked long hours. The expected learning and achievement of all the children, not just those who were blind, was beyond anything he had experienced or expected, but it helped explain to him how Jumapili had done so well.

Like the three blind children, Absko had never seen braille before, but once introduced, he became fascinated by its simplicity. He happily joined in the braille lessons, and through this he learned to read and write fluently, a task that had eluded him. But with this new-found skill he became a bit of a bibliophile, spending any spare time he had in the school library enjoying the books first collected by Joyce's father.

Jumapili was correct. Downsted Hall was an ideal place to learn echolocation, because while the shape of the house remained the same, the dynamics of each room were different, so they were easily learnt. To keep his pupils on their toes, Absko would constantly re-arrange the furniture so that a path taken one Monday might not be taken the next.

Slowly but surely Absko took charge of teaching the blind children. It is said that some people have a gift, a calling, and this could be said of Absko. For both Jumapili and Catherine, he was God-sent.

Absko watched Jumapili go for her early morning run on the playing field. He was amazed to see what he remembered as her gangly, and uncoordinated body now move with the grace and beauty of a gazelle. It was something his 'pupils', as he referred to them, should do too. After lunch and a rest on their beds, Absko had his troop on the playing field and started to teach them how to run. It was to lead to the biggest disagreement Absko, Catherine and Jumapili were to ever have.

While sitting around the fire pit one evening, after the three blind children had been put to bed, Jumapili broke the silence by unexpectedly announcing, 'Grace has to leave – she has to go.'

'Why?' demanded Absko, immediately coming to the defence of one of "his" pupils.

'She's not trying. She's not improving. She's not good enough.'

'What d'ya mean?'

Jumi's right,' said Catherine. 'Grace is not going to make it.'

'What d'ya mean, she's not going to make it?' asked Absko, confused.

'She's not up to our standards,' answered Catherine.

'Standards? What are you talking about, "standards"?'

'You do your very best. You try your hardest or you don't stay,' said Jumapili in a tone that suggested that this was not a matter for debate.

'It was Mr. and Mrs. Downsted's rule,' added Catherine. 'Lots of girls would start a new term, but after five or six weeks some would be asked to leave.'

'Why? I don't get it' said Absko.

'Because either they weren't clever enough or didn't work hard enough, but usually it was the two combined.'

'We must accept that poor Grace is not bright enough,' said Jumapili, 'but worse, she's not trying, and that's the thing I can't tolerate. Look at her running times. They're not improving. Not one bit!'

'Do you remember the day when Mr. Downsted yelled at you for not running properly?' asked Catherine repeating a memory they had often shared.

'Oh God, yes,' answered Jumapili. 'I'd never run anywhere before. I was so frightened my heart was in my mouth. I thought I was going to die.'

'We all did,' said Catherine amused by the memory. 'And there's the difference. Jumi tried and got better, much better by constantly trying to beat her personal best. Sadly, Grace doesn't have the initiative to even try, let alone get any better.'

'I'll talk to her. I'll tell her she's got to try harder. She must get better. She must improve,' said Absko using various synonyms to prove he had got the message.

'I'm really sorry, Absko,' said Jumapili sympathetically, 'but we really must be the best. If we don't strive to be the best, then we will fail.'

'Not everyone can be the best, not at everything,' pleaded Absko.

'I agree,' said Catherine, 'but they can darn well try, and she's not trying, not one bit'.

'I'll speak to her. I promise, I'll speak to her,' said Absko.

'Until I came here, apart from being in hospital, I'd never slept in a bed with a properly sprung mattress,' said Jumapili. 'You know what it was like. I'd never soaked in a hot bath until I was in hospital; we had very little to eat because we couldn't afford it; I couldn't read or write. I could just about play the mouth organ and recorder and that was about it. I can't tell you how hard I have had to work.'

'We all worked,' interrupted Catherine. 'The regime here, was tough, mighty tough but now, look, Jumapili has all of this.'

'But it was given to her!' protested Absko.

'Only because she deserved it,' retorted Catherine. 'If you'd known Mr. and Mrs. Downsted you'd have known they wouldn't have given it to her unless they knew she would do something with it. She deserves it because they believed in her, and they knew she'd use it properly.'

Three weeks later and with Absko's approval, Grace left the school. Her leaving hurt him so much that from that moment he took extraordinary care before accepting any blind student for training at Downsted Hall.

Chapter 94

'MISS MWANGI, PRESIDENT Moi's office is on the telephone,' shouted, the school secretary.

'What, who?' shouted back Jumapili from the hall. 'Did you say Moi?'

Jumapili didn't see the school secretary nod furiously as she placed the telephone in her hand.

'Hello,' said Jumapili.

'Miss Mwangi, I understand everyone calls you Jumi. May I call you Jumi?' asked President Daniel arab Moi.[46]

Jumapili said something indecipherable.

'December 12th [47] will be the twenty-fifth anniversary of our country's independence,' announced Moi. 'We're having a celebration concert in Uhuru Gardens, and I'd like you to be there to perform.'[48]

Jumapili mumbled incoherently.

'Thank you so much,' Moi continued. 'Someone from my office will be in touch with you over the next few days to finalise arrangements.'

---

[46] Daniel arap Moi CGH served as the second president of Kenya from 1978 to 2002. Moi previously served as the Vice-President of Kenya from 1967 to 1978 under President Jomo Kenyatta, becoming the president following the latter's death. In 1969, with the banning of the Kenya People's Union (KPU), Kenya became a one-party state with the Kenyan African National Union (KANU) as the only party. As a result, KANU won every seat in elections in 1969,1974,1979,1983 and 1988. On 21st March 1988, Moi was re-elected as president of Kenya without a vote being cast.

[47] 1988

[48] Uhuru Gardens are considered Kenya's birthplace. It is where, on 12th December 1963, Kenya's first national flag was raised on the country gaining its independence from Great Britain. The gardens were officially declared a National Monument in 1966 because of their historical importance.

He put down the phone. Moi's call to the next performer he wanted to invite was already on another telephone line waiting.

Jumapili had said very few words.

'You can't use your English band,' said Absko when he heard of Moi's invitation. 'You must use fellow Kenyans.'

'Why?' protested Catherine. 'They're good. We all work well together.'

'Is he going to pay you?' asked Absko.

'He didn't say. I doubt it. These things are normally for charity, aren't they?' answered Jumapili.

'Yeh, Moi's charity,' added Absko sarcastically. 'Your musicians, are they Black or White?'

'He's got a point,' interrupted Catherine. 'Who's going to pay to fly them from Britain and back?

'What do you mean,' asked Jumapili picking up on Absko's question.

'Moi won't want White musicians playing at his celebration concert,' answered Absko. 'You forget he was involved in kicking the Brits out.[49] He won't want them back, not on that day.'

It took Jumapili and Catherine six months to put together a twelve-piece band comprising Kenyans, Ugandans, South Africans and herself. It was a coincidence that they were all women. Apart from being female, the common factor was that they were all versatile musicians, skilled in more than one instrument, who could sight-read, improvise and, most importantly, could hear a piece of music played a couple of times and be able to repeat it.

There were delicate negotiations with the concert organisers for Jumapili's band to be paid their expenses, while Jumapili agreed to perform for free. Once these negotiations were concluded, the newly formed band moved into Downsted Hall where the front west room, with Joyce's piano in it, became their rehearsal studio. There is an expression 'practice makes perfect' and this was certainly the case for Jumapili's duodecet.

---

[49] Moi was part of the Kenyan delegation which travelled to London for the Lancaster House Conferences in 1960, 1962 and 1963 where the Kenya's first post-independence constitution was drafted.

It was Sefu Obasanjo, and his daughter Madina, who were going to have the greatest influence on Jumapili's concert performance. Sefu was an assistant producer with the Kenya Broadcasting Corporation. He was responsible for all the preparations for the concert from setting up the stage, sound, lighting, even down to the provision of changing rooms and toilets.

'That won't work,' pronounced Sefu when he saw what music Jumapili had proposed for their three-piece set. 'It's too English, too Western. Your songs, your music should be in Swahili.'

Kenya had just done well in the Seoul Summer Olympics, winning five gold medals. In recognition Sefu agreed that there should be one exception to his rule. Jumapili's band would play Vengelis's theme tune from *Chariots of Fire* while a video of the Kenya athletes winning their gold medals would be shown on a large screen.

'What are you wearing?' asked Medina bluntly at the same first meeting with her father Sefu. She rejected all the band's suggestions. 'You need a uniform, and it's got to be sexy, very sexy,' she ordered. 'And some of you better slim fast, cause if you're overweight you're gonna get put at the back'.

'Ella Fitzgerald and Aretha Franklin aren't exactly thin, are they,' protested one of the band.

'And you ain't no Ella or Aretha,' retorted Medina.

Five days before the concert, Medina turned up to see how rehearsals were going. She watched as they played their routine through twice.

'Well that ain't goin on. That's no good at all,' she said firmly.

Jumapili's band looked at each other aghast.

'You're an act, a flaming act. People ain't coming to watch statues. You guy's ain't got Kenya. You ain't got Kenya at all,' Medina complained.

'That's what I said,' interrupted Absko. 'They gotta move, gotta dance.'

Medina held up her thumb at Absko to signify her approval.

Their costumes were rejected as being too old and frumpy.

'We agreed sexy; these aren't sexy,' said Medina. It was now Absko's turn to hold up his thumb.

The next day a KBC choreographer and seamstress turned up at Downsted Hall. Their instructions were simple. Make 'em wiggle, make'em dance, make 'em sexy and starve anyone overweight. The choreographer and seamstress were probably more frightening than Medina, but it was the fear that they might get dumped at any moment which kept the duodecet on their toes and working their hardest.

It all paid off because not only was their performance one of the highlights of the evening, but at the final dress rehearsal they were the only performers invited on stage to play the Kenyan national anthem with the Kenya Army Band at the end of the concert.

'You need to come back on my show,' said Murade Ngesan who was one of the co-presenters for the concert.

'It would be nice,' replied Jumapili. 'It's been a long time.'

'Yeh, I know. You had a regular slot on the BBC didn't you?'

'Yes,' answered Jumi modestly.

'Well, they can't keep all the talent. We'll book you,' he said before walking away.

Jumapili didn't know, because she could not see, the joyous expression she had on her face when the celebration concert was broadcast around the world. It was picked up by news channels and newspapers everywhere.

The blind, orphan girl from the slums of Nairobi was no longer famous in just Kenya, but around the whole globe.

Chapter 95

IT WAS SAID that you couldn't choose Tristram Marsh as your agent, he would choose you, and Tristram Marsh had decided he wanted to represent Jumapili Mwangi.

Marsh was a lawyer who never practised law. Having studied the subject at Oxford University he had an aversion to contracts. It was why he never signed them. His word was his bond and he demanded everyone he worked with behave the same way. His honesty and ethics were a rarity in the entertainment industry. He prided himself on telling the truth even if it was harmful to his own cause. However, he thoroughly approved of sugar-coating the truth if it made it easier to swallow.

It was Marsh's family background and his education at Eton that enabled him to walk the hallowed corridors of influence, somehow jumping the queue for membership of the Garrick Club, the elite London private members club of actors, lawyers, and men of letters.

Such was the trust Marsh's clients had in his judgement that two of the nation's highest profile stars had worked together for over fifteen years under a complex contract designed to split everything fifty-fifty. Their lawyers had fought tooth and nail over each clause and had only succeeded in upsetting their clients. The contract was only signed when an important new final clause was added. It read: *Not withstanding any term of this agreement, any matter regarding either its operation or dispute shall be settled by the Parties on such terms and conditions as Tristram Marsh shall, in his sole and absolute discretion and from time to time, decide, and his decision shall be final and binding on the Parties without appeal.* It made the rest of the agreement null and void, but such was the trust in his judgement and the esteem he was held throughout the entertainment industry.

'Talent', as actors, musicians, and artists are called, wanted Marsh to represent them because he had offices both in London and New York, and an associate office in Los Angeles. These gave his clients a market reach not enjoyed by other talent agencies. Of course, it meant that when you said Tristram Marsh was your agent, and he would always take his clients' calls, it was his team of staff who really looked after you. But this team were excellent at their job because each was a sycophant by nature who loved being on the edge of fame.

As Marsh boarded the last aeroplane of the day from Heathrow Airport heading to New York, he was handed a newspaper. Three days later when he returned, he had in his briefcase just Page 5, neatly folded. The rest had been discarded. The page Marsh had kept was a black-and-white photograph of Jumapili laughing as she played at Kenya's silver jubilee celebrations. He knew nothing of her except this photograph, and in it he saw the opportunity for a unique product – a blend of Diana Ross and Stevie Wonder.

By the time Marsh got back from New York, his London office had secured a recording of Jumapili's performance at Uhuru Gardens and a videotape of her two performances on the Murad Ngesan's evening show on KBC. Learning that she had been a regular on the BBC Radio 4's Week Ending show, Marsh made a point of speaking to both of its co-producers, and they spoke approvingly of her talent and professionalism.

Marsh watched the videos time and time again to a point that came close to being obsessional. He knew he had found a rare and exceptional talent. He was seeing exactly what Joyce and Colin Downsted had seen when Jumapili was just eleven years old.

Making up the excuse of taking his family on a Kenyan safari, Marsh arranged to visit Jumapili at Downsted Hall. While she listened modestly and said very little, Catherine told Jumapili's story. It was, Marsh decided, a publicist's dream. It couldn't possibly get any better.

With Absko listening too, Marsh gave a list of the clients he represented and offered them as references. He set out his terms for representing Jumapili. Everything Marsh said was crisp and to the point.

She would have the stage name Jumi – nothing else. What she chose to play would be up to her and the record company she signed to. He would represent her and not her band, which it was her job to keep and maintain out of the income he was able to generate for her. He was an agent not a personal assistant. It wasn't his job to get her to a booking. She would use one of two accountants he would recommend so her tax affairs were always up to date and there were to be no hard drugs at all. One sniff and he would be gone. His fee was twelve-and-a-half percent of everything she earned, and he would not charge expenses. All her earnings would be paid into a separate client bank account in her name which he would maintain, and this would be emptied in favour of her bank account on the last day of the month, and within seven days of that, she would be given a statement showing all incoming and outgoing money.

The meeting ended with Jumapili thanking Marsh for coming and saying she would think about what he had said. Catherine was insistent that they would visit his London office before making any commitment. She had always believed that you could tell a lot about a man and his business by simply walking through the front door of his office or home. However, a bond was immediately struck between Marsh and Jumapili, which was never to end, when he wrote to her in both braille and script to summarise his proposal. No one had taken the courtesy of writing to her in braille before.

Soon after Marsh returned to London, he contacted International Music Artists, one of the leading record labels, and, based on his video collection of her work, he tentatively secured for her the offer of a three-album recording contract. Just as Jumapili and Catherine were packing to go to London, another letter arrived by courier from Marsh. His Los Angeles associate office had secured for Jumapili an audition for an emergency three-month cabaret contract at Caesars Palace Las Vegas. The band which supported the headline act was leaving, and if Jumapili wanted the job then she and her band had to get to Las Vegas by the weekend.

Immediately Marsh broke his own rules of not getting his clients to a booking. Instead, he worked furiously with Caesars Palace to get the necessary visas while Catherine worked equally hard at reuniting Jumapili's band and getting them to Las Vegas with all their instruments.

At Caesars Palace, just as happened with the Uhuru Gardens concert, Jumapili and Catherine lost control of everything except their performance on stage. Directors, stage managers and stylists were aghast to learn that Jumapili was blind because no one had told them. They thought this gave them the extra leverage they needed to take control, which they brutally exercised.

'Stop rolling your head like you're fucking demented,' commanded the stage manager after he'd watched Jumapili play the piano to accompany her first song. 'I can't fuckin' listen to what you're singing 'cause you're like fuckin' Noddy, and I'm wondering when your head's going to fall off. Also, the sound's hopeless 'cause your waving your head around in and out of the microphone.' He was talking to Jumapili as though she was a junior in one of his dancing troupe.

'Don't you dare speak like that!' shouted Catherine angrily.

'My stage, my rules' retorted the stage manager sharply 'You don't like the rules, well, you know where the fucking exit is.'

'It's all right Catherine,' said Jumapili calmly. 'Colin criticised me for doing the same thing. I'd forgotten I was doing it. It won't happen again.'

Jumapili was as good as her word because, for the next song, with her hendectet of musicians in full support, the stage manager was blown away by the beauty, purity and range of her voice. It had a power that was remarkable for one so slight in stature.

'What do you want them to play? Ask them to play anything?' demanded Catherine to prove the loss would be Ceasar's Palace and not theirs if they didn't perform.

'Anything?' asked the stage manager beginning to eat humble pie.

Catherine nodded.

'*La Vie En Rose*.'

'Edith Piaff, everyone knows that, too easy,' responded Catherine desperately hoping her bravado wasn't going to back fire.

'How about *Per Una Cabeza* by Carlos Gardel,' said the stage manager as Catherine's heart leapt into her mouth; she had never heard of it.

'The tango?' asked one of Jumapili's violinists before starting a few bars from memory, by which time every one of her musicians had joined in, each supporting the other. It was a masterpiece of improvisation. With the momentum now running in their direction, Jumapili moved seamlessly to start performing the first five songs they had planned for their evening set.

'Okay, you guys can perform,' agreed the stage manager, 'but you ain't Caesars Palace material, not yet! Here we sell sex appeal and you've got as much of that as a hot bikini wax. You'll have to work on your act. You Jumi, you're a petite sexy little thing, so if you've got it, why aren't you flaunting it? For Pete's sake, when you're sitting at your piano, sit bolt upright, tummy in, and stick your tits and arse out. And you others – you're all women, so for God sake, when playing your instruments, bloody well wriggle.'

'You can hardly wriggle over a double bass,' protested the double-bass player.

'And you can't over a cello either,' protested the cello player.

But the stage manager had no interest in their complaints. Just as happened when working with KBC TV, Caesars Palaces's choreographer took control of the on-stage image. She ordered a white trouser suit for Jumapili drenched in silver sequins and white dress suits for the band, with skirts which were far too short for decency. The cello player protested loudly and eventually the whole band was allowed to choose between ludicrously short miniskirts, reminiscent of a period twenty years before, or trousers.

It was at the full-dress rehearsal three days after they had arrived, and the directors of the casino came to give their approval, when everything nearly went wrong.

'Why's the kid on the piano wearing dark glasses?' shouted one of them.

'cause she's blind.' answered the stage manager.

'I know that, but that's not the question. Why's she wearing 'em?'

'I'm told my eyes roll and people don't like that,' answered Jumapili.

'Do they?' asked the director.

'I don't know. I'm blind. I can't see.'

'Take'em off, take your shades off,' ordered the director as he left his seat and climbed the steps to the stage.

On the stage the director studied Jumapili's face and her eye movements. 'You've got a right pretty face, but you're right, your eyes wander. It's off putting,' he said before asking, 'what happens when you close your eyelids? Can you sing with your eyelids closed?'

'Yeh, sure'

'Well go on.'

'Memories,' sung Jumapili teasingly, *'Light the corners of my mind. Misty watercolor memories, of the way we were.*

But the director didn't notice the dig in Jumapili's choice of song. His mind was gripped by her voice.

'Barbra Streisand!' he said. 'I love that woman. You must put it in your act.'

'We don't have a licence,' said the stage manager.

'Well get one.'

'Okay Jumi' said the director. 'Welcome to Caesar's Palace. You're on. Three months. Try singing with your eyes closed, not scrunched up, just closed, and we'll get you some smaller blue-grey tinted glasses so your eyelids can still be seen. We need to make your performance less Godfather more Chariots of Fire.'

Jumapili started playing Vengelis's theme tune, at which point the director, who was walking away, stopped in his tracks, turned, and put his thumbs up, but of course she couldn't see this.

'Catherine,' shouted the director before he left, 'anything you and Jumi want while you're here, just holla, OK?'

Catherine was thrilled with the changes Caesar's Palace had made to Jumapili's act. KBC and the Uhuru Gardens had improved their stage craft enormously, but by comparison Caesar's Palace had taken it into the stratosphere.

Chapter 96

THE EXECUTIVES OF International Music Artists, on hearing that their new potential signing was performing at Caesars Palace, were on their company's private jet flying to Las Vegas airport the very next day. They arrived unannounced and watched Jumi and her band perform. It was the confirmation they needed that Jumapili was a rare talent worthy of the three-record deal they had tentatively negotiated with Marsh simply on his recommendation and the few old videos he had sent them.

When Catherine phoned Marsh to say that the IMA executives were at Caesar's Palace and wanted to meet Jumapili, Marsh went incandescent with rage, not at them but with IMA. He tracked his contact down to the hotel room he was staying in and accused him of the most appalling bad manners, saying that any meeting without him being there would be an act of bad faith.

Jumapili and Catherine agreed with Marsh that they wouldn't meet IMA until he got there, but on reflection they decided that this was probably bad manners, so they met for a simple coffee and spoke about the weather and Las Vegas. They changed the subject every time IMA tried to discuss their contract, simply saying that this was something Mr. Marsh would be negotiating for them.

When Marsh saw Jumi and her band perform, which he did before meeting IMA, he was staggered. Thanks to Caesar's Palace, their act was a magnitude greater than he had ever imagined. It wasn't a support act anymore but, as IMA had recognised, they were worthy as bill headliners.

Immediately after seeing Jumapili's act and before he had started his negotiations with IMA, and with Caesar's Palace approval, Marsh set his team in New York the job of getting Jumapili and her band on one of the national late-night TV shows.

Success was achieved with the first phone call so when Marsh announced to the IMA team that Jumapili was appearing live on the Hester Logan Late Live Show, one of the US's most popular comedy sketch, political satire, and variety television shows, he had her ten points up in the amount they would pay in advance fees and twenty-five points up in her rider.[50]

Interestingly, so inexperienced were Jumapili and Catherine on the business side of the entertainment industry that, until that moment, they had no idea that rider terms co-existed alongside performance contracts.

---

[50] A rider is a document that sets out the essential requirements that a musician must be provided with at a venue so they can perform to the best possible standard.

Chapter 97

HESTER LOGAN WAS the co-creator and presenter of the Late Live Show which was broadcast nationally throughout the US. So high-profile was his show that even the most seasoned performer would be nervous. Logan was renowned for his acerbic wit.

No one had told Logan's production team that their end of show star performer was blind. All their efforts had been on getting a Steinway grand piano into the studio as required by Jumapili's rider. Logan was good manners and consideration personified. He took time to chatter with Jumapili and became so interested in Jumapili's ambition for her blind school in Kenya that the format of the show was changed. Rather than just playing the ending number they would discuss what it was like being blind. It was a heavy subject for a late-night chat show, but Logan proved to be an exemplar in both tact and easy wit when he came to discuss the problems of being blind with Jumapili.

'I can do almost anything you can do,' said Jumapili confidently as they chatted away in front of a live studio audience. 'I might not be able to see the red light of the camera to know that we're now on air, and I can't drive a car or fly an aeroplane but otherwise almost everything else is possible. It just takes me a little longer, that's all. The key is being methodical and having a good memory.'

'I'm told you have a unique skill called echolocation. What is it?' asked Logan.

'It's what bats use to see in the dark. They make screeches and then listen to their echo to work out where they are.'

'And you can do this?'

'Yes, I've started a school in Kenya with the specific purpose of seeing whether this is a skill which can be taught.'

'And you're happy if we do an experiment with you now? Is that okay?'

'Sure,' said Jumapili focusing her attention on sitting bolt upright, not allowing her head to sway, and keeping her eyelids closed as had been emphasised on her *ad nauseum*.

'There are six cameras in the studio, and you know where they are?' asked Logan.

'Yes.' Jumapili started clicking. 'There, there, there ...' She repeated, pointing in the direction of each camera in turn.

'Just in case the audience thinks we're cheating, we're going to blindfold you and we're going to play some music in your ears so you can't hear what's going on around you.'

'That's a first time,' said Jumapili as she laughed out loud. It was the laugh of someone having fun and it took the audience with her.

'And we're going to move some of the cameras around and you're going to tell us where they are. Are you okay with that?' asked Logan.

Jumapili sat quite relaxed, her face smiling as she tapped her hand on her knee in time to the music in her earphones, and the audience watched as three cameras were disconnected and wheeled out of the studio and the other three changed positions.

Logan helped Jumapili remove the headphones, but she kept the blindfold on.

'Where are the cameras now?' he asked.

Jumapili clicked her tongue and said nothing for things had most definitely changed. She knew that, but how exactly puzzled her.

'Can I stand up?' she asked.

'Sure.'

Standing up, Jumapili clicked her tongue, tapped her cane, and walked a few paces.

'There are only three cameras in here now. You've taken out three.'

'And where are the ones that are left?'

Jumapili laughed again.

'There, there and there,' she said.

Only then did Catherine and Jumapili's band start to breathe again, for like the audience, they had been willing her to be right.

'And you're definitely blind?' asked Logan, equally amazed.

‘It’s what they tell me.’ she said with a smile on her face and a flick of her head.

‘And this skill, echolocation, you think it can be taught to blind kids?’

‘I do, at least I think it’s worth a try,’ she said as she removed the blindfold.

‘Now, you and your band have got a three-month gig at Caesars Palace, and you’ve kindly agreed to play us out with something from your show there. What is it?

‘*Somewhere my love*. It’s Lara’s theme tune from the movie *Dr Zhivago*.’

‘Let me help you to the piano,’ said Logan as he gently took her hand.

Once seated comfortably, Jumapili started to sing:

Somewhere, my love there will be songs to sing.
Although the snow covers the hope of spring.
Somewhere a hill blossoms in green and gold,
And there are dreams all that your heart can hold.

Wherever you were, you had to stop and listen because Jumapili’s voice was captivating. It was exquisite in its purity, and she looked quite lovely. There was not a man or woman who saw her on the show that night who did not fall in love with her. In fact, the TV station controller was so captivated that he allowed the Late Live Show to overrun by over a minute, a rare honour in a television station dependent upon advertising revenue – but you only become a station controller by knowing exactly what your viewers want, and he was in no doubt they wanted to see Jumi and her band perform to the end.

Caesar’s Palace were thrilled with her performance because any free mention of them on television helped their sales. But it brought about two requests: firstly, they insisted that Lara’s Theme tune be added to the song list to be played at the end; secondly, they wanted to extend her contract. However, Marsh advised against it because IMA wanted her in the studio, and on tour as soon as possible.

Chapter 98

ABSKO LEARNT ABOUT Jumapili's performance on the Hester Logan Late Live Show through a large and sudden increase in enquiries from the press and parents of prospective students. From one appearance on a television show, Downsted Hall had been put on the map. Student recruitment would not be a problem for a considerable period.

Marsh quickly finalised Jumapili's contract with IMA. Immediately the ink was dry, she and her band were in a studio in Las Vegas to record their first album. They were pleased to be busy because, with just one show a day in Caesar's Palace, the rest of the time seemed to drag. There was only so much swimming, gym training, and music practice one could reasonably do.

IMA purchased a couple of original songs from an established music and lyricist duo for Jumapili's album, which they planned to release as singles. These songs turned out to be flops, but all the other tracks were covers of other people's hits and mirrored the Caesar's Palace programme. Jumapili's soft, pure, balletic voice produced music that people wanted to hear and buy.

Not knowing how hard it would be, Jumapili agreed to a sixteen-week tour working around the states in a clockwise direction starting in Chicago, going through Detroit, Boston, New York and all the way down to Miami and New Orleans. From there they crossed the country through Huston, Dallas, and Austin, before travelling north on the west coast via San Diego, Los Angeles, San Francisco, Portland and finally Seattle, a long trawl.

Venues seating three thousand to five thousand people were booked for evening performances from Wednesday to Saturday. That gave Sunday and Monday for travelling, and Tuesday and Wednesday for set-up and rehearsals. Then on Saturday night, after the performance, the set would be taken down, and on Sunday morning the whole roadshow would start all over again.

As Jumapili and Catherine were to discover, concert touring was a distinctly separate business from music production and distribution. It required people who were experienced in organising such things. Who knew that the distance from Austin to San Diego was one-thousand-three-hundred miles and would take nineteen hours of non-stop driving to complete?

Two luxury tour buses were hired for 'the talent', as Jumapili and the members of her band were called. These came complete with bunk beds so they could lay down flat and, of course, a toilet. However, the road and stage crew, who were responsible for sound and lighting set up and take down, were given a far less salubrious vehicle.

If a concert and the album was to be a commercial success it was essential Jumapili get interviewed on the local radio and television stations at the start of the week in each city where they appeared. There was a whole team at IMA booking Jumapili's appearances. Normally the pitch by a booker of an unknown artist would fall on deaf ears, but when they said the Jumapili had been a hit on the Hester Logan Late Live Show, the slots were easily secured.

Interviews with radio and TV stations was something Jumapili and Catherine did alone. For radio they took a CD with them so that could be played on air, and for television Jumi would sing and play the piano unaccompanied. She was never out of her trademark white trouser-suit, and every time she moved into the limelight Catherine would say to her jokingly: 'tits, bum and no wobble.'

There were some tense moments when IMA instructed Jumapili and her band not to play because the theatre had not paid over the ticket money as they should have done, but always, at the last minute, it would appear, often in cash.

Apart from the physical exhaustion which comes from being on the road, packing and unpacking, eating junk food and sleeping in a different bed every night, there were tremendous highs which come from performing live in front of audiences of several thousands of people.

The first cheer from the audience always lifted Jumapili and her band as they arrived on stage. Then as they relaxed into enjoying their performance, their energy and enthusiasm lifted both the audience and performers in a truly symbiotic relationship. It was obvious they were having fun together.

After every show there would be a clamour for Jumapili to sign CD's, T-shirts, baseball caps and programmes, all of which added to someone's profits somewhere. The adulation was something which Jumapili found strange and hard to deal with.

As positive reviews of Jumi's concerts spread, so did the opportunities for more work. But, although IMA and Marsh put offer after offer in front of her, she turned them down. After Seattle, she was going home to Downsted Hall. She had a school she wanted to get back to and a sports field whose grass she needed to feel between her toes.

Chapter 99

IT WAS A lovely Sunday afternoon and several months after Jumapili and Catherine had returned to Downsted Hall from their first North American tour. Together with the whole school, they had been to the little church at Tayiana for holy communion, had ice creams from the village shop and then enjoyed a traditional roast-beef lunch in the school dining room. Like all their pupils, Jumapili and Catherine had retired to their bedroom for a rest and some quiet reading before the afternoon activities started.

During their prolonged absence, Absko and Miss Marjorie Jones, a science teacher from a family with strong colonial roots in Kenya, had adopted the positions of *de facto* headmaster and headmistress. Under their joint leadership the school was beginning to do well. It had grown to twenty-one full-time boarders, three of whom were blind, and for the next term they already had twenty-eight places confirmed of which four would be blind students. Absko and Miss Jones had decided that a blind-to-sighted ratio of greater than one-to-six would be harmful to their ambition for the whole school.

Other people were contacting Downsted Hall to see if they could learn to teach echolocation, but Absko and Miss Jones kept delaying. It was not that they were jealously guarding a secret, but without an independent assessment of their programme they were not sure how successful they were being. Absko was one-hundred-percent certain their course was working, but he had no idea how effective it was when compared to what was happening elsewhere. As Miss Jones continually pointed out, he was incredibly selective about the kind of pupils he allowed on his course. They were the best and brightest; perhaps they would have thrived wherever they were.

As they lay on Jumapili's bed after lunch, just as all the pupils in the school lay on theirs, Jumapili read a long letter written in braille from

Marsh, while Catherine was studying the attachments which came with them.

'They've cheated us,' said Catherine, as she discarded the papers she had in her hand with disgust.

'Marsh says the same thing to me in his letter. Apparently, they've dumped the marketing costs of the record against the cost of the tour which they're not supposed to do. I had no idea IMA had set up a brand-new company with its own bank account just for the tour, did you?'

'Not until now. It's what Tristram has sent us. They're the company accounts for the tour. They've calculated the profits and set out how these should be shared between IMA and you, but it's nonsense. The royalty statement for your album sales is straightforward, you simply get an amount of money based on the number of records you either sell or are played on the radio or TV, but this touring business, well its open to every kind of trickery.' Catherine was getting cross.

'I'd no idea concert-touring was such a complex business, did you?' asked Jumapili.

'No. Thank God we just stayed inside the US. Can you imagine what would have happened if we'd toured the UK and Europe as they suggested?'

'I must do two more tours, mustn't I?' asked Jumapili dejectedly. 'One for each new record.'

'Yeh, well you're not going. If they think they can cheat you like this then they've got another think coming, said Catherine, her anger rising. 'I'm not having it. They're trying to take advantage of you because you're blind.'

'Catherine,' said Jumapili. 'We've been together for years now and you've never mentioned your money. We talk about my money and how I'm doing, but we never talk about *your* money. I know when you're paying out for me, but often you're paying out of your own money for us too. Even Absko notices how much you subsidise us. I don't know how you manage.'

'I don't, said Catherine and, to be honest, it's beginning to worry me too. As you can guess, being here with you means I have no income, no earnings, but my inheritance and the money I got from my divorce. It's nearly all gone.'

'But I couldn't manage without you! I couldn't do this on my own.'

'Yes you could. You just need someone else like me to hold your hand. Absko did it for years.'

'That's not true. Look how you put the band together and get everyone organized, tickets, itinerary everything, I couldn't do that.'

'No one's indispensable,' said Catherine. 'In any case, I so want Downsted Hall to succeed. If you remember, I set out the conditions at the start, and I feel responsible.'

'Can I not employ you, pay you?'

'No, it would change everything. We've become kind of partners, life partners and for me to work for you would give us a master-servant relationship. I don't want that.'

'But I pay Absko and he's not my servant. He told me he had to be paid if he was to stay.'

'Yeh, but he's your brother and you don't share a bed with him, do you.'

'We used to, when we were kids,' said Jumapili, 'but I know what you mean.'

They sat in silence for a little while, watching the dust dance in the sun beams that fell through the slats in the window shutters.

'We should be partners, equal partners,' announced Jumapili after a little thought.

'We couldn't be equal partners; that wouldn't be right, and what about Absko? He needs to be thought of too,' said Catherine.

'It's my money. It's my decision,' Jumapili said firmly but politely. 'You and me, we'll share in the music equally and here, Bottlesford Hall, we'll share that with Absko, one third each.'

Catherine leant across and kissed Jumapili very gently on the lips. 'Do you want me to ask Tristram to organise it,' she asked.

Jumapili put her hand to Catherine's face and kissed her back. She was using it to give her answer.

Chapter 100

AFTER A LOT of argy-bargy, Catherine and an assistant from Marsh's office flew to IMA's offices in New York. Jumapili had made it clear that there would be no second or third Jumi tours until Catherine had agreed the accounts, and she had been paid the money she was owed.

Over three days Catherine audited every item of income and expenditure included in the tour accounts. There was not an invoice or receipt she did not examine and categorise as either properly incurred, nothing to do with them, or to be negotiated. There were glaring errors. As Marsh had identified, album-marketing costs had been wrongly charged against the tour, but the other big mistake was that the accounts bore all the expenditure for the merchandise sales, but none of the income.

Catherine's work resulted in the accounts being altered by nearly five-hundred-thousand dollars, roughly thirty-thousand dollars for each concert city, in Jumapili's favour. It was an embarrassing 'mistake' for which Marsh demanded an IMA main-board apology because he wanted to make sure that there were no 'misunderstandings', as he referred to them, in any of their future business dealings.

On a clear understanding of their future business terms, Jumapili did another two albums for IMA as she had contracted. For the second album she toured only ten cities in the US but added six in the UK. For the third album, IMA London decided the supporting tour should be at smaller venues in Europe, and the UK.

Album Two did very well, but Album Three was a commercial and critical failure. For that reason and because Jumapili had never had a top-ten hit, IMA told her they were not renewing her contract. It was never said among themselves, but Marsh, Jumapili and Catherine had each assumed the real reason the contract was terminated was IMA's inability to make their usual super profits from dodgy accounting practices.

Marsh quickly found another record company, but by now the royalty flow from Jumapili's albums and the accumulated income from three years of concert tours was sufficient for Jumapili to live the rest of her days in modest comfort and to keep the blind section of Downsted Hall fully functional for several more years.

Jumapili's new deal had less aggressive targets with fewer cities and smaller venues, creating more intimate concerts. The size of her band was reduced, the loss of performing talent being made up by a brilliant sound technician who became a key member of their team.

A smaller group and lighter itinerary allowed Jumapili to make guest appearances in other artists' concerts, often doing duets, many of which went on to be recorded.

Although it was hard work, Jumapili insisted on touring the US and the UK every year but for one reason and one reason only: she hoped and prayed her daughter would see her and this would lead to them being reunited. It was the single thing that spurred her on.

Chapter 101

THE BRITISH AIRWAYS aeroplane had risen to its cruising height, the food service had been completed and the cabin lights had been dimmed. Nicki Williams had covered herself with a blanket, placed her cushion against the cabin wall ready to rest her head against it, and she was settling down to sleep.

Nicki had just completed a semester's study-abroad program at Regent's College in London and was returning to Chicago for Christmas with her parents. She was pleased to be leaving London because while it had been sunny and warm when she arrived in late summer, it seemed as though it had been cold, damp, and wet for days, making everywhere miserable.

Nicki unwrapped her airline headphones to listen to music in the hope that it would drown out the engine noise. She plugged them in, selected a channel at random and closed her eyes.

'My guest today is the renowned musician and singer Jumi Mwangi, famous for her pioneering work teaching echolocation to blind students at her school in Nairobi. Jumi, welcome to Desert Island Discs,' said the presenter.

'Thank you for having me,' said Jumapili by now almost accent-free.

'You were born blind in the slums of Kibera, in Nairobi and it was not until you were aged eleven did you learned the year and approximate month of your birth,' continued the presenter.

It was the word 'Nairobi' that drew Nicki's attention. She started to listen more attentively.

'You were badly burned by boiling water when you were just four-years-old, and on the same day your father, Odikinyi, went permanently missing leaving your mother, you and your brother, who was just nine-years-old, on your own. Three years later your mother,

Nyawira died from tuberculosis leaving your brother Absko, who was then just twelve-years-old to look after you. Tell me about those early years.'

Over the airwaves, Jumapili described how Absko looked after her, found her a safe place to sit throughout the day while he worked on the buses: how he gave her a harmonica with which she taught herself to play; how this led her to become a street busker so she no longer begged for money as she had a skill which people would pay for.

'So, what's the first record you'd take with you to the island?' asked the presenter.

'*The Skye Boat Song* sung by Kenneth McKellar, please. My first paid gig was to sing this song at a funeral, and I learnt how to sing it from hearing this version,' explained Jumapili.

The programme continued to map Jumapili's life. Her second choice was *Moon River* from the film *Breakfast at Tiffany's* because it was the first time she had become aware of style and had started to wear black sunglasses. Like Audrey Hepburn before her, these had subsequently become a trademark feature in her public life.

The third song was *How Great Thou Art* sung by Elvis Presley with the Royal Philharmonic Orchestra, which Jumapili used as a basis to praise Joyce Downsted and the impact she had had on her life.

Somewhere Over the Rainbow from the *Wizard of Oz* sung by Judy Garland was her fourth song, recalling the first time she sang on TV. She emphasised her belief in the lyrics - *And the dreams that you dare to dream really do come true.*

Her fifth song was *You'll Never Walk Alone* from the movie *Carousel* which she dedicated to her brother Absko, just as she had done on Murade Ngesan's Evening Show. It was at that point that she spoke about Downsted Hall, her ability to create spatial images from clicking her tongue, and their pioneering work in echolocation.

'Every time anyone writes anything about you, you get called 'the Batgirl'. Does that worry you?' asked the presenter.

'It's not very polite, and in most cases it's lazy shortcut journalism, but no, I don't mind,' she answered. 'I guess every time they say that, they're writing about my school's programme for blind kids so, on the whole, I think the positives from awareness outweigh any negatives.'

The sixth track was *Swingin Safari* played by Bert Kaempfert. That was for Colin Downsted whom Jumapili referred to as the 'best, most loving surrogate father anyone could have had', while mentioning how strict and demanding he was.

'At the age of fifteen you fell pregnant,' said the presenter, 'and your baby daughter was adopted. Tell me about that time and how you coped.'

Jumapili was not shocked by the question. They had agreed in advance that it would be discussed. Jumapili wanted it mentioned in case she said something that might allow her daughter to find her.

Nicki Williams' eyes shot wide open, and she twitched her head. Her ears strained to hear what Jumapili was saying.

'I didn't cope then, and I don't cope now,' replied Jumapili. 'It haunts me every day. I wake up every morning thinking of Kaweira.'

'That's your daughter's name,' interrupted the presenter.

'Yes. And I go to sleep at night thinking of her. Like every mother who has lost a child, I manage, I exist, but I don't think I'll ever be truly happy until ... well.'

'Did my parents change my name?' wondered Nicki. Had Kaweira been her birth name?

'So what happened?' the presenter asked Jumapili.

'I knew nothing about sex. Strange as it may seem, I had no idea how babies were made. It had never been discussed. There was this boy with a Scottish father and an Indian mother, he liked me, and I liked him and, well we were having fun, but it turned out not to be so funny after all ...'

Jumapili paused at that point, expecting the presenter to say something, but she didn't, so Jumapili continued speaking.

'Because he was over eighteen-years-old, the father would have been arrested and jailed for having sex with a minor and so, with his mother's help, he ran away. To make matters worse, his mother told me to my face that her son's bloodline was vastly superior to mine. She called me the "runt of the litter." '

'Runt of the litter!' exclaimed the presenter shocked.

'Yes. She said her family did not "breed with the runt of the litter". Those were her exact words.'

'What did you say?'

'I've suffered a lot of prejudice and unnecessary exclusion because I am blind, but that was the first time, and the only time I can remember, when anyone was deliberately racially vile towards me. It was a shock.'

'So your baby's father and his mother would have nothing to do with you and Kaweira. What happened next?'

'Colin Downsted, my guardian, was really keen for me to keep the baby. He offered me and my daughter a home, but he wasn't allowed. They said I was too young and blind, and he wasn't married and was too old. It was all fixed between Child Welfare Services in Nairobi and the Catholic Church. Just as we now know what they were doing in Ireland, selling the illegitimate babies of single mothers, the Catholic Church in Kenya was doing exactly the same thing.'

'I think it's time for your next song. What have you chosen?' asked the presenter.

'*Somewhere My Love* ... because the words are ...' Until that moment, Jumapili had been strong and determined, but now her voice rose higher in pitch and it waivered. She choked, and tears came to her eyes. Her pain leapt through Nicki's earphones, and she started to cry too.

'I understand this has become something of a theme song of yours,' said the presenter, her voice also touched by emotion. 'I gather you play it at the end of every concert because the lyrics 'somewhere my love ...' Suddenly, the presenter's voice choked and then stopped. She couldn't go on. She was crying too. '

............'*Somewhere My Love*, Lara's theme tune, composed by Maurice Jarre from the sound track of the film *Doctor Zhivago*,' said the presenter after the track had been played. Her voice was now composed as there had been a long break in the recording for tissues to be shared.

'There'll be a lot of women listening to this program, who know they've been adopted and are desperate to find their mothers and are wondering if that could be you,' said the presenter. 'I believe what you can say with certainty is that, if their adoption papers do not reference Nairobi and 1973, then you cannot be their mother.'

'That's right,' acknowledged Jumapili.

'Also, I understand your daughter has a special object which you gave her on the day she was taken away.'

'That's right but there's a possibility that my daughter and this item could have been parted, so I don't know. I just know I can't give up hope.'

Nicki knew she was born in Nairobi on 14th May 1973 and had been put up for adoption, but hundreds of other baby girls would have been born that year, but she had no special object, no special item that could prove a link between the two of them.

'I think we should turn to your eighth and final record,' said the presenter.

'It's the *Power of Two* by Indigo Girls,' said Jumapili.

'And why this song?'

'All through my life I have been supported by other people: Absko, Joyce, Colin and now my girlfriend and business partner, Catherine Delfont,' said Jumapili. 'It takes two to do everything I do, and if it hadn't been for Catherine I wouldn't have my music and singing career, and Bottlesford Hall would not be doing its pioneering work in the teaching of blind students. Everything squared is much stronger than something on its own and Catherine is the living proof of that.'

Nicki listened to the words of the song carefully because she had heard Jumapili describe Catherine as her 'girlfriend'. Were they romantically linked? she wondered, remembering how Catherine was also described as her business partner. Who were the Indigo Girls? Were they gay? She was no wiser when the song had ended.

'If the waves were to crash over the shore and were to sweep away all eight gramophone records, and you could only save one, which record would you save?' asked the presenter.

'*Somewhere my love*. It's my theme tune. It's dominated my mornings and nights for the last nineteen years,' said Jumapili.

Nicki stopped and rewound the programme to the beginning. Her heart was thumping hard. She had to listen to it again, and she did so time and time until the cabin started to be prepared for landing at O'Hare airport.

By the time the aeroplane's tyres kissed the tarmac, Nicki had a change of plan: she wouldn't be returning to college in the US; she would be doing another semester in London. She was certain she would find her birth mother there.

But did her adoptive parents have some kind of special item of hers which had never been discussed? It was a conversation she knew she had to have.

Chapter 102

IT WAS THE last concert of their UK summer tour. Over six weeks Jumapili and her supporting dectet of musicians had played twenty-three concerts throughout the UK, from Cambridge to Carlyle and all the cities north and south. They had lived cheek-by-jowl for eight weeks, as they had rehearsed together for two weeks before the tour had started. And now they were exhausted.

Thanks to the tour operators and Catherine Delfont's organisational efforts the concerts were a great success, never less than ninety per cent sold out. They had raised enough money needed to keep eight completely blind children at Bottlesford Hall free of charge for another year. It was, they all agreed, time to go home.

There were mixed feelings in the band when Jumapili started singing their last song of the show - *Somewhere, my love* - because they knew it signified the tour's end. It had been a happy time. The lyrics were engraved on Jumapili and her musicians' hearts, as they were on the heart of a young woman sitting in the audience.

'You'll come to me out of the long ago,
Warm as the wind, soft as the kiss of snow.
Till then my sweet, think of me now and then.
God speed my love, 'til you are mine again.'

On their last night Catherine noticed a young, attractive woman, immaculately dressed, sitting by herself in the middle of the third row of the stalls of The Corn Exchange Theatre in Cambridge. She had arrived early, as she had done for the previous twenty-three concerts and, on each previous occasion, she had stayed for several minutes after the concert hall had emptied, sitting reflectively on her own.

After several loudly applauded encores, Catherine decided to go down to talk to the young woman.

'I just wanted to say thank you for coming to all our concerts. You must've been to them all.'

'All of them – yes,' said the young woman in an American accent.

'Would you like to meet Jumi?' asked Catherine. 'Come around the back? You certainly deserve that.'

'I don't know; I'm not sure. She might not want me.'

'Nah, come on. You must be one of her biggest fans. You deserve at least a greet, meet and a photo.'

The woman loitered shyly behind Catherine as they made their way to the wings of the stage where Jumapili, her fellow musicians and the sound men were relaxing.

'Jumi,' said Catherine. 'You need to meet one of your biggest fans. She's been at every one of our concerts. What's your name, luv?'

'Nicola Williams – Nicki.'

Jumapili stood up and, taking her white stick, she tapped gently towards Nicki's voice.

'Nice to meet you,' said Jumapili offering her hand hesitantly because she sensed something was wrong.

'Can I ask a question? said Nicki.

'Sure,' replied Catherine briskly who, with her adrenaline burning after another successful concert, had fail to understand that the question was not for her but for Jumapili.

'Miss Jumapili,' said Nicki almost in a whisper, 'does this mean anything to you?' She produced a silver case a little bigger than a cigarette case with tiny bumps, and placed it in Jumapili's hands.

The moment Jumapili's fingers touched the braille on the mbugi she let out a wail, and she grasped out for Nicki, clinging on to her shoulder as her body started to cave.

'Can you see? Can you see?' she asked frantically. 'You're not blind? You've not lost your sight?'

'Did you have a daughter on 14th May 1973?' asked Nicki. The quiet calmness of her voice hid the turmoil she felt inside. It was the question she had been waiting a lifetime to ask.

'Are you blind? Are you blind?' repeated Jumapili. 'Can you see?' The urgency in Jumapili's voice was frightening to those who knew her well.

'Yes, I can see. I am watching you right now.'

Jumapili dropped her white stick and grasped Nicki with her other hand and bowed in grief before her daughter.

'It's just - I was born in Nairobi on 14th May 1973 to a blind girl who was aged just sixteen. I think that must be you,' said Nicki.

'I'm sorry. I'm sorry. I'm sorry,' wailed Jumapili and she fell to the ground, kneeling in front of Nicki. 'Forgive me, please forgive me,' she pleaded, as tears flooded from her eyes.

Catherine rushed forward and squatted down to take hold of Jumapili.

'It's Kaweira,' cried Jumapili. 'It's my Kaweira.'

'Your daughter? You're sure?'

'14th May 1973, Nairobi, with my grandfather's mbugi. It must be,' sobbed Jumapili.

'Come on, stand up,' commanded Catherine, before taking both of Jumapili's hands and helping to raise her up.

'Are you adopted?' asked Catherine, addressing Nicki with the official tone she always took when taking charge of a situation.

'Yes.'

'I think you two need to talk away from here,' said Catherine, conscious of the crowd that was now looking on.

With Catherine leading Jumapili by the hand and Nicki following behind, they found a small empty dressing room.

'I'll leave you in here,' said Catherine once Jumapili was seated in a chair.

'Can I touch your face?' Jumapili asked. 'Can I feel you, please?'

'Of course,' replied Nicki as she bent at her mother's lap.

Jumapili's fingers worked their way around Nicki's face, her skull and through her hair.

'You have lovely hair. You're lucky. You have your father's hair.'

'You know my father?' asked Nicki surprised.

'If I didn't you wouldn't be here,' chuckled Jumapili.

'You know where he is, I mean?'

'I know where he is, but he and I haven't spoken since he was told he was going to be a father.'

'Not once?'

'No, not once.'

'But he knows I exist?' asked Nicki.

'Oh yes.'

There was a pause as Nicki remembered the bitterness she had heard in Jumapili's voice when listening to her speak about her pregnancy on the aeroplane.

'Can I ask a question?' said Jumapili.

'If I can ask you one in return.'

'Have you had a good life? Have you been happy?' asked Jumapili. 'Were your adopted parents good to you?'

'Yes, the best life, and they're lovely. I've been lucky,' Nicki replied. 'They know I've come looking for you and they're happy about it.'

Tears flowed from Jumapili's eyes because her happiness was now gold-wrapped with an enormous sense of relief.

'Lara's song,' said Nicki. 'The last couple of lines: *Till then my sweet think of me now and then, God speed my love 'til you are mine again.* You sing them at the end of every concert wherever you are. Is this my song? Is it sung to me?'

'No one else,' sobbed Jumapili. 'No one else.' Then her face broke into a smile of joy and her arms reached out to hold her daughter. She was never, ever going to let her go again.

BV - #0008 - 221223 - C0 - 216/140/20 - PB - 9781915972217 - Matt Lamination